The Burning Sands

The Burning Sands

Carole Lehr Johnson

by

Carole Lehr Johnson

INK MAP PRESS

The Burning Sands

© 2022 by Carole Lehr Johnson

All rights reserved. No part of this book may be reproduced or used in any manner without written permission of the copyright owner except for the use of quotations in a book review. For more information, address: carolelehrjohnson@att.net

Published in Pollock, Louisiana, by Ink Map Press
www.inkmappress.com

Cover Design by Victoria Davies (vikncharlie on Fiverr.com)
Interior Design by Morgan Tarpley Smith (morgantarpleysmith.com)
Map by Artist Monica Bruenjes (artistmonica.com)
Cover Photos courtesy of the author

Scripture quotations are from the King James Version of the Bible.

Scripture taken from the New King James Version®. Copyright © 1982 by Thomas Nelson. Used by permission. All rights reserved.

This is a work of fiction. Names, characters, places, and incidents either are the product of the author's imagination or are used fictitiously. Any resemblance to actual persons, living or dead, events, or locales is entirely coincidental.

ISBN 978-1-952928-27-7
ISBN 978-1-952928-28-4 (ebook)

Publisher's Cataloging-in-Publication Data

Names: Johnson, Carole Lehr, author.
Title: The burning sands / Carole Lehr Johnson.
Description: Pollock, LA: Ink Map Press, 2022. | Illus. ; 1 map, 1 photo, 40 b&w images.| Summary: Still mourning the loss of her husband, Olivia travels to Cornwall to discover her grandmother's past and finds herself captivated by an old tavern and the story of a woman from the seventeenth century.
Identifiers: LCCN 2022907379 | ISBN 9781952928277 (paperback) | ISBN 9781952928284 (ebook)
Subjects: LCSH: Cottages—England—Fiction. | Grandmothers—Fiction. | Man-woman relationships—Fiction. | Taverns (Inns) —England—Fiction. | Widows—Fiction. | Cornwall (England)—17th century—Fiction. | BISAC: FICTION / Christian / Historical. | FICTION / Family Life / General. | FICTION / Women.
Classification: LCC PS3610.O36 B8 2022 | DDC 813 J64b--dc22
LC record available at https://lccn.loc.gov/2022907379

Printed in the United States of America
2022—First Edition

To Mrs. Vivian Griffin-Redd

Your encouragement and concern for a near-sighted, painfully shy fourth grader made a lasting impression. The memory has stayed with me these fifty-plus years.

Are not five sparrows sold for two farthings, and not one of them is forgotten before God?

Luke 12:6 (KJV)

**Other Books by
Carole Lehr Johnson**

Permelia Cottage

A Place in Time

Their Scottish Destiny
(co-authored with Tammy Kirby)

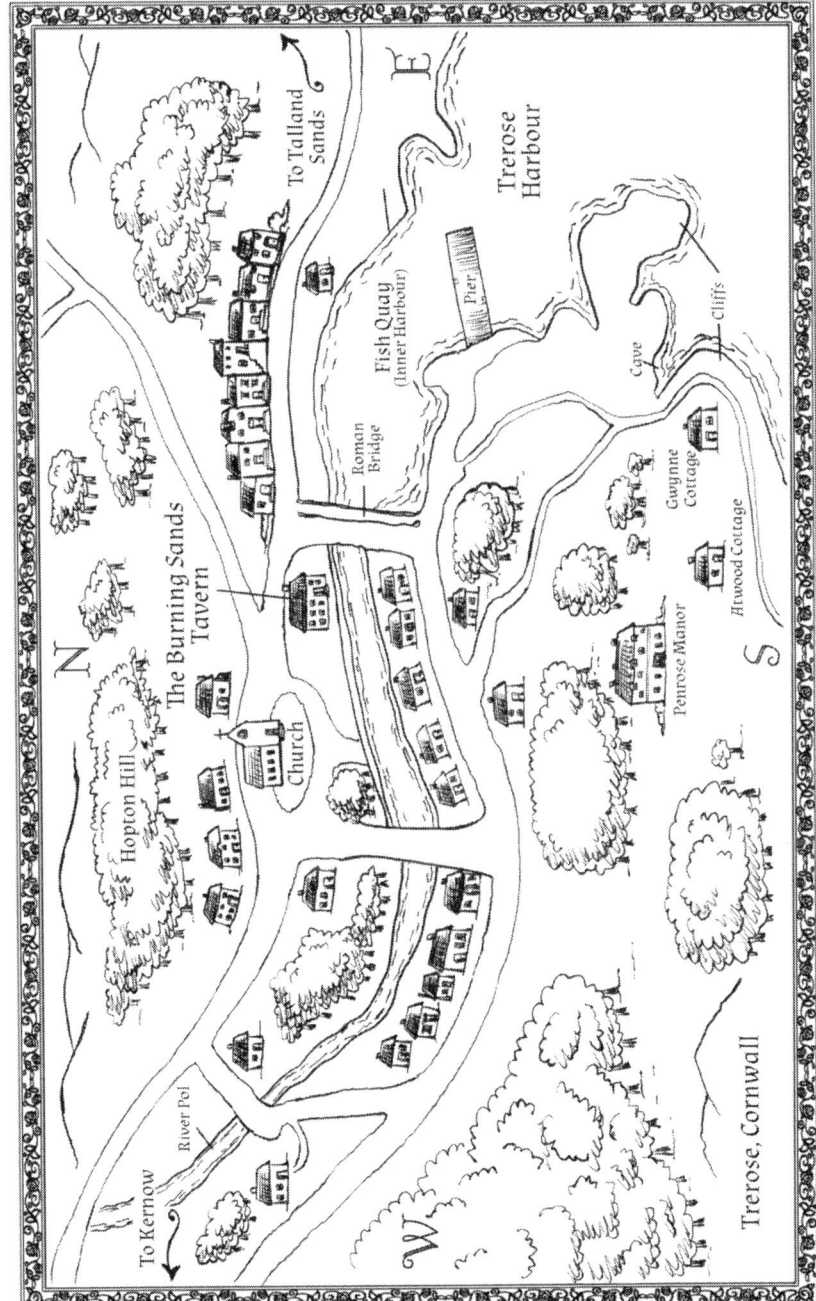

Prologue

Cornwall, England
September 1656

The girl's auburn hair glinted in the warm sun as she patted a handful of wet sand into a small pewter cup. A squeal of laughter brought her head up to peer at the boys running into the crashing swells. Wind caught her wild curls in a dance around her face, and at that moment, a series of waves grew in intensity. Her brother and his friend were swallowed by each pounding surge.

She held her breath until she saw her brother emerge with force, a look of fear crossing his face as he screamed, *"Nick! Nick!"*

Sebastian dove, and after a long while, resurfaced, eyes searching for his friend. He repeated the action many times before Grace ran to the edge of the beach, the cup clutched to her chest.

Her eyes remained on the massive rock a distance from where the boys had begun their usual race. They always swam from this stretch of sand to the rock and back as a game. Nick usually won.

Time stretched with each of Sebastian's dives, always coming up with no sign of Nick. Grace screamed, tears coursing along her cheeks. "Sebastian, save him, please save Nick!"

She dropped to her knees in the damp sand as the clouds darkened like great grey beasts flying overhead, screeching a warning of the impending storm. The wind rose, and Grace's eyes stung from the salt spray. Her tears became sobs, and after a time, slender trembling arms wound around her shoulders.

Sebastian's shaking voice pleaded, "I tried, Grace—" his voice caught on gasping breaths, "—I tried," before burying his drenched head against her small shoulder.

Huge drops of stinging rain slapped them with such force they sprinted for shelter beneath the overhanging rocks by the cliffs edging their favorite beach.

Grace would never remember it as such again.

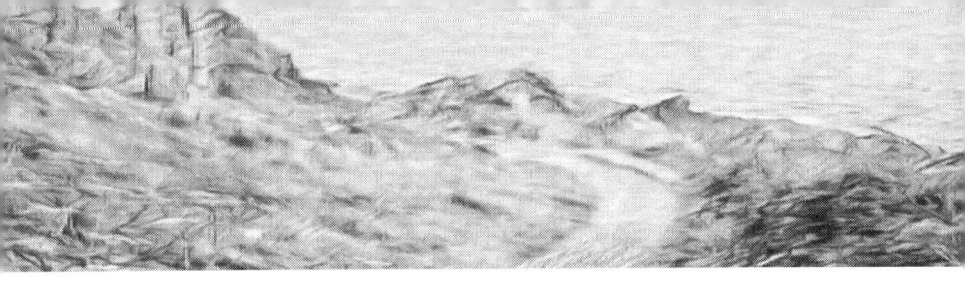

Chapter One

Louisiana
April 2022

The news hadn't come from a uniformed stranger.

Olivia Griffin opened the door to a bright spring day of blooming daffodils and the scent of lavender, a mild breeze playing with her hair. Her husband's closest friend, Sam, and his cousin, Billy, stood on her doorstep. Sam clutched the strap of a brown backpack slung over his shoulder.

The moment her eyes took in the bag and the pain on the men's faces the force of its meaning buckled her knees.

Reliving that surreal day came upon her with force like standing outside her present surroundings as a sad, unemotional bystander. She had sagged against the doorframe, Billy reaching out to steady her, his hoarse words still echoing in her mind.

"Livi, I am so sorry."

Olivia gripped the mug tightly, heat permeating her aching

hands. Her sorting and packing became a welcomed frenzy of activity. Anything to occupy her mind.

The chirping phone intruded on her thoughts.

"Hello." Her mother's cheerful voice now a new irritant. What was happening to her?

Olivia steeled herself for the forthcoming speech.

She attempted to sound as light-hearted as the caller. "Good morning, Mom. How are you today?"

"Splendid, dear, just splendid." Her mother coughed. "This is the most marvelous spring day. I hope you plan on getting outside for a while. Maybe putter around in your lovely garden."

Olivia almost laughed. It had not been a *lovely* garden since Ian . . .

She pulled in a fortifying breath. "Yes, Mom . . . I . . ." A knock at the door halted the excuse she was about to give. "Sorry. Someone's here. I'll call you later. Love you." She punched the button to end the call and sprinted for the door, guilt hitting her more than she'd felt in a while.

The petite blonde bounced across the threshold, her arms filled with containers of takeaway. The scent trailing her through the air elicited a growl from Olivia's stomach. She'd not stopped for breakfast, and when she glanced at the clock on the mantle, she noticed it was well past lunch.

"Come on, you slug." Angie turned and looked at Olivia. "You haven't eaten all day, have you?"

Olivia slumped into a chair at the table, pulled a drink toward her, and sipped. "You know me too well, Angie Timmons."

Angie huffed. *"Too well."* She sat across from Olivia and retrieved her own drink. "How's the tea? Did they get it right this time?" She sent her longtime friend a playful smirk, then glanced around the room at the stacks of boxes.

"I know. I meant to take those to the thrift store days ago." Olivia dropped her chin to her chest. "It's just so hard."

Angie patted her hand but said nothing for several moments.

"Guess I'll have to take the bull by the horns, or in this case, the bullheaded friend by the hand."

Olivia lifted her head. "How so?"

"After we eat, we'll load it up, and I'll take it myself. That way, you don't have to witness its departure. As long as you have it in front of you, you'll continue to grieve." She lowered her voice. "It's been over a year."

Olivia's eyes stung, and she dropped her gaze to her left hand. The deep pink, Asscher-cut diamond winked at her from the midday sun glinting through the kitchen window. Again, painful memories caused her emotions to cut more deeply each time they resurfaced.

She crossed her forearms on the table and rested her head on them, her shoulders quaking. A chair scraping across the tile floor brought her head up to see Angie come to her side and kneel beside the chair.

Angie rested her hands on her thighs, not touching Olivia. With tears in her eyes, she said, "Livi, I think there are too many memories here."

She opened her mouth to speak, but Angie held a hand up, palm out. "No. Say nothing until you hear me out." She exhaled, then continued, "I'm not suggesting you forget Ian. Just try to go forward with your life. You are young." She laughed and bumped her shoulder against Olivia's. "*We're* young. After all, we've only been out of college for twenty years."

Olivia sniffled. "Twenty-two years, my friend."

Angie sneered. "Twenty sounds better." She lifted her brows. "Anyway, you need a serious change of scenery. Sell the house."

Olivia's eyes widened, and her back stiffened.

"Okay, okay. Rent it out for a while. You can put your stuff in storage and travel."

"Well . . . I don't know." The thought had not occurred to her since she now had full control of her life. Half of herself was *gone*. The love of her life no longer existed. How could she ever recover from that?

Ian had been a wonderful man—a wonderful husband—except for one thing they could never get past.

She heard Angie speaking, but it was as if from far away like the PA system in an airport paging someone who wasn't paying attention.

Olivia refocused at the mention of her great-grandmother. "Excuse me? What were you saying about my grandmother?"

"Your *great*-grandmother. Didn't you say she was from England and your great-grandfather served there during the war and that's how they met?"

Olivia's mind reeled. "Yes, my great-grandmother was from a small fishing village in Cornwall on the east coast along the English Channel."

Angie rose, groaned, and staggered back to her seat. "Yeah, twenty-two years for sure."

They shared a laugh as Angie slid a plate toward Olivia. "Eat up while I convince you to go to Cornwall."

ॐ

Olivia waved to her friend as she backed her brilliant blue SUV out of the driveway, loaded with the boxes of Ian's life. She swallowed back tears. She would live again and would wish the same for him.

Trudging into the house, she looked at the few remaining containers. It had taken her six months to go through his belongings, sorting them into stacks of items his family may want, items to go to charity, or what she would keep—mostly photograph albums full of memories that mere objects could not convey—except for the collection of tiny seashells.

Their first trip together was their honeymoon, which they spent in the Caribbean. They walked the beach early every morning, the sun blazing orange and yellow with slashes of a near purple backdrop, searching for shells to take home. She could almost smell the salty air, hear the gulls screeching overhead as the sun rose above the sparkling water. They walked hand-in-hand until one of them spotted a prize, kneeling in the cool, wet sand. Each time they repeated the ritual, it ended in a kiss.

Later, in a souvenir shop, Olivia found a miniature crystal box and discovered the tiny shells fit perfectly. This one item now graced her desk, so she could look at it as she sketched or painted.

Since Ian's death, she had found solace in her work,

although she had given up her nine-to-five job creating art for a company that designed greeting cards and devotional covers. After the initial shock wore off, she began branching out with her creativity, knowing that she was the only one who would see it. Creating occupied her mind while taking her thoughts away from her husband.

The phone jangled, an intrusion to her thoughts. She picked it up and saw her grandmother's name.

"Hi, Grandma." She grinned, imagining the round, smiling face, always full of genuine happiness.

"Hello, love. How are you this evening?"

"I'm doing very well. And you?"

"Other than this arthritis, I'm brilliant." She giggled like a schoolgirl, and Olivia imagined she was most likely multi-tasking while they chatted. Her grandmother was a conundrum of epic proportions. One of her favorite sayings was, 'There is no logic in idleness.'

"Grandma, what are you doing right now—other than speaking with me?" She laughed.

"Well, my dear, I am baking your grandpa a batch of blueberry scones. Why?"

"No reason. I just like picturing you multi-tasking. It encourages me."

Grandma Knox tittered, "That is so sweet of you, dear. I believe God wants us to make the most of the time He gives us on this earth. Talking on the phone is not a burden, so why shouldn't I be doing something else while I chat? There aren't enough hours in the day after all."

"Yes, Grandma. You *are* right." Olivia paused, Angie's talk of her great-grandmother's life in Cornwall prompting her. "Grandma?"

The familiar sound of the oven door closing reminded Olivia of the countless sugar cookies she'd eaten in that kitchen.

"Yes, love."

She visualized her grandmother's pursed lips as she cleaned the kitchen while the scones baked.

"Would you be available for a *visitor* and go through my great-grandmother's mementos?"

Her grandmother cleared her throat. "Certainly. Give me a bit of notice and I'll make you breakfast, lunch, or dinner—or all three, if you'll stay a day or so."

The offer settled in Olivia's mind. A couple of days at her grandparents' house in the country might be what she needed. She no longer had any obligations. No job. Ian had made sure she was well taken care of. Her heart clenched, but before the tears came, she simply said, "I may just take you up on that." She switched her phone to speaker and began searching her calendar. Nothing for the next couple of weeks.

"What are your plans for the next few days?"

"Nothing of note. We have a church picnic on Saturday. You could come with us and see some old friends. How lovely!"

Olivia's gaze traveled to one of the framed photos on the bookshelf across the room. Her grandparents stood next to her and Ian while on a family vacation in the mountains about five years before. Her mother had taken the picture. It was an enjoyable week away, and Ian had promised he would do none of his extreme sports while there—no river rafting, mountain climbing, or hang gliding.

The trip had been good for her mother as well since her father died the previous winter. That getaway pulled her through. Her mother had not been as fortunate in marriage as Olivia. She refused to recall those memories. It was much too painful because it also brought back what else had been missing from her marriage—children. Fear of Ian dying and leaving her with children to care for alone was too great a risk.

"All right. I'll be there tomorrow afternoon."

They hung up with air kisses and goodbyes, and Olivia felt lighter than she had in a long time. Maybe Angie was right. Getting away, putting some distance between her memories of Ian, could help her move on.

☙❧

Olivia stretched lazily, awakening to a fully risen sun. She'd intended to take a turn on her treadmill before leaving, but she decided to forgo it for a light breakfast, a strong cup of tea, and Bible study.

Within two hours she settled behind the wheel of her mid-sized sedan, cruise-control set as she glided along I-55 toward the hilly, green countryside of north Louisiana. Even though she did not live in the crowded center of New Orleans, her little suburban world teemed with people, shopping, industry, and chaos.

At the mere hint of a hurricane, she and Ian shot north to her grandparents' house. Since her mother lived a couple of hours east of them, they would make it a habit of taking the long way back for an overnight stay.

The day was so mild, the cloudless blue-bird sky hovering overhead, lifting her spirits. She turned on music and listened to her favorite movie score. The series was filmed in Cornwall several years before, and the music took her to the rugged Cornish coast of her ancestry.

Angie had hit on something with her suggestion of ancestry and travel—even if Olivia wasn't yet convinced to go anywhere. She had, however, packed her passport and genealogy research just in case.

After a brief stop to grab a snack to get her by until she arrived for one of her grandmother's delicious lunches, Olivia forced her thoughts to Cornwall. Maybe she should take a trip to see where her great-grandparents met.

The closer she got to the small town, dark gray clouds gathered, and light sprinkles flecked her windshield. Slowing to turn into the long drive leading to the square white house upon a slight rise, she noticed a few daffodils peeking above the grass in a circle around the mailbox post. The yellow buds reached toward the rain, drinking in what the sun would soon dry up.

She parked behind her grandfather's dented and scratched old red truck. The front door of the house swung wide, and her short, stout grandmother sprinted down the steps. Susan Knox was a marvel at eight-one. As she would say, "There are no flies on your old grandmother!"

No, the flies wouldn't dare. She was too quick for them.

"Livi, my girl!" Elderly but strong arms encircled her in a hug. "It's so nice to see you." She pushed Olivia back. "You are much too thin. We'll have to fatten you up in the brief time you'll be with us."

A tall, steel-gray haired man took a slower descent from the porch, holding onto the railings and making his way to repeat the solid hug. "She's right, you know? You look a tad thin."

Olivia placed a kiss on his cheek. "Oh, Grandpa. I eat just fine."

"That's not what Angie said."

She started. "You've been speaking with her?"

Grandma Knox jerked when the door squeaked open. "Oh, my. Billy, I quite forgot you were still with us. Come see Livi."

Olivia watched Ian's cousin move lithely down the steps, his shirt sleeves rolled up to reveal tan, muscular arms—much like Ian's. They had both inherited the same olive complexion of their ancestors who had lived in the south of France for generations, departing for New Orleans with the first French settlers over three hundred years ago.

Her breath caught at his resemblance to Ian.

She'd forgotten how much they looked alike. Perhaps her hasty decision to come had not been thought out enough. Billy living next door had never entered her thoughts. She pulled in a shaky breath and willed herself to remain calm.

"Hello, Billy." She extended her hand.

He took it and placed an arm around her, pulling her into a side-hug. "It's so good to see you, Livi. I haven't seen you since—well, since the funeral." He dropped her hand but kept his arm around her shoulders. "I stopped by to look at your grandfather's clunker." He pointed to the beat-up truck. "And they told me you would be here soon. I wanted to stay and tell you, again, how sorry I am about Ian."

THE BURNING SANDS

She avoided his gaze. "Thank you. That's very kind."

Grandpa Knox glared at Billy. "That *old clunker* was built before you were born, my boy, and it'll likely still be running after you're gone." His tone was gruff, but Olivia knew the humor behind those amber eyes.

Olivia moved from Billy's hold and took her grandfather's arm, looking up into his wrinkled face. "You are an old marshmallow, Grandpa. I think you love that ancient truck more than you do any of us." She tugged his arm and pulled him to the house. "Come on. I'm starving for Grandma's massive lunch."

Her grandmother took her husband's other arm but glanced over her shoulder. "Billy, come along. You'll be eating with us, my love."

Billy shook his head. "Mrs. Knox, I don't think I'll ever get used to anyone calling me that." He laughed.

Grandpa Knox chimed in. "I won't either, Billy. She got that from her *mum*. It's meant to be an affectionate greeting for men or women, not romantic."

Billy shrugged, but even his olive skin couldn't hide the blush tinting his cheeks.

Ian would've turned it into a joke. Billy was more laidback and easygoing than Ian. Although their personalities were quite different, everyone liked them equally. She warmed toward him in that moment, her tension easing at finding him at her grandparents, allowing the connection between him and Ian to fade.

Olivia asked Billy how he and his family were doing and made small talk as they enjoyed the tender, delicious roast and vegetables her grandmother prepared. Compliments flew across the table as they consumed the mouthwatering meal.

After dessert of fresh apple pie and ice cream, they each groaned with varying degrees of fullness and stood to adjourn to the screened-in back porch overlooking the small lake surrounded by weeping willow trees.

Billy stood. "Thank you, but I really need to get back to work." He patted his flat stomach. "Although I don't know how much I'll be able to do with this load I'm now carrying on board."

Olivia's grandmother laughed. "Go on. As thin as you are and as hard as you work, you'll have that lunch worked off this very afternoon."

Billy eased his chair under the table. "I thank you, ma'am, but I'm not taking any chances. I can't do a thing about getting older, but I can avoid putting on extra pounds."

He slapped Grandpa Knox on the shoulder. "Here's a good example. Fit as can be."

The elder man returned the slap and grinned. "Kind of you to say, son. But these old bones aren't what they used to be."

"Couldn't tell it by looking, sir." Billy strode to Olivia. "Livi, it was a pleasure seeing you again. If you're staying a few days, maybe we can go get a cup of coffee or something."

It was her turn to blush at the invitation. She glanced at the floor and then met his eyes. "All right, Billy. Perhaps."

He walked toward the door with her grandfather following, chatting about the truck.

"Come along, love. I have tea waiting on the porch." She took Olivia's arm and drew her alongside, chatting cheerfully as they walked.

Olivia picked up a cup of tea and sat facing the water. Long shadows of the drooping trees rippled across the lake, a pleasant breeze sending them into a slow dance.

She loved the soothing aura of this place. Why had she not come back after Ian—*left*? Was it the long drive alone?

Ian had always said that it was the perfect time for them to discuss plans whether about a vacation, household projects, or the latest books they'd read. One of the many wonderful things about their marriage was all the things they had in common. Reading was something they shared—not always the same genre—but they enjoyed discussing plots, characters, scenes . . .

Tears welled, and she averted her gaze so her grandmother could not see them. She sipped her tea and cleared her throat.

"Grandma, when will we dive into my great-grandmother's life? I'm eager to get started." She chuckled. "After all, I don't think I'll be wanting dinner this evening after that enormous lunch."

"I understand. Your grandfather likes it when I make roast. He'll just want a sandwich tonight. Says there's nothing better than a thick roast beef sandwich." Her gaze shifted to the lake, a wistful gleam in her eyes.

Olivia straightened. "Are you well?"

"Oh yes, love. I remembered the first time I made him a nice roast. Well, it was nice but a bit on the chewy side. He never complained. I did some cookbook research after that and have made them perfect ever since." She reached out and patted Olivia's hand.

Olivia nodded with a tender smile. She and Ian had loved to cook together. Their synergy was incredible. Everything about their marriage was incredible—except his need for danger. A slow burning sensation began in her stomach and wound upward to her heart. His love of extreme sports had taken him from her.

The tears flowed too fast and free, and she clenched her eyes tight to staunch the flow, but it didn't work.

A warm hand cupped her shoulder, her grandmother's arm draped around her. "Oh, my love. I am so very sorry."

They sat this way for some moments, Olivia's sobs shaking them both.

"Oh . . . Gr—Grandma! I'm so angry with him. If he had stopped all the insane sports, he'd be with me now. I love him. I miss him!"

Grandma Knox wrapped both arms around Olivia and rested her head on her granddaughter's. "I know . . . I know."

Olivia remained in the comforting embrace until her grandfather returned from seeing Billy off and interjected, "What the devil is going on here?"

His gruff tone snapped them to attention. Olivia wiped the tears away with the back of her hand while her grandmother stood, moved to a small table, and retrieved a box of tissues.

She snatched a tissue and dabbed at her eyes before handing the box to Olivia and facing her husband. "Ben, why are you being so surly? Can't you see the girl is broken?"

He crossed his arms over his chest and sent them both a stern look. "It's not my intention, but it's about time you move forward, Livi." He pulled in a long breath and slowly released it, his voice softer when he spoke again. "You have mourned Ian for over a year. I understand you had an exceptionally good marriage. A godly marriage. But God would not want you to give up your future. Ian is with Him. You will see him again, but you need to *live* in the present."

The tall man dropped into a chair and put his elbows on his knees, letting his hands dangle. "Livi, Ian didn't die on purpose just to leave you. He was *living*. Those sports he loved were a part of him." He leaned back, and his gaze bored into hers. "If you had made him choose, how long do you think it would've been before it divided the two of you?"

She blinked, tears blurring her grandfather's face. A sharp pang gripped her chest. An epiphany condemned her. Was she still grieving because she was blaming Ian for his absence?

Olivia wiped her eyes. "I love you both, but I need to be alone. To think." On slow, unsteady legs, she left the porch.

She heard their muffled voices as she climbed the stairs to her room. The room she and Ian had always settled in when they visited. It had been her room from the time she was born.

Her grandparents made it hers. She felt at home there—more so than her own home now. Her mind whirled at her grandfather's declaration.

Maybe he was right, but no one else had the courage to tell her so. Angie had said things that pointed in that direction but not so forcefully. She could see the pain in his amber eyes as he forced himself to be honest. But could she be honest with herself?

CAROLE LEHR JOHNSON

Chapter Two

Olivia reclined on the window seat in her room, watching the sunset over the lake. A white crane glided over its surface, searching for his last catch of the day. An impulse to draw the creature urged her to grab her sketchbook, but she'd not thought to pack it. He was a graceful wonder to observe. The word *grace* settled in her mind, the verse about His grace being sufficient for the day.

God had given her plenty of grace. Those first days after Ian's death were spent in limbo with her living in a surreal state of numb unacceptance. He was *not* truly gone from her world. Then, those emotions gave way to anger.

The sun sank, leaving her in darkness. She stumbled to the bed, slid under the covers fully dressed, and welcomed oblivion. Just as she was losing herself to sleep, a soft knock sounded, and her grandmother's sweet voice asked if she needed anything.

"No, ma'am. I just want to sleep."

A long silence stretched before her grandmother's reply. "All right, love. Please let us know if you need anything."

"I will. Good night, Grandma."

"Good night."

Slow, measured steps faded down the stairs, and Olivia willed herself to slip into nothingness. The more her brain focused on sleep, the more it eluded her.

After tossing about for an hour, she rose, showered, and retrieved the bag that held all of her great-grandmother's things she'd brought with her. Tomorrow, she and her grandmother would pool their resources and get down to serious research. She trudged to the small desk and placed her bag on the top and unzipped it.

A blue accordion folder with tears and wrinkles caught her attention. When she pulled it free, it bumped the crystal water decanter on the corner of the desk. She settled it with a smile.

Her grandmother always left her favorite bottled water poured into this antique container next to a matching tumbler. Her finger trailed over the cut pattern.

Next to these was the ever-present crystal box containing tiny seashells. It had captured her attention as a child. She'd been extra careful to return them one by one. The box had prompted her to include Ian in the daily seashell hunt on their honeymoon when she'd found a similar crystal box in a souvenir shop. It was as if her great-grandmother had reached out to her from the past.

Olivia removed the folder and lifted the flap, thumbing

through the tabs, noting the organization.

When she came across her great-grandmother's name, she removed the inch-thick stack of yellowed paper with neat, small handwriting. Random notes on family genealogy with dates, places, and personal descriptions were scratched in unorganized paragraphs.

As she continued to flip through the papers, a newspaper article fluttered to the floor, torn by countless hands that had gripped it through the decades. She noted the year of 1941. It was an article about a squadron of American RAF pilots that helped Britain before the United States entered World War II with a list of pilots who were lauded for their bravery fighting the Germans. She scanned the names, stopping at her great-grandfather's, Lawrence Flowers.

She froze.

Her grandmother had never mentioned her father was a pilot—especially an American pilot in the RAF. Olivia retrieved her laptop and searched for details. Sure enough, even though they were threatened with losing their American citizenship and faced prosecution, many American men *chose* to aid Britain because they saw the handwriting on the wall of the coming world war. Less than a year later, it became reality.

Olivia leaned back in her chair, holding the ragged article in front of her. Family history fascinated her. She noted the time but still had no desire to return to bed and allow her troubled thoughts to replay, not wanting to drop the captivating discovery.

Her grandparents were early to bed, so she eased out of the room and quietly strode to the kitchen. She found her favorite mug. It was huge, and one side read, *one cup of tea is never enough*, in bright pink script, and the other showed a woman holding a cup the size of her head.

Olivia laughed as she put the kettle on and made herself a *cup* of tea. She placed it on a small tray along with a blueberry scone wrapped in cellophane and *Livi* written on the note next to it.

She returned to her room, settled at the desk with her snack, and jumped into the family history papers, hoping her grandmother could shed light on this surprising new slant on her ancestry. There was most certainly a story there.

❦

Olivia glanced up to see subtle light coming through her window. She didn't remember going to bed in the wee hours, but in bed she was. Her eyes burned, dry from hours of overuse. She squeezed her eyes tight to elicit tears to ease the dryness, and a yawn escaped. Rolling to her side, she saw a crane out on the lake shopping for breakfast.

A knock made her sit up abruptly. Before she could answer, the door inched open wide enough for her grandmother to poke her head through.

"Rise and shine, love." She pushed the door wider and stepped into the room, holding a large green tray laden with tea, toast, scrambled eggs, and jam.

"Grandma, you didn't have to go to so much trouble. I was going to have breakfast with you and Grandpa."

Olivia clasped her wrist with one hand and stretched her arms over her head.

Her grandmother laughed. "Dear, we had breakfast hours ago." She perched the tray on the foot of the bed and motioned for Olivia to lean back against the headboard.

"Go on. Get comfy." She waited for Olivia to obey, and when she did, she settled the tray onto her lap. "There's a good girl, now."

Grandma Knox sat at the desk. "I didn't want to wake you too early but knew you shouldn't sleep too late and get your sleep pattern wonky."

Olivia smiled, her cheeks likely resembling a chipmunk's, as she chewed her toast and nodded. "Thank you. That's true." She sipped her tea, remembering her discovery. "I couldn't sleep, so I did a bit of research last night. What do you know about your father being in the RAF?"

Her grandmother cocked her head and pursed her lips. "I seem to remember Mum talking about that. I was just a babe during the war. We'll get my family boxes out and get to work on that." She pushed herself up and stood beside Olivia.

"Why do you ask?"

"I found some notes in my family files—a newspaper article from World War II. Fascinating stuff." She continued eating, all the while watching her grandmother's expression.

"Yes. Families can be complicated. We'll just see what turns up. Maybe we have a spy in our ancestry." She waggled her brows and energetically left Olivia to her tea and toast.

For the first time since Ian's death, Olivia was happy to have something new to divert her attention. After breakfast, she and her grandmother sat at the large table in the dining room. Papers, memorabilia, and Olivia's laptop covered the surface. Each woman had a fresh glass of iced tea laced with lemon in front of them, heads slanted over the family trail of details.

Periodically, Olivia entered another piece of information into her grandmother's online family tree, verifying their source to be certain they had it thoroughly documented.

"Olivia," her grandmother began, "I've found something of interest."

The solemn tone of her grandmother's voice halted her search. The ragged piece of paper in her hand hovered over the table.

"I don't remember a lot about my mum as she died when I was a small girl. We had not been in the States for long." She paused, a catch in her voice. "Later, Papa said she had been very sick but said nothing to me at the time so as not to worry me overmuch."

A lone tear slipped along her wrinkled cheek and dripped onto the table. "My memory of her face is clouded, but I do recall she always smelled like a bouquet of spring flowers."

Olivia laid a hand on her shoulder. "I'm sorry you did not get to grow up knowing her."

Her grandmother nodded, her gaze on the object. A small brown book quivered in her hand. "I'd quite forgotten about this. When she died, I placed it in this box, promising never to read it."

"Why not?"

She sighed. "My childish mind thought if I did, all the happy memories of her would fade. I feared there was something sad inside this little book. Possibly the reason for her death." She handed the book to her granddaughter. "Maybe you should read it first."

THE BURNING SANDS

Olivia paused before gently taking the diary. The weight of it was a surprise. In design, it appeared to be from several centuries past. "How do you know it belonged to her?"

She shrugged. "It was in a drawer with her jewelry, which was sparse. She wasn't much for fripperies as she called them." The words brought a smile to her face.

Olivia asked in astonishment, "So you never opened it?"

"Just once. The handwriting was hard to read, and I was still a mere child, not having learned much cursive writing."

Olivia nodded, understanding. "Well, I have reading material tonight."

Her grandmother smiled, eyes now bright and clear. "I think we've begun to unravel our family history, my love. So exciting!"

೦೩೮

Olivia gripped her second cup of herbal tea, inhaling the sharp citrus aroma. Her grandmother could whip up a batch of her famous coconut oatmeal cookies in less time than it took Olivia to check her mail.

She leaned against the counter and watched her sling lumps of cookie dough onto a huge stainless steel cookie sheet in rapid succession, popping it into the oven and immediately began repeating the action on a new pan.

"Grandma, you are a conundrum."

Her grey eyes lifted. "What do you mean by that?"

Olivia shrugged. "It's just that you can do so many things—all of them well—and yet you never seem to be bothered by anything that goes wrong."

Her grandmother scrunched her face. "I'm still not sure what you mean. Of course, I get aggravated about things at times. But there's no sense worrying about something you have no control over." She slid another pan into the oven. "Give me an example."

Olivia quirked an eyebrow and thought for a moment. "You didn't hesitate when I asked if I could come for a quick visit with no notice."

"Ha! Like I'm going to question that. You could've called me from the driveway, and I would've been ecstatic to see you." She wiped her hands on a dish towel.

Olivia laughed. "Let me finish . . . I mean I call on short notice, and when I get here, you have a fabulous meal that would've taken me days to plan and right in the middle of your plans for the church picnic which I know you prepare for in advance."

"Will you pour me a glass of tea, please? It's in the fridge." Her grandmother sat and fanned herself with the towel. "I don't believe I could handle a hot drink right now. That oven heats this room up like nobody's business."

"Coming right up."

Olivia set her cup on the table, filled a blue tumbler with ice, and poured the dark brew, topping it off with a slice of lemon.

Grandma Knox took a long drink and released a pleasing sigh. "That's more like it." They chuckled and shared some memories of baking cookies when Olivia was a girl.

When Olivia's mother came up, she hesitated but worked up the courage. "Grandma, I know Mother and Dad didn't have a great marriage—and I don't fully know what all the issues were between them—but as far as I know, she never really grieved when he died."

The oven timer rang, and her grandmother rose, releasing a soft grunt with the action. She huffed and grabbed the oven mitt.

"It's a long story, love. Has your mother not shared any details?" Before Olivia could answer, she continued, "No. Of course, she wouldn't. Your mother doesn't handle sharing her emotions well."

She carefully placed the cookie sheet onto a large trivet on the counter. The sweet scent of coconut floated around them, making Olivia's mouth water. She could already taste the moist, spicy mixture melting on her tongue.

When Grandma Knox turned toward Olivia, she held a saucer with two cookies on it and placed it next to Olivia's cup.

Olivia reached for the sugary treat. "You always could read my mind."

"Only where these are concerned." She patted Olivia's arm.

"Now, about your mother. Don't concern yourself. Your father was a hard man. Self-centered and demanding. He kept those traits well-hidden until your mother married him. The first time they came here for a Sunday lunch, just days after their return from the honeymoon, it was most apparent the kind of man he truly was."

Her eyes glistened, and she drank a swallow of tea. "I was sad for your mother. But she was a good soldier and weathered through. I worked up the gumption to ask her about it once. She said God had put them together for a reason and would say no more after that."

"I see." Olivia knew she would get no more from her grandmother and changed the subject. "Now that your dessert offering is complete on to your savory dish for the picnic."

"Ah, yes. We're making a casserole that we can pop in the oven in the morning, so we can arrive at the church with a hot dish."

"Is it your lovely chicken and rice casserole?" Olivia lifted a hopeful smile.

"Yes, it is. So, you can begin by chopping—"

The kitchen door swung open, and Grandpa Knox came in. "Do I smell cookies?"

"What if I told you no?" Grandma Knox gave her husband a peck on the cheek.

"All right. *Could* I smell cookies?" He waggled his brows.

"Cheeky devil, you." She pulled out a chair for him and pointed to the seat. "I'll bring you a glass of tea to go with them. Looks like you've been hard at the yardwork, my dear."

"Thank you, Susie."

Olivia began her chopping duty as a sudden realization hit her. Her grandparents' marriage was much like her and Ian's. Solid, warm—oh, how she missed him.

૭૩ॐ

Olivia sank deeper into the calming lavender bath. The picnic had been pleasant enough, but Olivia had to endure the platitudes from old friends about how sorry they were. All were kind and understanding, but it wore on her. Billy was the only one that didn't fawn over her with sympathy, and they had had an engaging conversation before he was called away to help carry something. She had then entered the church sanctuary, sat quietly, and prayed.

She had longed to return to her comfortable room and dig deeper into her great-grandmother's past. She already stayed up too late reading the night before—or should she say *deciphering*—the diary.

The book was elusive, written in a script style from so long ago, it was difficult to read. What appeared to be an *f* was actually an *s*, and a *y* was in current writing an *i*. The list went on and on.

When she searched online about how to read old handwriting, she discovered it was called paleography, and with all the tips she found, she quickly grew overwhelmed. At this rate, she'd need to hire an expert.

Olivia finally removed herself from the bath, dressed, and propped against a pile of pillows, smelling of sweet, fresh air and sunshine, while she attempted reading the spidery handwriting. Just as she was about to close the book and let it slip onto the nightstand, the strangest name burst out to her as if lit up like the neon sign in a convenience store window.

The Burning Sands.

She scanned the previous pages but did not see the name a second time. A few more pages over she found a mention of *the Sands*, which if she used the context did seem to be the same name. It was a tavern—*The Burning Sands Tavern.*

Her phone rang. She answered Angie's call, and in no time, she had pulled her friend into the search for more about the *Sands.*

"Try an online search," Angie said with certainty. "I'm sure it'll hit on something. And you found it mentioned several times?"

Olivia cradled the phone against her shoulder and thumbed through the diary. "Yes, I found a few other places that refer to the *Sands*, but I can't make everything out." She huffed. "It's hard to read. In places, the ink has faded beyond reading, or there are spots where it pooled into little blobs."

She groaned. "And then there's the difference between some letters actually being something other than the way they appear."

Her friend's voice muffled, speaking to someone in the same room before she returned to Olivia. "Sorry, I've gotta go. Another fire to put out. Talk to you soon."

"Bye. Hope things calm down for you." The line hummed in response.

Olivia shrugged and started an online search for the tavern in Trerose, Cornwall. An ad popped up about real estate in Trerose, and as a distraction, she navigated the site looking at properties until a description of an available property drew her attention. There was no picture.

Former business in a seventeenth-century building. Renovated in the eighties but in excellent condition. Living quarters on first floor.

She knew that translated to the second floor in American lingo. She glanced at the cost, mildly surprised. It wasn't cheap, but it also wasn't exorbitant. She noted the fine print at the end of the ad.

Owners retired, price negotiable.

She continued scanning the section, noting a small cottage to let in the same village. Her mind whirled. What would it hurt to take a brief vacation? She'd not traveled since Ian died. A flash of encouragement presented itself—this was the first time she'd acknowledged that Ian had *died* and not just *left*.

Maybe this was progress.

CAROLE LEHR JOHNSON

I

Trerose, Cornwall

September 1671

Grace Atwood perched on the harbor wall, the moon casting an ethereal glow on the boats, nodding in the slowly receding surf. Feet flat on the top of the wall, her knees bent, she rested her head on them. The pungent scent of sea-soaked sand mingled with the stench of rotting fish.

Laughter echoed behind her as the last of the fishermen stumbled from The Burning Sands Tavern, signaling her to return and help with the evening clean up before going home. She sniffed in amusement. The dwelling she called home was a small cottage above the cliffs she shared with her parents and two siblings like a school of pilchards packed into a barrel salted for the winter.

"Grace! Where ye be gurl?" Her father's voice grated, and she winced as she slid off the wall, legs stiff from a long day of serving drinks and pasties to leering men reeking of the day's catch, or to sweaty dirt-covered miners.

"Coming, Father." She edged her way past the staggering men.

Radigan Atwood crossed his arms over a broad, muscular chest. "Been callin' ye fer a time." He cocked his head, brown eyes spearing her with a cruel glint. "Wilmont be doin' all the work clearin' up. Git your shiftless backside to the tavern."

Wilmont would *not* be doing all the clearing up. She had a bit of idleness about her she appeared unable to control. One more thing she must face, along with her family.

Would she ever be free of this place—and the guilt from her past?

"Yes, Father. I needed air for a moment."

Radigan released a mocking laugh. "Get to the tavern, or ye shall be needin' some air, gurl!"

What was it about the cruel-tongued man that made anger rise within her? Seemed she should have grown accustomed to it by now. Her mother had told her to pay nay mind to his rantings. It was just his way. She had feared him at one time, yet he nay longer towered over her, his height not much more than her own.

Nearing the age of two and twenty, she understood her father thought his attitude and ways were right—above all others.

Grace's legs tugged like the weights on the gillnets the fishermen used to capture their haul for the day. How she hated working for her father. Once in the tavern, wool-gathering occupied her mind from the odious task of cleaning after the crowd of men who sloshed their drinks onto the tables and floor after over-imbibing. All except one.

Eudo Cubert was not uncomely to look upon, yet he held no *attraction* for Grace.

Yes, he was well-formed—tall, muscular, and tanned with sun-streaked hair tied into a queue. He was friendly but not overmuch, only nursing one drink each evening, always surveying her as she worked. His smile was sincere, not ogling like most of the others.

Although, there was something about the man that made Grace keep her distance despite the constant promptings of her father. Radigan Atwood hounded her relentlessly about growing too old for marrying and that he would not support an old maid for the rest of his life.

Grace returned the broom to its place, reached for her cloak, and said to her sister, "Arabel, good eve. I am away."

Arabel brought her dark head up to peer at her sister. "Aye. Be safe on the cliffs. Wait for Sebastian at the fork as always." She bent her head to the accounts and dipped her quill in the inkpot.

"Always do, Sister." Grace smiled. "Good eve."

Before leaving, Grace stuck her head in the kitchen, careful to be certain her father was distracted.

She whispered, "Eulalia, do ye have Mrs. Braddock's bits and pieces?"

A tall, thin woman of middle years grunted and pointed to a bundle on the table. "Aye, there it be. Your father is busy talkin' to Eudo, so not to worry 'bout him seein'."

"Thank ye. Ye are a dear one." Grace patted her shoulder and eased out the rear door.

Grace trudged the street along the harbor wall, crossing the bridge where the River Pol flowed to empty into the inner harbor. She paused a moment to watch the moon glint on the water, rippling with the gradual release of the flow to the sea.

She shivered and pulled her black cloak tighter as she climbed the path to the cliff's edge. She sat on the bench, looking across the Channel.

"God, what would my life be like if I somehow escaped this one ye have born me into? Help me. I feel as if I shall drown. Just like . . ."

Grace shook her head to clear her mind and waited for God to answer like the countless times she had sat there, waiting for Sebastian.

The answers never came. Why had God abandoned her?

The moon had moved much, signaling Sebastian's lateness. It was not like him. She rose, clutching the package against her middle. A small distance before she approached Gwynne Cottage, its white front shining brightly in the moonlight, Grace started at the sound of pebbles crunching on the path. She turned to see her brother's tall frame approach.

"Sebastian, what kept ye?"

"Sorry, my dear. Got held up at the mine." He raised his hand to halt her forthcoming worry. "All is well."

Grace sighed. "Thank the good Lord."

He made to sit on the short, rickety bench by the door of the cottage.

"Nay need to wait since it is a short walk home." The word *home* stuck in her throat. Home should be a comforting word, a place of refuge and peace. It was none of those things. She nodded and drew her fist to knock on the old woman's door but hesitated.

Changing her mind, she said to his retreating back, "Wait for me."

Sebastian returned to the bench and wearily eased onto the splintered surface.

Mrs. Braddock met Grace with a wide smile. Her hands stilled over a ragged piece of fabric, needle poised in one hand.

"Good eve. Would ye like to eat now, or shall I place it by the hearth to keep warm?"

The withered woman blinked, intelligence in her gaze. Grace pulled a candle from her pocket, and from the table, she retrieved the stone Sebastian had found years before, the uniqueness of it being the round hole at its center. She placed the candle in the hole and lit it. The stone sparkled under the candlelight, casting dancing shadows in the tiny cottage.

"Leave it, dearie. Shall eat up later. Can ye stay for a chinwag?" The old woman's eyes glimmered with hope. Few visited her except Grace and sometimes Sebastian. Yet tonight there was something in his eyes that saddened Grace.

"Nay, ma'am. I cannot stay this eve. Yet I shall come around to see ye soon and have tea."

"Got nay tea, dearie."

"Oh, Mrs. Braddock. Not to worry. Tea I shall bring." Grace crossed the room in three steps and stooped before her. "Ye know, there may be some pasties to be had with the tea." She raised her brows, eliciting a chuckle from the old woman.

Grace patted her knee and rose. "Now, I must go. Has been

a long and tiresome day, and Father shall not take kindly to getting home before me."

Mrs. Braddock's face clouded. "Have a care. That man is not to be trusted." She coughed into her hand. "Ye know this?"

"Aye, I do." Grace opened the door, and Sebastian rose. "Have a good night and bolt the door before ye sleep." She eased it shut.

Sebastian stood and brought his gaze down to meet hers, his brown hair flopping over one eye. "How fares she?"

"Fine. I know she would like a visit from ye soon."

He took her arm and hooked it through his. "I know. Shall make the time soon."

They walked on in silence, the sea crashing below them, the glow above lighting their path until Grace stopped.

"Sebastian, what ails ye?"

He stared at the sea for a time and then turned and strode to a nearby stone. As soon as he sat, he dropped his face into his hands and heaved a loud sigh. He spoke into his cupped hands, muffling his voice. "Ye know what today is, do ye not?"

Grace moved to stand over him and lay a hand on his shoulder. "'Tis on my heart since yesterday." She hesitated. "For certain, 'tis always on my heart."

"I should have done more."

An owl glided overhead, revealing a pure white underside, its heart-shaped face and black eyes peering down at them. Something ghostly in its stare made her skin crawl.

"Ye nor I could have done naught." She trembled at the memory. "We were but children."

Sebastian looked at her as he straightened. "In my heart, I know ye speak truth, but in my head I believe not." He took her arm and pulled her up with him. "Let us be gone. It shall not please Father that ye are late."

Grace knew it only too well. She still bore the scar.

ଓଗ

A crash accompanied by a scream awakened Grace as the sun lightened the window in the loft where she slept.

"What do ye mean there be nay hot meal awaitin' me?"

Something shattered as Grace bolted from the bed. Her mother's timid voice shook. "Rad," she moaned, "'tis late. I could not keep it hot so long without it coming to ruin."

A slap echoed through the paper-thin walls of the cottage and up the narrow stairs.

Grace wished that Sebastian had not moved out a few years ago. He was the only one who could calm Father when he was in his cups, which always altered his caustic tongue from cruel words to more cruel actions. Her brother's impressive height and strength influenced their father, who was a bully in every sense. But he knew he was no match for a man of Sebastian's size. She would suffer for defending her mother, but try, she must.

Taking the stairs cautiously, Grace stopped on the bottom step and saw her mother cowering by the hearth. Her father held the broom handle overhead, ready to strike.

"Nay!" Grace catapulted herself toward him, grabbed the handle, and wrenched it from his grasp. He raised his hand and slapped her across the face hard enough to send her careening into the table.

The door crashed against the wall, bouncing back toward her brother, who grabbed it in one large hand. "What goes on here, Father?"

In two strides, Sebastian had taken their father by the shoulders and slammed him onto the settle.

Radigan looked up at him and smiled. "Me boy! What brings ye here?"

"How dare ye hit me mother and sister. Ye are a brute and need a beating! If ye do such again, I shall kill ye!" Sebastian shoved his face near his father's. "Do ye understand?"

The man's face paled. "I be sorry, me boy. Just had a few too many at the ole Sands. Ye don't begrudge me that, do ye?"

Through clenched teeth, Sebastian said, "I begrudge ye everything, old man. Ye are a flay-flinted old—"

"Sebastian!" Melior Atwood screamed at her son. "Please, stop."

He brought his gaze to Grace, who now held a cloth to her swelling cheek and, with the other hand, mopped blood off their mother's hand.

"He has been drinking. 'Tis all. Things shall be aright on the morrow."

Sebastian stormed to the door. "Nay, Mother. It shall not! It never is." He looked at his father with a murderous expression. "Lift not a hand to either of them again, or ye shall be sent over the cliffs. 'Tis not an idle threat." He stomped from the cottage and into the gray mist that had settled over the dawn.

Hours later, snoring came from the small bedchamber next to the lower kitchen and living area of Atwood Cottage.

Melior's eyes were puffy and her face red splotched. Grace handed her mother a cup of hot tea, made one for herself, and joined her at the table.

Grace wrapped her hands around the mug. "Mother, why do ye stay with him? I know not a living person who does like him. The small children in the village run when he walks the lane."

Melior would not meet her daughter's eyes. "Ye know not 'bout our past, my dear. He was once a lovely man. Even now, he is nice to look upon. Most women cannot say that 'bout their men. They grow old, fat, and lazy. Not Rad."

She brought a hand to rest atop her mother's trembling one. "That is not all that is important. Kindness has much more worth. Do ye not see?"

Tears slid down Melior's face, and she choked on a sob. She patted her daughter's hand and stood. "I have much to see to today. To the market first." She fetched her tattered cloak and limped to the door. "I must find what your father requests for his evening meal." The door closed gently behind her.

Grace sipped her tea, sorrow welling inside. If only she could earn enough money to find a way for them to leave their dreadful life. Sebastian had made a way, but he was a man. Women did not have that choice. Her father paid her stingy earnings for her time at the Sands, yet she hid away all she could. The tin box where she stored the farthings was well hidden. That she made certain of. The path she took would take her a lifetime to save enough to fund their escape. Their very lives depended upon her.

She shoved away from the table and took her tea outside to watch the seagulls circling overhead in their incessant search for food. They were most fortunate, flying anywhere they chose. Life was simple for them. Scripture that Vicar Olford read came to mind.

Behold the fowls of the air: for they sow not, neither do they reap, nor gather into barns; yet your heavenly Father feedeth them. Are ye not much better than they?

Why did God not feed them and give them shelter to leave her brutal father?

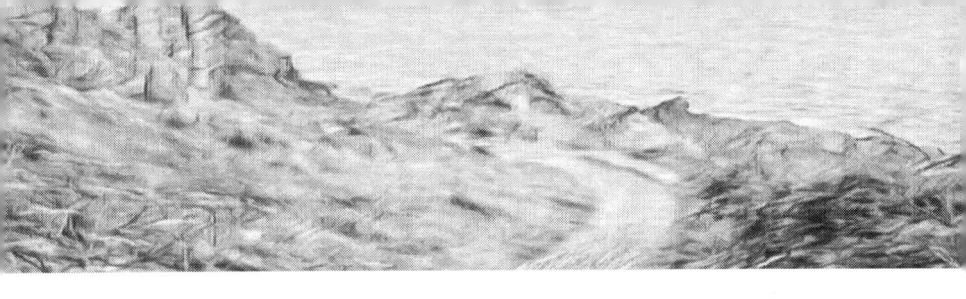

Chapter Three

May 2022

Olivia leaned against the kitchen cabinet, her customary large cup of tea in hand. Her gaze followed her grandmother as the sprightly woman buzzed from task to task. A sketch formed in her mind of a frazzled woman with a table full of children eagerly waiting for the delivery of homemade cookies. She made a mental note to form a rough draft of the scene for future inspiration.

Grandma Knox paused long enough to cock her head and peer at her granddaughter questioningly. "Isn't this a bit rushed, dear? I mean, we've only now discovered the tip of the iceberg of our genealogy. You don't have to rush off to Cornwall when you're not certain there'll be any evidence there at all."

She smiled to herself at her grandmother's occasional

Britishism. It endeared the sweet woman to her even more.

"I know. But this is the first thing I've really been able to cling to since Ian's death." She hesitated at the insult her words seemed to express. "I mean—to distract me." She slumped onto a stool.

Grandma Knox gave her a side hug. "No worries, my dear. I know what you meant. And I think it's marvelous to have something to focus on rather than your grief. Ian would be pleased. I am certain."

Olivia wasn't so sure. An interest in genealogy was one thing they had not shared. Not that it totally enamored her, but it had always been fascinating. She and her grandmother were of a like mind on the subject. Her mother, on the other hand, was a fanatic, which used to drive Olivia crazy when she lived at home.

"Do you think Mother may have information we don't?"

"Hmm?" Grandma Knox slid a plate of fresh teacakes across the counter to Olivia, who absently took one and nibbled.

"Dear, did you ask me a question?" Her grandmother sat at the table and sipped her own cup of tea.

Olivia shook away her thoughts. "Sorry." She took the seat beside her grandmother. "I was just wondering if Mother may have some genealogy information that we don't. Is she still hooked on her research?"

Grandma Knox heaved a long-suffering sigh. "I believe she is, although we've never been extremely close, you know?" She peered into her cup. "It shames me to say that since she left home for college, we never really communicated all that well. I tried." Tears glistened in her eyes. "I believe she tried as well."

"It's okay, Grandma. Being an extreme introvert, she had difficulty getting too close to people." Olivia shrugged. "I suppose I inherited a smidgen of that myself but not to her degree."

Grandma Knox dabbed at her eyes, then slapped her thighs and stood. "That is *not* something I've ever struggled with. Your grandfather would heartily agree."

Olivia also stood. "If you'll be staying in the kitchen for a while, I'll be glad to help you."

She cupped Olivia's shoulders, pulled her near, and kissed her cheek. "I'll be in here for the rest of the day, but I don't need any help. Why don't you get your laptop and keep me company? You can research your fabulous Cornish adventure and tell me all about it as you go."

Olivia wrapped her in a hug, then eased her to arm's length. "That sounds like a splendid idea."

Fifteen minutes later, Olivia tapped furiously on her laptop keyboard while Grandma Knox puttered around the kitchen, humming some unknown tune to Olivia's ears. The cottage she'd found was available to let for a few weeks because of a cancellation, and without hesitation, Olivia booked it before she could change her mind.

Completely captivated by its location in the small village of Trerose, she jumped when her grandmother spoke near her ear. "Oh, my! Isn't that charming."

Olivia pulled in a hesitant breath and released it. "I've booked it. Can you believe it?"

Grandma Knox patted her back and returned to her baking. "When do you leave?"

An uncomfortable quiet infused the cinnamon-scented kitchen.

"Olivia?" Her grandmother's voice drew out each syllable the same way she had done when she was a child, unsure what Olivia was up to while playing too quietly.

Timidly, Olivia answered, "The day after tomorrow."

Grandma Knox leaned against the counter, her eyes wide. "What! So soon?"

"I know it's sudden, but I wanted *that* cottage. There was a cancellation, and it would not be available again until December. I couldn't possibly be away over the holidays, now could I?" She offered a winning smile.

Grandma Knox tapped her chin with a forefinger. "I suppose that makes sense. But what if you can't get a flight?"

Olivia leaned back in her chair. She had given that point a lot of thought. "I realize it will be tough to endure, but I may just have to fly first class."

Her grandmother laughed, and then grew serious. "Won't that be horribly expensive?"

"Absolutely, but Ian made sure he left me well provided for. We loved to travel, and he wanted me to do as much as I wanted."

Another pang of sadness hit her but with less force than usual. She turned back to the computer. "Now to book my flights."

Over her shoulder, her grandmother added, "Don't forget a rental car. Cornwall is much easier to maneuver in a car than by train."

Olivia's brow furrowed. "How do you know that?"

"Your grandfather and I found that out the first time we traveled there. It was a few years before you were born." She smirked. "He even let me drive occasionally. I got the hang of it pretty quick. Surprised the dickens out of him!"

Olivia grinned, imagining her grandparents driving along a coastal path. She pictured herself driving that same coast in a few days.

The truth of it all rushed in. She was going to Cornwall.

ଔଞ

Two days later . . .
England

Olivia snuggled into her first-class seat on the last leg of her journey across the *Pond*. It felt extravagant to travel this way, but she was thankful to Ian for providing generously for her. Life had been so hard this past year. It was as if God was blessing her with a special gift of comfort.

She shook off the absurdity of her thoughts. God didn't *have* to provide anything but spiritual comfort in times of need. His mere presence was enough. Had she reacted that way after Ian died? No, she had not. She'd blamed God—*and* Ian.

The flight passed without incident as she alternately read and watched movies. Not once did she second-guess her decision to travel to Cornwall.

The sign signaled for them to fasten their seatbelts, and the captain came on the intercom alerting them to their landing at Heathrow. She looked out the window at the familiar landscape. Whenever she and Ian had made a trip to the UK, he said she was like a child on their way to an amusement park. Her love of England had spurred him to bring her to the country of her ancestors frequently, but they'd never made it as far south as Cornwall. Strange, since that's where her great-grandmother had come from.

Once out of customs, she sprinted to the Heathrow Express to Paddington Station, where she'd take a four-hour train ride to Looe. A rental car awaited her at the station. The short drive to Trerose would only be about fifteen minutes.

The landscape changed from tall, crowded buildings to undulating green hills gliding by with increasing frequency. Olivia's excitement accelerated with the train, the gentle rocking lulling her into drowsiness.

She first awoke in Cornwall when the train stalled at the small station in Saltash. Amazed that she had slept through numerous stops, she looked at her itinerary, noting there would be but one more stop before her change of train in Liskeard, taking her on to Looe.

Olivia gathered her things as her connection time was tight. She didn't relish the idea of driving after dark on unfamiliar roads.

A tall, thin young woman met her on the platform, holding a sign with her name inscribed across it. She explained about returning the rental car and handed over the car keys. After Olivia settled into the rental, she pulled in a ragged breath and straightened in the seat. "Into the fray!"

Although the ride took thirty minutes rather than the projected fifteen, she found the drive to be pleasant. Stone houses and cottages lay tucked along the road. Welcoming light glowed from their windows, illuminating her path toward the village, bringing a sense of peace—like a sign of coming home.

The directions from the owner of the cottage were spot on. She easily skirted the upper portion of the village and wound her way around the harbor, the rows of buildings shimmering in the clear night. She searched the cottages for the special light that would mark her destination. When the owner told her to look for a pink light, she'd know she was home.

Beryl said she would pop by the following morning to see if all was to Olivia's liking, and they could have a sit-down.

Olivia dropped her bag onto the small brown sofa facing the stone fireplace. Stepping slowly through the room, she flipped on lights as she went into the kitchen. Charming was the first word that crossed her mind. A narrow wooden table with four chairs sat beneath a wide paned window, a red toile valance hanging across the top. Far out, a light blinked and wavered across the English Channel.

At the table's center sat a plate wrapped in cling film, a note taped to the top.

Olivia,
Welcome to Gwynne Cottage. We hope this little treat of cinnamon scones will quick-start your stay with us. There is damson jam and clotted cream in the fridge. You'll find a nice variety of teas in the pantry.
Your hostesses,
Sheryl and Beryl

Olivia smiled at their thoughtfulness. She wasn't the least

tired after the long nap on the train, so she put water on to boil. While she waited, she took her bag to the bedroom and sorted her things, changing into a baggy sweatshirt and leggings.

As her tea steeped in a white teapot, she set out the jam, clotted cream, and lemon. Tugging back the cling film from the scones, the scent of cinnamon made her stomach growl. The last time she'd eaten was a hearty Cornish meat and vegetable pasty she'd picked up at Paddington Station and eaten on the train before the first stop at Reading.

A loaf of bread sat beside a covered plate of scones and small jars of strawberry jam and clotted cream on the table, and when she opened the fridge, there were also eggs, butter, and milk.

With the first bite of scone piled with jam and clotted cream, she closed her eyes and sighed. She chewed slowly, then washed it down with steaming Earl Grey. "Heavenly."

The word reminded Olivia she hadn't thanked God for her safe travels nor her food. She bowed her head. "Thank you, Lord, for bringing me here safely, and I'm sorry I have spent little time with you . . . lately."

She clasped her hands under her chin, the days and weeks before coming to mind and how she had kept God at a distance. She had been so angry after Ian's death and then numb in her grief. "I am so sorry for neglecting you, God. Please draw me near to You and help me to live again. I don't truly know how anymore."

A single tear slid along her cheek and dropped onto the table's surface. She braced herself to experience the extreme emotion of the pain of loss. To her surprise, she smiled. Ian had given her several years of joy, and rarely pain. That is—until he died. Memories of pleasant times spent in his company played through her thoughts like the scenes of a movie. A wonderful movie. She saw his bright smile, eyes twinkling with humor, and his laughter rang in her ears as if he were in the room.

Olivia inhaled deeply, released it, and finished the delicious scone. With a fresh cup of tea in hand, she stepped out onto the patio overlooking the sea. A cool, salty breeze tickled her face. She wrapped one arm around herself and drank the warm brew, breathing in the calm night air. God had brought her here to heal her spirit.

Olivia looked to the stars, a peace within spreading through her from head to foot, as she whispered into the night, "Ian, I know where you are and am happy for the years we had together." She lifted her cup. "Good night, my love."

Leaving the sea and the past behind, Olivia locked up the cottage and crawled between lavender-scented sheets. With the click of the lamp, semi-darkness engulfed her, the glimmer of the light she'd purposefully left on in the kitchen fading down the hall. And that night she slept as she had before the death of her precious husband.

છ৪৯

Olivia struggled with the dream, a pounding sound echoing through her sleepy haze. She opened her eyes with a groan and rolled over to see the time on the bedside clock. Seven?

Turning to regain sleep, the pounding became real. It was not a dream.

She bolted from bed and to the door, parting the curtain to

see who would call at such an early hour. Two elderly women stood on her doorstep clutching purple shopping bags. Both were short in stature, one sporting a pair of leopard tights topped with an alarmingly pink tunic that—thankfully—hung to just above her knees.

Wine-tinted hair spiked upward. Her companion's gray hair was also short but styled more sedately. She wore a pair of brown tailored slacks with a turquoise printed twinset—a term she'd heard her grandmother use for a cardigan and matching pullover sweater.

Olivia rubbed the sleep from her eyes and tried to clear her head. She flipped the latch and pulled the door open. "Good morning."

"Good morning. I'm Beryl Perry, and this is my sister, Sheryl Ford—we're twins." The gray-haired woman said with a little too much cheer for Olivia's befuddled state.

Though longing to return to bed, Olivia smiled and waved her hand to welcome then inside. "Please come in." She fought the urge to laugh at the extreme differences in their appearance. Though twins were not always created equal.

Olivia eased the door closed, and she overhead a stage whisper from the sensibly dressed Beryl as the sisters entered the small kitchen. "Sheryl, I told you we should've waited until this evening or tomorrow before we barged in on her. There's jet lag to consider, you know?" She huffed.

"Oh, Beryl, get your knickers out of a twist! No need to sleep the day away. There's adventure to be had."

Olivia wasn't sure she wanted to join in any adventures concocted by the eccentric sister nor would she admit she had overheard their conversation. The women placed the purple bags on the table and emptied them.

Sheryl offered a grin to Olivia, her bright pink lipstick that matched her top covering a mouth wrinkled with age. If Olivia had to guess, this woman would favor the paintings by Picasso or perhaps the work of Dali.

"Olivia, we've brought you a few groceries. We'll do our village tour as soon as you're dressed." Her gaze traveled from Olivia's face to her toes and up again. She clapped her hands. "Chop, chop, my dear. The light won't last all day now, will it?" She laughed at her own joke and turned to her sister. "Now, Beryl, let's get to it and make this lovely young thing some breakfast whilst she dresses."

Beryl sent Olivia an apologetic half-smile. "Please pardon my sister. She can be overly . . . excited."

Sheryl grimaced, but just as quickly, her expression brightened. "Yes! Especially when the *vicar* is around!"

Beryl's expression changed to one of horror. "Sheryl!"

She harrumphed. "Oh, lighten up. When Olivia sees him, she'll agree with me whole-heartedly."

"You're old enough to be his grannie, you old hag." Beryl blew out a puff of breath. "He wouldn't spit on you if you were on fire."

Olivia wondered if she should step in before they came to blows. Thankfully, the interaction calmed when Sheryl removed a bottle and plopped it on the table.

"Here you are, my dear. We know how you Yanks like your pop."

Olivia glanced to find a glass bottle of a cola soft drink and smiled. "That is very kind of you, but you've already left me so many things. I enjoyed the tea, scone, and clotted cream."

She was about to excuse herself from the tour, but the next sentence died on her lips with their sheepish grins of appreciation.

"Ladies, I thank you, but I'm moving rather slowly this morning. May I meet you somewhere in the village after I've had time to shower, dress, and have breakfast?"

Beryl's eyes widened. "Well, of course, my dear." Her expression changed as she peered at her sister. "See—I told you it was too early."

Sheryl didn't miss a beat. "Pfft! We'll make breakfast for her while she gets ready."

Not once did she address Olivia but began pulling out food and cooking utensils. "Now, Olivia, get on with it and prepare. We'll cook, and by the time you're done, we'll have a sit-down and eat."

Olivia was shooed from the kitchen, the banter of the two sisters following her down the passage to the bedroom. "Sheryl, you're such an old blighter! These young people need a firm hand. Lying about half the day while the sun's shining. There's too much to be accomplished. Get with it, woman!"

Olivia didn't hear Beryl's reply. She rushed into her room and covered her mouth with both hands to muffle the laughter bursting from within her—and it felt good indeed.

II

October 1671

The weather chilled overnight. Grace huddled beneath her cloak as she walked the coastal path to The Burning Sands Tavern. She struggled for weeks with the revelation of what she must do to flee her father's tyranny, but she feared she could not accomplish the task. Tonight would begin the first phase—much like a new moon.

When Grace arrived at the tavern, Eudo Cubert sat at his usual table. The presence of her brother next to Eudo was a surprise.

She nodded to Sebastian and sent him a questioning glance before going to the kitchen. Her father railed at Caye, the kitchen maid, who knelt, mopping a puddle of amber liquid.

Radigan Atwood stood over the girl, hands on hips, his face flaming. "That," he pointed to the tankards littering the floor, "will be taken from your wages!" As he turned to leave, he nearly bumped into Grace. His glare halted her movement, and he rushed from the room.

Caye settled onto her heels and tilted her head to look at Grace. Tears glided along her slender, pale face. "He be a hard man. How do ye live with he?"

Grace stooped to the girl's level and placed a hand on her shoulder. "Sorry I am that he treats ye so. Please have a care when near him. He is a cruel man to be sure. Keep your distance. It shall be for the better."

The girl nodded and returned to her chore.

Eulalia, the cook, released a sad sigh. "Aye, how do any of we live with the likes of he?" She smacked a large scoop of mutton pie onto a plate and handed it to Grace. "This be fer that looker settin' out there."

The cook took in Grace's frock and gave her a sideways glance. Grace swallowed at the woman's assessment of the forest-colored dress and hoped she could not smell the scent of lavender clinging to her. She picked up the salver and left without a word.

Sebastian's eyes widened as she approached the table, the salver balanced on her hand. He reached up as if to take the food from her, but she turned away.

"Nay, 'tis for Eudo. Eulalia did say so."

Eudo's brows rose. "Did she now?" He made nay move to take it from her.

Grace placed it on the table before him, and just as quickly, he shoved it toward Sebastian.

"Nay, Mistress Grace. 'Tis for Sebastian. I did hear him asking fer the mutton pie. I have nowt liking for it meself." He sent her a heart-stopping smile. "Tatties and leeks are more to my taste."

Grace stared at him, caught by the handsomeness of the man, his sun-streaked hair against tan skin. The man was undeniably fine to look upon, muscular, with a nicely sculpted face, not overly tall. Yet why did she not have a stirring within her? Most of the women of the village paused in their washing to watch as he passed. The thought came upon her not without humor. Eulalia had said to take the food to *that looker* . . .

She swung her gaze from Eudo to Sebastian. Eulalia thought her brother a looker? Grace peered at him through fresh eyes. He was pleasant looking. Many a girl had told her so. Why had she thought of Eudo rather than Sebastian?

Grace shrugged, sent Eudo what she hoped was a beguiling smile, and as she turned to leave offered her brother an apology. A round of men's laughter followed her to the kitchen. Eulalia huddled over an enormous iron pot, stirring slowly.

She took a plate and stood behind the cook. "Why did ye not tell me the pie was for Sebastian?"

A slow chuckle escaped the woman. "Ye did not ask who it be for." Her shoulders shook as she met Grace's gaze.

Grace extended the plate. "Tatties and leeks for Eudo please."

The woman guffawed. "Who did ye take it to, gurl?"

Heat infused Grace's face as she made way to deliver the meal.

Eulalia waved the wooden spoon in front of her. "Tell me who."

Grace hung her head and whispered, "Eudo."

The woman burst into laughter again. "Always thought ye did take a notice of the man. Jest proves me right." Her mirth tapered off, and she lowered her voice. "Your father would be that happy to know it. Are ye coming around to his way of thinking that ye should wed Eudo?"

Grace's head snapped up. "Why would ye say that? Just because my father wants it would not be why . . ."

"*Why*, my dear?" Concern now shone in the woman's face. "I would not want ye to marry fer what your father wants. Ye should love the man."

Love, thought Grace, was a luxury, and she had not felt love like that of a husband for any man—nor had she seen a trace of its kind between her mother and father. Could perhaps she and Eudo obtain it? Either way, with shame, she realized she would marry the man if she must to escape the wrath of her father.

◈

Sebastian's long legs, crossed at the ankles, jutted out onto the coastal path before Grace. She stood over him, arms hugging her chest, fixing him with her sternest look.

"Do ye not look the picture of innocence, Brother." She made to step over his legs and continue on her way.

He pulled her to sit upon the bench beside him and nudged her shoulder. "Grace, what have I done to cause such anger in ye?"

She glared at him. "Why did ye tease me so in front of Eudo?"

His gaze traveled to the crashing waves below. "I see how ye dressed and the smile ye gave him afore ye left. I have been your elder brother for a time, Grace. Do this not just because Father wills it. Have a care. Please."

Grace recoiled. "What do ye mean? How could ye know what I mean by this dress?" Her hands fidgeted with the parcel holding Mrs. Braddock's vittles.

"'Tis your best dress, and ye rare wear it 'cept to church." He glanced at her for a moment. "Eudo has long admired ye, Grace. Yet ye have never shown him nay mind 'cept to bring him ale and vittles."

Grace would not meet his gaze. "Ye do not understand."

"Ye have shown him kindness, as ye do all, yet nothing more. 'Til this eve. What has brought this change?"

A surge of anger mingled with a lifetime of fear overtook her. She jumped to her feet and stood over him. "I am sore tired of waiting to die in the house of a man who only knows bitterness, anger, and cruelty. I know not what has made him thus. Does not matter what has brought it about. 'Tis nay longer for me to bear. Should I wed Eudo I may bring our mother and little ones to leave this wretched life!"

She wheeled, leaving Sebastian behind, and making her way to Gwynne Cottage. For once, she did not cry, and her thinking was clear and focused. Eudo had never been cruel, whether in word nor deed. There was always coin on the table once he departed the Sands. Generously so.

Grace could only assume he would be generous to her and her family. Why should he not?

A hand gripped her shoulder. "Grace. Please hear what I

must say. Ye are my sister, and I love ye."

She faced Sebastian, her anger cooling. "It makes nay matter. 'Tis the only way out."

"Nay. 'Tis not." He pulled her into a brotherly embrace. "I have hidden money away. 'Tis yours."

Grace raised her head, his shirt damp where she had laid her head against his shoulder, unaware of her tears. "Nay, Sebastian. I shall not take your money. Soon ye shall have a wife and family and with it ye can build a home."

He shook his head, his jaw taut. "I do not want ye to marry Eudo."

She tilted her head. "Why ever not? I understood ye were friends and ye do work for him from time-to-time."

"Aye. But his coin does not come by pleasing means, and I would not have ye suffer for it."

Curiosity slowly stirred within her. "What do ye mean?"

"'Tis not for me to say. I do believe Eudo would treat ye with kindness, but what he does to earn coin may be of harm to those near him, even if they be innocent."

Grace took in all he said, unrest twisting within her. "I shall think on all ye said. Thank ye for your honesty." Something unsettling crept over her. "Are ye aiding him?"

Her brother's face clouded before he answered, "Be not concerned for me."

They arrived at Gwynne Cottage, and Sebastian sat on the bench and turned his gaze to the sea, resting his head against the wall.

Grace knocked on Mrs. Braddock's door and entered with

a smile to the older woman, who had not a soul to care for her if Grace did not bring her remnants from the tavern's kitchen.

An hour later, Sebastian walked Grace to the door of their family's cottage and bid her goodnight. She encouraged him to come in and speak to their mother, but he refused, saying he was weary from a long day in the mines.

Melior sat at the table with a cup of tea, another steaming cup across from her. Five-year-old Degory sat in her lap, large tears rolling down his cheeks, glistening in the firelight.

Grace hung her cloak on the peg by the door and joined them. She reached for her tea and brought it to her lips, speaking over the rim. "What has happened?" She sipped the soothing liquid, tension from her conversation with Sebastian easing.

Her mother lifted her gaze, meeting Grace's eyes, her head giving an imperceptible shake. "Degory had a tumble down the stairs." She cleared her throat. "'Tis better now." She brought a cloth away from the child's temple and dipped it in a basin of water. She wrung it out and returned it to his face.

The boy peered through thick, dark lashes at his elder sister. "Did not."

It was near a whisper, but Grace heard him clearly. Her mother's eyes filled with moisture, and before long, tears coursed along her face.

Passionate fury swelled within Grace. Something had to be done about Radigan Atwood.

"Mayhap ye should put Degory to bed. Sleep would be best for him." She saw the understanding in her mother's eyes.

"Aye." She rose and led the child to bed.

Grace noticed a piece of shattered wood by the stairs. He had used a stick to beat his son. She had never known her father to hit any of the younger children before this night.

With sluggish steps, Melior returned to the table. She moved as a woman twice her age.

"How did it begin?" Grace cringed, her words harsher than she intended.

Her mother sat quietly for a time, drinking the tepid liquid. She wiped her eyes with a tattered rag. "Degory has been ill for a few days. I wished to summon Doctor Keast, yet your father shall not allow it." She exhaled. "I, too, felt poorly, but Rad would not hear of wasting coin. Degory worsened, but it made nay matter to Rad. My mistake was to beg."

Grace's fury mounted, but she checked it for the moment.

"He threatened Degory with a beating if he did not work. Said he was a dawdler. A fit of coughs took me, and he turned his anger on me and said I was of the same cloth. He struck me." She sobbed into the rag.

Grace took her mother's hand and squeezed it. "Sorry, I am."

"My sweet boy came to my defense, he did." Melior flinched. "I could hear Alsyn crying upstairs. Degory and me both looked up the stairs at once. We knew what he was capable of. Before we could do aught else, he fetched a stick of wood and hit Degory on the head. He then made way to the stairs, but I grabbed him and pleaded he not go to her. He was in his cups, and I knew what he would do."

Grace knelt beside her mother and embraced her, rocking her like a child. "'Tis well now, Mother. He is gone."

Silence engulfed them for a while before Grace had the courage to ask what happened to Alsyn.

"I hung onto Rad and entreated him to leave her abed, telling him to beat me, not her." Her mother looked down. "He did so."

Grace's voice was near a whisper. "Where is he now?"

"Said he was to Kernow to see Mr. Tallow about more drink for the Sands."

Grace closed her eyes and prayed that God would send him over the cliff, as Sebastian had said. How could they go on? If Sebastian found out, he would kill their father. Though it might solve their problems, she would not see her brother go to the gibbet.

Once Grace had soothed her mother and tended her bruises, she guided her to bed. She soon eased herself into bed next to Degory and Alsyn. She couldn't bear to sleep in the room she once shared with Arabel and leave them unguarded.

Grace's plan to marry Eudo occupied her thoughts as sleep was not swift to come. If it would save her family, she would do almost anything. Perchance Eudo was an answer to her prayers.

CAROLE LEHR JOHNSON

Chapter Four

After a breakfast of eggs, sausage, toast with jam, and two cups of tea, Olivia rose lethargically from the table while watching the twins scurry about cleaning the kitchen, babbling incessantly.

She marveled at their energy level. They never ceased talking, constantly berating one another while wearing the warmest of smiles, which was baffling behavior, though most entertaining.

Sheryl took Olivia's cup before she finished the last sip. "Now, let's get to it, ladies. We have a lot to do before the sun sets."

Beryl was quick to share her thoughts on the matter. "Sister, we don't have to reveal every inch of Trerose in one day. I'm certain Olivia has much to do. Perhaps we could break it down into bits." She turned to Olivia. "My dear, is there something you had in mind upon your arrival?"

Sheryl crossed her arms over her narrow chest and widened her eyes expectantly.

Olivia looped her bag over her shoulder and stood. "Well, I had wanted to meet with the realtor about a building I saw for sale. But I haven't made an appointment, so that may have to wait."

Beryl's face brightened. "Please tell us which building is for sale."

Olivia took a tattered printout from her purse, unfolded it, and handed it to her. The wine-colored head tilted next to the gray, and they both released a soft *oh*.

Olivia frowned. "What? Is there a problem?"

Beryl was the one to answer. "Not exactly, dear. But it's a commercial property, not a home."

"I'm aware of that."

"You are?" Sheryl asked incredulously.

"Yes, ma'am." Olivia's confidence waned. "The building intrigued me. I'm considering my options."

"You plan to stay awhile?" This was from Beryl, who now seated at the table, her hands clasped.

"I'm uncertain how long, but, yes, I would like to stay for a while." It was the most confident decision Olivia had felt about *anything* since Ian. She would see where this path led, and if it was only back to the U.S. then so be it. "I believe the ad mentioned something about living quarters above the shop."

The sisters shared brow-raised looks, Sheryl's brows stark

gray compared to her colored hair. A laugh bubbled up inside Olivia. She cleared her throat. "I suppose I need to look at it before I plan further. Since you ladies are from here, you could be a wealth of knowledge." She smiled warmly. "Your help would be much appreciated."

She turned to the door. "May we go there now? I'll call the agent and schedule a meeting for later." She looked from one to the other.

Both women nodded, grabbed their bags, and headed for the door, simultaneously chiming, "Into the fray!" They lifted their umbrellas like batons as if going into battle.

Olivia couldn't suppress a laugh. She was in for a very interesting vacation.

ଓଯ

The building's neglected whitewashed façade appeared more gray than white. Morning sunlight highlighted the harbor side of the two-storied structure, revealing thick, dingy glass, and a gray slate roof. A plaque by the entrance noted in Roman numerals its establishment in the seventeenth century. Captivated with the possibilities of what had occurred in the aged building, Olivia longed to transfer the image before her onto paper.

Sheryl and Beryl stood on either side of her with hands-on-hips. Beryl leaned toward Olivia. "The old girl looks rather well, considering her age."

Her sister glanced at her, then quipped, "Wish I could say the same of you."

Olivia took a step back, thinking this may be the quelling blow.

Beryl returned the jibe. "Since you're older than me, I'd say I have the leg up, *Sister*."

They ogled one another and then burst into laughter. "Good one, Beryl!"

Olivia observed all in amazement. They actually *enjoyed* cutting each other to shreds. She wondered what the vicar thought of them.

Sheryl strode to Beryl and looped arms with her. "Let's walk the coastal path for a bit and work off breakfast, then we'll ask about the Sands building." She glanced at Olivia. "I guess there wasn't anyone available to answer the message you left."

Olivia nodded and strolled behind them, inhaling the fresh mid-morning air and its invigorating scents of wildflowers, the briny sea, and an unidentifiable smell of . . . *coconut or vanilla*?

"Ladies, what is that I smell? It's pleasant enough, but I can't place it."

"Gorse, my dear." Beryl halted their walk and pointed to a nearby cluster of shrub-like plants dotted with bright yellow blooms.

"Oh, that's right. I recall seeing it in Scotland when my—" She hadn't meant to bring up Ian, not yet.

"When you *what*, dear?" asked Sheryl.

Olivia closed her eyes but forged on. "When my husband and I toured there a few years ago."

Beryl patted her shoulder. "I recognize the pain in your eyes, Olivia. I've been a widow for near on twenty years. I am sorry. You are much too young to have experienced such tragedy. Do you have any children?"

Olivia took a sharp breath. "We . . . couldn't."

Beryl offered her condolences, and Sheryl seemed not to hear Olivia's answer.

Sheryl tut-tutted. "So true. That's why I've elected to never marry." She sniffed arrogantly. "So many men—so little time!" She strutted ahead.

Beryl's gaze held sympathy when she turned to Olivia. "Don't mind her, dear. She's an old crone who fancies herself a beauty queen." She glared at her sister's retreating form. "Always has."

The comment pulled Olivia into the present, and she chuckled. "You two are remarkable."

Beryl shot her a pleasant smile. "We aim to please."

By the time they hiked up the path toward the northeast and looped inland over pastures and through thickets and groves, Olivia's exhaustion overwhelmed her. These women had to be in their eighties, and they had worn *her* out.

With no shortness of breath whatsoever, Beryl said, "Sheryl, let's take Olivia to The Pilchard for lunch."

"Indeed. They have the most delicious pasties this side of Bodmin."

Lunch sounded heavenly to Olivia as well as something cool to drink. "I could go for a huge glass of iced tea with lemon right now."

The sisters exchanged glances, and after a moment, Beryl piped up, "Not likely to find the like here, but we'll see what we can do."

After the long, sunny walk, Olivia nearly stumbled through the pub's dark interior as she followed the sisters to a table by the window. Once seated, she watched the boats bobbing in the harbor, seagulls swooping to catch a meal.

Her stomach growled as the male server approached. Beryl immediately told him Olivia's drink of choice, and he said he would take care of it.

Olivia watched as Sheryl's gaze took in the young man's physique. All she could manage was a wide-eyed stare at the woman's bravado.

Beryl patted her forearm. "Not to worry. She's all bluff and nonsense. Likes to put on a good show and all."

Olivia didn't quite believe Sheryl's audacity wouldn't extend to making a pass at any good-looking man who came her way—no matter if they were likely a third of her age.

Their food and drinks arrived, and Sheryl winked at the server. "There's a love."

To Olivia's surprise, the iced tea was not half-bad. The hot beef and potato pasties were just the thing she needed to fortify her after trekking through the countryside. As they rose to leave, a tall, lean woman with straight blonde hair approached their table.

"Hello. Nice to see you, Miss Ford, Mrs. Perry." Her chin bobbed as she greeted each woman.

"Oh, so lovely to see you, Teffeny. How goes the plant business?" Sheryl asked.

"Quite well, actually."

"Would you have any cornflowers still, my dear?" Beryl inquired. "Ours seem to have lost their will to live. Rather sad looking at the moment."

"Oh my, we've failed to introduce you to Olivia." She motioned with a wave of her hand. "Teffeny Leverton, this is Olivia Griffin—and Olivia G—"

"Oh, for Pete's sake, Beryl. You're not introducing royalty!" Sheryl smirked at her sister and lifted her arm to hail their server. "Another round of drinks please, love? We are going to chat just a bit longer."

Teffeny added, "Nothing for me please. I'd finished when I saw you about to leave. I can only chat a moment." She settled into her seat. "So, Olivia, what brings you to Cornwall?"

Olivia opened her mouth, but Sheryl answered for her. "She wants a look-see at the old tavern. Fancies putting roots down in the village. Maybe open a *shop*." She whispered the last word as if it was scandalous.

Teffeny quirked her mouth. "Very nice. It's a lovely old place. Been well taken care of. Sure hated to see the Marlows leave."

"Why did they?" Olivia took a drink and cradled the cool glass in both hands.

"They were both getting on in age, and Mr. Marlow passed suddenly. Their son had no interest in the family business, so she moved south to live with her sister."

"What business was there?"

"A pub. Been in their family for generations. Looks like the end of an era." Teffeny cleared her throat. "Unless you're planning on opening a pub."

Olivia laughed. "Not me. I'm more of a books-and-tea kind of person."

"Is that our plan, to sell books and tea?"

They all chuckled and began drilling Olivia about types of businesses she could start there. Dazed, she listened intently and shared her grandmother's connection to Cornwall and their genealogy research.

"Honestly, initially, I just wanted to visit where my great-grandmother grew up. But when I came across the realty ads, something sort of clicked."

Olivia nervously toyed with her glass and shrugged a shoulder. "It's more of a diversion from—" She swallowed the lump that suddenly lodged in her throat. "I am a widow. My husband died last year, and this trip began as an escape from the memories that surrounded me."

Why had she shared that? Uncomfortable silence engulfed the shared space.

"I'm sorry. I didn't mean to drag down this happy party." She grabbed her bag from the arm of her chair and stood. "It was a pleasure meeting you, Teffeny." She peered at the twins. "Thank you both for a lovely morning. The tour was wonderful."

Olivia turned to go, but a gentle hand took her arm.

Beryl's eyes shone with unshed tears. "I am so very sorry, my dear. Here we've been dragging you up and down the landscape and chatting away like choughs. We were unaware of your sorrow. Please forgive two old biddies."

Sheryl sniffed and dabbed at her nose with a lacy vintage handkerchief. She stood and took Olivia's other arm. "Oh, stuff and nonsense! Keep moving, I say. It will keep the doldrums at bay."

Olivia stared at her for a long moment. A sense of relief gripped her, and she laughed. Before long, they were all laughing, turning heads around the pub.

Teffeny joined them. "I say we go have a look-see at that old building. I haven't walked by in quite a while." She sent Olivia a questioning expression, maybe sizing her up.

Olivia wondered if it were a challenge. "Yes, let's go."

They filed out of The Pilchard, along the harbor wall teeming with gulls, and over the old stone Roman bridge.

Beryl grabbed Sheryl's arm and steered her to follow Olivia and Teffeny. "Sister, we will not bother the vicar. He has too much on his plate already without having to fend off your misguided advances."

Teffeny tipped toward Olivia and whispered, "They are a pair, are they not?"

Olivia whispered back. "Why is the vicar *not* interested in Sheryl?"

Teffeny laughed. "He's about half her age."

"I see." Olivia's understood perfectly. "I'm glad Beryl can keep her in check."

"She's successful—most of the time."

The sisters lagged, arguing back and forth about Sheryl's behavior toward the vicar. Olivia caught snippets but focused so she could find her way later.

The mention of the vicar brought to her mind a verse from the twenty-third Psalm about God guiding his children. Olivia hugged her bag in front of her like a shield. Was this what *she* wanted or God? She hadn't asked God for direction before she sailed into a life-altering commitment. She would be sure to pray over everything

The building came into view, and Sheryl sauntered to the door and reached for the handle.

Beryl slapped her sister's hand away. "That's called trespassing."

"Pfft! Hugo won't mind." Sheryl glanced at Teffeny. "Will he?"

She lifted her brows. "Best ask him yourself."

Olivia looked a question at her.

Teffeny answered, "He's my cousin—an estate agent."

Olivia lowered her voice. "Does Sheryl have a *thing* for him too?"

Teffeny chuckled. "No. He's too *old* for her."

Olivia tightened her lips. "Really? How old is he—ninety?"

"No. He's fifty-five."

They exchanged an *aha* look.

Olivia turned to the twins. "Is Hugo as handsome as the vicar?"

Beryl frowned, but Sheryl perked up. "Hardly! But Hugo's an honest man. He won't allow you to be gazumped."

Beryl gasped. "Sheryl, the vicar is an honest man!"

Sheryl glared at her sister. "Beryl, I know that."

The two sparred, while Olivia and Teffeny watched in amusement. Olivia asked, "What is gazumped?"

Teffeny answered, "Just means making an offer on a property and someone else coming along and beating it."

"That's not fair."

"No, it isn't."

After a few more moments of listening to the verbal bout, Olivia asked, "Are they constantly like this?"

"Always," Teffeny said dryly. "And you're seeing them on a good day."

Olivia bit her lip to stop a laugh. She could not imagine this was a good day for the pair. She glanced at the building and then at Teffeny.

"Care for some tea at Gwynne Cottage? I'd love to ask you some questions about the village if you don't mind."

Teffeny smiled. "Sounds lovely. And don't worry about these two. They have Bingo later, so they won't follow us. Nothing interferes with that." She huffed. "And it's at the church."

They told the sisters goodbye and headed for the cottage.

"I need to know more about this vicar that Sheryl goes on about."

Teffeny laughed. "Yes, she's quite smitten. He's a wonderful chap. Takes their antics in stride as do the lot of us."

Olivia's breath became short as they climbed the steep incline toward her cottage, the thought warming her. *Her* cottage. "Who would you recommend for information about the local history? I'd like to know if there's anyone left that would have known my great-grandparents."

Her brow furrowed. "There's the local historical society." She paused. "Come to think of it, the vicar may help with that. He was born here and has a knack for remembering dates like no one I've ever met."

A thought gripped Olivia. "By the way—can you give me your cousin's number? I want to make an appointment with him to see the inside of the building."

Teffeny pulled her phone from her pocket. "Sure. Let's get settled with a cup of tea, and I'll give it to you." She pinched her lips together. "That is, if the twin hooters don't blast in."

Olivia's laugh burst from her chest. "Hooters?"

"That's what we call a car horn. Those two are like constant hooters going off. They can't seem to help themselves. Two sod duffers. But we hold them with fondness."

"Pardon me?"

"Sorry. Two irritating women."

Olivia clicked her tongue. "I see."

"I will say this about them—they are very generous. With their money and time."

"I've seen that. When I arrived last night, they practically stocked my kitchen." She smiled. "And this morning they showed up early with more groceries and made me a massive breakfast."

"Sounds about right."

Seated at the kitchen table with steaming cups, Olivia and Teffeny spoke of themselves, the sisters, and the village. She dearly missed her friend, Angie, but maybe she had made a new friend in Teffeny Leverton, and for that she was immensely thankful.

☙❧

A booming clap of thunder and rain pelting the window roused Olivia from sleep with a start. She glanced at the clock on the bedside table and groaned. *Seven*—now she'd never get back to sleep.

Resettling onto the fluffy pillow, she stared at the rain beating the glass. Too early to rise but too late to sleep in. She was to meet Hugo in the village and have a tour of the property at nine. She could take a long shower, make herself a full breakfast, pray and read her Bible, and still have time for a leisurely stroll down to Trerose. In the rain, it seemed.

Resigned, she rolled out of bed and staggered to the bathroom. Standing in the stream of warm water, she mulled over what her plan of action should be. This was the first time in her entire life she was flying by the seat of her pants. Ian would be shocked.

Ian. He was a planner too. They enjoyed their times of plotting out excursions and adventures even if only to a nearby town.

With sausage sizzling on the stove, she popped in bread for toast and poured a strong cup of Cornish Smugglers tea. Her first cup of the brew—made by Beryl and Sheryl yesterday—had forced her into alertness. It's just what she needed today. She guessed a smuggler *needed* to be alert. The stuff could probably hold a spoon upright in the cup.

Half an hour later, she was dressed and ready to go when a knock sounded at the door. She groaned. "Oh, no." If it was the twins—and who else would it be—she wondered how to get rid of them politely?

Holding her breath, she opened the door to find a fiftyish man with black hair and neatly trimmed beard.

"Good morning. I'm Hugo. I know we have an appointment

at the old pub, but I thought I'd pop 'round to escort you." He held a massive umbrella over his head and pointed upward. "This brolly will keep a crowd from a pelting. Though I hope you have your wellies."

Olivia blew out a breath. Would she ever understand their slang?

She smiled and invited him in. "That is very kind of you." He remained just inside the door, his dark blue raincoat dripping onto the rug.

"I'll wait here while you grab your things." Hugo rested the tip of his brilliantly hued striped umbrella within the confines of the rug and glanced around the room while Olivia grabbed her backpack and a light rain jacket.

"I'm ready. But I don't have any wellies."

He looked at her feet. "Well, nothing to be done for it. We soldier on."

By the time they had *soldiered on* to the old building, Olivia's feet were thoroughly soaked, yet she had to admit that the brolly had kept her dry otherwise.

While Hugo unlocked the door, Olivia peered through a large window and found only darkness.

Hugo flipped on the lights, and with a flourish, he waved his arm in a mock bow to usher her into the large open room. Drop cloths covered a few tables holding upturned chairs. To her left, a wide dark-stained counter ran along the wall that faced the harbor, the window offering a clear view of the water which stood between low and high tide for the morning.

Olivia crept around the room, taking in every inch of the space. Dark beams paralleled overhead, scarred with age and, most likely, stained by cigar and pipe smoke. When she crossed the room, she noticed a door at the end of the bar.

"Where does this lead?"

Hugo tilted his chin up. "Go on. Have a look-see." He pulled a chair from underneath a cloth, placed it on the floor, and sat. "I'll look through the papers on this old girl. I have a flyer of sorts that has details on the place."

"Thank you." Olivia lightly eased the door open and stood still.

"Light switch is on your left."

She found it, and the room flooded with light to reveal a commercial kitchen with all the modern accompaniments—impressive, though dated. But she wouldn't need anything like this. Her mind had focused more on a bookshop that maybe sold tea and scones. And she wasn't even certain about that.

The kitchen in the old building was certainly not teashop material, more for pub fare. Before exiting the kitchen, she peered through the window that overlooked a small garden filled with wilted plants. One side of it bordered the lane that crossed the narrow River Pol, passing under the stone bridge they'd crossed.

Olivia returned to the main area and found Hugo's head bent over his folder of papers. It appeared her tour of the bottom floor was complete when she saw the narrow staircase.

"Hugo, may I go upstairs?"

Without looking up, he said, "No worries. Just mind the cobwebs." He lifted his head. "By the by, there's a broom by the railing. Grab that and sweep the air as you go."

Olivia lifted her brows and clenched her teeth. She *hated* spiders but did as she was told, glad to have a weapon handy.

At the top of the stairs, Olivia halted on the landing and noted three doors. The first, to her left, opened easily. It was not an over large room and was empty of all furnishings. A limp lace curtain hung over the paned window. Although crusted with dirt, she could make out the garden at the back of the kitchen. Feeble light glinted off the flowing water emptying into the harbor.

Hugo shouted up the stairs. "Are you having a proper self-guided tour?"

Olivia strode to the opened door and called down the stairwell. "I'm fine. Give me a few more minutes, or come on up."

His slow steps sounded on the time-scarred stairs. She walked to the next room down the hall and found it much the same as the other, only larger. Hugh waited for her at the door of the third room, a black portfolio tucked under his arm.

With lifted brows and a small smile, he asked, "Well?"

Olivia sucked in a long breath, her mind whirling with emotions. She'd not given herself enough time to fully soak in the building—or grasp what she was doing here.

Hugo held up the old keys and jingled them enticingly.

Grace opened her mouth to tell him she wasn't quite ready to make such a monumental decision when he surprised her.

"Take them. Come back. Bring a picnic. But have some cleaning things in hand if you plan on staying a while." He shot her a lopsided grin and jingled the keys once more. "Keep them for a couple of days. No rush."

A loud clap of thunder rattled the windowpanes, and she jumped.

"Best be getting away before it comes again." He gripped one of her hands and forced the keys into her palm. "You don't want to be walking the coastal path in a downpour. Should you have a misstep, you'd be over the cliffs."

Olivia's heart skipped a beat. "Oh, right? Not much to do with the weather like this."

Hugo nodded. "If I had the freedom to do so, I'd have a good lay-about with a novel." He turned and led them down the stairs.

She agreed. "Perfect day for a good read and an enormous cup of tea."

"Indeed."

They stepped out into the stormy day. Though the rain was presently a gentle fall, the appearance of darkening gray clouds soon promised a downpour.

He faced her with pursed lips, hand outstretched, as they stood under the narrow overhang.

Olivia narrowed her eyes, not understanding until she realized she clenched the keys in her hand. "Sorry." She handed them to Hugo, and he promptly locked the door and returned the keys to her, which she dropped into her bag.

"Thank you for showing me the building. I'll come back tomorrow and do a thorough look around."

"No worries. Take your time. I have another set of keys should another buyer pop up."

"You are very kind, Hugo. Thank you."

He snapped open his *brolly* and tossed over his shoulder, "Best be getting up that thigh-killer before the clouds open."

She laughed. "On my way!"

A few steps from her cottage, the rain became a deluge, and even with her brolly she was soaked. She sighed. "Figures."

Once inside, she changed into dry clothes, made a cup of tea, retrieved a couple of biscuits and a novel, and settled into the cozy overstuffed chair by the large window overlooking the sea.

A sense of deep contentment enveloped her, and she rested her head against the back of the cushioned seat. She closed her eyes and tried to envision the property from the moment she stepped into the antique structure.

A plan formed in her mind. She would pack a lunch and with the old diary go there tomorrow. A smile curved her lips. *And* cleaning supplies. Her eyes grew heavy, and she settled deeper into the comfort, her novel sliding to the floor. Something about the building—the Sands—called to her, but she didn't yet know what all it had to say.

III

The small, cracked trunk at the foot of Grace's bed held all her worldly possessions. Kneeling before it, she lifted the lid, releasing a creak of protest. On top lay the green dress, one of her most precious treasures, until she wore it to entice Eudo. What had she been thinking? Desperation had driven her to consider marrying a man she did not love.

The dress was a gift from Mistress Ellery on the occasion of her ten and sixth birthday. When the woman placed the lovely garment smelling of lavender in her arms she had sobbed.

Mistress Ellery had always been as another mother to her, particularly since Sebastian and her son, Nicholas, were the best of friends until the tragedy. Nick had been gone some ten and five years. She would soon be two and twenty, not the girl of seven years when Sebastian lost him to the churning sea.

Grace ached with remembrance of that horrid day, helpless on the shore as Sebastian dove underwater again and again.

She thought of Nick often. He had always treated her with kindness. What would his appearance be as a man of five and twenty? Would he have married and left Trerose? Would he and Sebastian have remained friends? They were only questions without answers for he was lost to them.

Her gaze returned to the dress. Mistress Ellery had been slightly larger than Grace, and she had since grown enough for the frock to fit her well. Whenever she wore it, something in her shifted. She gained confidence. Not because of the glances from the men at the tavern. Wilmont, a serving girl, garnered their attention far more with her curvy figure, raven hair, and gray eyes. A year younger than Grace, she had yet to marry as well. She was much too fond of all men and what they could buy her. Wilmont was not a bad sort and could be kind-hearted for the most, yet even she could not garner Eudo's attention.

When Grace wore the dress, she also thought of Mistress Ellery, who was gone from them for some years as was her son. She had been a godly woman—full of compassion and generosity. And what of Mr. Ellery? Nay one saw much of the man. Wealthy though he may be, he kept to himself since Nick's death, which appeared to have crippled him. Only those who delivered goods to the manor had news of the man. His servants were most protective and would not reveal in what state he was. His wife's death had sent him further down the chasm of grief that had begun at the loss of his son.

Grace fingered the satin fabric, pushing sad memories away. How she wished to have one more of a different color and could wear it proudly to remind her not of the past. Green was Nick's favorite color. She tucked the garment beneath her belongings, stirring its floral scent, and retrieved the small book—another gift from Mistress Ellery—in which she kept her daily writings. She admired its lovely parchment, crisp and clean. Once her father had caught her writing in it. He railed at her. "'Tis a waste of time." His large hand grabbed the book and he hurled it across the room. "Do not let me see ye writing in that again."

Her finger traced the cover, now marred with the force of being slammed against the rough stone wall.

"Grace!" Her mother called from below, not in urgency, yet Grace started at the interruption. She strode to the doorway. "Aye, Mother."

"Your father sent a boy over to tell me he would not be home for supper."

Grace hesitated, not remembering that her father had ever sent word he would not be home. He merely arrived when he saw fit. Sometimes it would not be 'til dawn's light. A flash of curiosity grabbed her, and the trunk's lid closed with a squeak. She bolted down the stairs and snatched up her cloak.

"I forgot to take Mrs. Braddock her vittles. Do ye need me to fetch anything while I am out? I shall not be long."

Her mother shot her a questioning glance. "Nay, my dear." She turned away, then quickly faced Grace again, and said in a whisper, "Why do ye not fetch us a treat of some such? Shall be our secret." She hesitated. "Say naught to Arabel."

Grace knew what her mother was thinking. Arabel was Radigan's golden child. She could do nay wrong because she had a way with numbers. He gave her a fine room of her own at the tavern and never railed at her—unlike the rest of their family. Grace had even seen him slip her coins upon occasion. To the rest of them, he offered nothing but grief.

"Aye, Mother."

Melior pressed a few farthings into Grace's palm. Her eyes grew wide. "Shall not Father want to know where the coins have gone?"

A sly smile crept across her face. "He knows not. When he is senseless from drink, I filch a few bits from his pocket."

Grace grabbed her mother in a fierce hug before slipping into the night and down the path to the tavern. When she arrived, she took care not to bring attention to her presence. She hunkered under the kitchen window and peeked inside. Wilmont perched on top of the table, legs dangling, telling Eulalia about a *fresh* man who had just left the tavern for the night, saying he was 'right purdy.'

Grace rested her head against the plastered wall and closed her eyes, waiting for the right moment to steal another glance into the room. As Wilmont chattered on and the cook grunted replies, she peeped through the window. Her father entered the kitchen, and all talk ceased.

Radigan stood in the doorway, muscular arms crossed over his chest. "What the blue blazes are ye jawing 'bout?"

Wilmont hopped off the table and stood nearly eye-to-eye with Grace's father. "Jest taking a break from that mob." She lifted a slender finger to point toward the other room.

Radigan stared her down, yet she did not flinch before she turned and spoke to Eulalia. "I be gone fer the evening." She nodded curtly at him and sashayed from the room.

By this time, the cook had returned to her mutton pasties.

"Ye let that gurl put on airs just cause the men like her." He grabbed a pie and bit into it, glaring at her.

"Makes nay niver mind to me what she says. She be a good worker and rare complains." The cook banged the blade of a cleaver into a head of cabbage and chopped it skillfully.

He watched her work, then his gaze flickered to the window. Grace dropped to her knees, a sharp stone piercing her leg. She slapped a hand across her mouth to stifle a cry.

A moment later, she scuttled from the window and ran around the tavern, the sound of the River Pol trickling into the quay. Suddenly, strong hands gripped her upper arms. Her head snapped toward the man who held her, his cavalier hat shadowing his face.

"What ails ye, Mistress?" The tall stranger looked over her shoulder. "Are ye running from harm?"

His cultured voice did not hold the tone of a local, yet there was a familiarity to his accent that she could not place. Trerose Harbor greeted sailors from various places, and Grace had heard many manners of speech through the years.

"Nay. I am well. Ye startled me was all." When he dropped his hands and stepped back a pace, the glow from a tavern lantern revealed half of his face. Was this the man Wilmont had spoken of? He was, most assuredly, handsome in a rugged, seafaring way. Grace bit back a laugh, thinking of Wilmont going on about the 'purdy man.'

He slanted his head. "Did I say something of good humor?" He rested his hands on his hips, and the side of his mouth that she could see curved into a smile.

She laughed. "'Tis of nay concern. I am sorry to bother ye."

She made way to go around him, but he stepped in front of her.

"Ye have a delightful laugh, Mistress. I have heard nothing so amiable for some time."

Heat coursed through Grace. Nay man had spoken thus before, a different sort of flattering speech indeed, yet she did not feel ill at ease.

Footsteps, and her father's curse, sounded behind her. She shuddered and pulled her hood to hide her face.

The man gave her a curious stare and took her arm. "Methinks ye are afraid of something." He crooked his elbow. "Allow me to escort ye home, Mistress."

Her father grew closer with each step. She took the stranger's arm and thanked him. "'Tis kind of ye, sir."

When Radigan appeared, giving them nothing more than a cursory glance, she walked forward into step behind her father.

They walked on for a time, and when her father topped the hill, he knocked on the door of Richard Bassett's cottage—a scoundrel who had barely escaped the gibbet a number of times. She frantically glanced around, her gaze landing on Mrs. Pittard's bakery. Though the shop was closed, Grace knew the woman would welcome her.

Grace halted in front of the building. "Thank ye, kind sir." She nodded and pulled her arm from his.

"My pleasure, Mistress." He took a step away. "Pardon me, I have not introduced myself." He offered a bow. "Rig Cooper, your servant."

She had nay choice but to respond with a curtsy. "Grace

Atwood." Though the light was dim she could see he was a young man, his brown hair long enough to be tied at the nape of his neck.

"Grace. A lovely name to be sure."

"Thank ye." She dipped her chin, a sudden surge of shyness overtaking her, but when she looked up, he stood a pace nearer—close enough to see his hazel eyes.

"Good eve to ye. Mayhap we shall meet again." He tipped his hat and headed the way they had come.

The door of the shop opened, and Mrs. Pittard stood in the opening, wearing a curious expression. "What brings ye here at this hour, me gurl?"

"Good eve, Mrs. Pittard. My mother would like something . . . anything ye may have left from the day." Grace removed the money her mother had given her and extended it to the baker.

The woman glanced at the offering, her gaze softening. "Keep your farthings." She disappeared into the cottage and returned with a small package. "Take this to dear Mellie. 'Tis a gift."

Grace opened her mouth.

"Shush, child. Your mother has a hard enough life. This shall bring her spirits up. Tell her to save the farthings for a time of need." She bid her good eve with a fond smile.

Grace hugged the bundle to her chest. Mrs. Pittard was a dear. A waft of yeast and honey filled her senses, and she breathed in the welcome scent. The sudden sound of men's lowered voices halted her mid-stride. She stepped back into the shelter of the cottage doorway. Her father kept pace with

Mr. Bassett, his voice dropping to a whisper.

When they rounded the corner leading out of the village, Grace followed, keeping as close as she dared. When they left the path and passed into the woods, she stopped, unsure if she could go silently enough not to reveal her presence. Hesitancy captured her for a moment before she squared her shoulders and continued until she heard the crunch of footsteps behind her. She ducked into a stand of undergrowth and knelt, holding her breath as the man passed her hiding place.

He held a torch, and as he walked by, she saw his face clearly enough to know she had seen him before.

An angry voice growled from the darkness. "What the blue blazes are ye about, man? That torch will be telling the whole village our where 'bouts."

The man released a few swear words and quickly doused the flame in the nearby stream.

"Come on." Mr. Bassett, a fisherman, said coarsely, "Come on. Time be wasting."

Grace watched as they took the wooded path down the hill, away from the village and to the cliffs. She wondered why they had not merely gone back through Trerose, which was much closer and less difficult to traverse. Immediately, she chastised herself for her naivete. They were doing something for which they wanted nay witnesses.

On their downhill descent, she hung back, but her foot loosened pebbles, and they skid in front of her, startling a small animal to dart across her path.

Her father's voice cut through the night. "Did ye hear that?"

One man said, "Jest a critter."

She froze, holding her breath, and waited. Their movement resumed. She exhaled and carefully continued her pursuit.

The trio eased downward onto the hillside path that ran above Lansallos Lane, and the salty scent of the harbor grew closer. Darkness deepened with the night, and she could barely make out the men ahead of her as they worked their way down the side of the cliff.

Why were they going to the cave at this hour? The entire village knew of its use by smugglers. The villagers who valued their safety never went near it. Though Sebastian said they would harm not a soul except the excise men who tried to hinder their trade. To scare off intruders, they bandied a warning about what would happen to those who interfered with them.

What was her father, Mr. Bassett, and the stranger doing there? A chill slithered through her. Radigan Atwood was not an honorable man, and this was yet another nail in his coffin.

ଔଯ

When Grace returned to the cottage, she handed a flattened bread to her mother. They both stared at the mangled treat and laughed.

Melior patted her shoulder. "I know of unpurchased goods to be sold at a reduced cost, but even this is beyond the pale."

Grace shrugged. "Well, 'tis not that. I had a mishap and damaged the cake upon my return home." She gave the farthings to her mother. "Mrs. Pittard refused payment." She placed a slice of the sweet bread in front of her mother. "And 'tis newly baked. Was warm when she did give it me."

Melior's eyes widened. "In truth?"

"Aye. She is a kind woman." Grace spoke not of what the woman had said. Her mother cared not for pity.

Melior cast her gaze on the cake and muttered, "Aye, she is."

Grace cut herself a piece and sat. "Where are Degory and Alsyn?"

Her mother said, "They are abed."

"This early?"

"They did not wish to be downstairs when Rad came home." She took a bite and slowly chewed. "They fear him now more than afore."

Grace closed her eyes, the shared laughter with her mother now a distant memory, and fought back the hatred she felt for the man who fathered her. She prayed for forgiveness but could not shake the loathing. Sebastian's thoughts on the situation returned to her—why had her mother stayed once he began beating her? Living from hand to mouth in a cave would have been better than this.

She squared her shoulders, pushed the cake away, and plunged in. "Mother, why have ye stayed with him all these years? Ye could have returned home and taken Sebastian with ye. Grandmother and Grandfather would not have let him take ye had they known how he treated ye."

Her mother's expression grew cold, staring at her eldest daughter in a way foreign to Grace. "Do not speak of what ye know not. The choices I made were the only ones I had." She placed her hands flat on the table and pushed herself up.

"Put the bread away where your father shall not find it. I

shall give some to the others once he leaves for the Sands tomorrow." She walked from the table, dry-eyed and stiff.

At the foot of the stairs, she paused, "Grace, ye and Sebastian know nothing of what has passed. 'Tis of nay concern of yers."

Speechless, Grace watched her mother's sluggish steps on the stairs until she disappeared altogether.

Her brother. Grace must find Sebastian. It was time for her to learn of what happened in the past to unite her mother with such a horrid man for a husband.

CAROLE LEHR JOHNSON

Chapter Five

Olivia stuffed a blanket and pillow into her brown backpack, bulging with supplies that would see her through the afternoon. Although she'd not heard from the twins, she hoped for another day on her own. She needed solitude to digest plans that had not fully formed in her mind.

She hummed a tune from the television show she had watched the night before, a historical drama with a sweeping soundtrack, set in Cornwall interestingly enough. The show's breathtaking cinematography reminded her that those views were literally outside her door—she just had to go. Slipping on her backpack, she left the cottage.

The morning sea air restored her with each breath. Gulls circled overhead, screeching as if in communication with one another. Clumps of pink thrift were scattered alongside the pathway, and other wildflowers Olivia didn't recognize. Their scents mingled with the salty air brought memories to her, yet this time melancholy wasn't what lingered. Happy thoughts of Ian made her smile—memories of him pushing aside his wavy windblown hair, green eyes shining with mischief.

Movement on the path ahead caught her attention. The mild weather had brought out several tourists, but the man in her direct vision walked ahead of her with purpose. His back to her, she only saw his lean build in jeans and a dark blue shirt and his tawny hair, the sun shining off streaks lightened by the sun. His long strides took him away from her before they reached Trerose.

Olivia noticed the small tearoom ahead tucked between a gift shop and a market and decided to stop for something to eat. It was still early, and she had skipped breakfast in order to avoid the twins. A bite of guilt nipped her conscience, her stomach growling perhaps as punishment. Noting the bold black lettered OPEN sign attached to a violently purple door, she reached for the handle.

The door jerked inward, nearly sending her to nosedive forward into the room.

A man's calm, deep voice reached her ears. "Pardon me."

Olivia glanced up and met sea-blue eyes rimmed in gold, a surprising contrast.

"Did I hurt you?" He lifted a hand toward her shoulder as if to steady her but abruptly pulled back.

Still mesmerized by his unusual eyes, Olivia muttered, "No. I'm fine."

"Allow me." He held the door wide to allow her to pass, their proximity unsettling her.

By the time she'd regained her senses, the door had closed with a jingle of the old-fashioned bell hanging above it.

A server approached, seating her at a two-chaired table by the window facing the street. She hadn't even gotten a good look at the man's face. His eyes had held hers, and she recalled the fresh scent of the salt-infused sea air clinging to him.

A glance out of the window revealed a tall man in jeans and a dark blue shirt strolling away from the tearoom—and he had tawny hair. It was him, the man on the path.

As Olivia ate breakfast, he lingered in her thoughts, and a moment later, with pencil in hand, she sketched a man walking the cliffs. She couldn't help but hope their paths would somehow cross again.

෪෧

Olivia inserted the key into the worn door and struggled until finally it gave way with a satisfying click. The sun sent shafts of cheerful brightness through the window from the east on the harbor side and illuminated the old building's main room. She cleaned a table and chair by a window, deposited her backpack on the floor, and sat with an irritated squeak, then retrieved the old diary, a notebook, and a pen.

When she opened the notebook, her gaze landed on the name she'd discovered at her grandmother's—The Burning Sands. She glanced around the dusty room, hardly believing this building could possibly be the old tavern.

Flipping to a clean sheet of paper, she jotted down a heading—*Things to Find Out*. The first item on her list was about the name. Next, she would ask about her great-grandparents. Surely the twins knew of them since they'd lived in Trerose all their lives. The last item was to inquire about the local historical society. Satisfied with her list, she opened the diary and fought to read it once more and settled in to decipher the difficult faded script.

When the light dimmed, Olivia pushed the diary aside, along with her feeble notes on what she *assumed* they meant, and retrieved her lunch. The rickety chair groaned in protest, so she moved to her blanket, which she spread on the floor under the window and leaned against the wall. With a sandwich in one hand and the diary in the other, she chewed and gave thought to what she was reading.

The dates at the beginning of each new day were fairly clear as numbers weren't that hard to make out. One of the many articles she'd read regarding tips on reading old handwriting came to her. It recommended looking at each letter carefully rather than trying to make out whole words at once.

Sometimes, a *s* and *f* appeared to be the same. *Y* could be for *i*, and *j* and *i* could be interchangeable. She studied the next page, then sat upright. A name rose from the text—*Sebastian*.

She attempted to figure out why the man's name was mentioned, but after several minutes, she slapped a palm to her forehead. "This makes my head spin."

Olivia needed help, but she was ecstatic to find the name. Tomorrow, she would try to locate someone who could help her translate the documents.

A yawn escaped. She glanced at her phone and found it to be only three in the afternoon. Leaving all her materials where they lay, except for the diary and notebook, which she stuffed into her backpack, she stood and stretched like a lazy cat.

Could the building really be The Burning Sands? Olivia was determined to find out. She wandered around the room a moment, willing it to somehow release its secrets to her, but the dark wood walls were silent.

Fighting back another yawn, she decided more caffeine was want she needed, so she grabbed her bag and returned to the tearoom from that morning. Her gaze roamed the room for the man in blue, but he had disappeared again, likely a tourist on a solo stroll.

The Cornish tea and cream scones revived Olivia, and she headed back to the *Sands*, as she was determined to call it with a spring in her step.

The sun crested and headed westward, leaving the main room of the Sands in filtered light, shadows stretching along the scuffed wooden floors. Olivia flicked on the lights, casting a warm, ethereal glow over the room. She once again settled herself under the window, finding it more comfortable than the old chair.

Reopening the diary, she inspected the first page and was unable to make out the name of the diary's owner written on the inside cover. She remembered seeing a website with examples of each letter written in seventeenth-century style. After a few minutes of searching on her phone, she found it and compared the first letter to the alphabet chart. It was definitely a *G*.

Olivia noted the *G* on the paper and carried on until she'd found each letter.

Grace. That was it.

The last name was her next endeavor, but her eyelids grew

heavy, and the sun had abandoned the eastern sky. It was time to get back to her cottage. She packed her belongings, but an unidentifiable tug kept her there.

Olivia moved from room to room, turning on all the lights, then went up the narrow, antique stairs. Each room brightened as she illuminated them. The pull of untold stories gripped her. Every chamber had its own tale, and it was as if they called for her to discover and reveal their long-forgotten past. What were they trying to tell her?

With a laugh she shook her head to clear it. "Girl, you have finally gone nuts."

After a final pass through the rooms, she couldn't shake the sensation she was missing something. She shrugged it off, locked up, and stopped by the market to pick up a few items.

With a shopping basket slung over one arm, Olivia scoured the shelves. When she rounded the end of the aisle, her basket collided with another shopper's.

She jumped back with a gasp. "I'm so sorry," she stuttered. "These aisles are so narrow, and I—" Her gaze met gold-rimmed blue eyes that held a hint of amusement.

Olivia was *not* amused. This was the third time she'd seen him, and it couldn't be a coincidence. Her ire rose, and a hand went to her hip.

"Are you following me?"

His brows arched, smile fading, as he took a step back while holding his hand up. "Excuse me, but I am *not* following you." His demeanor shifted. "Maybe *you* are following *me*?"

Olivia sucked in a breath and straightened her shoulders, watching his expression. Handsome men always made her nervous. This one was not only too good-looking for his own good, but the tiny wrinkles around his eyes told her he was always smiling—or loved to be outside. Although his clean-shaven face didn't appear tanned enough for that. Was that a spark of mischief that flashed in those strange eyes? Was he *flirting*?

Another surge of anger jolted her. "You, mister, are insufferable!" She turned on her heel with a grunt and rushed to the check-out counter. She would absolutely *not* sketch the man on the cliffs—nor did she wish to see him again.

ଓଃଔ

The sun slipped past the rise as Olivia approached the cottage. A light shone in the kitchen, and she didn't recall leaving it on. When she tried the door, it was already unlocked, and a clattering sounded from the kitchen. The twins had arrived.

"Olivia, love!" Sheryl exclaimed, her gray brows drawn together. "Where have you been? We've worried buckets for you."

"So sorry we've neglected you," Beryl chimed in. "Other commitments and the like." She presented Olivia with a steaming cup of tea. "Fortification, dear."

Olivia nearly sighed, but she took the proffered cup, offered her thanks, and tamped down the irritation of having her temporary home invaded. She sat beside Beryl and sipped the tea, considering what to say without hurting their feelings.

Beryl frowned at her sister. "I told you we should've called first. It's unseemly to just barge in. This is currently her home—not ours."

Sheryl shot her a murderous glare. "You're daft."

Olivia's gaze rotated from one to the other. "Please don't quarrel because of me. I'm rather enjoying being on my own. Honestly."

The sisters exchanged questioning glances. Beryl smiled in understanding, but Sheryl hitched her hands onto her thin hips and scowled. "You don't want us to come round?"

Olivia flinched. "No, I don't mean it that way. You are so kind. I appreciate all you've done, and I know you're just trying to make me feel welcome." She placed her cup on the table and sighed with feeling.

She ran her hands across her face, then through her hair and motioned for Sheryl to join her and Beryl at the table. "Please sit."

As soon as the leopard legging-clad woman settled into a chair, Olivia began to share about the past—from the time she and Ian met until when she lost him and the recluse she had become in the past year.

By the time she finished both women were in tears. Surprisingly, Olivia did not cry, though moisture rimmed her eyes. Maybe it was a sign that she was truly healing.

"Now, you know," she said, a weight sliding from her shoulders. "This decision to come to Cornwall was the first one I've felt right about since Ian's passing. The further truth is that I have no idea what the future holds beyond being here right now. I know God will reveal it to me in His time."

Beryl placed a hand over Olivia's. "Oh, my dear, I am so sorry for your loss. How awful we have been, never considering you were here for nothing other than a holiday or business."

"Please forgive us, Olivia." Sheryl's face held remorse, but a hint of secrecy lurked behind those violet eyes. We shall no longer pop over without calling first."

Olivia stared at Sheryl, then Beryl. "I was not aware that you both have such lovely eyes. I don't think I've ever seen anyone with violet eyes before."

The twins beamed.

Sheryl cocked her head. "Are you changing the subject?"

"Not at all. I've only just noticed, I'm sorry to say. I can be so unobservant." She shrugged. "And me an artist."

"An artist?" Beryl asked with interest.

"Yes, by profession. Well, before Ian died, anyway. After he died, I quit my job. He left me well off enough that I don't have to work." Only then did she realize had he not been so thoughtful, she would still be working, and maybe the distraction of a day-to-day job would have helped her heal faster.

"Oh, may we see some of your work, dear?"

Sheryl rolled her eyes. "I doubt she's lugged canvases across the pond, Beryl."

Olivia laughed. "I brought my sketchbook and a few supplies. I've considered sketching—or painting—in the front garden with its stunning view over the cliffs and sea."

Beryl clapped her hands. "Please do."

"Yes, do," Sheryl echoed. "I'm certain Mr. Jones has paint supplies in his shop. It's just across from the market. She struck a pose. "And if you are in need of a model, you know where to find me."

Beryl stood and put a hand on her sister's shoulder. "Come, Sister, let's leave Olivia to her evening." She pointed to the Aga. "We've left your dinner warming, and there's dessert in the fridge."

Olivia gave them each a hug and thanked them for their generosity. "You are spoiling me."

Sheryl huffed. "Rightly so. Seems you are due for some spoiling."

The twins bid Olivia a good night, promising they'd not intrude any longer as they backed out the door into the cool evening air.

Olivia watched them go with affection. The pair had certainly made the trip eventful so far. She settled at the kitchen table with a Cornish pasty on her plate. She prayed over her food and bit into the flaky pastry, the warm savory filling satisfying.

Her phone chimed, and Angie's voice sang out, "Olivia!"

"Angie, how are you?"

"Me, silly woman? You're the one in Cornwall basking in the south of England's perfect summer weather. You lucky duck."

"You could've come with me." Olivia teased. "Two single ladies on the loose."

Angie snapped, "Oh, yes, but some of us have to work for a living." Her voice sobered. "I'm sorry. You know I meant nothing by that."

A knock sounded at the cottage's front door, invading the quiet. Olivia jumped. She wasn't expecting anyone. She looked around the kitchen to see if the twins had forgotten something.

"Olivia, are you okay?" Angie's voice held concern.

Olivia recovered with a hand pressed to her heart. "Someone just knocked. I'm so sorry. May I call you tomorrow?"

"Oh, Ms. Popular, I see. Don't forget about your old friend, okay. Will a call about ten o'clock your time tomorrow night work?"

The knock sounded again, a little louder. She grabbed her backpack and headed for the door.

"Of course. I'll call you then. Bye."

"I expect a full report. Bye!"

Olivia cautiously peered out of the window to see Teffeny's smiling face. She held up an overstuffed paper bag. "I come bearing gifts."

Her smile fell when she saw Olivia with the backpack. "Oh, no. I'm sorry. I should've called. Are you going out?"

Olivia laughed and widened the opening. "No, I wasn't. I'm ashamed to say I thought you were the twins, and if I had my backpack in hand it would be an excuse that I was leaving."

Teffeny's expression scrunched in confusion. "You're going to the beach dressed like that?"

"No—the old building. Hugo gave me keys." She relayed the story and details of her earlier visit.

"Well, based on what I've brought, I should fit right in. May I join you?"

Olivia welcomed her new friend, but a twinge of privacy-invasion stabbed at her for a moment before she chased it away. "Certainly. Let me lock up."

"What are you trying to accomplish by sitting in a musty old place half the day?" Teffeny halted on the steps, eyes narrowing. "Wait! You're going to buy it, aren't you?"

It took Olivia a moment to grasp the allegation. "I . . . uh . . . don't believe so." Yet the idea took hold. "I've no idea what I'd accomplish there."

Teffeny smiled, her pale eyes briming with excitement. "For one, you could live up top and open a shop below. Sell teas from around the world, cups and pots, and books and your artwork." She touched Olivia's arm. "What about imprinting cups and teapots with your artwork? Brilliant, I'd say."

ଔଞ

Two days later, Teffeny's ideas for a shop still turned over in Olivia's mind. She wrote them in a notebook.

When she had shared with Teffeny about the old diary, her new friend immediately suggested selling antique-style diaries in her *shop* with artwork scattered throughout the pages. Olivia made a few notes in the margins about what sketches might look best in the diary.

She scooted her chair away from the kitchen table just as the phone rang. Beryl's name flashed across the screen.

The twins hadn't returned since she revealed why she was in Trerose. She hoped she'd not hurt their feelings.

"Olivia! So sorry to have abandoned you" Beryl's tone was overly chirpy "Event planning is such a joy and a chore, but we soldier on, I say."

"Just get to it. You're burning daylight!" Sheryl urged her sister in the background.

Olivia smiled. "Is there something you wanted?"

"Yes, dear. The church fundraiser is taking place in a couple of weeks, and we would like to know if you'd do a painting or something for us to have for the raffle."

Taken aback by the request, Olivia said, "You haven't seen my work. How do you know it's good enough?"

Beryl thought the comment was humorous enough to share with Sheryl, so Olivia listened to them discuss the subject. Muffled shuffling sounded, and Sheryl spoke directly into the phone. "You are such a silly cat, Olivia. Of course, it'll be splendid. Will you do it?"

Olivia, deeply flattered, wasn't sure how long she'd be in Cornwall and told her so.

Sheryl sniffed. "Indeed. You will be here. We already know that." More shuffling. "Make a list of supplies and we'll get them to you as soon as is expedient. There's a love. Tootle-loo!"

Olivia blinked in confusion. She was being railroaded by two very eccentric old women. Although likeable. They were adorable in a strange, quirky way. She thought about their request and decided to get to it, especially since she would not be here in two weeks' time.

After breakfast, she returned to her handwriting research. An hour later, she gave up and told herself she must contact the local historical society. The feeling that the diary would reveal something important wouldn't let her go. She would find out about this woman named Grace.

CAROLE LEHR JOHNSON

IV

The Burning Sands Tavern rumbled with activity. Two days prior, a tremendous catch of pilchards brought a great deal of excitement to the village. The catch was most unusual for October and made the difference for the poor to survive the winter.

Grace reached her two and twentieth year, yet the occasion held nay happiness for celebrating. Not that anyone would laud her birth. Downheartedness engulfed her.

The stranger who rescued her the night she discovered her father's recklessness sat in the tavern tending a lone drink the entire evening—much like Eudo. His eyes followed her—much like Eudo. Yet, this man's attention did not unsettle her in the same manner. Over the past nights, he had arrived early, his sun-bleached brown hair tied with a length of dark leather.

The door opened, and a blast of icy night air chilled the room. Another stranger. This man was near as tall as Rig

Cooper but had dark skin and short curled hair. Something about him kept drawing Grace's attention. He was a fine man to look upon. At that moment, his gaze met her appraisal, and he presented her with a smile that lit his coffee-hued skin.

Rig raised an arm and called out, "Adam!"

The man strutted to Rig's table and with much grace eased himself down. He leaned close to Rig, and his lips moved as they shared something in confidence. Grace served a man a few feet from them, and Rig's deep voice called to her.

"Mistress Grace, would ye kindly bring my friend a plate?" He looked a question at Adam.

"Aye, Mistress, may I please have eggs and cheese with a fruit tart?"

The man's cultured voice surprised Grace. She nodded. "Would ye care for a drink, sir?"

His eyes twinkled. "Aye. Coffee with milk if ye please."

This, too, surprised her. Rare did any man come into the Sands and not request ale or stronger drink.

"Aye, sir." She turned to leave, but Rig nodded toward the other man.

"Mistress Grace, may I present my friend, Adam Gittens?"

The man rose with a bow, took her hand, and kissed the back of it before she could blink. "'Tis a pleasure to meet such a lovely young lady, Mistress Grace."

Heat rushed to her cheeks.

"Grace!" a voice bellowed across the room.

She jerked and brought her gaze around to see her father standing at the door, a cold gust trailing him into the room that had grown silent at his entrance.

Grace offered the two men at the table a stiff smile and swiftly left the smoke-filled room with a tin salver under her arm.

She slammed the door open with a bang, bringing Wilmont and Eulalia's heads up.

"What the devil do ye mean?" Wilmont asked sharply. "Ye startled the life out of us."

Grace set the tray on the table with a clatter. "My father is a beast. I . . ."

"Grace Atwood!" Rad stood barely inside the doorway of the kitchen, eyes flashing with anger. "What mean ye letting that man paw ye like a common trollop?"

Wilmont gasped. "She did what?"

"Keep out of this, wench!" He turned to glare at Grace.

Fury seeped into Grace's very soul, and she tossed all caution into the air before her. "I let nay one paw me, *Father*!" She fisted her hands. "How dare ye accuse me of such!"

"The rogue kissed your hand in front of the whole tavern!" He puffed out his chest and drew closer. "Shall not have my daughter's name bandied about as a—"

"Father! Stop this, now." Sebastian's tall frame entered the kitchen. "Your barking shall make naught better."

Her brother towered over Rad, offering Grace the courage to stand up to their father.

"Ye are not so certain of yourself when there is a man big enough to fend for the weak—are ye, Rad Atwood?" She spat his name like a curse and stormed away.

Her brother's final words met her ears from the doorway. "Father, I do believe ye have gone one step too far this time. One day, your actions shall take ye over the cliff."

Grace cringed at her brother's threat. Their father would avenge his pride, yet she did not care at present. She longed for home.

The kitchen door slammed, and she quickened her steps to cross the Roman Bridge, leaving her brother behind as well. With his long strides, he made pace with her by the time she reached Lansallos Street.

"Grace, what were ye thinking? Ye know he shall have his pound of flesh afore the week is out."

She turned tear-filled eyes toward her brother.

Grace was glad he did not share their father's resemblance nor his character. Sebastian was a caring man. Radigan Atwood cared only for himself.

"Aye. He will." Her voice broke, and sobs gave way until he stopped and embraced her.

After a long moment, Grace wiped her eyes and sniffed. "Sebastian, nay longer can I stomach being in the same room with him." She released a shaky sigh. "Not since he—"

Sebastian eased her to arm's length, yet she would not meet his eyes. "He *what*?"

Fear gripped her at what he would do to Rad if she shared the beating he had given Degory.

"Tell me, Grace."

She met her brother's glare and shook her head, remaining tight-lipped.

Sebastian scowled, his fury shifting to concern. "I shall discover the truth."

Grace grasped his arms. "I fear for ye, Sebastian. Please do not question me further. I shall take care of it in my own way and time."

"That does concern me, Sister." He released his hold. "Ye are nay match for that brute, and I shall not see ye come to harm."

She lowered her head. "He has not harmed me except with words."

"Have a care." He took her hand and led her alongside the fish quay and to the steps that climbed the hill to the cliffs. "Ye must go home. Sleep in the garret. He shall not find ye there."

She nodded, thinking of the hidden space in the attics and the secret door behind the wardrobe her brother had fashioned years ago when their father had been away a fortnight. Grace and her siblings had spent many a night in hiding until their raging father fell into a drunken slumber.

"'Tis not a pleasant place but better that than what the swine could do to ye."

Grace squeezed his hand. "He shall not forget my words this eve, and he shall seek me out."

Sebastian shook his head. "He was full of drink—of that I am certain. He shall not remember what ye spoke."

Grace pondered his words until they reached Gwynne Cottage. She halted and tugged at his hand. "Oh, my. In my haste, I forgot Mrs. Braddock's supper."

Her brother patted her shoulder. "Get ye home. I shall attend to it."

Grace nodded. "Thank ye, Brother. Ye take such good care of us all."

"Make haste. Tell Mother what has taken place and hide." He turned on his heel. "Take Degory and Alsyn with ye."

Grace nodded and raced for the cottage, her mind turning over what she must do. She opened the cottage door and crept inside. Her mother sat mending by the fire. She looked up at Grace's entrance.

Melior laid the garment aside and offered Grace a sad smile. "How are ye this eve, Daughter? I trust all is well at the Sands."

The mother and daughter shared a long, knowing look. Tears welled in Grace's eyes, and she rushed to her mother, flinging herself in her arms.

"Mother, I know not what is to be done. Father was especially cruel this eve, and I spoke when I should not have. Though I mean it still." She cried on her mother's shoulder until she remembered she must hide.

"Where are Degory and Alsyn?" Her gaze traveled up the stairs. "Are they abed?"

"Nay. They are at Mrs. Braddock's. I thought it best they be away for a time." Sorrow and pain crossed her mother's face. "Your father rare asks after them."

She led Grace to the settle and pulled her to sit. "Now, what ails ye, dear?"

Grace recounted what raised her father's ire and her response to his accusations. Melior dropped her head in her hands, her shoulders trembling.

"Oh, what have ye done, Grace? He shall kill us all."

"Nay, Mother. Sebastian said he was deep in his cups and shall not remember it. 'Tis as always. Ye know he forgets all when he has drunk his fill."

Her mother's anguish lessened. "Aye, 'tis true." She straightened. "Aye."

"I am glad ye sent Degory and Alsyn away. We know they shall be safe—for now."

Her mother nodded, the sorrow in her eyes breaking Grace's heart. She had to bring her plan to fruition and must find a way for her family to be free of this terror.

A knock sounded on the door, and they both started, arms tightening around the other. Seconds later, Sebastian strode inside with the scent of salt and sea, his expression grave.

"Father shall not come home this night."

Grace seized her mother's hand. "What has happened?"

Sebastian sat on the settle across from them. "He be laid up at the Sands, black and bluer than a Cornish night. Can scarce walk." The smile that spread across his lips held a tinge of satisfaction.

He clasped his hands behind his head and leaned back. "When I went to fetch Mrs. Braddock's meal, Wilmont did tell me he made to go after Grace, but he was much into his cups and stumbled over her foot." He laughed aloud. "I believe she assisted him a touch. He fell against the table and near knocked the sense—what little he may possess—out of him."

Grace squeezed her mother's arm. "So, he shall not remember what I said."

Sebastian dropped his hands to his thighs. "Nay, he shall not. When he rose, there be a knot on his head like them eggs

Mrs. Braddock's hens do lay."

He roared with laughter. "Yet, 'tis not all. He made to follow Grace, even though he staggered like a drunken sailor." He yawned. "By the time I returned from Mrs. Braddock's, I sought Eudo to share a drop, but he was not there. I did chance to become acquainted with two sailors new to Trerose. Said they were here whilst they made repairs to their ship. Might be here a fortnight or longer."

Sebastian sighed. "Rig Cooper and Adam Gittens. Afore long, a commotion came through the door, two men carrying Father."

Melior scooted to the edge of her seat. "So, he is yet alive?"

Grace could not miss the unmistakable hopefulness in her mother's voice. She held her breath, wishing he perished, guilt tugging at her insides.

God forgive me.

She could not help but think if her father were to perish those she loved would be free.

Chapter Six

What had she gotten herself into? Olivia stood at the window overlooking waves and sea-soaked sand, her spoon hovering above a half-eaten bowl of oatmeal. Her mind kept straying to the conversation with Teffeny about opening a business in Cornwall. She wouldn't know where to begin. Certainly, there was a tremendous amount of red tape to be unraveled for a non-UK citizen to not only own property but operate a business too.

Teffeny told her she believed a US citizen could start a business in the UK without having residential status or living in the country, but the stipulation was that the company must be registered to a UK address. Olivia had reconfirmed the information on the British government's website.

Of course, Teffeny had an answer for everything. Olivia had to hand it to her—she was well-versed on a vast number of subjects. *And*, if she purchased the Sands, she would live there as well.

The clock perched above the gray stone fireplace chimed the hour. Olivia glanced at the time and groaned. Teffeny had invited her to church, and she initially shied away from being bombarded with a slew of new acquaintances all at once. She'd shared as much, but her new friend said she understood and would meet her outside the church right before the service to put off the meet-and-greet until afterward.

The lone walk to the village offered Olivia time to collect herself, not wanting to admit she had avoided church overmuch since Ian's death.

Her ankle twisted slightly, and she winced. What possessed her to wear heels knowing the route was rock infested? By the time she arrived, Teffeny stood alone by the church door, her face written with worry lines that shifted to relief at the sight of Olivia.

Between rapid breaths, Olivia said, "I'm sorry. I didn't calculate for extra travel time in these shoes." She lifted a blue kitten-heeled pump.

Teffeny doubled over in laughter. "Very nice. But who on God's green earth would consider walking that path in those?"

Olivia grinned, her spirits rising a notch. "Thanks. I feel horrid at being late. I'm never late for anything."

Teffeny waved for Olivia to follow her to the door. Before she opened it, she whispered, "The service has started, so we'll quietly slip in and sit in the rear." She took Olivia's arm and, with the other, eased the creaking door open, pulling her along. She led them to the empty back pew, and they sank onto the green gold padded seat in relief.

Olivia smoothed the skirt of her taupe dress, composing herself, and when she glanced at the podium, her gaze met the sea-blue eyes belonging to the vicar.

༺༻

The vicar and the man from the cliff were one and the same.

Olivia still couldn't believe her eyes as the service carried on with a wonderful message given by said vicar. Embarrassment rolled over her, stomach clenching, and she wanted to run before being formally introduced to him by Teffeny.

Her friend nudged her gently with an elbow. "Are you all right?" she whispered. "You sat there like a stone during the benediction."

Olivia sighed, unsure what to say, because *I called your vicar insufferable to his face so please don't make me meet him* wouldn't work.

"I'm fine. I'm—well, I was thinking."

Teffeny offered a sidelong look. She wasn't buying it.

A small crowd filed past. Several nodded in greeting. Olivia stood and pasted on a faux smile. She had to get this over with as painlessly as possible.

They were the last through the door and into the bright day, the vicar waiting on the top step.

"Teffeny, how nice to see you."

The vicar shook her hand with a smile, then turned to Olivia and extended his hand to her. She straightened, mustering up what little gumption she had left, yet it deflated when he met her eyes with a knowing look. She timidly accepted and stared back at him.

Before he could speak, Teffeny touched Olivia's shoulder. "Vicar, this is my new friend, Olivia Griffin."

"Olivia, this is Luke Harper."

During their introduction, he kept Olivia's hand gently clasped between his. Her face heated, and she slid her hand free. Though as soon as she did so, a sense of loss filled her, and she nearly reached to retake it. What foolishness.

His gaze stayed on her. "Our paths have already crossed." This time, the twinkle in his eyes was unmistakable. "It's a pleasure to officially meet you, Miss Griffin."

Olivia's insides twisted. "Nice to meet you, V*icar*."

His brows rose at the inflection in his title. He cleared his throat.

Teffeny's eyes narrowed. "Well . . . I suppose . . ."

"Vicar!" Sheryl bounded forward with prancing steps from inside the church, holding a large container. "I'm sorry they held me up. Mrs. Shandy and I were discussing the fundraiser and lost track of time."

She stepped through the doorway, and Olivia gladly stepped back to allow her room to stand before the vicar and shove the gift against his chest, leaving him no recourse but to accept the offering.

"Thank you, Miss Ford. It's very kind of you. But if you keep spoiling me, I'll be as large as the bell tower."

Beryl strode to the doorway beside her sister. "Not to worry, Vicar. It's just another of my sister's famous fruitcakes that you may use as a doorstop."

Sheryl sent Beryl a murderous glare that could curdle milk but batted her false eyelashes at the vicar. "Pay her no mind, Vicar. She's just a fusty old hen."

The vicar glanced at his watch. "Thank you again. I must be away to the Smythe's for Sunday roast. Good day to you all." He disappeared into the church, fruitcake doorstop in hand.

Teffeny shared a look with Olivia but before she could say anything, Olivia quickly asked, "Where's the best place for Sunday lunch? My treat." She had never been so thankful for the eccentric Sheryl and her fruitcake.

⊰⊱

Olivia woke early, Grace's diary and conversation with Teffeny in her thoughts. The lunch they'd had the day before, just after church, left her with much to contemplate—not only the diary but the possibility of having a business in Cornwall.

Could she leave her family behind? Her grandparents would miss her, but they would understand. Her mother would not likely bat an eye.

Olivia rolled onto her side and took in the cerulean sky— such a magnificent shade of blue. The vicar's eyes flashed before her. Sitting upright, Olivia shoved thoughts of the intolerable man to the back of her mind. "So, what if you're a vicar? You're still insufferable!"

Stuffing her feet into oversized yellow slippers, she mustered the energy to put the kettle on, but soon realized she was out of tea. She had forgotten to go by Carew Market after church. Seeing the vicar had completely thrown her off.

No matter. She'd dress and have tea in Trerose and then go

do her shopping. In no time, she was out the door with list in hand and into the clear, bright morning.

The descent along the cliffs reminded her of the promise she'd made to the twins for the artwork. She hadn't seen much of them lately. The fundraiser had certainly been keeping them busy.

Maybe she would pick up some art supplies and get started.

Once she finished tea and scones at the tearoom, Olivia found the shop the twins had mentioned, but they didn't have what she required. She would have to return to the cottage for her rental and drive a few miles to a neighboring town. Before doing so, she purchased groceries and walked back up the coastal path.

Seeing Teffeny ahead, she called out to her. Her blonde head turned around and she stopped, hands on hips. "Hello. Again, I should've called." She reached for one of Olivia's bags. "Let me help."

Olivia thanked her, and together, they trudged uphill. She inhaled the floral-infused breeze, and she peered at the water far below. The jagged gray rocks took the force of the waves, spilling over and rippling down in streams.

"Beautiful day, isn't it?" Olivia closed her eyes for a second. "So, are things slow at the nursery today?"

Teffeny shrugged. "Not really. But not busy either. I left Ethan in charge. He's a good egg."

"What brings you up the mountain?"

Teffeny's brow twitched. "Is that what you call it now? Thighs giving you a burn?"

"Not anymore. I think they've become accustomed." Olivia

remembered her task. "Want to go shopping?"

"Shopping? Whatever for?"

"Art supplies. I only brought a sketch pad and watercolor pencils, and the twins requested artwork for the event."

She angled her head. "I'm game."

After unloading the groceries, Olivia drove them in the Vauxhall down the tight lane to the main highway, tall hedges closing them in on both sides. She used every ounce of concentration to maneuver the compact car.

"I'd be happy to drive if you haven't gotten your driving legs yet."

"No, I'm fine. It's just that I haven't driven since I arrived, and I need to focus until I can familiarize myself again." She looked carefully before easing onto the busier road. "Have you ever driven in the US?"

"Yes, I have, actually." She laughed. "Had a minor incident my first day behind the wheel on the *wrong* side of the road."

"Want to share?"

"Of course. I know how to laugh at myself." She shifted in her seat. "I pulled into the car park of a market and zipped toward a spot, but a man was crouched tying his shoe. I slammed the brakes and stopped inches before I parted his hair."

Olivia's mouth dropped.

"I felt so foolish, yet then I realized *he* was the one at fault. And I told him so."

"What did you say?" Olivia asked, wide-eyed.

"I said something to the effect of, 'You imbecile. I could've

123

killed you! Why stop there?' And in a most casual tone, he said, 'I needed to tie my shoe.'"

"Seriously? That's all he said?"

Teffeny paused while the GPS gave them directions to their destination, and they pulled into the car park. Olivia slipped into a slot, killed the engine, and draped her right arm on the wheel, and smiled. "Continue."

Teffeny laughed. "He straightened to his full six-foot height, and I realized he was rather dishy. It caught me quite off guard."

Olivia leaned in. "Then what happened?"

Teffeny leaned her head against the seat with a sly smile. "He asked me to have a cup of coffee. So, I did. That was six months ago, and he's coming to Cornwall in a few weeks."

"You've got to be kidding me? What a meeting! Better than a speed dating service. You sped right to him."

Teffeny burst out laughing followed by Olivia until they both held their sides. It felt good, freeing.

After regaining control, Teffeny glanced expectantly at Olivia. "I'd love for you to meet him. Will you still be here?"

Olivia opened the car door and stepped out, her gaze on the sky, birds wheeling overhead. She thought of the Sands, her draw to the building and the diary like the tide pulling into harbor and gave the only answer that made sense at the moment.

"Possibly."

☙❧

When Olivia wound the Vauxhall up the lane to her cottage,

the sun dipped into the horizon behind them. Lights flickered on from inside the cottages along the lane, sending welcomed warmth into the darkening sky.

As she parked beside the cottage, Teffeny yawned.

"At least your knees aren't knocking with fear from my driving skills."

"Hardly. Brilliant job, you!"

They hauled Olivia's art supplies inside the cottage. She turned to her friend with a smile. "Thanks for going with me. It was nice. You're welcome to stay for dinner if you'd like. I've been to the market, so we can throw something together quickly."

"I'd love to, but I need to return to the nursery and make sure they secured everything for the night."

"You said Ethan was a good egg. Won't he have done all that?"

"He will have done it, but being the owner, I'm a bit OCD." Teffeny poked around in one of the shopping bags. "Will you be seeing Hugo tomorrow?"

Olivia handed a bottle of water to her. "Possibly."

Teffeny laughed. "That's the same answer as before."

"I know." Olivia took a long drink of water, ashamed to admit the truth. "I'm praying about it first. It's been too long since I've really talked to God and asked Him for guidance."

Teffeny held up a floral-handled paintbrush, flicking the bristles against her thumb. "And about returning to your art?"

Olivia acknowledged the statement with a nod. "It has been nagging my conscience ever since . . .

The wind picked up, and the kitchen window rattled. Olivia's gaze traveled to the swaying tree branches outside. "I should've taken you in the car."

"No worries. It's not that long of a walk, and I always welcome further exercise." Teffeny closed the top of the shopping bag and straightened. "I'll ring you tomorrow afternoon." She strode to the door, then paused. "*After* you've talked to Hugo." She raised her eyebrows with a grin before closing the door behind her.

Olivia shook her head and smiled. "Thank you, Lord, for bringing me such a delightful friend just when I needed one." She snatched up the new pink satchel and began placing her supplies inside. Pink wasn't her favorite, but it served the purpose of being noticeable, so she wouldn't leave it behind.

Rather than prepare a meal so late, she strolled to The Pilchard for dinner. She wished she'd had the idea before Teffeny left, thinking she may have joined her before checking on the nursery.

"Ah, twenty-twenty hindsight and all." She muttered as she grabbed her flashlight as well as a lightweight jacket from the hook by the door.

The further she walked, the more thankful she grew to have the slight covering. The wind had lessened, but the temperature also dropped, a chilly breeze blowing at her back. She breathed deeply of the unsullied air and focused on the cozy lights in the village below. The whole scene before her of harbor and village at dusk was as a painting come to life with a depth of contrasting strokes of dark and light. A thrill coursed through Olivia. Her ancestors were from this very place, the thought invigorating her to find out more about them, the area's history, and new possibilities for her future.

She made her way into Trerose to the two-storied structure steeped in history rising before her. The rough exterior of The Pilchard was whitewashed, black shutters flanking the windows. A pair of black iron lanterns with sputtering bulbs to mimic candles hung on each side of the door like drop earrings. Laughter and music met her before she reached the entrance. She thought of the *Sands* and considered how it must have held a similar appearance some three hundred years before.

When she pushed the door, it resisted until finally relenting, and the interior noise suddenly grew more intense. The battered, dark beams overhead reminded her of the *Sands,* which was only a short walk around the corner at the other side of the harbor.

A thump against her calf and two barks brought her gaze toward the floor. A wiry-haired terrier, tongue lolling lazily from one side of its mouth, peered up at her.

She petted his head. "Hello, there. And who might you be?"

"That'd be Uno."

Olivia looked up to find Hugo standing in front of her, a bottle of soda in one hand and a raincoat draped over his shoulder. "He's a right fixture here. The Pilchard has always had a dog in residence. If you'll notice, he barked twice upon your arrival—always alerts them to a new customer."

"Truly?" Olivia took one step closer, so she could hear more clearly. "This would never do in the US." She shrugged and asked, "Why Uno?"

"So, you do not approve?"

"Not at all." She patted the dog's head again and moved as the door opened behind them, Uno offering his two-bark salute.

Hugo tipped his chin toward an empty booth. "Come. I'll show you the ropes so to speak." Before guiding her through the room, he leaned in at her shoulder. "It's Uno because he knows he's number one around here."

Olivia laughed, and they settled themselves into the comfortable corner, the sides of the booth muffling the surrounding din.

"What brings you into the night?" He took another swig of his beverage.

"I didn't feel like cooking."

Hugo rose. "Pardon me." He walked to the bar. When he returned, he handed her a laminated menu. "Have a look-see. I've just eaten, but I'll keep you company for a bit."

Olivia thanked him and perused the choices, which were many, and decided on the tiger prawns in garlic herb butter with salad, chips and a soda. She'd not had French-fries since her and Ian's trip to the UK several years ago. They were a favorite of hers.

"What'd you settle on?" Hugo asked.

She told him, and he again excused himself to go to the bar. When he returned, he said, "Your order will be up soon."

Olivia thanked him and rummaged in her purse. "What do I owe you, Hugo?"

He shook his head. "No worries. It's the least I can do for a client."

At that, she smiled. "But I'm not your client." Retrieving

the keys to the *Sands*, she slid them across the table. "Thanks for letting me spend some time there. It really is a charming place."

He pushed the keys back to her. "No need. And I'll get you an extra set once the papers are signed."

Her gaze fell to the table, the keys lying on the weathered wood, reminding her of the dark walls of the Sands. They seemed to whisper—*I belong to you.*

The server arrived with the food, and though she said *thank you*, her eyes stayed on the keys—or perhaps her future.

Hugo glided the bottle of soda toward her until it nudged her hand. "Have a sip. Fortification, you know." He paused and then apologized that he needed to go.

Olivia acknowledged his words in parting and said her own goodbye. Alone in the booth, the world around her carried on as if she didn't exist. She sipped her drink, then shook her head to release the fog that had settled around her before slipping the keys into her bag.

CAROLE LEHR JOHNSON

V

Grace watched Sebastian, still holding one arm tight to their mother. "Father is alive for certain?"

"Aye. He is and the same old teasy as afore." Her brother drank from his steaming cup of strong tea. "'Tis unfortunate."

Grace's stomach sank. Her insides twisted like a sailor's knot. Sebastian was correct—her father had always been ill-tempered. Was this the moment to act, to bring her family to safety?

"He shall not be home for a time. Ye shall have some manner of peace. Someone did beat the man without mercy. He had each clout coming to him."

Grace rose to prepare tea for her and her mother, the carefully laid plans shifting in her thoughts. Her father may not be the wiser for days, yet the preparations were not complete. She did not have time enough. "How long have we yet? And who is caring for him?"

"A few days. Nay more. Doctor Keast has been summoned,

and 'tis to be arranged for a woman from Talland to care for him. Nay one in Trerose is willing." He stood and placed the cup in the washtub. "'Tis known far about for his cruelty. Yet, 'til then, the tavern girls said they would bring him food, but that was all they shall do."

Grace stood and embraced her brother. "Thank ye for bringing the news. 'Tis sad it has come to this. Someday it may not end so well for Father."

"Aye." Sebastian hugged his mother and slipped out into the night.

When Grace turned to her mother, she stared into the flames, an eerily calm expression on her lovely, yet worn, features. She turned her gaze to her daughter.

"I must ask forgiveness of God, Grace. I want Rad dead." She did not shed tears, yet her face appeared aged beyond her years.

Grace put an arm around her mother. She did not voice her agreement.

The next morning, Grace found the tavern running smoothly, more so than ever. Rad's absence allowed for a more jovial atmosphere, and therefore, coins were more freely spent.

Wilmont offered Grace the full account of how the men found her father bloodied and bruised, lying on the northern coastal path.

Grace asked, "Where is he?"

Wilmont lifted the food-laden salver and jerked her chin up. "He be lying upstairs, moaning and groaning. Can barely talk because they busted his jaw—and other parts." She bumped the door open with her hip. "Doctor says his foot be broke. He shall not walk for a time."

Hearing the truth a second time did not lessen Grace's relief at her father being confined to bed for the next days. Lord, forgive her.

Eulalia, lips quivering, struggled to fight back a smile. It seemed not a soul missed Radigan Atwood.

A twinge of regret gripped Grace for being unsympathetic to someone in pain, yet the man had inflicted pain on others.

Eulalia broke through her thoughts. "Gurl, what be wrong with ye?" She tossed the dishcloth over her shoulder. "Ye wear the strangest look."

"Fine. I am fine. I just thought of something I need to take care of. Could ye do without me for an hour?"

"I believe so. Worry not about your father's anger. He shall never know. Take yourself off and do whatever it is ye must." She dipped her head toward a large salver filled with eggs, toast, jam, and steaming coffee. "Afore ye go, would ye take this salver to them purdy men Wilmont goes on 'bout."

Grace moved to take the salver when a scratching sound came from the window. She glanced up to find a chaffinch pecking at the breadcrumbs Eulalia put out for them each morning.

The cook cleared her throat. "That little fellow does fret 'bout nothing. He be patient 'cause he knows God shall provide. 'Member the scripture 'bout the sparrow?"

Grace pulled her attention from the tiny creature. It was amazing how the woman could near read her thoughts. "Ye are right. God shall take care of all."

She picked up the heavy salver and entered the main room. The men, Rig and Adam she recalled, sat at the same table as before. Rig looked up at her approach, eyes meeting hers, and offered a slight smile.

Adam rose, greeted her with "Good morn," and reached for the salver.

"Ye have not to do that."

"Oh, 'tis my pleasure to assist a lovely lady." He gently took the salver from Grace and placed it on the table.

Rig chuckled. "Adam, sit yourself down."

The man did so with a scowl. "Rig, did ye leave your gentleman's ways at our last port?" He grinned at Grace and whispered, "Pay him no heed. Too much time at sea, I would say."

"Aye." Rig's gaze met Grace's. "I suppose."

Grace looked from Rig and spoke more quickly than she intended. "If ye need anything, Wilmont shall be pleased to assist. I must be away."

Rig cocked his head, eyes slightly narrowed. "Did ye not just arrive?"

"Aye, yet there is something I must attend to."

He peered at her curiously. "I heard your father met with ruffians on the path. How fares he?"

"He is abed for some days." She clasped her hands in front of her, uncertain what more to say. "Enjoy your meal. I bid ye a good day."

Grace headed for the kitchen with the tray before either man could pursue further conversation. She bid farewell to

Eulalia, pulled on her cloak, and eagerly stepped out into the crisp autumn morning.

The cry of gulls circled the harbor, and people ambled about the village, attending to tasks and errands. She retraced her path to the cottage and found her mother hunched over a lump of dough on the flour-strewn table, humming a jaunty tune. The room was filled with the scent of warm, yeasty bread.

She paused at the door to watch her mother, shoulders not slumped in defeat, lines in her forehead not as severe. She seemed lighter this morn with her husband's absence.

Melior looked up in surprise. "Are ye well? What brings ye back so soon?"

"Mother, have ye spoken to the doctor about how long Father shall be abed?

"I have not seen the doctor." Melior focused on her task, slapping the dough against the floured surface.

Grace pulled a chair from the table and sat before her mother as she continued to work the dough. She clasped her hands, summoning courage. "Mother, with Father abed, we must make our escape."

Her mother's hands stilled, and Grace plunged ahead with her plan. "I have some coin put aside, and Sebastian shall give us more to help us leave this place."

A light shone in her mother's eyes, yet in their depths there was hesitation and doubt.

"Mother." Grace reached out and lightly gripped her hand. "This may be our only chance."

"Where could we go that he would not find us?" Melior

dropped into a chair, her floured hands gripped together on the table.

"We must decide soon. I shall speak with Sebastian. He can help us. He shall know what to do."

Her mother nodded, and Grace embraced her. When she reached the door, she paused and turned back. "I do love ye, and I want a better life for us all. That shall never happen so long as Father lives, or we stay here. Please think on that."

She took another route back to the Sands by way of the doctor's cottage. When he opened the door, he offered a timid smile. "Good morrow, Grace. How may I assist ye?"

"I want a word with ye about Father."

He closed the door behind him and joined her on the path. "I am calling on the vicar. Please walk with me and speak of your concerns."

As soon as they were on the path, Grace asked, "How long shall Father's injuries keep him abed?"

The doctor appeared deep in thought. "His leg is broken, nearly lost his foot. He shall be abed for a fortnight." They ambled along Fore Street, nodding to those they met along the way. "The man is a stubborn old fool and may try to leave his confinement too soon."

Plans of escape flittered in and out of her mind. She had little time to lose. "Do ye think he shall perish, doctor?"

The doctor slowed his pace. "I am uncertain."

She thanked him, and they bid each other farewell.

Arriving at the tavern, Grace spied Sebastian heading for the entrance. She called out to him, and he turned back.

"I must speak with ye."

He jerked his head toward the Sands. "Can ye not speak here? I have yet to break my fast and have just come from the mine."

Grace's shoulders fell, yet she would not deny her brother a meal. "After ye eat, we must needs speak privately. Not in a crowded tavern."

"Must we?" He raised his brows in question, then offered her a sideways grin.

To her surprise, Rig and Adam were still at their table, steam rising from their cups. As they neared the table, Grace inhaled the rich aroma of the coffee, an expensive drink her father must have bought from smugglers to avoid the taxes.

Sebastian asked her to fetch him a plate from the kitchen to bring to Rig and Adam's table. She glanced at the two men watching her and leaned in at her brother's shoulder. "How well do ye know them?"

"We have fished together. Their boat is in dock for repairs. May be here a while."

Grace nodded. "I see."

"My stomach is making more racket than the crowd in the corner." He notched his chin in the direction of Eudo and two other men locked in a game of cards.

She laughed, gave him a gentle shove toward the table, and strode to the kitchen. Wilmont, Eulalia, and Caye gathered around the worktable, preparing plates each laden with either bread and cheese, mutton pie, or scotched scallops.

Eulalia looked up from scooping a generous portion of mutton pie. "Ye not be gone long."

Upon seeing the pie, Sebastian's favorite, she remembered his request. Grace turned to Caye. "Please take a portion of mutton pie to Sebastian." She slid a mug of ale to the girl. "This as well."

With a smile and flushed cheeks, Caye nodded.

Grace prepared plates and filled mugs while addressing Eulalia. "I spoke with the doctor, and he said Father would be abed for at least a fortnight."

Wilmont loaded plates onto a salver. "Perhaps we shall have a few days peace."

"Even one day without Rad would be a holiday," Caye said, then burst into laughter. "Now would be the time to poison his food while he is abed and knows not what we do."

Wilmont gave a curt nod, her eyes narrowing. "Perhaps we should speak with Mrs. Braddock as she knows much about herbs and such."

Grace grew silent. She knew she could not bring herself to harm her father, yet the hardness in her heart resulting from his cruelty made her wish to end their turmoil.

Eulalia broke into her thoughts. "Are ye going to see him, Grace?"

She frowned. She did not care to see him. "Why should I go to the man who beats my mother—and now his young children?"

The cook's eyes widened. "Has Rad beat Degory? Little Alsyn?"

Grace grimaced, realizing she had spoken aloud. "Please say nothing of this, Eulalia." She glanced at the two women, but they had their heads together, whispering and giggling.

"I should not have told ye, and I do not want to make more trouble for Mother. Degory was only defending her. Father was deep in his cups and lashed out at him."

Eulalia fixed Grace with a stern look. "We well know he can do such whether or not he be in his cups." The woman laid a gentle hand on Grace's arm. "Not to worry. I shall say naught. That man shall pay for what he has done in this life and the next. God shall have him account for his wrongdoing."

Eyes filling with tears, Grace dropped into a chair as Wilmont and Caye left the kitchen with laden salvers. She imagined her father beating her mother and could do naught to stop him. "Mother can take little more, and Degory is but a boy and deserves this not."

"We both seen him when he be angry, not a pleasant thing." The cook swung her gaze around the room. "'Tis amazing. This tavern's been here this long. With he in charge. Most ignore him, and they know not the whole of it. Jest keep their distance an' mind their own business."

"Thank ye for all ye have done. I know not how I would have managed without ye all these years." Grace embraced the woman. "Ye have been there for me when my mother could not. Grateful I am for your kindness to her because I know the two of ye have been friends a long while."

An idea came to Grace, and she took one of the woman's hands. "This time of day ye shall not have to cook until much later. Why do ye not carry yourself to the cottage and have a cup of tea with my mother? She would enjoy it. There would be nay danger of Father interrupting. Take your leisure, Eulalia. Please go see her. Take some of your wonderful food to share with her."

Gratitude brightened Eulalia's face. She stared at Grace a moment, a slow smile lifting her lips. She glanced at the oven.

Grace smiled, "I shall take care of the bread. Fear not, I shall not let it burn. And if a man needs something, I do know how to cook."

"Thank ye, child." She removed her apron, handed it to Grace, and scurried around the kitchen gathering items into a roughly woven basket. She looked at Grace once more before leaving. "Thank ye."

As she closed the door, Sebastian walked into the kitchen, Wilmont and Caye following. They skirted around him and paused on the opposite side of the room.

"Well, Sister." He smiled and drew closer to Grace. "Where would ye like to speak?"

Wilmont and Caye straightened and presented him with their most becoming smiles. Grace could not fight the urge to roll her eyes. She knew her brother was fine in appearance, yet did all the girls have to act like dolts?

Grace cleared her throat and glanced their way. "I'm sure ye have other duties to tend outside the kitchen." They shrugged and left the room. She pulled out a chair and sat as Sebastian prepared two cups of tea and joined her.

"Sebastian, we must talk most seriously. Doctor Keast said Father would be abed for at least a fortnight, though he may try to rise earlier. We may have but a sennight without him. Now is our chance."

He raised his brows. "What do ye mean, Grace?"

Grace leaned forward, arms on the table. "I want to take Mother and the children and leave this place. He cannot chase after us whilst unable. But where shall we go that he cannot find us, because find us he would. And should he, ye know what shall happen—what he is capable of. Oh, Sebastian, I need your help to do this."

Sebastian squared his shoulders, his eyes glinting in the candlelight, a flicker of inspiration in their sea-blue depths. "Perhaps, ye shall travel far enough."

CAROLE LEHR JOHNSON

Chapter Seven

Olivia stood before her easel on the spit of sand that curved past the entrance to the harbor. Facing the village, her stand and supplies were ready to take advantage of the low tide. The small fishing and pleasure vessels lay on their sides like children's toys abandoned in the middle of play. Seagulls swooped over the pockets of shallow water that had not escaped the out-flow, forming a cluster of saltwater puddles.

The sweet-laced breeze tugged at her hair, annoying tendrils whipping around Olivia's face hindering her vision. She rummaged in the bag to find her hair clasp and pulled the offending hair from her face, securing it into a messy bun.

Forcing herself to rise early, Olivia came to the harbor to get the full effect of the morning sun and the limited time for low tide. Seeing the boats dipping precariously on the wet sand touched her artistic mind. Today, her choice of medium was watercolor. Although she was not as skilled in it as she was in oils or acrylics, the picturesque theme summoned her. In watercolor pencil, she sketched the harbor with its leaning boats, gulls circling, and the sodden sand beneath.

"Olivia . . . Olivia!"

A groan escaped, and regret immediately followed. She looked upward and whispered, "I'm sorry, Lord. I don't mean to be so easily irritated with them."

She spun and waved as the twins approached. Wobbling on the sand, their arms looped together to steady each other.

"So glad to find you." Sheryl's breath caught with the exertion. "We received no word from you about your supplies, and here you are at the ready."

"I told you we could bank on her support." Beryl huffed and pointed at Olivia's set up. "Look at that wadge of materials. Brilliant!"

Sheryl propped one hand on her hip insistently. "But you must allow us to reimburse you."

Beryl nodded her agreement. "Yes, please. We must do so, Olivia."

"There's no need, ladies. I'm happy to do it. It's been too long since I lost myself in art. You've done me a favor by asking for my contribution."

Both women's faces lit with pleasure, and Olivia again regretted her irritation at their intrusion.

"I'm sorry to cut you off, but I have but a short while before the tide comes in, and I want to capture this scene." She mustered her warmest smile and returned to her work.

"Come along," Sheryl whispered to Beryl. "Let us not

disturb our artist any further."

Olivia paused, her brush hovering over the canvas. "Tell you what—why don't you come for dinner tonight? I'll cook this time. It's the least I can do for all your kindness."

Their expressions cheered, and they agreed and asked what time.

Olivia cocked her head. "Let's say sevenish?"

Sheryl clapped her hands. "Splendid. See you then, dear."

Once they'd gone, Olivia added color to her sketch while thinking about what she would cook for the twins.

Time flew like the curious gulls overhead, and before she knew it, she was cleaning her brushes and packing.

"Good thing you're closing up shop now."

Olivia, spun around to find the vicar behind her, his arms crossed over his chest, gaze on her work. She narrowed her eyes. "Looks like you *are* following me after all."

"On the contrary." He pointed to the cliffs behind them. "I live a half mile past Widow's Cottage."

Olivia's memory flashed to the day she'd seen him walking ahead of her on the path. Then she recalled the day they'd collided at the tearoom. She stared at the man. How was she to react? The irritation that grew every time she saw him puzzled her, and all she wanted to do was leave. Keeping her gaze averted, she continued packing, yet she could not help but ask, "Where's Widow's Cottage?"

This time he laughed, its unhindered warmth and purity catching her unawares.

"Where you live," he finally answered, amusement lacing

his tone.

Olivia gasped. Widow's Cottage was *her* cottage?

But it was *Gwynne* Cottage on both the website and the sign on the cottage itself. She met the vicar's gaze. He didn't seem to be teasing her, yet was he? Had the twins told him she was a widow?

Certainly, a man in his position wouldn't joke about a subject so sensitive in nature. There had to be an explanation. She would ask the twins.

He took one step closer. "Are you all right, Miss Griffin?"

Her irritation flared. "I'm fine, thank you."

Guilt riveted her. "I'm sorry. That didn't come out the way I intended. I have a lot on my mind." She gathered her belongings and forced herself to meet his eyes.

"Excuse me, Vicar, but I must go. I'm cooking for the twins tonight and don't have a clue what to make."

He fell into step beside her, his hands clasped behind his back. "Casserole. And please call me, Luke."

Olivia paused. "Pardon me?" She most certainly would *not* call the vicar by his given name.

"Sheryl and Beryl are partial to casseroles. Especially ones loaded with cheese. Never met anyone who cooked with cheese more than the Ford twins."

The vicar sent her a charming smile—straight, white teeth gleaming. Another wave of irritation surged over Olivia with a flutter in her stomach. Her face heated, and she made to hide it by offering a swift 'thank you," and walking away, but he added a final tip.

"Top it off with a salad and anything disgracefully sweet for dessert and you will have made enough points with them to last you through the new year."

Caught off guard once more, Olivia laughed. She dipped her chin. "Again, thank you and have a pleasant afternoon." Before he could say anything further, she nearly sprinted up the rocky path.

Her mind raced between their encounter and planning the twin's dinner. She stowed her art supplies in the cottage and returned to Trerose, shopping bag in hand. When she stepped up to the market door, the vicar was coming out. Would she ever be free of this man?

Olivia stepped past him. "Excuse me, Vicar."

He stopped Olivia with a gentle hand on her arm, his touch sending a shiver through her.

"Miss Griffin, have I offended you? Each time we meet, you appear ready to remove my head from my shoulders."

Olivia sucked in a trembling breath. Was he right? Had he offended her? She looked intently into the sea-blue eyes and read nothing but sincerity. "No, you haven't. I apologize if I've acted as if you have."

The vicar released her arm, and Olivia side-stepped to allow a woman to enter the market, giving her time to prepare what to say next.

Luke waved a hand away from the door. "May we step aside for a moment?"

Hesitantly, Olivia shifted to stand in front of the multi-paned window of the shop. A couple passing by greeted the vicar and nodded toward her before continuing down the street. She watched them a moment before facing the vicar, his expression earnest.

"Please forgive me for being so bold, but I must know how I've slighted you." His eyes twinkled. "It isn't seemly for the vicar to go around insulting the locals."

She smiled at that. "I'm not a local, Vicar."

"You've gone and done it now." His arresting smile stayed in place.

"Done what?" Olivia's fist tightened around her canvas shopping bag, dread building within her.

"I'll grant you that you're not a local, but I still would rather not alienate anyone—local or no." He held his hands out in defeat. "And I did make you smile."

The vicar shifted the direction of the conversation. "May I call you Olivia?"

This did not make her smile. Her Christian name on his lips made a strange, warm sensation ripple in her stomach. He was *flirting*.

Olivia opened her mouth to call him out on it, but the strangest thing occurred—she was afraid. It was more than a year since Ian's death, and the thought of another man taking his place was laughable and unthinkable, all rolled into one. For the second time that day, he asked her if she was well.

"I'm just fine. Please excuse me. I have two hungry ladies to feed." She turned on her heel and rushed into the market without another moment's hesitation.

When she'd finished shopping, Olivia peeked out the shop window to be sure the vicar was not waiting. Hugging her shopping bag as if it were a life preserver, she power-walked all the way to the cottage, her gaze straight ahead. She unlocked the door, slammed it shut, and leaned against it. Knees weak, she took her purchases to the kitchen and put the kettle on.

With a cup of steaming Earl Grey in hand, she prepared a hot bath laced with lavender oil and reclined in the pungent water, her tea perched on the edge of the tub.

Her phone rang, and she jumped. Relieved to see it was Angie, she answered, "Hello."

"Hello, *you*. Why haven't you called?"

The thin thread holding her emotions together snapped. "Oh, Angie!" The unbidden tears trickled into the warm water, mingling like the narrow river that ran through Trerose and emptied into the sea.

"Olivia, what's wrong? Are you ill?" Angie's panic-stricken voice pealed in her ear.

She blubbered and reached for the dry washcloth hanging over the rim of the tub and dabbed at her face. "I . . . I'm so confused."

Angie sighed heavily. "I'm so sorry. Is it about Ian? Just remember us poor slobs who have never had that kind of relationship. You were blessed."

At that revelation, Olivia sobbed harder. "I know. That's what scares me. I may never have it again."

"Oh, dear. I am so sorry." Tears laced Angie's words.

Olivia pulled herself into an upright position, the water now tepid. "Angie—" She stopped.

After a few moments, her friend said, "Please calm down. Do you have a cup of herbal tea?"

"Earl Grey," she replied.

Angie blew out a breath. "Caffeine won't do. You need something calming."

"I can't. I'm cooking dinner for the Ford sisters tonight." Remembering Luke had called them that brought another round of moisture. *Luke.*

"Who?"

"The twins. That's their maiden name. The vicar called them that this afternoon."

"The *vicar*?"

"Yes. I ran into him."

"Is this the *dishy* vicar that Sheryl is after?"

Olivia laughed through the tears. "Yes. One and the same."

"What does he look like? Must be pretty old to have attracted an eighty-something old woman."

Olivia reached for her tea and took a sip. It was as tepid as the water she sat in. She grimaced, stood, and wrapped a fluffy white towel around her.

"He's at least half her age. She fancies herself a cougar, I suppose."

"For real?" This brought a round of laugher from Angie.

"Yep. Quite a woman. The poor vicar has to keep a low profile to avoid her, I'm sure."

Angie said cagily, "*So*, what's he really like?"

A long silence followed before Olivia answered, the fear she'd felt earlier resurfacing. "He's nice enough, although a bit irritating."

"How so?"

Where to begin? "He's always running into me. It's like he's following me, but I know that couldn't be so. He's the vicar, for Pete's sake."

"Do I detect a note of panic?"

"What do you mean by that?"

Olivia could hear her friend's fingernail tapping against something. Angie had done that since they were girls. When she was contemplating anything, she'd tap her fingernail against the closest hard object, creating a sort of Morse code.

"Are you attracted to this man?"

Olivia deciphered the code. She sucked in a painful intake of air. The fear she'd felt at the market returned. Was she?

೦೩೮೦

The bubbling casserole satisfied Olivia's cooking sensibilities. She settled it onto a trivet, grateful her wandering thoughts hadn't caused it to burn. She focused on chopping ingredients for the salad.

Storing the salad in the fridge, she arranged the table and poured herself a glass of sparkling water laced with lemon and rested against the worktop.

The conversation with Angie came flooding to her. It was unthinkable to consider an attraction to any man other than Ian. But she must admit Luke was rather handsome. She chuckled, recalling what she'd said about him being dishy. Yes, Sheryl would most likely call him that.

Olivia straightened at the loud knock on the kitchen door. As she made her way to answer, Sheryl and Beryl stepped inside.

"Good evening, ladies."

"Good evening!"

"My, but it smells divine in here." Beryl's gaze swept the area. "Doesn't the table look lovely, Sister?"

Sheryl agreed and made herself at home, pouring each of them a glass of what Olivia was drinking. The two women settled into their seats while Olivia fetched the salad and dressing.

When Olivia sat, she asked if one of them would care to say grace. Sheryl flicked a hand in her sister's direction, and Beryl said a very short but moving blessing.

After the initial tasting, Sheryl gave her meal review. "Olivia, this is marvelous."

"I have tasted nothing so delicious in a while, love." Beryl agreed.

Olivia warmed at the compliments. "Save room for dessert. I have it on good authority that your weakness is of a very sweet nature."

Both women looked at her, wearing identical expressions, but it was Sheryl who enquired, "And who might that be, dear?"

Olivia crawfished as fast as she could. "Well, I, um . . ." She took a sip of water to buy a moment of time. "It's nothing. I ran into the vicar and mentioned you were coming for dinner and—"

"Oh, the *vicar*. Why didn't you say so, love?" Sheryl's voice dripped with honey.

Heaven help her but Olivia rolled her eyes, eliciting raucous laughter from Beryl. Sheryl shot her a toxic look, but this did not deter Beryl's enjoyment.

Sheryl turned her gaze on Olivia. "Please enlighten me why you and the vicar would discuss us."

"Oh Sheryl, lighten up. Olivia didn't mean a thing by it."

"Sheryl, I apologize. After you left me at the harbor, Lu . . . the vicar passed and stopped to chat, but I had to excuse myself to shop for our dinner and told him so."

Sheryl studied her for a while. "That I will yield to, but why did you roll your eyes?"

Olivia sent a pleading look to Beryl, but her head moved from her sister to Olivia, as if watching a tennis match. Finally, she said, "Sheryl, why wouldn't she? Everyone in the village—no—in the county is fully aware of your twisted fascination with the vicar." She cleared her throat. "Or with any other man half your age that is still upright."

Sheryl's eyes blazed, and she shoved her chair back. "How dare you!"

Olivia silently prayed for God's intervention. Why were they always so harsh with one another?

She stood and stepped around the table and placed a hand on each of their shoulders. "Ladies, why must you always bicker? You are sisters. I just wanted to make dinner for you as a thank you for being so kind to me. Please don't quarrel. I have made a labor-intensive, *sweet* dessert for you to show my gratitude."

Beryl patted Olivia's hand, but Sheryl's expression brooked no budging of her stubbornness.

Olivia dropped to her haunches and faced Sheryl. "I apologize for rolling my eyes. It was an innocent reaction . . .

to . . . your fascination with him." She hurriedly added, "Although I can see why you'd be attracted to him. After all, he is *dishy*, isn't he?" She wiggled her brows for emphasis.

Silence suspended for a time, but then Sheryl giggled. "Yes, indeed, he is."

Olivia attempted to further calm the waters. "I mean, no matter a woman's age, she's still a woman and not blind. As long as we don't get carried away with it. We're all in agreement that a nice-looking man can be admired, but not allow it to become—" She was in deep water now. "You know. Not become lustful, as it's a sin."

Beryl jumped in, seeing her struggle. "That's correct, my dear. It's like looking at a beautiful painting, admiring it, then moving on, keeping our mind on—" She cocked her head in deep thought. "Ah, yes. It's in Philippians . . . whatever things are true, whatever things are noble, whatever things are just, whatever things are pure, whatever things are lovely, whatever things are of good report, if there is any virtue and if there is anything praiseworthy—meditate on *these* things."

Sheryl's face lit with pride. "Beryl, you always were good at memorizing things. Brilliant!"

Olivia released a sigh of relief. Flames doused. Thank you, Lord.

Dinner continued in a cordial atmosphere, and Olivia honestly enjoyed their company. Over dessert—sticky toffee pudding—she gleaned a lot of information on the area including some genealogy information about her great-grandparents. They remembered Susan Flowers from their childhood.

Olivia was ecstatic to learn of this and bombarded them with questions. She excused herself to get her notebook. When she returned, they were yawning, and she knew her moment had passed. At least for this evening.

She blew out a breath. "I'm sorry to have kept you so late. It's been great fun sharing the evening with you."

They agreed with enthusiasm. "It has been splendid, dear." Beryl pointed to her pen and paper. "Perhaps we can get together soon so you can take heaps of notes."

"I'd like that." And she meant it.

After goodbyes, hugs, and promises of gathering all their childhood thoughts for another day, the twins parted into the growing darkness. Olivia was thankful they'd have enough time to get home before the path grew inky.

While cleaning up Olivia admitted to herself once the hostility dissipated the evening was a tremendous success. It seemed the vicar was right. The extra-sweet dessert was well received. And she had to admit, her opinion of *Luke* had sweetened a bit as well.

CAROLE LEHR JOHNSON

VI

Fear overwhelmed Grace, her hands fisting at her sides, a bitter taste on her tongue. "We have nay horses nor cart in which to escape."

Sebastian's tone was firm. "Yet if ye sailed, he would never find ye."

A tiny flame ignited a spark of hope within Grace. She assumed they would depart by land. Why had she never considered by sea?

Her brother stood abruptly. "I shall speak with Rig and Adam and discover when their ship shall depart. Perhaps they can take ye away."

Grace started. "They would help us?"

"They are honest men, Grace." Sebastian smiled. "I believe they would do anything to help ye."

"Why? They know me not nor ye."

"There are times when ye know ye can trust someone, and

when ye cannot," he said with conviction. "I trust them."

Grace crossed her arms and considered the possibility. Should they place their lives in the hands of strangers?

Sebastian rose and stood at her side, leaning to kiss her cheek. "Please, Sister. I have coin enough for ye to start a new life."

She grasped his arm. "But what of ye? Ye must come with us."

When her brother met her eyes, his expression was solemn yet resolute. "Nay, my life is here. I do not fear Father. If this is your chance, ye must take it."

෨෩

Grace stirred a pot of porridge and recalled her brother's words. Was this their chance? Furthermore, could she leave Sebastian? Her chest ached at the thought. Their family had suffered greatly—yet to be parted from him would bring more pain.

Wilmont and Caye's strained voices rose behind her in argument, returning her to the kitchen and her task.

"Who shall take food to him?" Caye's voice wavered. "I shall do it nay more."

"Nor me," Wilmont spat out. "The last time I fetched something for him, he threw it in my face. The man is a beast. 'Tis why that woman from over Talland way chose not to come care for him. She heard tell of his ways."

Grace faced them, hands on hips. "'Tis sorry I am ye must be at the end of his sharp tongue and tossed porridge." She grabbed the salver and climbed the narrow stairs to the upper floor of the tavern.

When she arrived at his room, he sat propped up in bed, foot elevated on pillows, wearing a deep scowl. "Why haven't ye been afore now? My daughter should care for me."

Grace settled the salver on his lap and walked beyond his reach. "Nay one shall come because ye are a cruel, sharp-tongued man. Why would anybody want to be around ye?"

She pointed a finger at him. "Do not think of throwing that salver. If ye do, I shall not clean it up." She glared at him. "Ye may stay here and smell the foul stench and not have another bite of food"

Her father's face reddened, veins throbbing at his temples. When he spoke, his voice rose to a shout. "Ye have a sharp tongue, and I have done nothing to ye."

"Ye have harmed those I love and made us all live in fear," Grace said with a snarl. "My time of cowardice is over. Ye have made your bed and now ye lie in it. Ye had it coming, Father." She spat out the word as if it fouled her mouth.

Grace made for the door before he could throw anything at her. When she reached it, he shrieked at her back, "Grace! Ye shall not speak to me in that manner. Do ye hear me, gurl? Ye *shall* pay for your words."

She slammed the door, her breath coming in gasps as anger rushed through her. "Oh, dear Lord, please forgive me. I should not have spoken thus. Yet how many years must a person face such cruelty?" She leaned against the wall and buried her face in her hands. Closing her eyes, she began to pray.

Every part of Grace ached from the day spent on her feet

and the ache in her heart. All she desired was to lie in her bed, knowing her father could not shatter the eve with his drink-laden rants and beatings.

Only a handful of men were present as Grace cleaned. The stale odor of unclean men and tobacco hung in the air. Her brother still sat with Rig and Adam, their heads bent in conversation. He should have been abed long before now as the hour to return to the mines drew nigh.

Grace trudged to their table and placed a hand on the back of her brother's chair, allowing her weary body a moment's rest. "'Tis time for ye to be off. The Sands is closed."

Rig gazed at her, a mix of compassion and pain in his dark eyes.

Sebastian drew a chair out and motioned for her to take it. "Sit, Grace. Ye look near to swoon."

Fatigue won out, all eyes on her. Her brother slid his drink toward her with a nod. Hesitantly, she complied. The cool liquid restored a fraction of her strength, and she rested her forearms on the table. Sebastian slipped a brotherly arm around her and drew her to him. She dropped her head onto his shoulder and sighed.

Sebastian's voice vibrated low near her ear. "Now is the time to speak."

Too weary to lift her head, she nodded, yet Rig's assured voice captured her attention, and she raised her head.

"Grace, we are more than willing to help ye. Our ship shall be in port for a fortnight, perhaps longer with all the repairs needed. We shall take ye somewhere safe—to our first port of call or wherever else we are bound. 'Tis your choice. Your father shall find ye not."

Adam studied her and nodded. His speech was different than Rig's—partly that of a Cornishman, partly she assumed as those from the West Indies. "Our captain is a kindly man. If ye have money enough to feed yourselves, 'tis all he would seek. Shall be tight quarters yet offers more comfort than living with that man upstairs."

Surprised at his revelation, Grace stared at him. Sebastian had told them of their father's treatment of his family?

The crash of a platter brought their heads around, and Wilmont stuck her head out the door. "Pardon. Cleaning up, Grace."

They returned to their conversation, each of the men offering suggestions to aid her.

Grace rose yet kept a steadying hand on the table. She met Rig and Adam's eyes. "Thank ye for your kindness. I shall give this great consideration."

Sebastian took her hand and tugged her to sit. "Grace, I believe ye dozed a mite while we spoke." He chuckled and tapped a finger under her chin the way he used to do when she was small. "Should ye agree to accompany Rig and Adam, we would need a place to hide ye all until the ship is ready to sail."

Her eyes widened, but she held her tongue, noting the quiet confidence in the men's expressions. A memory came to her of Sebastian and Nick as boys. That same look brought adventure, not likely a safe undertaking.

Rig's hazel eyes brightened. "Because your father may be up and about before a fortnight ye must hide soon. He must believe ye left earlier than is truth, and perhaps not pursue ye at all."

Sebastian patted her arm. "We found a most ideal place."

She brought her gaze to her brother's. "How shall we hide in the village? Someone is bound to see us." A single tear trickled down her cheek. "All know every crevice that would shelter us."

Rig retrieved a handkerchief from his pocket and gently wiped the tear away. "They do not know this place. Tomorrow eve we shall show ye."

She watched him fold the finely woven cloth with care, noting finely stitched initials in one corner. Though she could not make them out.

Hope flared in her. "May we go now?"

Adam said, "Ye are too weary. Do not toil as hard on the morrow as it is a taxing descent."

Grace stared at the man. Her mind turned over the local places he could be speaking of.

Sebastian nudged her shoulder. "Ye must rest. We shall be certain to take ye tomorrow eve." He helped her to stand, his arm supporting her. "Come, dear sister, I shall walk ye home. This mayhap be your first step into freedom."

○ℨ☙

The morning dawned on a cool breeze, newness in the air. Grace prayed it was the scent of hope.

Eulalia greeted her as she entered the kitchen. "My gurl, did ye sleep over long this morn? Was worried 'bout ye."

Graced donned an apron and sent the cook a warm smile. "Yesterday was near my undoing. Was a rabble last eve." She retrieved a stack of salvers and absentmindedly wiped them with a damp cloth.

The cook shot her a curious look. "What ails ye, gurl?" She punched a lump of dough with her fist and held Grace's gaze.

Grace blew out a long breath. "I was so weary when I left. It was good that I had a companion home or else I may have tumbled off the cliff."

The woman chuckled. "'Tis good that Sebastian is a caring brother."

Grace nodded. "Aye, he is. I know not what I would do without him."

"I seen him and them two new lookers out and about together a lot of late."

Grace noticed the glint in Eulalia's eyes. She sought gossip, but Eulalia was not one to bandy about what she discovered. Of that, she was certain. She could always trust her to hold a confidence.

"They have formed a friendship. Sebastian believes them to be honorable men."

Caye stormed in, Wilmont on her heels. "There be a bite to that wind this morn." Caye shivered.

Wilmont laughed. "Gurl, ye be cold in midsummer." She jerked a thumb upward with a frown. "Who be feeding the ole bear in the cave this morn?"

Nay one spoke until Eulalia huffed. "After the scorching he gave Grace, I best be doing it this time. He knows better than to mess with the likes of me." Eulalia reached for a bowl and slung a huge dollop of porridge into the bowl. Caye cut off a hunk of warm bread and slathered it with butter and put it on the salver as Wilmont poured a cup of coffee.

Grace followed Eulalia upstairs, carrying the heavy salver, but stopped by the closed door of her father's prison. When the cook knocked, a disgruntled response told her to enter. She handed her the salver, and Eulalia strode into the bear's lair. Grace listened to see if Rad would abuse the kindly woman. When she only heard soft grumbling, she slipped down the stairs.

For the remainder of the day, she did as Rig bid her. Mostly, she sat at the worktable and chopped vegetables for Eulalia, made bread, poured drinks, and tried not to be upon her feet overmuch. Caye and Wilmont waited on the tables.

Sebastian told her to meet him at their usual place atop the cliffs, and she would do just that after delivering Mrs. Braddock her evening meal.

The old woman asked for news from the village, and Grace shared about her father.

Mrs. Braddock's eyes brightened. "'Tis time the man got what was comin' to him. Humph!" She scowled, her wrinkles deepening. "Your mother shouldna have wed Rad. Told her that meself many a time. 'Tis a day she now laments."

Mrs. Braddock leaned back in her chair, tugging her tattered brown shawl closer around her bony shoulders. "Nay, your mother shoulda wed Gerry."

Grace straightened on the stool, eyes narrowing. "Gerry?"

Mrs. Braddock bent toward the fire, grabbed the fire fork, and angrily stabbed at the peat, sparks flying. Her voice was low when she spoke again. "It matters not, gurl. 'Tis a long time afore."

Who was Gerry? Did he love her mother once? Grace wondered how different life would have turned out for Melior if she had married *this* Gerry.

What had happened? And what further sparks of her mother's past now dwindled to embers?

CAROLE LEHR JOHNSON

Chapter Eight

Olivia groggily slung on her bathrobe while the incessant rapping on the door grew louder. A glance in the mirror revealed her disheveled hair. She peeked out the window and saw Hugo doing battle with a wayward, early rising bee attracted to the profusely blooming roses surrounding the entry.

She opened the door and quickly ushered him inside, shooing the bee away. "Hugo, what are you doing here at such an hour?"

Hugo propped a hand on his hip. "Indeed. It is all of half ten, Olivia."

"Honestly?" Olivia glanced at the clock and saw that it *was* ten-fifteen. "I'm sorry." She tugged the belt tighter around her waist. "Come on, let's have tea."

He yanked the portfolio from underneath his arm. "Won't

say no to that." He added, "Do you know how to make a London Fog?"

Olivia blinked. "I've never heard of such a thing." She put the kettle on and took two cups from the cabinet.

Hugo laughed. "I'll see if I can find the accouterments to display my talents." He tossed the folder on the table and rummaged through the cabinets and drawers as another knock sounded.

"Well, for Pete's sake. Who could that be?" Olivia made her way to the door again and opened it to find Teffeny swatting at the persistent bee. She darted in before Olivia could greet her and eyed Olivia with curiosity.

"Are you unwell?" Teffeny lifted a blonde brow.

Fighting the urge to roll her eyes, she said, "No. I entertained Beryl and Sheryl last night and slept in."

"Hmm" was Teffeny's response. The sound of clattering metal triggered another elevated brow. "Am I interrupting something?"

Olivia's face flamed. "No!"

Hugo came into the room holding what looked like a wand over his head. "Eureka!"

Teffeny's mouth twisted. "Why are you sword-playing with a frother?"

"A *frother*?" Olivia asked with a frown.

"I want a London Fog." Hugo lowered the tool. "Would you like to join us?"

Teffeny brushed past Olivia, Hugo behind them.

Olivia leaned against the doorframe. "Do you two mind if I

get dressed?"

Hugo laughed. "Of course not. By the time you return I'll have the tea ready."

"Thank you." She pointed toward the refrigerator. "And there are scones and clotted cream too."

Fifteen minutes later, Hugo was as good as his word. Three steaming cups sat on the table, along with a plate of scones, jam, and clotted cream. He stood over his offering and ceremoniously waved a hand. "Prepare to be amazed!"

Teffeny playfully slapped his arm. "So, what brought about this meeting?"

Hugo slid the portfolio across the table toward Olivia, saying nothing. She unzipped and opened the folder and glanced at the top of the first page.

OPTION AGREEMENT

Her heart skipped a beat. How could he have done this so quickly? Could she go through with it? There were no plans in place, inventory, furniture, or insurance. A small voice inside her said, *"Ian left you very well off. You could live off a fraction of that for a year or more while you get the business in place."*

Olivia's shoulders hunched. "Hugo, I've not given you any of my financial information." She waved the paper in front of her. "This cannot be legal."

Teffeny smiled. "Don't worry. It's just an option agreement to put you at the top of the list. The price is fixed *if* you choose to buy it. And they can't sell it to anyone else. It has a time limit.

Hugo stirred a small pot on the stove. In a few minutes, he returned to the table and poured vanilla syrup followed by foaming milk into each cup. He smiled at Olivia. "Try this."

"Hm. Not bad." She took another sip. "I rather like it." She replaced the offending paper on the stack and focused on the tea. "Hugo?"

"Yes, love." His gaze studied her over the rim of his cup.

"If I give you all of my information, but ask you not to do anything that would lock me into this purchase, can you do that?"

"Certainly. I know you need to be cautious. Who wouldn't, considering the amount of money and the commitment you'll be making?"

Olivia noticed Teffeny's serious expression during the exchange while she prepared a scone.

"Yes, it is a commitment I'm not sure about." Olivia sighed. "Yet."

Hugo pulled a small stack of stapled papers from the back of the folder. "If you'll fill these out and return them to me tomorrow, I'll put the information in the system and create a few loan options for you." He slipped a pen from its loop on the portfolio and poised to write. "At first inclination, what length would you like the loan to be?"

Olivia shifted her gaze from Teffeny to Hugo. "Well . . . I . . ." She stammered, stopped, and collected her thoughts. "A loan won't be necessary."

Hugo's mouth dropped. "But you just said—"

Teffeny's gaze held Olivia's for a long moment. "Hugo, don't get auncy. I think she means she'll pay for it in full."

THE BURNING SANDS

Olivia could only assume *auncy* meant angry or upset. Whatever the case, the comment calmed him. She dropped her chin. "Yes, Teffeny, that's exactly what I mean." Why did she feel embarrassed to have the money to pay it all?

Hugo let the pen slide to the table. "It's nothing to be ashamed of, love."

Olivia felt she must tell them. "I'd like to share something with you, but I ask that you keep it in confidence." She met their eyes. "Please."

Hugo and Teffeny agreed without hesitation.

Forcing courage to tell her sad tale once more, Olivia squared her shoulders. "My husband, Ian, died a little over a year ago. A boating accident. I really don't want to go into any details. Bottom line is—I now have more money than I know what to do with." She laughed mirthlessly. "I suppose that's not entirely true. There are a lot of things I can think of to spend it on but don't have the desire."

Hugo nodded. "Until now?"

Olivia released a heavy sigh. "Yes. Though it comes as a surprise. Seems I've come half-way round the world to find I want to buy a three-hundred-year-old pub."

"Tavern," Teffeny said matter-of-factly. "They called them taverns then."

"Picking nits now, are we?" Hugo tossed at Teffeny.

Teffeny stuck her tongue out at him, and he returned the sentiment. They acted more like siblings than cousins. Their child's play endeared them to her on the spot, making her feel the warmth of new friendships she hadn't felt in a while. Angie was her stalwart friend to be sure, but in the short time she had been in Trerose maybe she had made new ones.

Olivia scanned the forms. "I'll get these back to you this afternoon."

His brows rose. "If you wish, but tomorrow is fine."

"No," Olivia said, her voice resolute. "I've decided it's time for me to step out in faith and see where God leads me."

♦

Olivia completed the forms as promised, gathered Grace's diary and the genealogy papers, and strolled to the village. Hugo wasn't in his office, but his assistant accepted the papers and promised he'd give them to Hugo the moment he returned.

She made the short walk to the local museum. The building stood at the edge of the inner harbor, its weathered gray-white façade showing its age. Upon her entrance, the door set off a shrill bell, but no one greeted her. Fifteen minutes into her self-guided tour, a male voice spoke from a darkened corner. "Hello. Are you enjoying the museum, Olivia?"

Olivia squinted in the dim light, and a man moved out of the gloom. *Luke Harper*. She frowned. "Do you haunt every single corner of Trerose?"

He laughed. "Usually." He drew closer and moved as if to embrace her. She took a step back and bumped into the wall as he reached over her shoulder and flipped a switch.

With the room now illuminated, she saw a bulky wooden table where he'd been *hiding*. The back of a computer faced the door. Luke motioned toward the office area. "When I've a headache, I prefer to do my computer work in the dark."

Olivia willed her insides to calm. "Makes sense."

"How may I help you?" Luke Harper crossed his arms over his chest, his head cocked.

"Teffeny said I should ask someone from the local historical society to decipher an old diary that belonged to my great-grandmother." She opened her bag and carefully retrieved the book. "She was from Trerose."

The vicar's eyes widened, and he reached for the diary. "May I?"

Olivia released it into his hand. "So, am I to understand that you're an expert on old handwriting?"

Luke gestured toward the desk. She followed, and they positioned themselves in front of the computer. He shifted the keyboard to his right and lay the book in front of them.

When he opened it to the first page, Olivia pointed out Grace's name. "I did enough online research to confirm these letters spell out *Grace*." She felt a slight bit of accomplishment at having gotten this far.

He repositioned a small lamp to further illuminate the writing and took a magnifying glass from the drawer. After careful inspection, he placed the glass on the desk. "You're right. Proper job."

Olivia smiled. "I suppose my unanswered question is now solved."

His brow furrowed, then relaxed, a corner of his mouth lifting. "No. I am not an expert but a novice at best."

She tapped the diary with a finger. "Would you be willing to give me a crash course so I can move further along? I want to discover if this belonged to one of my ancestors."

Luke studied her. "Are you familiar with genealogical research?"

"Absolutely." Olivia removed the family records from her backpack and lay them in front of her. "My grandmother and I are the family genealogists. These papers are most of it, but I have digital files on my computer."

"Excellent. An *organized* genealogist." His smile was appreciative. "You'd be amazed at the people who come in bearing scraps of paper with a piece of a pedigree chart and ask us to locate their missing link."

Olivia chuckled. "Sounds like my mother. When I'd ask her a family question, she'd scribble it on the remnant of a grocery list."

His countenance sobered. "I don't want to offend, but do you mind if I ask a personal question?"

Olivia's pulse quickened. "I suppose not. But I reserve the right to refuse an answer."

"Fair enough." He leaned back in the creaking desk chair. "Why have you spent so much time alone in the old tavern?"

Olivia blinked. "It's going to sound strange, but when I did an internet search for Trerose, a real estate website was a top search result, so I clicked on it." She shifted in her chair. "I thought it a good way to see what the housing in the area looked like. The old place grabbed my attention right away."

"I certainly understand the draw to the place. It was the same for me with my cottage." He leaned closer until Olivia nearly shoved her chair back. "But why go so many times?"

Olivia bristled. "How do you know that?"

"*Olivia.*" He spoke her name with such familiarity it caught her off guard. "I'm the vicar. I walk these lanes several times a day. That's why we keep running into one another."

Olivia considered this. "Oh. I see."

He prompted her with a stare. "So, why go back?"

Olivia sighed. "I can't explain it. When Hugo took me there, it affected me." She looked around the room. "You'll think me strange, but buildings—places—it's like they're calling me."

"Déjà vu?"

Olivia considered the question. "No, not really. Just a connection."

"I've heard the same from many people who come in here. I suppose it's an ancestral thing. There are many unexplained phenomena we won't understand this side of Heaven."

Grace shrugged, uncertain how to respond.

With the growing silence, Luke inspected the diary again. "Ah, see this?" He used a pencil to point to what Olivia thought an indecipherable word. "I wouldn't know where to begin with that one. Looks like a drop of water landed on that one word."

At first inspection, she had assumed the ink had faded and told him so.

"I can see why you'd assume that. A number of years ago I attended a course on antique handwriting. Mind you, I'm not certified, but it gave me a leg up on things I would've otherwise overlooked." He continued to study the writing.

"Such as?" Olivia prompted.

"Oh, sorry. It's so fascinating." He placed a folder in front of Olivia. "The first tip says to read through the entire document to grasp the content, even if you don't understand some of it. Then, write out the alphabet mimicking the author's handwriting."

She interrupted, "What if you can't make it out?" She pointed to a letter she couldn't read.

He strained to see, then shot her a sideways look. "That's an *s*. Notice the surrounding letters and do the process of elimination as to the nature of the entire word. Keep in mind that lowercase *c, e, h, r, s,* and *t* are the hardest ones to recognize, especially in seventeen-century documents."

Olivia opened her mouth to speak, but his stomach growled.

"Pardon me. I passed over lunch. You were about to say?"

Up close, his eyes astonished her even more with their shade of blue ringed with gold. She cleared her throat. "It wasn't important." She glanced at the clock above the door. "I'm sorry to keep you past closing."

Olivia gathered her things and slung the bag over her shoulder. She stumbled, and his hands gripped her arms, bringing them much too close. She staggered toward the door. "Thank you for your help."

With her grip on the handle, he said, "I was thinking of going to The Pilchard for dinner. Will you join me?"

The question was like a punch in her middle. A lump formed in her throat, and she stared at the square panes of glass on the door, seeing her own reflection. Wide fear-filled eyes faced her. What was she afraid of?

Olivia closed her eyes. "I *am* hungry." His response was not immediate, and she wondered if he hadn't expected her to agree.

She turned to see him smiling. "Splendid. Why don't you go ahead and grab us a table. I'll lock up and join you in about fifteen."

"All right. I'll do that." Olivia stepped into the early evening light, unaccustomed to the sun setting past nine. When she rounded a corner to change direction, she sighted Hugo a few paces ahead. He turned as if she'd called to him.

"Olivia, love, all right?"

"Fine, and you?"

"Doing well. Thank you for being so prompt with the papers."

"You're welcome. Thank *you*."

He sidled up to her and kept pace. "Seems we're heading in the same direction. Where you off to?"

Olivia answered softly, "The Pilchard." She held her breath, hoping he wouldn't invite himself to accompany her.

Hugo leaned closer. "Sorry?"

She repeated her destination and sure enough—he did. What could she say? Dare she tell him who was joining her or let it be a surprise? While she fought with herself, he chatted on about the *mizzle* coming tonight.

Once they were seated in the pub, Olivia was about to enlighten Hugo that the vicar would arrive soon when she looked up to find Luke standing in the door. Thankfully, Hugo was speaking to the woman who brought their drinks, his back to Luke. He spotted her and moved toward the table. She sent him an apologetic smile. For a moment, she thought disappointment crossed his features.

He slapped Hugo on the back. "All right, Hugo?"

Startled, Hugo looked up. "Vicar! Fine. Join us?"

The vicar nodded and greeted her as if they'd not just spent time together. "Olivia. Nice to see you."

"Yes, please join us, Vicar." She felt the laugh in her throat building, grabbed her water, and took a gulp. What had overcome her?

The two men chatted, Hugo asking about the upcoming church fete. Olivia steered clear of the discussion, mulling over her own confusion. When their food arrived, she forced herself to join in the conversation, hoping she sounded coherent. Hugo was the first to leave, but she wasn't sure if she was glad or not.

Olivia declined dessert, but Luke ordered the berry trifle. Her eyes widened at the size of the layered sponge cake and custard.

"Would you like to share? I have to do takeaway when I order it."

The server looked at Olivia. "Would you like another plate?"

Luke spoke for her. "No, just another fork, please."

She chose not to respond, believing he would think her rude, yet wasn't their eating from the same plate a bit too intimate?

A flashback came to her of how she and Ian shared desserts at every restaurant they'd been to through the years. He always saved her the last bite. She swallowed hard, refusing to let tears come.

THE BURNING SANDS

It was only a dessert. There was nothing more to it, she told herself, as she picked up her fork and cut a small piece of the trifle. She savored the bite and dabbed a napkin to her mouth. "This is simply amazing."

"I'm glad you are enjoying it."

They ate in silence for a time until their forks clinked as each made to cut a bite from the one large piece left.

Embarrassed, Olivia placed her fork on the table. "Please, take it. I've had more than I need already."

He pushed the plate toward her. "This will be the first time I've left this place without a container in hand."

Olivia thoughts strayed to earlier. "I'm sorry I didn't have a chance to let Hugo know you were coming until you'd arrived. He pretty much took over the evening."

"No worries. Hugo's a splendid chap. I like him." He took the last sip of his drink. "And Teffeny. We aren't the same age, but we near grew up together. Few of us left in the village."

"Left?"

"Most who grew up here left to go to uni and never came back."

A brief pang of homesickness fluttered in her stomach. "I sort of did that myself. Although I didn't leave the state. Just the rural area where I grew up."

He raised his voice to be heard over a group of boisterous men watching sports on the television in the far corner. "Where do you live now?"

"New Orleans. Not in the thick of the city. Ian and I agreed on that before we married." Olivia stiffened. Why had she told him that? What happened to the carefully guarded wall she'd erected around her past?

The pause in sporting cheers quieted just as Olivia heard his hard swallow. He spoke in a low voice. "I was not aware you were married." He straightened in his seat, shifting away from her a few inches.

"Vicar!" Sheryl called from across the room, making her way in their direction, Beryl right behind her.

Olivia watched the approach with dread. Luke rose, tucked his chair under the table, and faced them. "Good evening, ladies." Olivia noted the tenseness in his tone.

"You have come at a most opportune time. Hugo just left us, and now I must be away. Will you keep *Mrs*. Griffin company? She has her dessert to finish." He then strode from the pub without a glance at Olivia.

VII

Dusk painted a slow fade to night on the top of the cliff path. Stars sparkling in the inky sky disappeared like a gradually released curtain. Grace sat on the bench she and Sebastian so often shared after her day at the tavern and his in the mines. When he worked days, she rested here for a moment from the uphill climb before visiting Mrs. Braddock with the bundle of food. She had not seen him, Rig, nor Adam the entire day.

After their conversation the previous eve, she wondered if it were a dream. Rustling sounded behind her, and she turned to see Sebastian. Her brother offered an engaging smile, and she wondered why he had yet to marry. Girls in the village—especially Wilmont and Caye—thought him a handsome man.

He drew closer, and despite the smile, fatigue etched his features. He motioned for her to follow him. "Come, I must show ye the way."

The darkness seeped around them so none could see where they were to go. Sebastian took her hand and guided her along the side of the cliff on the seldom used rocky path. "We go to the cave."

They walked on in silence, from time-to-time pebbles careening under their careful steps, skittering into the waves lapping against the rocks below. At the opening of the cave, Sebastian stepped in several feet before he ignited a lantern. Casks hugged the rock walls to their far left—smugglers' goods. Grace tapped her brother's shoulder and glanced at the contraband, his gaze following hers.

"'Tis of nay concern." He pulled her along, deeper into the cavern.

Grace allowed her brother to prod her forward, but timidity gripped her. "What if we are seen? Shall not our presence anger the smugglers?"

"They shall not discover us." The assurance in his voice urged her forward.

"How can ye be certain?" Grace jumped at a distant sound. The further they went, it grew louder. She thought them surely near the back of the cavern by now. The noise became soft voices, and she heard the scrape of footsteps against shale. Sebastian took her to a narrow passage she had not known existed.

Grace kept her voice to a whisper. "Who is speaking?"

Sebastian's grip tightened. "Wait, Grace. Be patient."

They walked on for a time, and she worried about being so far back in the cave. He stopped and placed the lantern behind a large rock, then extinguished it and guided her sideways through the slight opening, blackness enveloping them. A fleeting moment of panic surrounded her as one hand slid along the slippery stone.

Dripping water coupled with the sweet smell of fresh air piqued her curiosity as they stepped into a dimly lit cavern. "Sebastian, what is this place?"

Sebastian turned to her. "We pray nay one knows. I found it quite by accident when I was a child and have never shared it with anyone." He hesitated, and when he spoke again, his voice was hoarse. "Except Nick." He exhaled sharply. "'Tis difficult to find. Well hidden by the cleft we passed through. The angle of it shall not reveal lantern light. Do not forget to snuff your light on this side of the cleft. Ye must pass through in the dark, or the passage may be discovered."

Someone cleared their throat. Grace shifted to see Adam holding a lantern. Rig stood in front of the light, a glow encircling him. Adam extended an arm behind him in an elegant bow, the light held high in his other hand.

"This way, my lady." Rig shot her a disarming smile, and her breath caught. Something about that grin weakened her resolve.

When he moved aside to allow her to pass, what she saw astonished her. In a corner of the cavern, rocks supported a wooden roof. It covered a wide area to house four hammocks, a table and chairs, small iron stove, a trunk, and a crudely built open cupboard containing tins, boxes, burlap sacks, dishes, cups, and utensils. In the opposite corner stood a large barrel.

Adam picked up a burlap sack and walked to the other side of the cavern across a natural stone bridge. Clear water shimmered in the lantern light.

Grace saw a small shelter with a door. Sebastian whispered in her ear that it was their privy. Her mouth parted in amazement. They had thought of everything and must have worked days to achieve it.

When they reached the living area, Rig stood beside her. "We have made for ye a hiding place. Once ye come here, there shall be no need to leave unless ye want for the wind, which we advise not, other than when the night is moonless. Ye shall be safe until our ship sails." He paused, the first moment of hesitance she had observed from him. "Can ye bear to live in such a place with your family for this brief time?"

Why was this man—these *men*—being so kind? She stammered, "Ye did this for us? For me?"

Rig kept his eyes focused on her. "I—*we* did."

"But ye do know us not. Why should ye do this?" Grace stared into his hazel eyes, the dim light revealing the green in them.

Sebastian took her arm and drew her away from Rig. "Take it, Grace. 'Tis kindly meant by good men."

Not wanting to seem ungrateful, Grace whispered to Sebastian, "We don't know these men. How can ye be so certain of them?"

Her brother's eyes held such calm reassurance she could do nothing but trust his judgment. She knew not Rig and Adam, yet she knew her brother and trusted him with her life and future.

"Very well." Grace faced Rig. "Thank ye. I shall do as ye bid." She took in all the details they had attended to and dipped her chin. "Rig, Adam, how could ye have done this in such a short time?"

Seriousness settled over Rig, yet tenderness dwelled there too as he looked at her. "When the need does arise, ye do what must needs be done."

When Sebastian escorted her up the cliff path again, Adam and Rig parted ways, returning to their ship.

Grace looked at her brother. "Why did ye say that ye shall not go with us? Sebastian, ye are my brother. Ye must go."

He pulled in a deep breath of the night air. "Ye can trust Rig and Adam."

Grace took his arm and tugged him to a stop. "But how do ye know that, Sebastian?"

"Do ye think I would send my family off with men I do not trust? They shall see ye properly settled someplace safe, far from here."

She remained silent for a moment, pondering what to say. "How can we know when the smugglers shall not go to the cave? Should we happen upon them, they may do us harm."

"We know when they shall be about their business, so do not come here without one of us. Please." He looked to her for agreement.

Grace nodded but saw a flicker of something undefinable in his gaze.

Over the next two days, she planned with her mother on what belongings to take. She and Sebastian moved them, a few at a time, each eve.

In the cave, Grace knelt before the trunk containing her personal possessions. Sebastian had left her there to arrange things to her liking, cautioning her to stay nay longer than an hour. She surveyed her surroundings thinking of the next days she would spend in the dark cavern. They had lanterns, but the men said it would be wise not to use them overly in the eve should some unknown crevice reveal them.

Grace completed her task, placed the lantern on the natural ledge at the inner cave entrance, and extinguished it. She inched her way along the passage as quietly as possible. Footsteps softly echoed, but she could not determine from which direction they came. She shivered, fear gripping her.

Pressing her back against the cool stone, she held her breath. The footsteps were not stealthy, as though they cared not should they be discovered, and she wondered if it was Sebastian. She shifted her weight, and a pebble slid across the path.

The footsteps halted, and a deep voice whispered, "Grace?"

She released a breath, the drip of water echoing in the space, and stepped from the wall. "Rig, what are ye doing here?" Her voice seemed breathless even to her own ears.

"I brought something for ye." He took her hand and pressed a small paper package into her grasp.

Grace caught the slight hitch in his voice.

"'Tis kind of ye." Total darkness hindered her vision. His voice grew closer. He brushed against her, and her breath caught.

"Is Adam with ye?" She hoped—yet feared—he was.

"Grace," he whispered but did not complete the sentence.

The hair on her neck rose, though not in fear. She could not identify the cause of the flutter in her stomach. It was but the two of them. In the total blackness, only their voices were evidence of their presence.

"I wanted to speak with ye a moment. Alone. Since we have happened upon one another . . ." He faltered. "I know ye don't know me, but . . ."

She heard his shaky intake of air.

With hesitancy, he said, "Well, there's nothing for it . . ."

The heat of his nearness shifted something within her, drawing her to him. No feeling had ever encompassed her thus.

"I must speak my peace and leave it with ye. But I want to walk ye home as 'tis not safe for ye to be about at this time."

Boldness gripped her, unladylike though it was. "Rig, what do ye want to say?"

He moved closer, yet he did not touch her. "We shall have a long voyage ahead. Yet before we depart, I would like to know more of ye."

Grace hesitated. "I know not what to say."

"There is nay need to say aught at this time."

Wishing she could see his face, read what lay in his eyes, she rested against the wall to place more space between them.

"I have grown fond of Sebastian. Nearer the feelings of a brother."

Grace measured her words. "Ye are kind, generous, and caring. My brother trusts ye, and he does give his trust sparingly." A chill overtook her. "There are few men of such conviction that I have been acquainted with."

His voice lowered. "Of a certainty not your father."

"'Tis truth." Her heart ached at the thought of her father.

Sebastian's face flashed in her mind. "I know not why Sebastian wants to stay in Trerose."

"Your brother must make his own decisions, Grace. But ye can have a wonderful life somewhere else far from here, and nay one shall know. Trust me please?"

She knew if he could see her face, it would reveal the pain in her heart.

"His reasons are his own. When the time is right, Sebastian will tell ye. He cares for ye. Although I do not understand why he says Arabel shall not come nor will he ask her yet. Said she may reveal our plan to your father."

Grace swallowed. "My father has turned her against us. He tells her lies and treats her kindly because of all she does for him in the tavern's running. She has long been skilled with numbers."

"Yet she sees not what he does to the rest of ye?"

"Oh, she does, yet he always explains that we have wronged him and deserved the punishment."

"Seems she is much too innocent." His voice moved nearer.

Grace stammered as his breath caressed her face. "He plies her with gifts, and she has her own room at the tavern. 'Tis nicely furnished." A different kind of hurt stabbed at her. "He buys her pleasing clothes and the like." She swiped her hand over her worn skirt, and a tear slipped down her cheek.

"I must ask ye one other thing, Grace." Sadness tinted his speech. "Sebastian says your father wants ye to marry Eudo."

Grace's head snapped up. "Oh, that he does, yet I do not agree."

Rig's voice tightened. "He *appears* to be an honest man."

She caught the change in his tone. "So, it seems. All the women do like to see him coming. He is pleasant to look upon, and he leaves coin on the table when he departs."

Rig chuckled. "I know the ladies take a fancy to him. I hear them tittering when he walks into the tavern, and they rush to him," his voice lowered, "except ye."

"Aye. They do Sebastian the same."

"Ye have said that ye do not agree with your father about marrying Eudo, but how do ye feel about him?"

"If ye ask if I find him—agreeable—aye, he is kindly to all. 'Tis only my father's idea of marriage. I will not marry a man I do not love. At two and twenty it has yet to happen." She faltered. "Nay man I have met has ever been what a proper husband should be—except perhaps my brother and the vicar. A true man should respect others and care for those weaker. My father has not set a good example for either virtue."

"Of a truth. I can see this." His feet shuffled on the pebbles. "And I like not to disparage another. Have a care. Eudo is not all he appears."

She flinched with the revelation. "Ye just said he seems honest. What do ye know of him?"

"Adam and I sit and watch." He chuckled. "And we listen. When we are about, we have come upon things of which ye would not approve. Things Eudo is involved with, but 'tis not my story to tell, and how ye may learn about the details is not for me to say. I would not have ye come to harm." His voice grew hoarse. "If he does ever make to harm ye, I will have something to say."

Grace bristled. "What concern is it to ye? Ye know me not.

I am aware of more than ye think."

"It would vex me a great deal. And Sebastian. He has shared how close ye have been to him since ye were children."

"We have always been quite close, even more so after . . ." Her words trailed off, remembering that unbearable day long ago.

"What happened that changed ye?"

"'Tis not a tale I care to speak of. We can do nothing about the past. I was but a small girl when it happened, and I must needs leave it be. Just as Sebastian does try, yet he cannot, for he is older than me." Grace's shoulders slumped, and she stammered, "He feels responsible that he did not do more."

"'Tis a story of which I would like to know. Yet I shall wait until one of ye reveals it. Our friendship is yet new."

Silence lengthened between them, the sound of the waves muffled in the distance.

Grace listened to the plop of water dropping from the cavern roof into the pool. She shivered, remembering the first time she had collected water to wash their utensils, and her hand felt the icy liquid.

"Grace?" His voice was yet closer.

Her breath caught, and she felt warm lips on her cheek, and she closed her eyes, savoring the sensation, he then took her hand and led her from the cave in the darkness.

Rig Cooper was unlike any man she had ever met, and perhaps she wished to know him better as well.

Chapter Nine

The pub door slammed behind the vicar, and Olivia was left with her mouth hanging open, Sheryl and Beryl crowding around her.

Sheryl's eyes widened. "My, he was in a bit of a rush."

Beryl added with a nod. "As much as I hate to agree with you, it seems he was cheesed off."

Olivia pressed her lips together and peered at her. "Why do you say that?" She paused, confusion growing. "What does that mean?"

Sheryl huffed. "He's annoyed about something."

Beryl dismissed her sister's comment with a wave. "We've known him since he was a lad and recognize all his moods." Beryl studied her. "Olivia, love, are you unwell? Your face is a tad flushed."

Sheryl leaned toward Olivia and placed the flat of her hand

on her forehead. "She feels a bit hottish, Sister. Perhaps we should escort her home and put her to bed."

Olivia stood, grabbing her bag in a white-knuckled grip. "No. Please. I'm fine."

The twins stood with her, clearly intent on seeing her home safely.

Beryl leaned in and whispered, "Did the vicar say something to upset you?"

Sheryl eyed Olivia with suspicion. "What were you talking about when we interrupted?"

Beryl bristled. "That is none of our concern, Sheryl."

Olivia's stomach roiled. The last thing she'd said to him was clearly what spurred his abrupt departure. Her careless declaration made him think she was married. She'd put him in a risky situation. A married woman sitting in a pub having dinner with the vicar. How careless she was. She should have explained immediately that she was a widow.

Forgetting she was not alone, she jumped when Beryl put an arm around her waist and led her to the door.

"Come, child. Sheryl and I will take you home. You *are* unwell."

She followed the twins like a wayward schoolgirl. How could she be so blind? If this caused gossip in the village, guilt would eat her up. He had been nothing but kind to her, and she felt she'd betrayed their growing friendship. Weakness forced her to follow the women into the cottage.

Sheryl unlocked the cottage door, and Beryl led Olivia inside. "Now, now, dear. We will lock up for you. Get some rest and we'll pop over in the morning." She glanced at her sister. "But not too early, mind you."

A surge of gratitude calmed Olivia. "Thank you. You're such dears."

They smiled, patted her shoulder, flipping the light off as they parted, whispering all the way.

Olivia's thoughts strayed to the misunderstanding with Luke and his immediate reaction. Oh, how she wished she'd rushed after him and told him about Ian's death. She would seek him out tomorrow.

A wave of fatigue overwhelmed her, and she fell into a fitful sleep. When she woke, moonlight spilled through the curtained window, casting a silhouette of lace across her covers. She rolled onto her back and stared at the brilliant moon. The intensity of the quiet weighed on her until all she could hear were the angry waves crashing below.

With great effort Olivia slipped on her robe and made a cup of lavender tea. She cradled the mug between her palms and stepped onto the stone patio, the briny breeze lifting from the sea. For the past year, her life had been a nightmare from which she couldn't seem to awaken. She placed her mug on the patio table and strolled to the path, peering over the cliff edge to the rugged gray rocks below.

Moonlight cast eerie shadows on the surging white foam. Some ethereal longing swept through her . . . riveted her. The wildness of the pounding waves made her think of the dangers Ian liked to experience. It was the only thing they could not agree on.

Olivia wanted to scream at the waves, to tell them she hated them for what they were, for how the lure of their wild elements had enthralled her husband—and taken him from her. She had grieved him so fiercely, but at this moment, it occurred to her that maybe she had not grieved him properly, which was why she couldn't let him go.

She dropped to her knees, glaring at the moon, its hazy glowing orb reminding her of the watercolors on the harbor painting.

Tears fell in a torrent, shifting to heart-shattering sobs. She wanted her husband, needed him, not only the ghost of his memory. She cried out in a loud voice that was drowned out by the waves.

"Why, Lord, did you take him from me?"

⊙≫

Olivia woke shivering, her bed much harder than she remembered. She opened her eyes to the dark blue sky above a half-circle glow, its base an endless horizontal ribbon of gold—she'd fallen asleep on the path! She groaned, then listened to the sound of the waves, but they didn't fill her with anger as before.

Her body ached, and when she inched onto one elbow, pain shot through her side making her groan. Stiffness stretched along her entire form. It took her several moments to stand, but when upright, her gaze stilled by movement on the path past her cottage. She could have sworn she'd seen a man there but shook off the disconcerting feeling of being watched and hurried indoors. After a shower and quick breakfast, she yanked her backpack from the sofa and went into the village.

Her mission was to find Luke and finish her story.

For once, she didn't bump into him anywhere. An idea

nipped at her, and she called the twins. No answer. They were most likely working on the church fundraiser. It took only a few minutes to walk to the church, and that was exactly where they were—with many others. There was no way she could talk to the vicar among all the hustle and bustle.

Beryl rounded a corner of the church, and Olivia hailed her. "Good morning, Beryl. Have you seen the vicar?"

"Good morning, love. You look much better. How do you feel?" Beryl's tender tone melted Olivia's heart.

"Thanks to the wonderful nurses I had last night, I'm perfect." She was grateful for their care, even if they were a bit quirky.

Sheryl found them. "Who's perfect?"

"Olivia is, Sister."

Sheryl placed a hand on her hip. "Well, of course! We took care of her."

Olivia's affection for them grew. "You did that and more. I am much obliged to you both."

Sheryl's face wore satisfaction and Beryl's gratitude.

She stepped closer to the twins, but someone came around the opposite corner facing them and halted. Luke's eyes met hers. He gave an imperceptible nod and retraced his steps, slipping out of sight. It was as though she could read his thoughts. He felt deceived. And she couldn't blame him. If only he'd let her explain.

"Olivia, you look ill again." Beryl chewed her lip.

"It's okay. I just remembered something I must do. Please excuse me." She sprinted after Luke just as her phone rang. She glanced at the display, then answered. "Hugo, may I call you back please?"

His voice wavered. "Uh, yeah, sure. But I wanted to ask if you would stop by my office as I have news."

She jerked to a stop. "Good or bad?"

He cleared his throat. "Well . . . not necessarily *bad* . . ."

"But not necessarily *good* either?" Olivia saw Luke ahead, now too far for her to catch up.

Hugo's tone stiffened. "In a word—no."

Olivia huffed and resigned herself to temporary defeat. "I'll be right over."

ᛞ

Hugo sat at the desk, speaking in low tones into his phone, yet he smiled and waved for her to be seated. In moments, his assistant returned with a small tray holding two cups of tea and a saucer of biscuits.

He raised his brows, pointing to the receiver while she sipped her tea. Olivia liked Hugo, just as Teffeny said she would. He was a nice-looking man, neat in appearance, not over tall, and for some unknown reason, thought of Angie. They would make a lovely couple and would get on quite well.

A noisy exhale sounded. Olivia glanced up to find Hugo inspecting her. "What?"

"Oh, Olivia. You look so peaceful sitting there sipping tea and all." He took a drink from his cup and released a pained sigh.

"That tone tells me much, Hugo."

"Yes, as it should—as it should." He opened the file before him and tapped an index finger against it. "We have a tiny problem."

She leaned forward and placed her cup on the desk, waiting for an explanation.

"Word has gotten out that you've bid on the property."

Olivia bit her lip. "How did that happen, and why is it a problem?"

"You see—the local historical society has long had their eye on the building for their future museum." His brows pinched. "They're weary of the cramped space they possess and want a building that *is* historic."

"So why have they not bought it before now?" Olivia's mind whirled as to why, after all this time, they decided they wanted *her* building.

"Funds, my dear. Funds." He grimaced. "I think they merely want to scare you off to buy themselves more time."

"I don't understand."

"They don't have the pounds and won't for a while. But they don't want any prospective buyer lurking about, and they know you intend to plant roots here. They're hoping you'll move on to the next old fishing village to set up shop and so they made a higher bid."

"But my family came from here. I already have roots." Olivia grew suspicious. "How many locals are on the historical society committee?"

Hugo flipped papers. "Five."

Olivia lifted a brow. "Who's the chairman?"

He cleared his throat. "Luke Harper."

Stunned, Olivia swallowed. Her suspicion grew rapidly,

her stomach roiling. "When did this offer come in?"

He glanced down. "This morning."

"Hmm... I see." She contemplated this. "So, they think I'll fold because the price is more, yet they can't afford it. Correct?"

"*Yesss...*" Hugo drew out.

Olivia leaned back in her chair and tented her hands under her chin. "Tell them you accept their offer."

He notched his chin up. "What?"

"Yes. If they don't have the money, they'll have to back down, and I'll take it as planned." She slapped the surface of the desk. "So there!"

Hugo stared at her with a glint of humor in his eyes. "May I ask why you are so piqued?"

Olivia stood, ire rising, and paced the room a moment before turning to Hugo. "Because *Luke Harper* will not scare me off. The Burning Sands is mine!" She flounced to the door, bag in hand. "And tell the *man* I will top any price he can name!"

All she heard before the door slammed behind her was Hugo saying, "Yes ma'am," and chuckling.

Olivia stomped along the lane. The utter audacity of the man. She had hurt his pride, and he was attempting to pay her back. He felt duped, and she felt horrible. She had not intended to hide anything from him. How dare he! Anger gripping her, she barely heard her name over the din of tourists turning out for their evening meal, the streets frenetic with activity.

"Olivia! Wait for me!"

She turned to see Teffeny bouncing toward her, breathless. "You can really move!"

"That's what happens when I am ticked off!" Olivia regained her pace, Teffeny striding along with her.

Teffeny's eyes widened. "Well! I cannot wait to hear this one. Let's go to dinner before everything is packed tight."

Suspecting the vicar would not return to The Pilchard so soon after their encounter, Olivia changed course and strode to the pub. Soon, they greeted Uno and placed their orders.

Teffeny leaned back in her chair and crossed her arms over her chest, eyes slanted suspiciously. "Give over. Who's ticked you off?"

Without hesitation, Olivia said, "The vicar."

Teffeny stared for a long while before she laughed.

Olivia said nothing.

Her friend leaned toward Olivia. "Do be serious. Who is it really?"

"I am serious." Olivia relayed the series of events, beginning with the museum visit and his help with the diary. By the time she'd finished, their food arrived, and they dug in.

Between bites, Teffeny said, "I'm missing something."

"Don't you get it? We had dinner together, and he thinks I'm married, and I'll ruin his *vicarish* reputation."

"Hmm." Teffeny groaned. "Nice word."

Olivia smirked. "You know what I mean."

"I kinda see your point. Why didn't you just tell him you're a widow?"

"He didn't give me a chance. When Sheryl and Beryl

appeared, he fled."

Teffeny nodded. "Right."

Olivia cocked her head. "So, you see the impression he left?"

"Yes. *And* his avoiding you at the church this morning." She slid her empty plate to the side of the table. "I've known Luke most of my life. He's never had a serious girlfriend that I'm aware of. Unless it was while he was away at uni. But he never brought one home to meet his mum. And a vicar needs a wife."

"Aren't you the Victorian?" Olivia teased, her anger easing.

"Ha-ha." Teffeny pulled a face, making Olivia laugh. "You've got to admit there's less gossip about a married vicar if he behaves himself."

"True." Olivia considered this. "Still—I'm angrier that he's retaliated about his hurt ego and trying to snatch the Sands from me."

Teffeny's eyes widened. "How do you know it's him?"

Olivia thought about it. "Hugo said he's the chairman of the historical society. Who else?"

"Ask Hugo who called and made the offer."

"All right. I will." Olivia thought that was the least she could do.

The two women parted ways outside the pub, Olivia promising she'd speak with Hugo the following day. She breathed in the salty air and admired the village. The warm glow of windows filled with light dotted the darkness and reflected off the receding tide in the harbor. She really had grown fond of this place in such a short time.

As she took her first step on the path, her gaze fell on the museum across the harbor. The large window was well-lit, and she wondered if it could be Luke, though they would've closed hours prior. The sudden urge to go make her thoughts known to him nearly overtook her better sense.

"No!" she told herself. A couple passing by gave her a worried look, and she pulled a face and shrugged, eliciting a chuckle. The light across the way extinguished, and Olivia waited to see who would exit. It *was* him. A sense of urgency pushed her to dash up the hill toward the cottage. She knew he'd be traveling the same path and didn't want to encounter him. Although judging from his behavior at the church, he would probably just sprint right past her without a word. That was fine. She wasn't ready to tell him anything—*yet*.

Olivia picked up speed and topped the crest overlooking the cliffs. The sky rapidly darkening, she twisted at the fork in the path to her right, and her heel caught on a jagged rock, sending her to fall and roll toward the precipice. On instinct, she grabbed a small gorse bush, the thorny spikes pricking her palms. She cried out in pain but was able to pull herself to a sitting position.

Rustling in the dusk brought her head up, eyes squinting to see the source. An animal, perhaps? Or a person. She leaned over onto her elbow, trying to hide behind the offending bush. Embarrassment tightened her stomach, and she clenched her jaw.

"Olivia, I know you're here. I saw you on the path ahead of me." The words grew closer with each utterance. "Are you hurt?" This time, the tone rang with concern.

Olivia returned to her sitting position and tried to stand

but found her legs weak. Instead of continuing the effort, she pulled her knees to her chin and peered across the water, watching it ripple in the waning, sinking sun. When the vicar reached her, she avoided his gaze.

He stood over her, feet planted wide, and laughed. "What in blue blazes are you doing?"

His laughter irritated her beyond the pain in her palms. She stood on trembling legs. Heat flamed in her cheeks, battling with the cool wind whipping her hair. Her gaze caught on a clump of pink thrift, and she snatched a handful and tugged it from the dirt. She stumbled in her hurry to rise, toppling toward him. When she hastened to correct her stance, the direction of her fall shifted, and she teetered backward—toward the precipice.

Luke's quick reflexes saved her from certain death over the cliff. He wrapped both arms around her and backed onto level ground. "Olivia! What were you thinking!"

Without a second thought, she raised the handful of crushed flowers to his face. "Just picking flowers."

His brows rose. "Picking flowers?"

The moment stilled. Her words gave no heed to her brain, and they poured from her lips before she could process what she was saying. "I'm not married, Luke. My husband died more than a year ago."

As if stabbed by a knife of anger, she spouted, "You could've at least asked rather than snubbing me since dinner at The Pilchard last night."

She flattened a palm against his chest and pushed him away, this time sending him teetering toward the path where he promptly fell onto his backside.

His smile wide, he rose and dusted his hands. "What a pair we are, misunderstanding after misunderstanding since the moment we met." He wiped his hands on his jeans-clad thighs and presented his right hand to Olivia. "Good evening. I'm Vicar Luke Harper. It's a pleasure to meet you."

Olivia cocked her head, amused by the gesture. Hesitant, she gave him her hand. "Good evening, Vicar. I'm the *widow* Olivia Griffin, who just arrived in Cornwall. It's nice to meet you as well." When he squeezed her hand, she grimaced.

Luke gently twisted her hand and studied her injury. "That looks painful."

She shrugged. "I'll wash and disinfect it when I get home." She paused before saying, "Which I really must do now."

"Are you free to come by the museum tomorrow morning?" He hurried on. "I found a few genealogy items about your diary owner."

Olivia perked at the news. "Indeed? I can't refuse that offer."

The vicar gave a half-nod. "Splendid. See you around half-nine?"

"I'll be there." She stepped around him but turned back. "Thank you, Luke."

His smile was warm, eyes shining, as he looked at her. "You're most welcome, Olivia."

A grin tugged at her lips, and on her journey home, her step was lighter than she remembered in a very long time.

CAROLE LEHR JOHNSON

VIII

Grace and Rig stilled at the edge of the path leading to Grace's home, the sea surging below the cliffs. He pulled in a breath. "Please take nay offence at my behavior in the cave. I have been wanting to do that since the first day I saw ye standing in the lantern light at the tavern." Gently, his fingertips caressed her cheek where he had placed the kiss. "The night ye were following your father."

Grace did not respond, yet his touch sent a shiver through her, and her voice shook as she said, "'Tis time I was home."

Rig stared at her for a long moment, their eyes searching one another's. Grace could hear her own quick breaths, her emotions warring inside. Would he kiss her? Nay man had done so—yet a memory flashed from years before.

Sebastian and Nick were running into the waves on Talland Sands beach, wearing only breeches, their young, tanned skin glowing with health. She could see their brown sun-streaked hair curling from the seawater. Judging by their appearance, they could have been brothers. Though not by blood, yet most certainly by nature. They shared everything.

Grace saw it all in a memory as if she still sat on the rock-sheltered beach building a castle from the sand. She could near see the small pewter cup she had used to create her castle. Burned into her very soul was the image of her father's scowl when he discovered she had taken the cup from the tavern. That was her first recollection of his anger.

By chance, he encountered them on the path home that eve. Now she saw it was with cunning that he had sent the boys on ahead and then pulled her into a copse of gorse.

Her father had pressed her back into the shrub, the spikes pricking through her dress and into her skin. He was not altered by her tears as he slapped the pewter cup from her tiny hand, bruising the delicate skin. His voice was low and menacing, telling her she was a thief, grabbing the front of her dress, his large, rough hands lifting her, the spikes cutting into her skin.

Once he was through berating her, he dropped her to the ground and stormed away, the little cup tight in his paw-like grip. Grace had curled into a ball and cried until the day's light began to fade, and a low voice interrupted her sobbing. Nick had returned down the path after walking Sebastian home and found her beneath the gorse.

When he questioned her, she said she had fallen. He held her in his arms until she stopped crying, not once asking anything more. It was from that day she loved him. Though she was but a child, she could see his true character as he kissed her tear-streaked cheeks.

The sea air flowing through her hair roused her from the

memory, and she looked into the sparse light. She could not meet Rig's eyes, nor could she understand what had happened but a short while before. The tender way he treated her brought the bittersweet past to her. How she missed Nick.

Rig stared at her, his gaze roaming her face. Words would not come, uncertain how she felt about his attentions. Her insides still quivered from the contact, though brief it was. How did he know she was following her father that night?

She stepped away, and Rig made to go with her. "'Tis nay need for ye to walk with me."

His tone was unyielding. "I shall see ye safely home."

The cool, moist air surrounded them like a mist. Grace glanced at him and trembled from the cold—or *was* it the cold. He walked with her but said nothing as the cottage came into view. She stopped on the path and faced him. "Thank ye. Good eve."

When she turned away, he took her arm in a gentle grasp. "Grace, I have nothing to offer ye. I have nay home but the sea. Yet I would like for ye to know my feelings, but it shall keep for now."

She nodded, and he released her. Inside, she found the house asleep, the flicker of firelight bathing the room in golden warmth. Her mother left the fire for her to bank upon her return. The trudge upstairs drained what little strength remained.

When she sat upon her bed, she remembered the gift Rig had given her. The crisp brown paper crackled as she carefully opened it. A piece of paper lay atop a small brown book. In the dim light she read:

May this book distract ye on your journey to freedom.
– Rig

Grace opened it to find a collection of poems. She hugged the book to her chest.

☙❦❧

The following day, Grace found Sebastian waiting for her outside the cottage. "Should ye not already be down the mine?"

"Be not concerned at present." He rose from the bench and lowered his voice. "'Tis time for ye to move to the cavern."

She released a weary sigh. "'Tis hard to think on it. I lay awake the night thinking of all the responsibilities I shall step away from. Yet . . . trying to look toward a life without constant turmoil and pain. I fear for Mrs. Braddock. Who shall care for her?"

"I shall make sure she has food enough. Eulalia shall help."

"But when ye depart to join us, whenever that is, who shall care for her?"

"Grace, God shall provide. And I shall speak with the vicar and the doctor. They can be trusted to keep our confidence."

Grace frowned. "But *we* feed her. Though I know Father has kept us fed, yet he hoards away all that he can rather than giving to his family. We have just enough to get by. Should he know I pilfer food from the tavern to feed her, I would feel his wrath." She rubbed her arm, remembering the times he had grabbed her.

Her brother's eyes softened. "There are many who love the old woman who would help if they know we shall no longer be

THE BURNING SANDS

here, but I shall care for her in your absence."

A flash of worry crossed his handsome face.

"Sebastian, what do ye keep from me? Why shall ye not come with us?"

"Grace, I told ye. If I disappear, Father shall be more settled on trying to find ye. With just ye, Mother, and the children gone, it shall not look as suspicious. I must stay here and attend to some things. Trust me please?" He cocked his head, pleading. "Trust me."

Grace's thoughts tumbled. What did he conceal? From the time they were children, they shared all. Why was her life in such disorder? They reached the tavern, and Sebastian strode to the main room. She helped Eulalia with meal preparations for the morn and asked after her father. Eulalia told her the doctor had already come and gone for the day, saying that Rad had attempted to rise, but stumbled and hurt his injured leg.

"Ye should have heard the doctor railing at him. Telt him he was an old fool and would be abed longer 'cause of his stupidity. Naturally, your father railed at him like a wild beast. The doctor took it in his stride and telt him to sit there and rot if he would like. Your father gave him a good cursing as he stomped out. Heard it all from here, most likely the whole tavern did." She placed the food-laden plates on a salver. She slid it across the worktable toward Grace. "Here ye be. Take this out to them comely lads afore Wilmont arrives."

Grace gripped the salver. "What?"

"That Cooper fella, his friend, and your brother. They be back from Dickie Steve's. He telt them 'bout some thieves that coulda been the ones what hurt your father. Seems they may be working for Eudo." Eulalia cut portions of venison pie onto a plate. "I know your brother works for Eudo from time to time, but that do not mean your brother would ever do aught not proper." The woman's gaze surveyed Grace. "What? Ye think Eudo be above doing somethin' like that? Ye be thinking he was all niceness? Ye be naïve at times, child."

Grace winced. "I know not what ye mean."

"Have ye never wondered why your father wanted ye to marry him? Well, I believe he wanted ye out of the house to be rid of ye 'cause he did not want another mouth to feed." The woman shook her head and smiled. "'Tis not me to telt ye what to do or not to do. Just be on your guard with one of them purdy boys like Eudo. A purdy man that talks about what they got to hook a gurl, most likely will not be purdy on the inside."

Grace blew out a breath. "I wish ye would tell me, Eulalia. Speak freely. Ye are like a second mother to me. I trust ye."

The woman sighed deeply. "Grace, Eudo may be nice on the outside, and well to look upon, yet there are things he does ye know nothing of." She ladled a scoop of stewed beef. "Not sayin' he would be cruel to ye like Rad. He may treat ye most kindly and shower ye with baubles as he has coin for it. He be a fisherman. How can he have the coin for much of anythin' 'cept gettin' by?"

Grace glimpsed the honesty in the cook's face and saw the sincerity present. It was true Eudo wore clothes that a simple fisherman could not afford. How had she not seen it before now? Was Eulalia right? Was she naïve?

Chapter Ten

Olivia gripped the sun-heated door handle of the museum and pushed, but the weathered wood refused to budge. She peered through the window and into darkness.

She slipped her phone from her bag and checked the time, confident they'd settled on half-nine, as the British say. He was five minutes late, so she dropped onto the beat-up brown bench next to the entrance and flipped through her messages. There wasn't one from Luke. It seemed strange to call him by his given name, being the vicar and all. Her cheeks flushed at the way his piercing eyes and his arms held her the previous evening.

Thankful they had reconciled over the misunderstanding she still contemplated why it had bothered him so much. She knew a vicar had to be careful to separate himself from any appearance of misconduct, but they had only been having dinner. He *assumed* she was married and thought he must separate himself from her with haste.

Olivia couldn't fault him for that. She supposed she'd overreacted as much as he had. Why was she so insecure in his presence? Could Angie be right? *Was* she attracted to him?

Her name sounded from across the harbor, and her head snapped up. "Olivia!" Luke stood in front of The Pilchard, waving his arm. "On my way."

He walked briskly along the angle of the harbor and across the curved stone bridge with confident athletic movements. Guilt stabbed her conscience at her misinterpretation of him in the beginning. She liked the way the sun displayed the sandy streaks in his tawny hair, the waves stopping at his collar. The closer he got, the more her heart fluttered.

She muttered through clenched teeth when he was but a few yards away. "Get a grip! You are not an air-headed schoolgirl."

Luke halted in front of her, head tilted downward. "Did you say something?"

"Just thinking aloud." Olivia mustered a bright smile.

He sat on the bench, his eyes intent on her. "About what?"

Olivia pulled her gaze to a brown bird gliding overhead. She'd never been much at bird watching, but when one caught her eye, she always marveled at the diversity of God's creation.

Luke followed her line of sight. "Lovely tune that."

Olivia asked, "What is it?"

"A crested lark. They have a liquid, warbling tune that always makes me smile. They're rarely seen here. Best enjoy it while we can." He rested his head against the rough wall and closed his eyes, listening to the songbird as he floated on the morning wind away from them.

"Yes, I agree, and . . ." her voice trailed off as she studied his profile, much like she'd done the lark when his words came back to capture her. *Best enjoy it while we can.* He had a straight nose, lightly tanned complexion, and with closer inspection the subtle shades of auburn streaking his hair were apparent. A powerful impulse caught her off-guard, and her hand slowly lifted. She envisioned running her fingers through the shining strands.

Ian's face appeared in her mind's eye, and her hand dropped to the bench. Had she truly enjoyed Ian while he was with her? It seemed she was always on edge about his extreme sports—what he loved more than life itself, what had taken him from her. She had loved *him* more than life itself. But had her attitude about his hobby stolen something from their relationship? If she had not badgered him about it, would she now be more at peace?

Without opening his eyes, Luke nudged her shoulder. "You were saying . . ."

"Oh. Sorry." She struggled to remember what they were talking about. They sat in silence before she answered.

"I must get a grip and enjoy my time here before it's gone. I have yet to find out much about my great-grandparents. I'd like to see where they lived for one." She drew in a shaky breath. "Would you mind helping me?"

ೞಏ

Olivia and Luke leaned over the notes he'd taken about the old diary, the tip of the pencil hovering above the fragile page.

"Grace mentions a Mr. Ellery here." He twisted in his chair to retrieve a sheet of paper and placed it in front of Olivia. "If I've gotten my translation correct this may be a good tip about the manor's relationship to the tavern."

Olivia tilted the paper to catch more of the light and read.

While walking upon the path late this eve, I came upon Mr. Ellery. He appeared to be much afflicted. He has not been the same since Nicholas's death these many years. I but wonder why he has not married again. And what exactly was his connection with my mother? Mrs. B___ said it was a sad tale.

Luke's breath tickled her ear as he read along with her. "I couldn't make out the letters here. It seems to have gotten wet, and the ink smeared."

Olivia sniffed and reached for a tissue from her bag. "They were tears." While she dabbed her eyes, she felt his stare, and her gaze met his.

He leaned in closer rereading the notes. "How do you know that?"

"I suppose only a woman would read between the lines."

When he peered up to stare at her, she pulled a face, eliciting a chuckle from him.

"Women's intuition and all?"

"Something like that." She could feel the pain in those lines Grace had written so long ago. But who was this woman? And why had this diary come into her great-grandmother's possession?

The affectionate touch that grazed her cheek was like a

whisper as Luke gently wiped away a tear. She should have pulled back, but instead she leaned in, absorbing the tenderness, grasping the sensation she believed was only in her past.

When his fingers slipped away, she felt abandoned—again.

Luke cleared his throat. "I apologize. That was inappropriate." He moved his chair away a few inches and cleared his throat again. "You are still in mourning."

Olivia squared her shoulders and boldly met his eyes. "I'm not sorry."

His eyes widened for the briefest moment before he rested back in his chair, awaiting her next words.

"Ian's been gone for more than a year." She notched her chin up and took a deep breath before continuing. "As Angie—my closest friend—keeps telling me, it's time to move on. I needed that to remind me she was right."

His face softened, and he blinked several times. "I've wanted to do that nearly since the first time we met."

She crossed her arms and peered at him. "Would that have been the day I nearly bit your head off?"

His laugh was hearty and filled her with happiness until she reached out and caressed his face much the same way he'd done only moments before. His laughter faded, and his eyes sought her lips.

She scooted her chair closer. "Vicar, I do believe you are having the *un-vicarly* thought of kissing me."

One side of his mouth lifted. "Yes, Mrs. Griffin, you are very perceptive." He tipped his head. "May I?"

"That is more like it, *Vicar*." She angled toward him. "A

gentleman always asks first."

His brows lifted. "Indeed. What if the *lady* kisses him first?"

"Hmm . . . that's entirely different. After all, it's the *lady's* prerogative."

Olivia closed the space and pressed her lips to his, the kiss tender and pure, yet igniting the spark of undeniable attraction between them.

When they parted, Luke whispered, "Well worth waiting for."

Olivia sighed. "Indeed."

She held his gaze for a long moment until she carefully stacked the research papers. "I'm starved. It's probably well past lunch."

He regarded the clock above the door. She couldn't seem to keep her eyes from him.

"Sorry. We've worked through lunch."

"Is that what you call it these days? I'm out of practice." She sent him her most innocent smile.

He caught on. "Yes, did you not know that?" He wrapped an arm around her. "We could stay here and have more *lunch*, if you'd like."

"While that sounds lovely—" She kissed his cheek. "—I'm hungry." She moved away from him and retrieved her bag, the diary, and papers. "Are we safe to eat in public now?"

The door creaked open, the bell signaling a customer.

They both sighed.

He whispered, "Go on and save a table at The Pilchard. I'll

be on shortly."

She squeezed his hand and strode to the door, meeting a couple, and smiled a greeting before entering the beautiful sunshine. Her spirits soared as freedom gripped her. Freedom from guilt, mourning, and loneliness. She lifted her eyes to take in the glorious day. "Thank you, Lord, for this blessing."

For that was what this unexpected turn in Olivia's life truly felt like—the blessing of a second chance at love.

ఇఁ

Olivia sipped water while she waited for Luke to arrive for their late lunch. She'd been there about a half hour, and he had yet to appear. Was he having second thoughts? She'd give him fifteen minutes more.

The door opened, but it was Hugo. He immediately spotted her and strode her way with purpose, sitting opposite her without an invitation.

"Who was the committee member that made the offer on the Sands?"

His head jerked back as if she'd slapped him. "Come again?"

"Hugo, you heard me." She crossed her arms.

He blinked a few times as if trying to remember, then lifted his brows. "If memory serves, I believe it was the committee's secretary."

"And who might that be?"

"Gertrude Bigsby." He stood and held one finger in the air. "Be right back." He sprinted to the counter and returned sipping a fizzing soda.

Hugo released a loud puff of air. "I needed that!" He sat with a thud. "Now, why the question about who made the offer? She's just the messenger, so don't shoot her right off."

Olivia smirked. "I see your point."

"Good. Because the entire committee has to approve something like that, not just one member. Not to mention the entire historical society membership has to vote on the transaction first."

Her thoughts traveled straight to Luke. He'd made no mention of it to her, and he knew her interest in the building. As if conjuring him up, he strode through the door wearing a broad grin. She glared at him and stood.

When his gaze landed on her, a look of unease replaced his smile. Her pace quickened, and he lifted a hand as if to touch her.

As Olivia drew near, she only paused long enough to whisper through clenched teeth, "How dare you attempt to take it from me," before she flounced from the pub without a glance over her shoulder.

Olivia stomped along the lane, her annoyance growing with each step until the heat flooding her reminded her of their kiss. She halted on the stone bridge, people skirting around her. Confusing emotions of pleasure and pain consumed her, neither winning. A stab of betrayal took over as hot tears welled.

A hand at the small of her back made her gasp and turn. Confusion shone in Luke's eyes.

"What did I do, Olivia? What have I taken from you?"

The anger rose. It was so unlike her to lose control and yet while in Cornwall, it had happened more than in all of her past.

"*Vicar*," her voice strangled on the word, "you knew I wanted the *Sands*, yet you are part of the committee trying to take it from me. Hugo told me."

Olivia froze, a revelation coming to her—perhaps he voted against it.

"Did you vote to make an offer?" She clenched her hands into tight fists.

Passersby edged around them, near enough to take in the private discussion. When he touched her arm to gesture they move to the wall overlooking the harbor, she jerked away, causing a deeper expression of hurt to cross his face, but she did as he wanted. She propped stiffly against the wall and hugged her bag to her middle.

He sat but kept some distance between them.

"Olivia, I voted to make the offer. The historical society has had its eye on that building for a very long time. Since I was a boy."

"So, you admit you agreed to steal it from me?"

"*No*," he said with force, and raked shaking fingers through wind-blown hair. "I didn't know you were trying to purchase it."

She straightened and moved toward him, until their legs nearly brushed. "How can you say that? I told you how I felt about it, and yet you still did this?" The scorching tears released, and again, she saw the pain deepen on his features. She didn't want to hurt him, but he had wounded her to the core.

Before she knew what was happening, he'd grabbed her hand and pressed it between his, pulling her closer.

He lowered his voice. "Olivia, you never told me anything. Only about the time you'd spent there and how it drew you in. Never did you say anything about *buying* it."

Her stomach churned as she replayed every conversation they'd had—including the one where she'd told him off. Her knees trembled, and searing embarrassment made her feel as if she would be sick.

Luke eased her onto the harbor wall. "Are you okay? You're pale."

Olivia couldn't speak for fear of embarrassing herself further. She gripped the edge of the gray-blotched stone, focusing on its roughness beneath her fingertips instead of focusing on him.

He slid an arm around her shoulder. "Do you want a bottle of water? Or a sweet drink?"

There was no resisting the concern in his voice. "No. Thank you. I feel a bit shaky is all."

"When was the last time you've eaten?"

"Breakfast."

"Olivia, that was six or more hours ago." He stood, keeping a hand on her shoulder. "I'm sorry I was late for lunch. Two tourists kept me talking, and I couldn't get away." He sent her a timid smile. "Let me fetch us a bite of something. Stay here. Please?"

She'd calmed now that the revelation of his involvement in the property offer was settled, but her stomach continued to churn.

"All right. But just a small *lunch* will suffice."

At the playful use of the word *lunch*, he brightened. "So, I'm forgiven?"

Olivia sighed, then nodded. "You've done nothing to be forgiven for. I have though and reacted before thinking it through." She dipped her head in shame. "I'm sorry, Luke."

Luke crouched in front of her, angling his face, so he could look up at her. He wiggled his eyebrows, mischief in those sea-blue eyes. "If you'll join me for *lunch*, all is forgotten."

ଔଓ

Olivia and Luke perched on a group of rocks overlooking the jagged coast below, the surf slamming into the cliff base. She peered across the water toward France.

"It's so beautiful here."

Luke tightened his hold on her as she lay her head on his shoulder. "This is really nice." He kissed the top of her head. "It's been such a pleasant evening and a wonderful day."

Olivia lifted her head and spoke toward the sea. "Except for my little breakdown."

"Don't be so hard on yourself. You've been through a lot in the past eighteen months."

She heaved a sigh. "But that's no excuse to take it out on you." She chuckled.

"What's so funny?"

"I've just realized that you're the only person I've gotten angry with—except for Ian." The weight of loss pressed in on her for a moment before she released it. When she looked at Luke again, he wore a thoughtful expression.

"He's not here for you to release the anger on, so your emotions are substituting me for Ian. You aren't able to take out your frustrations on him for leaving, so I'm the stand-in, a way of putting it behind you—to heal."

She nudged his arm with her shoulder. "Aren't you the psychiatrist?"

"No, just the local vicar."

They sat in silence for a while, taking in the lightening horizon and enjoying each other's company.

When the sky darkened and stars appeared, the temperature cooled, and Luke stood and pulled Olivia up with him. He hugged her close.

"Want to go see my cottage now?"

"Vicar!" Olivia mocked. "I'm ashamed of you. 'Twould be unseemly."

He laughed. "Nothing unseemly about it—I have no etchings. Just a cottage of historic proportions."

She smirked, letting the reference go. "Really? How old is it?"

"Well, over three hundred years."

Oliva's interest was piqued. "Honestly?"

"Yes. I've found some interesting things while renovating." He added, "So, I guess I do have some etchings of a sort." He pulled her closer.

Olivia flattened her palms on his chest and pushed him back a few inches. "Sir, I shall not be enticed. I'll come tomorrow during the daylight so as not to cause a scandal."

He cocked his head with a deep sigh. "So, it must be."

Olivia poured strong tea into two cups, handing one to Teffeny. She needed advice from a friend and one who knew Luke, so she invited Teffeny over for lunch. She relayed all that happened the day before from the museum kiss to the romantic sunset viewing.

"So, you're going to the vicar's cottage unchaperoned in broad daylight?" Teffeny poured milk into her cup, her eyes held on Olivia.

"You really are a Victorian at heart, aren't you?" Olivia looked at her over the rim of her cup.

She sniffed. "Not a practicing one, my friend. I merely like to point out the possibilities."

Teffeny used her index finger to edge the rim of her cup, head bent. "*Sooo, you* and the vicar, hmm?"

"Why do you say it that way? Since the day we met, you've hailed his praises. Has something changed?" Olivia took a sip of tea. "Wait a minute . . . are you taken with *our* vicar?"

Teffeny's head shot up. "Hardly!"

"Then why the *tone*?"

"Just being sure. We don't take kindly to some American chicky breaking our vicar's heart."

Olivia laughed. "You are so amusing."

"*And* I heard you two were being very cozy on the harbor bridge."

Olivia's brows shot upward. "Where did you hear that?" She held her hand out. "No, wait. Was it Hugo or the twins?"

"Neither."

"Well?"

Teffeny wore the cat-ate-the-canary smile. "It was me."

"*You*?" Olivia's hand froze above the biscuit plate.

"I'm just teasing. Although I saw you sitting there in intense conversation. I knew something was up. Unless you were having a confession."

"Don't be silly. I told you what happened when Hugo came into the pub." She hung her head. "It was a misunderstanding that was all my fault."

"Let's change the subject. I'm certain the vicar is happy you'll be opening a business here."

Olivia nibbled on a biscuit. "He seems to be."

"The way I've seen him look at you, I'd say he is ecstatic."

"Really?"

"Certainly. He has that *I-want-her-for-lunch* look."

Olivia choked on the treat, grabbed her tea, and gulped it until she could speak.

"What did Luke tell you?"

Teffeny frowned. "Tell me what?"

"That comment you made about lunch."

"What about it?"

Teffeny appeared genuinely perplexed. Olivia didn't press her further, but her heated face took a good while to cool.

◦₃₰◦

Olivia approached the vicar's cottage with a little trepidation. Was she ready for another relationship? Ian had been the love of her life, and now she was stepping into unfamiliar territory.

It frightened her. She was no ingenue. Her marriage had lasted over twenty years, and she no longer knew how to act when approaching a new romance.

She paused before knocking, closed her eyes, and prayed for guidance and strength, wanting God's will in her future.

Her hand fisted and raised, the door jerked open, and Luke stood before her, wearing a wide smile. He stepped back and waved her in. "Come in, love. Come in."

She took one step and stopped, her questioning gaze on him.

Luke took her arm and eased her into the room. "I've been wanting to call you that since you accused me of following you. Is that acceptable?"

Olivia hesitated, then answered, "I rather like it when you say it. Better than Hugo."

"Cheeky monkey." He pulled her into an embrace.

She allowed the affection. "Are you certain it's okay for the vicar to have female company without a chaperone?"

"Olivia, it's the twenty-first century." He shook his head and had the audacity to roll his eyes.

"I believe I've been hanging around Teffeny too much. She's a Victorian wannabe, you know."

Laughter rumbled from Luke. "Seriously?"

"Yeah."

He took her hand and led her into the kitchen, where a savory aroma seized her. "What's that? It smells delicious."

"Chicken curry. My mum's recipe."

"I'm impressed. A vicar, psychiatrist, historian, *and* chef."

With an elaborate bow, he pulled a chair from under the table and motioned for her to sit. "At your service, madam."

Luke poured sparkling water into crystal stemware. The light glinted off the bubbly liquid.

She took a sip and nodded. "My favorite."

He turned to the stove and stirred the pungent dish, tossing over his shoulder, "If you'd like lemon in your water, it's in the fridge."

"I would. Thank you." She added a piece of lemon to her glass.

When she returned to her seat, she noticed a Bible perched at the edge of the table. She slid it toward her and observed the intricately embossed cover—dark blue, nearly black, etched with a square over-lapping circle grid. Embossed in the bottom right corner was the name *Brayden Harper*.

"Who's Brayden?"

His gaze fell to the Bible on the table. "That's me." He turned back to his task.

"Enlighten me. What's your full name?"

"Lucas Brayden Harper. I was called Brayden until I was seven. By that time, I was convinced they must call me by my first name but shortened to Luke. It was then I discovered I wanted to be a vicar."

Olivia interrupted, "Seriously?"

He sent her a solemn look. "Yes, seriously. I decided Luke was the only way to address a vicar." His smile melted her.

"Tell me more." She pointed to the Bible and gave him a questioning look. When he nodded, she flipped to the dedication page of the Bible.

To my little apostle, Luke. With love, Mum.

He scooped two servings of the curry onto plates and brought them to the table.

"My mum loved to tell tales about me. She claimed I lined my sister's dolls into rows and preached to them. Her tallest tales involved me using the cats as my congregation."

Olivia laughed until her shoulders shook, tears welling. "I bet you were adorable."

"Indeed."

He sat next to her and stared as if he watched the most beautiful thing he'd ever seen.

"You're staring, Luke."

"I know." He took her hand, then bowed his head.

"Lord, I thank you for bringing this treasure to me. You are the Lord of impossible things. I never dreamed someone this wonderful would come into my life. Thank You for this food. Use it as nourishment that we may be better able to serve you. Amen."

Olivia was unable to remove her gaze. He was wonderful too—so was Ian. Could this truly be her second chance at love? He appeared to be everything Ian had been to her and more.

Luke squeezed her hand. "Hope you like it." He took a bite, his eyes on her as she did likewise.

Olivia tasted the butter chicken. "Delicious."

"Honestly?"

"Yes, honestly. Your mother taught you well. I'd love to meet her."

His face darkened for a second. "I'd love for you to meet her too, but I'm afraid it will have to wait until we're all in Heaven."

It took a moment for the truth to sink in. "I'm so sorry. She must've been an amazing woman to have a son like you."

"She was, but it had nothing to do with me. I was a handful until . . ."

"You?" Olivia took another bite.

"Yeah . . . me." He pulled a face. "Even though I was determined to be a vicar, I strayed from time to time, but always returned to God. Thankfully." A sheepish smile crept across his face.

"Out with it. You cannot wear that look and *not* tell me what's in your head." She tapped his temple with the tip of her finger.

"If I must."

"You must."

"When I was told to give a book report in class, I winged it."

Olivia's face scrunched. "How so?"

"I stood in front of the class and gave a whopper of a long synopsis of a book I'd never cracked."

"How did you do that? You must have known something about the story—or saw the movie version."

Luke shook his head. "Nope. Not a clue. Just made it up."

Olivia stared at him wide-eyed. "How did you get away with it?"

"I didn't." He shrugged. "She gave me the lowest grade for

creativity though. Better than a zero."

She narrowed her eyes. "Sneaky man." Before he could respond, she said, "What about your dad? Was he like your mother?"

"No. I never met him."

Caught completely off guard, Olivia remained silent allowing him time to explain.

"Mother met him at uni and had a fling. He never knew I existed. She was a rare breed though—finished school, got a smashing job, and raised me alone until she met my stepdad. He was a true father to me and taught me what being a Christian really means as well as my mum. She always struggled with her past, and he told her the only real forgiveness she needed was God's. Nearly broke me when he died. They passed two years apart. Him first."

"How painful." Olivia grabbed his hand and squeezed.

"It was. But my sister has been a brick."

"Cats and all?" She smiled.

He laughed. "Cats and all."

CAROLE LEHR JOHNSON

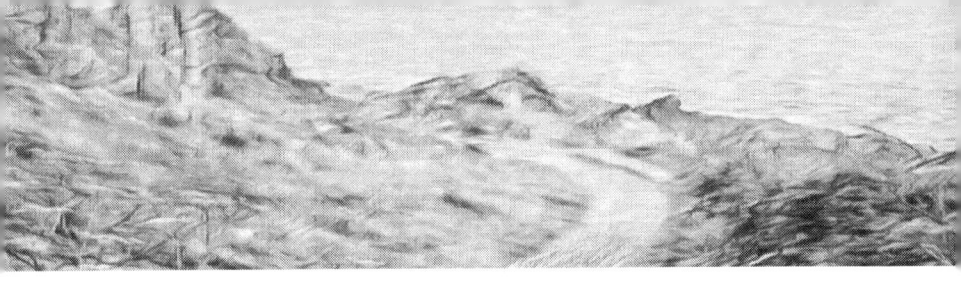

IX

Grace focused on the Vicar Olford who stood at the front of the small stone church, the stained-glass windows on either side shooting shards of colored beams crisscrossing behind him.

"And I say to ye today, are ye living the way Jesus told ye? Are ye being salt and light to those in your path? Why should God, therefore, answer your prayers if ye are not living in His will? Let us have a great esteem in the Lord's prayer. Let it be the model and pattern of all our prayers. Hereby mercies requested are obtained, for the apostle assures us that God will hear us when we pray according to His will."

Grace squeezed her eyes shut to fight back tears. She had prayed to God often, yet her condition had yet to change. Her father continued to abuse his family and held a particular hatred for Sebastian beyond her understanding.

The vicar continued with passion, "God is the best Father because He alone can reform His children. When an earthly father's son takes wicked courses, a father knows not how to make him better, yet God knows how to make the children of the election better as He is able to change their hearts. When Paul breathed out persecution against the saints, God soon altered his course and set him praying."

Grace wondered if God had forgotten her. The vicar's sermons never failed to touch her, yet with all of her prayers going unanswered, she considered if she had merited God's wrath.

The vicar's tone rose with fervor. "None of those who belong to the election are so roughcast and unhewn, yet God can polish them with His grace and make them fit for the inheritance."

Why had God not hewn and polished Grace's father into a better man? Perhaps she would speak with the vicar. She bowed her head in silent contemplation as the vicar spoke on. Her thoughts had been so entangled in her own problems that she missed the rest of the message and flinched when the singing began.

On the last note, they filed out of the church like sheep following their shepherd. Pretending to gather her shawl, she hung back in order to be the last leaving the vestibule. When she reached the door, she halted to face him. "Vicar, may I speak with ye privately today?"

The short, apple-faced man gave her his constant bright smile. "Of course, my child. My wife shall have tea *and* coffee at the ready for three o'clock. I must admit I have grown fond of the afternoon ritual." He leaned closer as if to reveal a confidence. "With, of course, my wife's lovely gooseberry pie." He clapped his thick hands together, a twinkle in his kind eyes. "We shall both look forward to your visit."

Grace thanked him and strode down the path not wanting to walk with anyone, keeping her thoughts to herself to consider all she would confide to the vicar. His gentle wife, cousin to her by marriage, would leave them to their privacy. Someone abruptly joined her side, and her gaze lifted to meet Rig's. Her face heated, and she glanced away.

Rig stepped closer, studying her face. "Are ye well, Grace?"

They walked shoulder-to-shoulder along the path to Fore Street and slowed to follow it past the Sands and homeward. He took her elbow, but she kept her pace.

A longsuffering sigh escaped. "Rig, I must get home." She stepped back, breaking their contact.

His expression hardened. "My apologies, but I would speak with ye. When are ye free to do so?"

Grace halted in front of him, resigned to do as he asked. "Meet me on the path at the bench this eve. *After* dark. I would have nay one see us alone." What did this stranger want with her? What did he wish to speak of—their escape or their intimate moment in the cavern? She swallowed hard, relishing the memory of his lips on her cheek.

Rig's expression softened, yet he spoke not for a time. "As you wish it." He bowed slightly and departed. She watched his retreat and glanced around to see if anyone had witnessed their interaction.

Her emotions lay scattered before her like a catch of pilchards on the sand. She disliked watching them gasp for air, flipping along the sand waiting to be placed in a basket to be salted down for winter. It was all the difference between life and starvation for many in Trerose.

Once home, Grace and her mother ate with Alsyn and Degory, then the children left to play on the beach. Their freedom was something they could all taste. They saw little of Arabel since her father had ensconced her in an exalted position at the tavern. As if reading her mind, her mother said, "I had always hoped ye all could have a proper education."

Grace patted her mother's hand. "Ye taught us well. The schooling ye passed on to us has sufficed."

Melior's tired eyes brightened with the compliment. "That was one thing your father could not take from me." She pushed her plate away and crossed her arms on the table. "Though I have noticed that my speech has become ragged around the edges in these last years."

"Ye were raised in a noble home and all can see your refinement." Grace smiled. "Nothing can take that from ye."

"'Tis kind of ye, child. I was once a lady." Moisture formed in her eyes.

"Ye remain so." Grace cleared her throat. "And ye shall always be."

Their small mantle clock chimed the hour, and Grace bolted from her seat. "I must go for a time, Mother, but shall return before . . ." She halted, remembering she was to meet Rig. ". . . just after dark."

Melior sent her a curious look, eyes narrowed. "*After dark?*"

Before Grace could answer, her mother said, "Oh—going to the cave?" She rose and retrieved a small tin box. "Please take this. 'Tis a few keepsakes I do not want to forget." She smiled at Grace. "Have a care."

"Certainly." Grace tucked it under her arm and left her mother clearing the table. She rushed along the path, descending into Trerose, careful to slow at the cliff's edge. Upon reaching the vicar's cottage, her breath came in gasps.

Mrs. Olford answered the door with a cheerful smile. "Come in, my dear."

"I am that sorry to be late, ma'am." The sweet scent of pie brought long ago memories of visiting the Sands when she was a girl. Eulalia would greet her with a flour-covered hug, and Grace would come away wearing a goodly portion of it.

Mrs. Olford patted Grace's shoulder as she waved her into the cottage. "Not to worry. The tea steeps, and I have sliced gooseberry pie for ye both."

"Shall not ye be joining us, Cousin?" Grace always enjoyed visiting with the amiable couple.

"Oh, nay, Enidor said ye wanted to discuss something with him, and I dislike interfering with his flock and their concerns. Not my place." She took Grace's arm and led her to the modest parlor where the vicar waited and left her there to collect the tea.

He stood when she entered. "Right on time, Grace. Most punctual of ye."

Grace looked at the ornate clock and noted he was correct, realizing their own paltry clock was most likely not properly set. She sat on the settle, suddenly timid. They briefly shared pleasantries about family until Mrs. Olford returned with a laden tray.

Out of courtesy, Grace took a bite of the pie before complimenting Mrs. Olford on how it was. The woman beamed with pride and quietly left them alone.

"Aye, my wife is an excellent baker. Can make most anything she ever tasted—and without a recipe."

Grace sipped her tea. "She is most talented, sir." They stared at one another. How could she share more of what her life was like? And the lives of her mother, brothers, and sister.

He coughed. "Now, my child, what would ye care to speak of?"

Grace fidgeted in her seat. "Vicar, I am aware ye know of the struggles in my home." She cleared her throat. "Can ye tell me why God does not answer my prayers for relief from my father's cruelty?"

His face turned grim, and he examined his coffee with care.

"My child, dear cousin, it is not for me to know God's will for another. If I did, I would be on His level, and that I am not. I do not have His mind. He has a purpose for all that happens to His children. All works for His good and to further His kingdom." He clasped his hands together and looked at her, sympathy in his eyes.

Grace breathed in deeply, her anger rising. "Why does He allow a brute of a man to beat his wife and children?" She sniffed. "Can ye tell me that, Vicar?"

The man startled at the passion in her voice, but he did not respond at once. "My dear, I can understand your suffering for my father was of a similar nature."

Taken aback by this disclosure, Grace leaned toward him, mouth agape.

"Aye. Yet his reasons were not those of your father. Although there is no good reason to beat anyone, he felt his punishment was God's will. To teach his children the rod of discipline. 'Twas taking scripture and twisting it to salve his own hurts. Aye, a father must discipline his children, yet only when they have done wrong. He felt he should beat his children—and his wife—daily so as not to allow them the chance of doing wrong."

Grace stared, incredulous. Sorrow gripped her to know that he, this kindest of men, was treated so cruelly. "What did ye do?"

"There was naught I could do. I took the pain and left home as soon as I was able, running away to the sea."

Her eyes widened, wondering why her mother never shared this family secret.

"I vowed I would study the scripture and prove that his ways were not God's. It did not take long to discover my father's error. We are to treat one another with kindness, forgiveness, and gentleness."

Grace gripped her hands together. "Why does God allow such injustice?"

"Because, my child, God has gifted us with making our own choices. It all started in the Garden of Eden when man made the wrong choice, and evil entered the world. The apostle Matthew said, 'for He maketh His sun to rise on the evil and on the good, and sendeth rain on the just and on the unjust.'"

A sense of unease fell over Grace. She understood of what he spoke, yet she still did not understand why so many had to suffer, and she told him so.

"'Tis a hard truth. Someday, we shall see God's glory and know what goes on that we are unable to see. Mayhap He saves ye from something far worse. Your father is a broken man. Therefore, he breaks others."

Grace straightened. "So, ye mean because someone has treated him so, he in turn treats others the same?" She shook her head. "But ye are not like that, Vicar. Ye treat all as ye want to be treated." She lifted her chin. "As the Bible does say."

"Aye. The Golden Rule. But not all live by it, and that is their choice." He leaned back in his seat and rested his clasped hands upon his generous middle. "Grace, should I choose to eat many slices of my wife's delectable pie, I grow more portly." He patted his stomach and grinned sheepishly. "That is my choice, yet I must suffer the consequences of *my* actions. Just as we all shall."

She considered all he had spoken, her understanding coming slowly, pulled in a ragged breath, and rose. "Thank ye, Vicar. Ye are most helpful."

His tender gaze fell upon her. "Just remember to pray about everything. God *is* listening, and He will answer in His good time."

Grace sent him a sincere smile and departed to meet Rig. She had time to deliver her mother's box to the cave before she met him, though Sebastian told her not to go alone. Dusk neared and yet she did not have night's covering, she pressed on. As she entered the narrow cleft in the rock leading to the hidden cave, she heard unfamiliar voices coming from behind her. She slipped into a depression barely concealing her presence.

"I be telling ye that I seed that Atwell gurl coming in here jest a few minutes ago. Should she find our plan, she may go telt the magistrate."

The man's graveled speech was familiar, yet it would not settle in her mind.

A more cultured voice asked with an edge of rage, "Are ye sure ye have not been drinking too much to know what ye did see and what ye did not, man?"

Grace froze. It was Eudo's voice. She assumed he was likely involved in smuggling, but she had never heard him angry.

A shaft of light flashed near her hiding place, but nay one came down the concealed tunnel. She held her breath as they passed close by, their voices trailing away from her. Once gone, she slipped into the hidden cave, deposited the box, feeling around in the dim light from the overhead shaft, rather than lighting the lantern.

With great care, she made her way back to the opening, listening for voices. Nothing sounded, so she crept out of the narrow space and saw that the sun had set enough to hide her exit. She climbed the steep path, moving with care, stopping often to listen. When she topped the rise she halted to see if anyone stood overlooking the cliff. The silhouette of a man sitting on the bench made her breath hitch. She strained to see and be certain it was Rig.

He stood and whispered, "Grace, is that ye?"

She kept her reply to a whisper. "Aye."

Rig strode to her and took her hands. "Were ye in the cave?" They were close enough for her to see him scowl.

She tried to pull her hands from his grasp, but he did not relent. "I was putting something there for my mother."

Rig pulled her to the bench. "Ye should not have come alone. Did Sebastian not tell ye so?" Annoyance tinged his voice.

"I am fine." She did not mention her near encounter with Eudo.

"Nay, ye are not. I saw Eudo and Mr. Bassett going to the cave. Ye could have come to harm."

Grace flinched in surprise. "Ye saw them?"

He gave a brief nod. "Ye should not have gone. If something had happened to ye . . ." His voice trailed off, pain reflecting in his dark eyes.

Her irritation got the better of her. "Why did ye want to speak with me?"

After a brief hesitation, he moved a step closer and held her gaze, as if searching for something. Time slowed as he brought his hands to gently cup her cheeks, eyes on hers. The low, mournful coo of a dove drifted on the night wind.

"*Grace.*" Rig's whisper sent chills along her spine, more a caress than the mere uttering of her name.

When she did not draw away, he brought his mouth to hers. Tenderly at first, then overcome with emotion he shifted to fold her into his arms, and Grace kissed him back.

He spoke her name against her lips, and she felt his smile. "Is this what ye wanted to *tell* me?"

Continuing to hold her, he answered, "Aye," then repeated the kiss. "And nay."

Grace laughed and took a half step back, her hands on his shoulders. Her head slanted. "'Tis not an answer."

"True." Rig embraced her once more and spoke into her hair. "There is something I would tell ye of myself, but 'tis hard to form words."

The quick thumps of his heart against her ear soothed her along with the scent of the sweet sea breeze that tickled her hair.

A voice loud and laced with anger broke their intimacy. "What goes here?"

With quick and fluid movements, Rig moved Grace behind him, a knife already extending in front of him.

Eudo faced them, hands on hips, legs braced in a wide stance. Grace had never seen such fury—not even on her father's face.

CAROLE LEHR JOHNSON

Chapter Eleven

Olivia dried the plate, and Luke handed her another. "That's the last one." He took the cloth from her and draped it over the handle of the Aga door.

"It was a delicious meal, Luke. Thank you." She retrieved her bag from the chair, slipping the handle over her shoulder.

Luke eyed her suspiciously. "Where do you think you're going?" He wrapped his strong fingers around the strap, and her eyes met his.

"Home, I suppose." Olivia paused in front of him and released the bag. "Although . . . I suppose I could go to the Sands and see what I can ferret out for my research."

He wrinkled his nose. "There's nothing in there. What could you possibly *ferret* out?"

"Hmm . . ." Olivia looped her arms around his neck. "If I'm to buy it, I could start by ripping out walls to see what secrets lay inside."

His expression didn't alter. "That has possibilities. I'm certain I have tools that could make the job easier."

She lifted her heels and planted a soft, quick kiss on his lips. "I think we're going to be fast friends, *Vicar*."

Luke snorted. "I see the lay of the land. As long as I agree with whatever you say, our relationship will be smooth sailing. Huh?"

Olivia smiled benignly. "You catch on quick."

He suddenly stepped away, dropping his embrace, and she reached for him. "Luke, I'm only joking. What's wrong?"

A look of embarrassment flashed on his face before he smiled at her. "Sorry, love, it's just that I remembered I haven't shown you my findings from the renovating." He sprinted into the adjoining room, and before Olivia could sit, he placed a two-foot-long box on the table. He pulled out a chair and motioned for her to take a seat, then sat next to her.

"You do the honors, love." He scooted his chair closer to hers and looped his arm over the back.

Olivia lifted the lid and peered inside. "There are a lot of items in here. I feel like I'm in an art supply store."

Luke grinned like a boy at show-and-tell. "I suppose for me it would be a box full of antique diaries."

She laughed, then asked with one hand hovering over the treasures, "May I?"

He nodded, moving his arm to encompass her shoulders.

Olivia raked her gaze over the items, longing for one thing to capture her attention. It took mere seconds before she spotted a small brown book containing poems and a pewter cup nestled into one corner of the box. Reverently, she picked it up and found it filled with tiny seashells.

As she cradled it in her palm, she brought her gaze to Luke's. "Where did you find this?"

He placed a hand inside the box and retrieved a small, modern notebook. Removing his arm from her, he flipped through the pages, and keeping his index finger on one line, he smiled.

"Once I began finding more and more items, I decided it may be wise to keep a journal of sorts to chronicle where I found each thing. The pewter cup was upstairs in a cordoned off section of the attic. It appears to be some sort of hiding place."

"How did you discover it?" She examined the cup carefully, twisting it to see if there were any identifying marks.

"I was working on the narrow bedroom attempting to repair an area of plaster when my tool drove completely through the wall. I figured the damage was done so curiosity got the better of me, and I cut out enough to see what was behind the wall."

Olivia held the cup between them. "And this is what you found?"

"That and a lot more."

Olivia's own curiosity piqued. "Describe it to me."

"I'll do better than that." He rose and took her free hand. When she made to return the cup to the box, he said, "No, bring it."

Without releasing her hand, he led her up the narrow stairs

and into the bedroom, allowing her to go first. She entered the pleasant, comfortable space with its chalky white walls and lace curtains billowing with the evening breeze, the fresh air wafting through the room.

A twin bed with a moss green comforter and white pillows stood in the corner. A stained desk and chair sat in the opposite corner, and a narrow chest of drawers flanked the little fireplace. As her eyes took in the room, the reflection in the mirror above the chest caused her to pivot and face a short door gracing the opposite wall.

Luke strode to the door and opened it. "Come see."

Olivia stooped to enter. What a fascinating thing to behold. Someone, centuries ago, had built rough bunk beds—enough to sleep five people. In her semi-crouched position, she turned to look at Luke. "So, there was no door here?"

"No, I built the door and have kept it clean but made no changes whatever. It just seemed disrespectful to tamper with it. Someone needed a hiding place for protection. That much is clear." He shrugged. "At least it seems so to me."

She nodded, but her eyes kept scouring the space. If only she could unravel the story behind it.

Luke tapped her shoulder. "Take a look at this."

They returned to the bedroom, and he dropped to his haunches, pointing to the wooden floor in front of his newly constructed door. He ran his fingertips along two separate lengths of scars in the wood running parallel to the wall.

"See these gouge marks? It appears there was something heavy against this wall. A cabinet or armoire and, when shoved away, created these lines. Perhaps there was a door—

or opening—here."

Olivia grazed the indentions with a tender touch. "And a later owner walled it up again."

"I suppose so. Not sure why. After all, they could've incorporated the hidey-hole into this room and created a much larger space." He cleared his throat. "I chose not to sand it smooth and refinish it. Something held me back. It's like a long-lost history I didn't want to gloss over."

"This is where you found the pewter cup?" She held it up, and the light from the window glinted against the matte pewter.

"Yes, and most of the things downstairs in the box. They were lined up on the crossbeams of the walls like built-in shelves."

Olivia shook her head in disbelief. The reality of something from centuries past gripped her. How could they begin to unravel this mystery?

"Luke, do you know the history of this cottage?"

He sat on the bed and patted the comforter beside him. She rose and joined him, the cup still in her hand. The image of tiny shells encased in a small crystal box loomed in her mind's eye. She supposed collecting tiny shells was a common enough ritual, but she connected to this small village by blood, and her great-grandmother's habit of collecting comparable shells awakened a curious sentiment.

"Some. I have my folders at the museum, so I can continue my research while working."

Olivia lifted one corner of her mouth. "May we go now?"

"Now?" He glanced out the window at the waning light that

cast shadows on the bed covering. He shrugged. "Why not?"

His gaze took on the wicked visage of a man up to no good, his brows lifting. "Now that I've plied you with food . . ."

Olivia laughed. "A vicar with an agenda. How quaint."

His musical laugh softened the mood, and she leaned in and kissed him. "You are a true gentleman . . . unable to hide the truth of your *vicarishness*."

"You are a gem, love. But we should enjoy a cup of tea and the dessert I've labored over all afternoon before I walk you home."

Olivia surveyed his face, caring more for this man than she could imagine. Her thoughts strayed to where her emotions were only a few weeks before her trip to Cornwall. Of their own volition, her arms flung around his neck, and she hung on. She spoke into his neck. "Luke—thank you."

His arms wrapped around her, but he said nothing, burying his face into her hair as they clung to one another.

⁜

Olivia and Luke hovered in front of her cottage door neither wanting the evening to end. She toyed with the edge of his collar, her eyes on his throat.

She sighed contentedly. "I've had a lovely evening."

Luke tipped her chin up with his finger until their eyes met, then he leaned in to kiss her. He broke the contact, unlocked her door, and said breathlessly, "Good night, love. I'll see you tomorrow."

All she could manage was a nod. She opened the door, and as he walked into the night, she remembered to ask him something. "Luke!"

He turned on his heel and was by her side in an instant. "Yes." His lips curved. "Must I kiss you again?"

The inquiry halted her, and she placed her hands on her hips in mock irritation. "*Must?*"

Luke reached for her, but she pressed her palms against his chest and shoved him away. "No, sir. I merely have a question I keep forgetting to ask." His expression sobered, and she laughed. "Why is this," she waved her hand behind her, "called Widow's Cottage?"

Luke's smile returned. "Ah, that?" He took one step closer, and his fingertips grazed her cheek. "It's a long story, but I'll give you a tidbit to hold you over until I can do justice to the entire story." He leaned against the doorframe.

"The original owner of the manor built it for his aging steward, and when he died, his widow lived here, and thereafter, the family allowed destitute widows to live out their last days here."

Olivia's curiosity grew by the moment, but the hour was late, and she needed sleep—as did the vicar of Trerose.

"I can't wait to hear the entire story. Will you be at the museum tomorrow?"

"Sadly, no. Poor old Mr. Tedley has taken a turn for the worse, and I must visit him in hospital. Afterward, I must help with the fundraiser. We have but a few days until the event."

"I'll see if I can help." Olivia teased. "Perhaps I'll call on the twins and have Sheryl bake you another fruitcake for all your hard work."

He released a painful sigh and hung his head. "And I

thought we were friends."

She eased the door closed. "We are, but I know your antique cottage could always use another doorstop."

Luke's laughter faded through the thick wooden door.

⚜

Olivia strolled toward the lovely stone church. The flawless weather amid the many colorful flowers that bloomed all around, birds chirping overhead brought a contented sigh to her lips.

Everything about the day was perfect. She began to hum a cheerful tune and nearly stopped mid-stride. She used to hum that particular song only when she felt happy and completely in love with her husband.

Was she in love? Her feet stilled on the pebbled path this time as the revelation hit her with force. *Was she in love with Luke?*

Loud chatter flowed from behind the stone structure, and she shook off the life-altering consideration. She changed course, winding her way to the rear of the church. The sight before her was a sea of women clucking about like hens, some on short stepladders, a few hanging garlands from temporary arbors, and more who stood to the side giving orders. Sheryl perched at the center of the drill sergeants pointing and voicing her instructions.

When Sheryl twirled to bark out a command to one of the few men helping, she caught sight of Olivia. Her eyes lit with joy, and her hurried, mincing stride caused her maroon hair to bounce until she halted in front of Olivia.

"Oh, how perfectly lovely to see you, my dear. Sister and I

have been so busy with this," she waved her arm theatrically toward the bustle, "venture, that we've not had the time to visit you. Please forgive our negligence."

Overtaken with affection for the kind but quirky women, Olivia gave Sheryl a quick peck on the cheek. "I've missed you both."

Sheryl's rapidly blinking violet eyes reflected genuine astonishment. Her hand came up to touch her cheek. Beryl broke their moment, her steps hurried but wider than her sister's. "Olivia! So nice to see you."

Olivia kissed Beryl's cheek to the same surprised reaction as her sister. "I've come to see if I may help."

Each woman took one of Olivia's arms and introduced her to every single person present with pride. They had their own resident artist and obviously wanted to show off. Within a short time, she was helping an elderly woman in a wheelchair create the cedar garlands she'd seen hanging about the courtyard. "I appreciate your allowing me to assist you, Mrs. Atwood."

"Oh, please call me Hortense. I always feel so old otherwise." She snickered, the silver-gray bun at the base of her neck shivering. "Near on ninety, but I do not give in to that."

Olivia studied the tiny woman as she wove the cedar together, securing it with flimsy wire. The elegant, aromatic scent reminded Olivia of Christmas. "If you don't mind me saying so, you certainly don't look your age." She smiled and added, "Hortense."

The woman reached across their makeshift worktable and

patted Olivia's hand. "I don't mind at all, dear." Her quivering giggle warmed Olivia's heart, reminding her of her own grandmother.

Olivia's hands stilled over her work. "Atwood. That name seems familiar to me somehow."

Hortense nodded. "You may have seen it at the museum." She worked on, not missing a beat in her task. "My husband's family has been in Trerose since the fourteenth century."

"Perhaps." Olivia's thoughts continued to unravel the recognition of the name. It badgered her until she forced it to the recesses of her mind when a new question arose.

"Mrs.—*Hortense*, would you remember someone from Trerose by the name of Flowers?"

This time, the woman rested her work on her lap and tilted her head back in concentration. Olivia waited patiently.

"I remember a girl named Elizabeth. Mind you, she was not a Flowers but married one. A handsome young man named . . ." Her eyes glazed briefly, then she nearly shouted, "Larry! That was his name." She gave Olivia a cheeky smile and raised a brow. "Dishy fellow."

Olivia's squeal startled Hortense, and she apologized. "You do not know how excited that makes me. I've wanted to discover someone who would remember either of my great-grandparents." Heads turned in their direction, and Olivia smiled an apology.

"Nothing to worry yourself over, dear. I'm happy to be of service."

"What a lovely scene to see the two most beautiful women in Trerose sitting in this lovely garden." The voice above her head caused her to jerk, so she angled in her chair to find Luke's smile on her.

Hortense beamed at Luke. "Vicar, I knew you'd be here, eventually." She drew back and examined Luke, then Olivia. "Is this the young lady you've been speaking of?"

Olivia shot a questioning look at him and narrowed her eyes. "Is it—*Vicar*?"

"He never told me your name. Only that there was a pretty creature that had caught his eye but refused to say more. I'd say it must be you considering the way his eyes sparkled when he saw you."

Olivia's face heated, and it spread all the way to her middle.

Luke squatted next to the old woman's chair. "Now, Hortense, you're embarrassing her." He turned his gaze to Olivia. "I apologize. Hortense is like a grandmother to me, and we share our thoughts."

Olivia understood, but it galled her to be the topic of discussion. She wondered how long ago he'd shared his feelings with Mrs. Atwood. By the time he'd chatted with the elder woman for a while, Olivia had calmed, but she would interrogate him when they were alone.

For the next hour, Luke made rounds to all the volunteers but returned to take Hortense home. He gripped the handles of her wheelchair and told Olivia he would return shortly. Mrs. Atwood invited Olivia to have tea with her the following afternoon, and she heartily agreed.

When Luke returned, Olivia was saying goodbye to the twins and others she had met. Luke took her arm, and they ambled from the church grounds together. After he held the gate open for her, Olivia looked up and found Sheryl giving her a narrow-eyed glance. Beryl watched the perusal and sidetracked her sister by motioning for her to look at something one of her minions had done.

Luke quirked his brows. "What's wrong? You look as if you've just seen a train wreck."

Olivia shrugged. "It's nothing. I suppose my imagination is a bit too vivid where you're concerned."

He frowned. "How so?"

"I think Sheryl just shot me the evil-eye."

Luke roared. "Honestly?"

Olivia smirked. "Oh, Luke. You know she thinks you belong to her?"

"Dear, I care about both of those two eccentric old women. I admire them on many levels. You seriously don't think I'm concerned she thinks I belong to her?"

"Of course not. But I also don't want to cause problems."

Luke stopped, glanced around, then pulled her into the tall hedge bordering the church grounds.

Olivia stumbled as he tugged her toward the hiding place. "What are you doing?"

"I don't want anyone to see us." He placed both hands on her shoulders and gently gripped her, so she couldn't escape, and he kissed her passionately.

Olivia kissed him back with fervor, then tucked her face against his neck, lingering in his arms.

Luke murmured in her ear. "I'm going to say something I told myself would have to wait until I was more certain, but the ardor that wells in me will not be contained."

Olivia's stomach clenched, and she swallowed the lump in her throat.

Luke eased back, an arm still around her, his other hand moving to cup her cheek. His sea-blue eyes mesmerized Olivia with their vulnerability and depth of emotion.

"I love you, Olivia. The only time I've ever had this feeling of destiny about was when I was called by God to be a vicar. Now I know God has destined us to be together. He has led us to this moment. Can you not see it?"

Luke pulled in a deep breath. "Will you marry me?"

CAROLE LEHR JOHNSON

X

Grace clutched the back of Rig's brown coat like a lifeline as the unrestrained waves hurtled against the rocks below. Her fingers chilled with the night air. Had Eudo discovered her in the cave and followed?

"None of your concern, Eudo." Rig ground out the words. "What do ye want?"

The stout man behind Eudo backed away as he took one quick step toward Rig. "I want what is owed me." His gaze lingered on Grace, his eyes hard.

Rig held his knife higher. "And what may that be?"

"Rad did give me the gurl. She be mine." His chin notched in Grace's direction. "'Tis well past time we were wed."

Trembling with anger, Grace moved from behind Rig and stood at his side. "What do ye mean, he *gave* me to ye? Are ye mad?"

"Nay. 'Tis time to take what be mine. Ask your father." His handsome face twisted in rage. He was not the man she knew after all. He repeated, a threat in his voice, "Ask your father."

Grace glared at him. "I shall." She had to get away before the trembling crippled her, and tears poured like the fall of the River Pol into the sea.

Rig addressed Eudo through clenched teeth. "I have nay quarrel with ye, so let us leave it here."

Eudo's wicked laugh rang across the cliffs. "For now. But I shall have what is owed me. Remember that, Rig Cooper." His footsteps crunched on the pebbled path as he strode toward Trerose.

Grace nearly ran toward the cottage, too angry and ashamed to think of nothing but escape. She burst through the door, and her mother spun from the fire, a small iron kettle in her hand. When she saw Grace's face, she set it down and came to her.

Melior placed a palm on her daughter's forehead and frowned. "What ails ye?"

"Oh, Mother!" She flung herself sobbing into her arms. She allowed her mother to guide her toward the settle and mop the tears from her cheeks with a damp cloth. She took the cloth and wept into it.

When Grace composed herself, she told her mother what had happened, omitting the kiss. "Why is Father so cruel? How could he *give* me to that man?" She pulled in a trembling breath. "Eudo said it was past time we were wed. What does that mean?"

Melior dipped her head, studying her clenched hands, but said nothing.

"Mother," Grace whispered. "Tell me."

Her mother swallowed hard and averted her eyes to the fire then rose and made them a cup of tea. "Please say nothing as I am uncertain. A thought came to me as soon as ye finished your story." She handed Grace a cup of tea and took a sip of her own. "I fear your father received coin from Eudo for your hand and has yet to deliver ye to the man." She shivered. "I considered Eudo may be responsible for your father's ill treatment."

Grace absorbed this revelation, incredulous that men would behave in such a vile manner. She did not condone what Eudo might have done to her father—should he be found responsible—but she also had a twinge of regret for believing he deserved the treatment.

"Mother, I am away to bed." Weariness overcame her, and she lifted leaden legs to trudge up the stairs.

"Grace, ye must needs eat a bite afore sleep."

Halfway up the stairs, Grace stopped. "Nay, Mother. 'Tis too much a bother to make the effort. I must work out things in my mind."

Her mother's brow furrowed, but she said nothing more than 'good eve.'

Grace prepared for bed and slipped between the lavender-scented sheets. She and Alsyn had picked and dried the flowers during the summer, enjoying the rare moments of pleasure. The small, crowded cottage garden held a sense of peace for her. It was a place her father never ventured into. They grew many purposeful flowers, vegetables, and a few fruit trees. The cottage sheltered it from the salty breeze and tempestuous winds.

She lay awake, hands behind her head, and recalled the kisses she and Rig had shared. The sensation of his lips on hers, his arms about her, was indescribable. A tear found its way across her temple, and she brushed it away, remembering his tender caress.

Grace imagined Eudo taking her into his arms as Rig had and kissing her. She shuddered. Why had her father agreed to this arrangement?

She thought of Rig, and how fiercely he had wanted to protect her from Eudo. What would it be like to be promised to a man like him? And, in truth, what was it he wished to share with her?

ଔଞ

Unable to sleep, Grace rose early and readied herself for the day, leaving early to go to the tavern. Still troubled with the scene of last eve, she crept from the cottage, forfeiting food and drink. The song of the lark met her as she marched the path as if to her death, the bird's beautiful warbling melody following her. How could such a perfect day occur with her world in such turmoil?

When she arrived at the Sands, Wilmont stood at the kitchen table pounding a lump of dough. The room smelled of heady yeast, and her mouth watered.

"Good morrow, Wilmont."

The woman jumped and released a shrill scream. "Ye scart the life out of me!"

Through her current troubled mind, Grace managed to smile. "I am that sorry. 'Twas not my intent."

Keeping her eyes focused on Grace, Wilmont returned to

the dough. "Ye do not look well."

Grace pulled a salver of fresh bread to the edge of the table, cut herself a generous slice, and placed it on a plate. "Where is Eulalia?" She tied on an apron. "I do not remember her ever being away in the mornings." She slathered a dollop of butter on the hot bread and bit through the crusty exterior to the soft center.

"Fetching more mutton." Wilmont gently pushed a cup of steaming tea next to the bread and sent Grace a sly grin. "Ye look as if this may help."

"Thank ye. I am certain it shall." She took a healthy gulp and continued eating, watching the dough being formed into loaves. Her friend's kindness and the repetition of her movements sent a calming surge through her.

Swift stomping footsteps echoed in the tavern, and Caye darted through the door. "Eudo jest thundered in like one of them great storms. He be headin' up to see Rad."

Grace's chest tightened, and she swallowed, the contents of her stomach churning. She gripped the edge of the table, and her head swam. What should she do?

A calming intake of breath urged her to dash from the room and cautiously slip up the stairs behind Eudo. On the landing, she listened as the bedchamber door slammed shut. She crept toward the door and pressed her ear to the crack. A heated confrontation took place. Her father cursed Eudo, and he returned the rage.

"Radigan Atwood, ye have not met our agreement. Your daughter belongs to me. Ye agreed when I accepted your offer to aid me in the smuggling trade. 'Tis only right and proper ye meet our bargain. Ye have made much coin on my account."

"Eudo, 'tis none of my doing. I cannot force her to marry ye. Ye were to woo her."

"What in blue blazes do ye think I be doing? Been here each eve pretending to be all vicar-like with little drink and leaving a guinea as a gesture to my goodwill toward her." His voice rose. "I be the best gentleman I could, and she still pays me nay mind."

The bed creaked, and Grace imagined her father shifting uncomfortably. How could they speak of her as if she were a cask of brandy smuggled from France? Heat warmed her face, and she clenched her hands into tight fists. She thrust the door open, and it crashed against the wall.

"How dare ye both! I be not a piece of merchandise to be bandied back and forth to the highest bidder."

Her gaze moved from one man to the other, aiming hatred at each. "*Father*, I shall never forgive ye for this, nor any other evil ye have done me and our family all these years."

Eudo shot Rad a querying look, brows raised.

Grace turned her rage to Eudo. "And I shall never marry ye. Ye are a vile snake, Eudo Cubert!"

Her attention returned to her father. "Sebastian is right, ye should be at the bottom of the cliffs."

Her glare swung to Eudo once more before she rushed to the door, slammed it behind her, and raced down the stairs, through the kitchen and out into the fresh morning air. The horror-stricken expression of Eulalia as she rounded the building's corner and saw Grace impressed upon her the danger of what she had done. What consequences had she set

THE BURNING SANDS

into motion?

Sorrow engulfed her, and she knew she had not pleased God with her words and actions. All she could ponder was why God had tossed her to the wolves.

The unhurried flow of the River Pol calmed her spirit. The melodic sound of running water brought her peace and cleared her mind. Mrs. Braddock's caring face came to her. Halfway to Gwynne Cottage, she wished she had taken time to collect something to bring the dear woman. This morning, still in its infancy, Mrs. Braddock met her with a scone, a cup of tea, and a questioning glance.

"Ye be looking a mite wretched, me dear."

Grace kept her gaze on the rippling liquid in her cup suddenly questioning where the poor woman had obtained tea. She peered at her with lifted brows.

"Not to worry. Been squirreling back the tea ye did gift me 'til a moment such as this."

Grace gave the woman a grateful smile. "But how did ye know I would be here?"

A long moment passed before Mrs. Braddock's eyes glinted with mischief. "I cannot tell ye a lie. I took a wee walk down the path and saw ye drooping along the lane from the village. The way ye hung your head telt me all I need to know."

Grace slumped in the chair, fatigue weighing her body as a sack of flour on her shoulder, her body longing to give in to the weariness. She looked at the scone, knowing she must fortify herself for the day ahead and the consequences.

"Aye, dear. Eat up. 'Tis a long journey ahead of ye."

Grace flinched. "What do ye mean?" Clearing her throat,

she treaded carefully, repeating her question. "What do ye mean?"

Mrs. Braddock's gaze did not falter. "It be a long day to travel through when ye be ailing. If ye will telt me, I mayhap have a tonic."

Grace's shoulders relaxed. Should she share her folly? The woman was most trustworthy and wise. She timidly told her tale, beginning with the conversation between her and Rig. She included how they were interrupted by Eudo and what he had revealed about her father's arrangement. The kiss she shared with Rig was still kept close to her heart.

Mrs. Braddock crossed her arms and chewed on the inside of her lip. Grace ate her scone, poured herself another cup of tea, and remained silent until the woman spoke.

"Grace, not all things are as they appear. Have a care. Your heart is most delicate, and ye have had a coarse life fer one so young." Mrs. Braddock poured herself another cup and took a few sips before continuing, "I would not have ye marry someone ye were not meant to be with—like your mother." Her face sagged as if in defeat.

Grace reached across the table and gripped her forearm. "Ye are such a dear. I—my family is most fortunate to call ye friend."

Mrs. Braddock patted her hand. "Ye are all precious to me. I have known your mother since she was but a babe and sadly lived to see the day she did marry your father."

Grace pulled her hand back and gripped the cup tightly to steady her trembling. "Why did she marry him? In truth, I would like to know."

For a time, the woman did not answer, then she released a somber sigh. "Your mother was set to wed William Ellery."

Nick's uncle? Grace's eyes widened, her curiosity piqued, and she leaned in to hear more.

"They was a lovely couple and in truth had eyes but for one another when Master William was called away to war. The Ellery family did treat Melior most kindly during his absence, but when his letters stopped, they grew anxious. Your mother 'specially so."

"He died in the war?"

"'Tis what we all suspected as he was never heard from again."

"But how long had he been gone when they thought him dead?"

Her gray head tilted, her eyes on the ceiling. "'Bout two months, I believe. I telt your mother 'twas not long enough to be certain and not to worry, but she was most distressed. Even made her sick."

The detail captured Grace's attention. "What do ye mean—sick?"

"Poor gurl, pale and weak-like." She shook her head.

"What happened?"

"A letter came from the Admiralty telling her William had died at Naseby." She paused to ponder something a moment. "'Twas not long after she wed your father. A shock it was. The whole of Trerose be most curious why she did lower herself. Seemed that was when your grandparents turned against your mother. Tried to force her to wed Gerry rather than Rad."

"Who is Gerry? You mentioned him before."

Mrs. Braddock's expression changed to one of sadness as if she was uncertain she should share the information. After a time of rising for more tea, remaining quiet while it steeped, she poured them a fresh cup and resettled into her chair, then began to tell what she knew.

"Gerence Ellery, Nicholas's father."

Grace's mind clouded. "In truth?"

"Aye. Gerry had been in love with Melior since he was a lad. Doted on her, protected her, and was always by her side. Your grandparents and Gerry's parents were great friends. When William died, they withdrew from society. Mrs. Ellery not as much as her husband, but she withdrew in her own way. Both was never the same."

"How soon after William died did she marry my father?" Grace's fingers toyed with the handle of her cup, thoughts running down many paths, but none converged. "So, you say that my mother refused to wed Gerry but married my father instead? Why would she marry either if she didn't love them?"

The woman brought her gaze to Grace. "She once telt me she could not wed Gerry because it would be like looking into William's eyes every day and would pain her to do so."

Grace dipped her gaze to the table. "I asked her once why she married my father. She said he was a very handsome man, and he was different then. She would not say what changed him."

They sat in silence for a time before Grace asked, "Do ye know the reason for the turn in him?"

Mrs. Braddock lowered her voice. "Mayhap I have said enough. Ye should ask your mother. Appears to me the torch has been lit, my child, and all is about to be brought to light considering the to-do you had with Eudo and your father."

Grace's head snapped up. "Why do ye say this?"

"Radigan Atwood and Eudo Cubert are two men who are of a nature not to be trifled with. Ye best ask your mother if ye want all the truth 'bout your father. 'Tis her story to tell. I have jest filled in the holes on what's passed."

Grace sorted through the pieces. Her mother may or may not want to divulge the rest. She thanked Mrs. Braddock for her hospitality, noting to bring her more tea.

The scent of rain hung in the air, heavy and foreboding. Movement caught her attention, and she glanced toward Penrose Manor to see a tall, stooped man trudging toward the cliffs, still on manor grounds. He gripped his hands behind his back, much like Nick did as a child.

Upon closer inspection, she realized it was Mr. Ellery. She had not seen him in a long while. He appeared much older than his years, just as she'd heard told throughout the village. How it saddened her. Why would her mother wed Radigan Atwood, a tavern owner, rather than a man of great standing? And why should she marry him if his brother had been her true love? There was no sense nor understanding in it.

None of what Grace knew made sense. Mrs. Braddock was right. She must inquire of her mother to learn the truth, no matter how painful it was to hear, nor the pain it caused her mother in the telling.

CAROLE LEHR JOHNSON

Chapter Twelve

"What did you say?" Olivia whispered, unable to believe what she'd heard.

Luke angled his head down to peer deeper into her eyes. "Olivia, I'm asking you to marry me"

She opened her mouth to utter something—anything—for her to gather her senses, but she was speechless.

He dropped his arms and stuffed his hands into his pockets, eyes searching hers. "Either I've stunned you beyond measure, overwhelmed you with joy, or the thought of marrying me is absurd." His shoulders slumped, and he murmured, "I was praying for the second option."

Olivia pulled in a shaky breath and released it. "Will you give me a moment to digest what you've just asked?"

His head popped up, eyes sparkling with hope. He combed his fingers through already disheveled hair. "Of course. Take all the time you need."

Voices drew closer to their hiding place, and he touched a finger to his lips.

"Beryl, did you not see the way the vicar and Olivia were interacting?" Sheryl sniffed loudly. "At any moment, I thought he was going to grab her hand and hang on. Disgusting! A vicar acting such a way in public no less."

Olivia could almost see Beryl roll her eyes and bristle at her sister's comments. "Sheryl, you have got to understand that our vicar is a godly man and would do nothing improper, and holding hands is not improper. Why should you—or anyone else for that matter—care if he finds someone to love?"

A dead, calm silence hung around them. Olivia held her breath as her gaze froze on Luke's. When her eyes shifted toward the twins, she saw the back of a wine-colored head. If it were not for the absurdity of the situation she would've laughed.

Sheryl's shrieking tone startled her. "Love! He just met her. How could he love someone he's just met and not love someone he's known for years?"

Her pained sigh hurt Olivia's heart. The poor woman was delusional.

Could she be dangerous? From what others had said, she'd been stalking Luke for a long time. Instead of anger, all Olivia felt was sadness, and a low sob crawled from her throat. She slapped her hand over her mouth.

Two arms slammed through the branches of the hedge, parting the leaves, and a wild, maroon-colored head shoved toward Olivia's face. "What in blue blazes are you doing in there?" She grabbed Olivia's arm and yanked her through, twigs scratching her arms and face.

Beryl screamed, "Sheryl! Stop it right *now*." She wrapped an arm around Sheryl's waist and bodily wrenched her from the foliage.

Sheryl's face was a mask of delirium, her eyes wild, lips twitching, but no sound came out.

Luke burst from the hedge behind Olivia and placed himself in front of her to block Sheryl's forthcoming attack.

"You cannot take him from me. He's mine." Sheryl's eyes sought Luke's, and her visage softened. "Tell her."

Luke's desperate gaze rotated from hers to Beryl's, begging for instruction.

Beryl appeared almost in tears, yet her voice was calmer than Olivia imagined it would be when she said, "Vicar, if you'll please take Olivia home and see to her scrapes. I'll assist Sheryl home and call the doctor."

Sheryl's head twisted toward her sister. "The doctor? Why are you calling him? He's an old coot."

Beryl looked into Sheryl's eyes and spoke to her in a soothing tone. "Dear, don't you remember? He's coming to dinner, and we must be ready. You know Dr. Cranford has always had a thing for you?"

Sheryl stilled. "He has? Oh, my. I must repair my makeup and hair." She turned toward Luke and Olivia. "I'm sorry, but we must leave now. We'll see you tomorrow." She patted Olivia's cheek and sent Luke a peaceful smile.

Olivia saw the moisture in Luke's eyes as he leaned to give the old woman a gentle hug. "Please take care of yourself,

Sheryl."

The woman nodded. "I shall, Vicar." She took Beryl's arm, and they strolled away as if nothing had happened.

Luke pulled Olivia into his arms. "You're shaking. Are you cold?"

Olivia hugged him tightly. "Not cold, just unbalanced. I hate confrontations. That was horrifying seeing Sheryl like that. What could've caused her to become so disturbed?"

Luke blew out a long puff of breath. "I've seen it before with the elderly when they are in the early stages of Alzheimer's."

Olivia shivered. The dreaded disease was something she prayed would never happen to her grandparents. It broke her heart to see its effects.

"I know she's eccentric, but I never dreamed she may be afflicted with Alzheimer's."

"Let me look at your arms."

Olivia extended them, and he traced his fingertip over the long scratches, thin lines of blood already clotting.

"Let's get you home and see to these." He wrapped an arm around her shoulders and led her to the path.

Once at the cottage, Luke cleaned and treated her wounds, which were minor, with such care. Olivia studied him as they sat side-by-side on the sofa in the dim lamplight, each holding a cup of tea. He met her eyes.

"I suppose this would be an inappropriate time to bring up the abrupt end of our conversation." He ducked his head.

Olivia played with the cup's handle, watching the amber liquid vibrate from her quivering hand. "Luke . . ."

He waited patiently while Olivia's thoughts hurtled through her, reminiscent of shooting stars across the night sky. She closed her eyes and prayed for God to tell her what to do. The earlier revelation that she was in love with Luke kept circling in her head. A current of peace flowed in and around her. His unanswered question still hung among that peace, but the fact that she loved him grew.

Olivia lifted her head to find him watching her. "Luke, I love you too."

His posture straightened, and he took her cup and settled it next to his on the table before them. "That's a beginning." His lips on hers, welcoming and protective, was all the promise she needed for the time being.

෴

Olivia and Luke snuggled on the couch well into the evening speaking of all manner of things and nothing at all. Before he left, they reached an agreement. A future together stretched ahead.

With a final goodnight kiss, Olivia closed the door behind her husband-to-be. She pressed her back to the wooden barrier and lifted her eyes to heaven. "Thank you, God, for sending Luke Harper to me."

The phone trilled, and she answered, "Hello."

"I miss you already."

Olivia laughed. "You just stepped out of my door, silly."

"True. I'm leaning against it right now." Luke paused for a moment. "I thank God for sending you to me too." With a shaky breath, he added, "Good night, love."

Olivia ended the call, and her stomach growled, so she ambled to the kitchen and rummaged through her food supply. She settled on a can of soup and relaxed in front of the television. Her mind was so full of Luke she barely registered her favorite historical drama as it played before her. One actor bore a striking resemblance to Luke, so she roosted in and concentrated on the scene, before long drifting to sleep.

She woke to brilliant morning light streaming through the front window of the cottage, she blinked until fully awake, taking in the magnificent sunrise. She rested against the sofa, wrapping her mind around the events of the previous day. The pain she'd seen in Beryl's eyes at her sister's breakdown saddened her.

Olivia hurried to shower and dress. A visit to the twins would be her first task of the day.

She ate a scone and popped a tea bag and water into her travel mug, grabbing her bag on the way out the door, nearly running headlong into Luke.

"Whoa, love! Where are you off to so early?" He wrapped his arms around her waist and kissed her long and thoroughly.

Olivia drew her head back and looked at him. "After that kiss, I don't remember my own name."

"I aim to please." He lifted a brow.

She took his hand. "Walk with me to see the twins."

He nodded. "We're of the same mind. I was about to stop and ask you to accompany me. The poor old dear must be in a bad way. I dread what her episode may lead to."

As they walked hand-in-hand, Olivia shared what she'd

read about Alzheimer's. "The grandfather of a friend of mine, Angie, had a similar breakdown, and though he'd already been diagnosed with the disease, he snapped one day. The doctor told the family that a trauma of some sort could speed up the symptoms."

Luke asked, "Like what?"

"Well, Mr. Timmons had a fall and broke his ankle. Since he lived alone, he had to go to rehab for a few weeks until he got his strength back. His physical health was still excellent until the fall, but the trauma of leaving his home and moving into strange surroundings propelled him over the top, and suddenly he grew emotional and angry."

"That's too bad."

Olivia chuckled. "I know it's not really funny, but Angie went to see him one day, and he thought she was his daughter. He told her to give him her purse, and she did just to keep him calm. When he got it, he took out all of her cash and car keys. He then told her he knew what she'd been up to the night before and would not have that behavior repeated."

"And?"

"Apparently, his daughter and girlfriends drove to a large mall about seventy-five miles away to go shopping. Being only seventeen, he didn't think that was very smart—or safe. Angie just played along, apologizing, and said she'd never do it again. She stayed and had lunch with him, and when he took his afternoon nap, she retrieved her things and left."

Olivia grimaced and sighed. "That was the mildest of his flareups, sadly."

Luke wrapped his arm around her as they walked.

When they reached the twins' small, modern cottage, he knocked, and Beryl answered. Her face was drawn with dark circles under her eyes.

"Vicar. Olivia. It's so nice of you to stop by." She waved them in. "Sheryl is sleeping. The doctor gave her a sedative."

Luke and Olivia took the offered seat on a brilliantly hued sofa, much the same shade as Sheryl's hair. It nearly made Olivia weep. The woman was a *pill* as her grandmother said, but she was fond of her and didn't want to be the source of her distress.

"Beryl, I'm so sorry we caused what happened yesterday." Her face heated at being caught in the shrubs with the vicar.

"Oh, my dear. You weren't the cause." Beryl pulled a lacy handkerchief from her sweater pocket and dabbed at her eyes.

Olivia rose and sat beside the elder woman, giving her a one-armed hug. "I am so very sorry. How long ago was it diagnosed?"

Beryl's face scrunched. "Diagnosed?"

Olivia whispered, "Alzheimer's?"

Silence hung in the room while they stared at one another for a long moment. Beryl burst into fits of laughter, and it took her a while to compose herself. "Is that what you thought?" She patted at the tears rolling along her wrinkled cheeks.

Luke held Olivia's questioning gaze and gave a one-shouldered shrug, quirking a side of his mouth upward.

Beryl inclined her body toward Luke, tugging Olivia with her, and lowered her voice. "Before we went to the church, she had a nip or two of her *sherry*." She mouthed the emphasized word rather than saying it aloud, straightening in her seat. "I told her not to do it. She usually only partakes when we stay home, but she said she needed fortification before she . . ."

They waited for her to continue, but she pressed her lips into a straight line.

Beryl stood and flapped her hands in the air. "Enough said, my dears. Needless to say, she will not be happy with herself when she discovers the vicar saw her this way. That stuff makes her loopy." She raised an index finger next to her head and twirled it in a circle.

Olivia bit the inside of her cheek to halt the laughter screaming to be released and nodded.

"Now, be comfy. I'm off to make tea. And we have fresh cake to go with it."

Luke's eyes widened, and Olivia's resolve not to laugh nearly undid her. She shook her head at him but addressed Beryl. "Would it happen to be Sheryl's famous fruitcake by chance?"

Beryl laughed. "Good heavens no! That doorstop. I made Victoria sponge."

Olivia and Luke released a collective sigh, which Beryl caught but reassured them. "Not to worry. Everyone in the village feels the same." She turned to leave but pivoted on her heel and looked at them.

"In three hundred years some archeologist is going to dig up dozens of Sheryl's fruitcakes buried all over the village and wonder what in the world they are."

CR8O

By the time Olivia and Luke left the Ford sisters' cottage, the afternoon was well under way. Beryl had kept them in stitches, telling them of Sheryl's behavior *without* the sherry.

"So, what's on your agenda for the rest of the day?"

Olivia retrieved her phone from her bag and opened her calendar. "Tea with Mrs. Atwood in about two hours."

Luke groaned. "More tea?"

"I can't hurt Mrs. Atwood's feelings by saying *no tea*." Olivia squeezed his hand. "Are you coming with me?"

His brows rose. "For more tea?"

Olivia elbowed him. "Surely you'll be ready for more in two hours."

"I suppose." His tone was long suffering.

"Speaking of Mrs. Atwood—that name keeps creeping into my thoughts as if I've heard it before I knew Hortense."

Luke shrugged. "You should have."

Olivia stopped. "What? Why should I have?"

"It's in Grace's diary."

Olivia's mind reeled through what little they'd deciphered so far but couldn't recall the name being there.

"I'm not remembering that," she said hesitantly.

Luke glanced at his watch. "I don't have an appointment before tea with Hortense, so let's go to the museum and look at our notes. I'm certain I saw it in there and thought you did as well."

Olivia agreed. "Luke, why don't I remember us discussing the name?"

Without meeting her eyes, he said, "You were probably so enthralled with me. I saw you surveying my person the first day we worked on the diary."

"So sure of yourself, are you?"

His blue eyes glinted with humor when he turned his gaze upon her. "Honestly . . . I was terrified you'd recognize I was enchanted by *you* from the moment you ran into me the first time."

"Me? I'm not much to look at with this uncontrollable wavy mess of hair."

He touched her hair and ran his fingers along a strand. "It's beautiful. Just like you." He brought the lock to his nose and inhaled. "And your signature scent has never left me since that day."

She smoothed her palm across his cheek—speechless that a man could be so romantic. Even Ian, as special as he was, didn't come close to Luke's care of her.

Olivia kissed his hand, which still held her hair. "Thank you."

His face clouded. "For what?"

"For making me live again."

Luke smiled. "You've already thanked the one who brought it about. God."

☙❧

Olivia scanned the page of the diary with the eraser tip of a pencil. "Is this what you were referring to?"

Luke flipped through a tattered notebook, the corners of the pages curling from overuse. He landed on a page, put it next to the diary, and tapped one line.

"See the worn areas here? I wrote this out in the notebook

and underneath played with substituting words that may or may not complete the sentence."

Olivia read the broken sentence aloud. "Today I was so angry with Sebastian ____wood__, unable to understand why he would not meet me _____ and cannot leave___."

Luke tapped her hand. "Maybe she was saying she was angry with him because he would not meet her *at the woods*, or his last name is *Atwood*."

Olivia chewed on her lower lip, then said, "I don't know. Seems a stretch to me. I wish she would've just put her last name in the diary's front."

"The easy way out. A detective's dream." He gave her an evil smile.

She narrowed her eyes. "So, this is the brilliant revelation that I should've remembered?"

He reclined in his chair and crossed his arms. "Sorry, it's all I've got."

"Wait. You said something about the history of Trerose and the name Atwood."

"Well, only as far back as the tavern goes." Luke's face paled, and he stood so quickly his chair tipped backward and landed against the wall. He stood over Olivia and angled his gaze downward. "You, my love, are a temptress and made me quite forget the history of the Sands." He bolted from the room, and Olivia heard the thump of items being shoved aside before a final crash.

Several minutes passed and finally Olivia called out, "Luke, are you okay?"

He stormed into the room, hair disheveled and his face

flushed, holding an enormous book over his head. "Eureka!"

Olivia laughed, her excitement escalating. "What have you found?"

He slapped his palm to his forehead in mock surprise. "How could I have forgotten this tome of history?"

"Where was it?"

"Keeping Sheryl's fruitcake company by holding a door open."

Olivia's phone chimed, and she took it from the desk and glanced at the reminder. "It's time to go to Mrs. Atwood's." She deleted the alarm. "I'm sorry."

"Not to worry, we'll take it with us. Hortense may have some thoughts on what's in here about her Atwoods."

CAROLE LEHR JOHNSON

XI

Grace's mother was not at home when she arrived, but Degory and Alsyn sat at the table eating bread and cheese. Their eyes widened at seeing their sister at midday. She stood between them with a hand on each of their heads and ruffled their hair affectionately.

"Where is Mother?"

Degory's large innocent eyes peered up at her. "She be at the cottage of Mrs. Pittard's daughter helping her give birth." He grimaced and squeezed his bright blue eyes shut as if to block out the thought of something so gruesome.

"When is she to return?"

Alsyn had grown quiet since the night their father had hurt Degory, and Grace had to admit that even her brother was not the lively child he had once been. The girl timidly pointed to a piece of folded paper on the table, her gaze on the food.

Grace sat between them and read the message.

Degory touched his sister's arm. His sweet, innocent face

melted her heart. "Mother bid me to fetch the letter to ye after we ate. Ye are here now, so there is nay need."

Alsyn looked at her, a tiny spark of the old light shining in her eyes. "I think she knows it, silly brother."

The boy reached across Grace and playfully hit his sister on the shoulder, eliciting giggles from them both.

The letter said little more than Degory had revealed except to ask Grace to return home with them when Degory brought the message, fetch their evening meal from the tavern, give them their daily lessons, and if she came home at all that eve, it would likely be late. She asked that Grace be certain they were abed at the usual time.

Her mother was more relaxed of late with Radigan laid up. She never would have gone away, even to help someone, for she knew she would pay should he discover her absence. He was not one to help others unless he gained something for it.

"Would ye like to come with me to the tavern? I believe Eulalia has baked apple tarts."

They answered with enthusiastic nods and wide smiles. Grace gathered them into a hug. "Ye are the sweetest and are about to become sweeter once ye have a few tarts." She tickled them—the happy sound music to her ears.

The scent of rain now stronger, she took their hands, and they skipped down the hillside toward Trerose.

"We best hurry or else we shall be soaked." The sudden downpour turned their walk into a race amid more laughter. Grace kept up with the children until the village came into view, then she slowed and watched them pick heather for Eulalia, Wilmont, and Caye, in the now gentle shower.

By the time they reached the tavern a light mist had settled, and a ghostly fog rolled into the harbor.

Degory arrived at the kitchen door first and held it open for his sisters, a courtesy taught by their mother along with kindness. The action brought back the memory of what Mrs. Braddock had said about Grace speaking to her mother regarding her choice of husband. Seeing Mr. Ellery that afternoon had stirred many emotions. Why would her mother want to marry anyone so quickly after William's death? And of all people—her father?

"My loves!" Eulalia dropped to her knees with arms wide. "What ye be doing here? 'Tis a brighter day fer seeing ye."

They ran into the cook's arms and squeezed her until she tumbled to the floor, the children falling on her with squeals of joy.

Grace's thoughts dissolved at the scene before her. If only their life could be more like this every day. A flash of lightning brightened the room, a crash of thunder following. They sobered and straightened.

Eulalia took the children by the hand and led them to the table as Wilmont and Caye entered the room bearing trays of soiled dishes. The children met them with equal happiness.

The two women pulled the children onto their laps as Eulalia fussed over them with tarts and milk.

A bellow drifted down the stairs. "Where the blue blazes be my drink?"

The children started, each grabbing tight to the women holding them.

Degory's eyes widened, arms clutching his middle. "Is that

Father? Will he come down?"

Grace knelt before him and stroked his cheek. "Nay, my pet. Father is hurt and cannot leave his bed."

His face relaxed, and he rested his head on Wilmont's shoulder, who told him, "Not to worry, my precious little monkey. We would not let him harm ye."

Degory nestled his head into her neck and whispered, "He has afore."

Wilmont's face flamed with anger, and she brought her questioning glare to Grace.

Grace nodded, wishing she did not have to admit the ugly truth. She saw the seething anger in Wilmont's eyes.

A familiar voice from the tavern's main room caught their attention, and a moment later, Doctor Keast stepped in, his smiling face greeting them. The recent rain left him glistening in the light and his damp gray hair blown askew. He mopped his face with a handkerchief. "'Tis a right and proper storm out there."

Grace ruffled Degory's hair, then directed her attention to the doctor. "I trust ye are well this eve?"

"Well enough. Came to examine your father."

Grace felt sorry for the man, having to deal with Radigan Atwood.

"Do not look so bereft, my dear. Your father's rantings like the devil merely roll off my back as the rain does—for the most part." He coughed. "I am here to see how he progresses."

"When ye have completed your examination, will ye have a moment for a cup of tea and one of Eulalia's tarts?"

The elder man's eyes brightened. "It would be a pleasure." He gave a slight bow and trudged up the stairs.

Grace prepared their repast as the children finished theirs, and Wilmont took them into the small parlor near the kitchen. While she readied the table for the doctor's tea, she mulled over the possibilities of moving to the cave. Would Degory and Alsyn be able to cope with life away from the sun and beach? Would she?

The doctor cleared his throat, bringing Grace back to the present.

"Please have a seat." She gestured to the side of the table she had laid for them.

Doctor Keast groaned as he sat. "This cold, damp weather is hard on the bones of us oldies."

Grace laughed as she poured his tea. "You will never be an oldie to me, Doctor."

He took his first sip and sighed with pleasure. "This shall warm me nicely." He took a bite of the tart and repeated his sigh. "Knew I should have married Eulalia when I had the chance." He sent the cook a shy smile.

Eulalia's head snapped up, and her face reddened. "Go on, ye old goose."

His eyes twinkled with mischief, but Grace thought she noticed a flicker of something else hidden in their brown depths. She glanced at Eulalia and glimpsed the same.

The doctor coughed. "Well, now. Ye shall want to hear my report on your father's progress."

Grace straightened in her chair, fear welling inside.

"It will not be more than a few days, and he shall rise from that bed whether or not I approve." He took another bite and watched Grace's face, unfettered concern showing there.

"Thank ye for warn . . . telling me." She wrung her hands in her lap, tears threatening.

Doctor Keast eased his plate away, took his last sip of tea, and rose. "Thank ye kindly, ladies, for the tea and sweets." He turned to the cook. "Ye are an excellent cook, Eulalia, and would have made a fine addition to any restaurant in London. Probably would have been famous."

He spoke the words with utmost sincerity, bowed, and midway to the door he stopped. "I near forgot." Stepping back to the table, he placed his bag on the worn surface, opened it, and retrieved a small amber bottle. He glanced around and lowered his voice. "Place a few drops of this in Radigan's ale and be certain he drinks it all. Do this each eve, so ye may all have a more peaceful night." They nodded in understanding.

Grace said goodbye but kept her gaze on Eulalia. The woman's face softened, and her eyes misted. She busied herself avoiding Grace. Was there once something between her and the doctor? Was there still?

ଔଓ

A few days later, Arabel Atwood stood in the middle of the kitchen, papers in one hand, the other on her hip. She cocked her head. "Eulalia, why do these receipts appear to be too costly for what was delivered?"

Grace swung her gaze to her sister's. The stern expression she wore was one seen many times on their father. They were much alike. Radigan's hair was the same dark brown but now flecked with gray.

Eulalia halted her task, patiently wiped her hands on her apron, and faced Arabel icily. They stared at one another for a few moments.

"Well, gurl. Are ye gonna tell me what's got your shift in a twist?"

The girl slammed the receipts onto the worktable, a pewter cup skittering across its scarred surface. "When ye have the inclination to review these, explain to me the reasoning behind the purchases." She tossed her long, dark hair over one shoulder and dashed from the room, her footsteps pounding up the stairs to her father's office.

The cook pulled the papers toward her, releasing a huff of irritation. "What be this?" She pointed to the cost of thirty-four hogshead of beer. "We never did serve that much in all the winter."

Grace gasped. "I know not when we ever ordered that much." She leaned over the woman's shoulder to view the items, noting the costs. Nothing appeared out of the ordinary at first. She slid the tip of her finger across a line of writing.

"Do ye notice this line," she moved to another area, "and this line are of a different hand?"

Eulalia squinted and took it in. "Aye, 'tis strange. Would not the style be the same?"

Grace nodded and pulled another receipt from the stack, perusing it in the same manner. "Consider this . . ." She removed one after another until they compared each receipt. "All have been altered. A proper job yet changed to appear to be more costly."

Eulalia's eyes danced with mirth. "Ye be a clever gurl. Yet

what means it?"

"It means someone wants the keeper of the numbers and the magistrate to believe items for the tavern were purchased legally."

"And not smuggled goods." The older woman grinned. "So 'tis to appear he did pay dearly to serve fine things like tea, coffee, and sugar to his customers like them fancy coffee houses in London?"

Grace patted her on the back. "Aye, my friend. But whose writing is this?" They brought bewildered gazes back to the papers, scattered before them. She knew the questionable handwriting seemed familiar . . . but to whom did it belong?

Radigan's voice boomed from the upper floor followed by Arabel's. Grace had never heard her sister raise her voice to their father. Moments later, a door slammed, rattling the seashells lined up on the kitchen windowsill.

Her sister stormed into the kitchen, snatched the papers, and made to rush out again, but Grace grabbed her arm.

Eulalia crossed her arms. "Seems a good time for a cup of strong tea." She set about with the preparations, keeping out of their conversation.

"Arabel, calm yourself a mite and allow me to tell ye something." Her sister glared, fire blazing in her eyes. Grace refused to release her, pulled a chair from the table, and eased her onto it.

"Listen to me please." She stacked the receipts neatly and pointed to the first, noting the two different styles of writing. "The top of the paper would have to be in the original owner's writing, but near the bottom, it lists new items in a different fashion. Though it appears the author tried to copy the original."

Arabel shrugged. "So, what if 'tis different?" She kept her eyes on the paper, scanning the lines.

Grace sat beside her. "Do ye not find it curious that the added items on each receipt are for more costly goods? Goods that taxes must be paid."

The girl finally brought her gaze to Grace, a flicker of light shining. "Tea, coffee, sugar, brandy . . ."

"Aye. Taxes are most dear on those goods."

"Yet why have they not been present in the past?" She quirked a brow. "The Sands has been serving them for some time now."

Grace met her gaze again. "I know not, but we must have a care. We cannot trust our father."

Arabel opened her mouth to speak, but Grace cut her off. "Sister, please listen to me. He is not a stable man. Never has been. Ye have lived here too long, and he has quite taken advantage of ye and made ye believe he is kindness itself. While, in truth, he is dangerous."

Grace hesitated to reveal what may upset her, but she did tell what their father had done to Degory. Her sister's eyes widened. Grace then told her what he had done to their mother for years, about Eudo, and what else had transpired the past few years while Arabel lived at the tavern.

Eyes downcast, Arabel straightened the papers repeatedly. "Grace, how could I have been so blind?"

She put an arm around her sister. "Because Father was clever, and ye have a talent he used for his own good."

The young woman, for that was what Grace now saw her as, hung her head, tears falling onto the lovely lavender dress their father had bought his *darling* girl. Grace fought the bitterness welling inside her at the generous treatment he had given Arabel yet not her.

Grace was too much like their mother and Arabel more like him. The path of thought brought her back to Sebastian. She had yet to ask Melior about what Mrs. Braddock had shared with her about the past.

Eulalia placed a salver in front of them with three cups of tea and a plate of tarts. "For my gurls."

Grace and Arabel found her kind eyes on them, and they thanked her. The three women sat in companionable silence, Grace mulling over what would follow. She leaned in and whispered, "We must find out who changed the receipts. They must not fall into the hands of the excise men, or else they shall take the tavern from Father."

"If Father is gone, how shall we run the Sands?" Arabel waved an arm into the air. "We must keep our living."

Eulalia cleared her throat. "'Tis of nay concern. Your father mere collects the coin whilst we all do the work. Has it not run smooth these past weeks?"

Grace and Arabel shared a look of agreement.

Eulalia laughed mirthlessly. "We all jest know our place and do it without being told."

"She is right, Grace." Arabel's smile was sad. "But Father shall be up soon. How shall we discover who did this thing afore he is about?"

Grace shook her head. "I know not." She rose and eased the

chair under the table. "Let me speak with Sebastian. He may have thoughts on it."

Arabel handed the receipts to Grace. "Please take these and hide them."

"Why?" Grace stilled. "What were you and Father fighting about earlier? We could hear ye shouting."

"I showed him the receipts and told him I questioned the amounts. He said it was none of my affair and to jest care for the accounts afore..."

Eulalia moaned. "Oh, my. 'Tis as I suspected. Is that your father's writing?"

The sisters gaped at one another, yet Arabel answered, "I think not. Even if he should try to copy the original hand, I do not believe he could do this. His hand is most erratic and unclear on the best of days."

Grace nodded. "'Tis truth. Father has not much education in writing, and his hand is poor. Perhaps he did pay someone. We must make a list of those willing to aid him and have a fair hand." She turned to Arabel. "Please create a list of Father's acquaintances who may be a candidate for this task? Then we shall take one name at a time and discover whether we may cross them off the list."

Arabel's smile was a mixture of sadness and pride. "Excellent idea, Sister."

Grace returned the smile. Though, she loathed their reconciliation was brought on by their father's frightening choices.

CAROLE LEHR JOHNSON

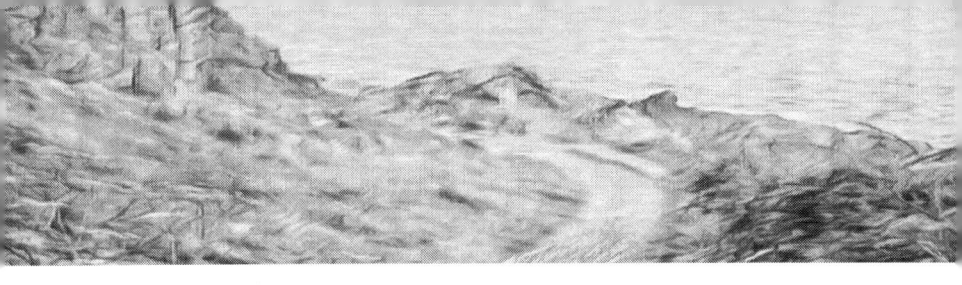

Chapter Thirteen

Olivia took in Hortense Atwood's square, white-washed cottage. The charcoal slate roof dripped moisture from the previous night's gentle rain, a clean scent infusing the air.

"Luke, does Mrs. Atwood live alone?"

He unlatched the black iron gate and stepped back to allow Olivia to walk through first.

"No, her granddaughter stays the nights with her until she completes her schooling. During the day, Laura Medlin, a woman from the village, takes over the running of the house and tends to Hortense."

The echo of Luke's rapid knock remained in the air when the door clicked open. Surprised, Olivia peered down into the eyes of the wheelchair-bound Hortense.

Olivia smiled. "Good afternoon."

Luke parroted the greeting, and Hortense ushered them to

a narrow kitchen filled with sunlight and the smell of fresh-baked scones. A large blue-willow teapot sat on the cloth-covered table, steam rising from the spout.

The chair shuddered as Luke placed the enormous book on the vacant seat with a thud.

Hortense gave him a pointed look. "Vicar, I hope you will not read that to us over tea."

He laughed and occupied the chair next to the book. "Hardly. It's historical. Olivia and I want to ask you some questions about the area, and I thought this," he patted the cover fondly, "may guide us and stir memories."

She huffed. "I'm not as old as that."

Olivia's gaze flew to Luke, hoping she didn't have another Sheryl on her hands. When she returned her gaze to the woman, a mischievous smile graced her lips.

"Vicar, may we have tea first?" Hortense reached for the teapot and began pouring the brew. "I've made smuggler's tea. It has enough body to get you through the afternoon."

Luke teased her. "And into the next, I'd say." His eyes widened as he peered into his lifted cup. "It's blacker than the smuggler's cave."

The old woman hooted at the comment, and she gave his arm a friendly slap. "You do make me laugh, Vicar. That's one of the many things I like about you. A brilliant sense of humor."

They chatted over tea and scones for a half hour, then Hortense asked if they'd prefer to stay where they were to look over the vicar's doorstop—as she referred to the massive book.

Choosing to stay put, Olivia removed her notebook and

pen, and they began.

Luke leaned over a page of the book. "Hortense, the information here says the Atwood family first came to Trerose in the fifteenth century. They fished for a living until the sixteenth century, when some of the family started a tavern. It doesn't mention The Burning Sands but skips ahead to the seventeenth-century history of the area and doesn't mention the Atwood involvement with the tavern after that."

The old woman scoffed. "Well, it should have. My husband was adamant that the old Sands has always been in the Atwood family."

Olivia and Luke shared a glance that Hortense did not miss.

"I'm not senile, you know." Her eyes shifted from one to the other. She wheeled her chair away from the table and held up one hand. "I'll be back." With more agility than Olivia expected, Hortense sped from the room, the repetitive squeak of wheels fading down the hall.

Shortly, loud shuffling sounded from another room. After a few moments of silence, the sound of wheels zipped into the kitchen. Perched on Hortense's lap were a couple of thick dilapidated ledgers. She rolled into her spot at the table with a pleased expression.

Hortense picked up one book at a time and slammed them onto the table in front of Luke, a few bits of parchment floating into the air. "Look at these and see if you can find anything of worth."

Olivia watched as Luke perused the cover, then opened the first book. His face registered shock.

"Hortense. Where did you get these?"

The woman wore a look of smug satisfaction. "They've been passed down along the Atwood family for generations."

Luke shook his head. "These are museum quality items. How have you stored them?"

Olivia heard the astonishment in his voice.

Hortense huffed with indignation. "In an acid-free box, of course!" She jerked something from her pocket and threw cotton gloves in front of Luke. "And be sure to use these."

Luke stared at the enigmatic woman. "You do know studies have shown that as long as your hands are clean, gloves are no longer needed?"

She shot him a glare, ignoring his comment. "I wasn't in the historical society a couple of decades before you were born for nothing."

Olivia choked on her tea, sputtered, and cleared her throat. "You what?"

Hortense sent her a long-suffering look. "You wouldn't have known, my dear. You're American after all."

Luke's eyes widened. "I've not seen in the records or heard that you were a part of the society. Why is that?"

"We were a very informal group, and I've never been one of those snobs that worked by the book."

"Not to worry, Hortense." Luke pulled on the gloves. "I'm amazed by your accomplishments. How has this escaped me all these years?"

Hortense nodded sagely. "Youth, my dear, youth. I know how it is to be self-absorbed. To quote George Bernard Shaw,

'Youth is wasted on the young.'"

☙❦

Olivia strolled beside Luke as they departed from Hortense Atwood's cottage, the sun barely beginning its descent into the western sky.

"She is an amazing woman, isn't she?" Olivia slanted her gaze toward Luke, who awkwardly tucked the *acid-free* box beneath his arm.

"That she is."

"What do you make of her revelation of the Atwood family's connection to The Burning Sands?"

A silence hung between them, and Olivia attempted to grasp what was running through Luke's mind.

"Are you okay?"

He blinked. "Sorry?"

"I know your thoughts are muddled right now because of Mrs. Atwood's revelation, but what do you think is behind this news?"

"I'm sorry. I'm amazed at what she'd been hiding all these years from the village's past. What *else* hasn't she revealed?"

Olivia gave thought to his comment. "That's something I'd not considered. What are you thinking?"

Luke paused on the path and faced her. "I apologize for being too caught up in the mystery." Because of the burden he carried, he used his other arm to draw her closer.

"My dear fiancée." He considered her with a long stare. "I know we cannot reveal that detail of our relationship just yet, and I am sorry this matter has quite taken my attention away from you."

His gaze lingered on her lips. "Why Hortense should keep these details to herself for so long baffles me."

Their eyes held. He then leaned in and tenderly kissed her, stealing her breath.

"Vicar?"

"Yes," he said against her lips.

"I think we're drawing a crowd."

He lifted his head, face close to hers. "What?"

Olivia cleared her throat and whispered, "Look to your right."

Luke twisted to see Teffeny and Hugo eyeing them suspiciously from the stone bridge by the harbor. He groaned. "Guess the cat's out of the bag now."

"Seems so." Olivia agreed, taking in the astonishment in Hugo and Teffeny's expressions. "Seems so indeed."

ଓଝ୭

With the prized ledgers between them, Olivia tucked into a booth next to Luke at The Pilchard across from Teffeny and Hugo.

"So, you see why we want to keep this under wraps for a while?" Luke told them.

Hugo eyed Luke. "Not really."

Teffeny elbowed Hugo, and he yelped. "I understand completely. After all, *our* vicar suddenly engages himself to a stranger in Trerose after only a few weeks. What's not to see?" She crossed her arms. "And whose business is it anyway? You fell in love at first sight and away we go!"

Olivia choked on her soda. "Love at first sight? Really?"

Luke laughed. "We were at odds from the beginning. I thought she was going to bite my head off."

Hugo burst into laughter. "Seriously?" His gaze went to Olivia's. "Did you?"

Olivia lifted one side of her mouth. "I told him so. In the middle of Carew market."

"I'm glad for the sake of the future of the old Sands building," Hugo said, relief in his voice. "The historical society can never purchase the old girl and do her justice. Whereas Olivia can open a successful business and keep the integrity of the building."

Luke's grin faltered, his intense gaze lighting on Hugo, something burning within it. "And the historical society can't do that?"

Hugo drew back with both hands raised "Don't get riled, my friend. I'm just saying that the organization will never have the funds to get the building and renovate it to its full potential. Olivia has the means. Let her have it."

Olivia's insides tightened. Her gaze shifted from one man to another, Teffeny keeping pace with her.

Luke straightened. "Hugo, I'm not saying I don't want Olivia to have the building. I just think it better suited to be our museum because of its antiquity." He grasped Olivia's hand under the table and squeezed.

Olivia's emotions twisted and turned, uncertain how to react—or feel. She examined Luke's eyes for clues. Had she misjudged him? Certainly not, given he was the vicar.

"Luke, are you saying you do *not* want me to buy the

Sands?"

He flinched. "No, I mean, it's not that I don't want you to have it. I've always thought it of such historical importance that it should be our museum. Trerose doesn't have another building of its significance."

Luke held her gaze, and she recognized the message he attempted to convey. A gift shop was not a necessity to the history of the village. A new museum in a historic building was.

Olivia released his hand, and he attempted to retrieve it, but she pulled away. "I need to get home. It's been a long day."

Luke's face expressed his disappointment, and a stab of guilt pierced her.

"Let me walk you home."

She fumbled with her bag. "Thank you, but no. I need time to think."

Teffeny stood and took Olivia's arm. "I'll walk with you."

Olivia wanted to protest, knowing Teffeny's house was in the opposite direction, but held her tongue.

Luke stood and kissed her cheek, but his movements were rigid, turmoil in his eyes. He sank onto the booth as Olivia departed with Teffeny on her heels.

Her friend barely let them leave the pub before she asked, "Why did you react to Luke that way?"

Olivia's head snapped up toward her friend. "How so?"

"You were so adamant that you have to buy the Sands. Is it that important to you?"

Olivia mulled over the question. "I'm not sure. It's some

niggling feeling I have that it's connected to my genealogy. So far, I have no proof."

Teffeny nodded but said nothing.

"I can't explain it. Have you ever been sure of something, but you have no evidence?"

The night closed in on them as they reached the cottage. At the door, Olivia asked, "Would you like to come in?"

Teffeny considered for just a moment and agreed.

Olivia locked the door behind them. "Why don't you stay the night? I've a lot on my mind, and I would appreciate another woman's point of view."

"Truly?"

"Truly. My emotions are all over the map since Luke asked me to marry him. We've known each other for such a short time, and I actually said yes. It was as if something internal urged me to accept."

"Whoa. That's deep."

They ambled toward the sofa and dropped in opposite corners. Teffeny curled her legs beneath her. "I'd say we need food and drink to get us through this night of emotions."

"I've enough cookies—sorry, biscuits—tea, popcorn, and so on to last the night."

"May I borrow nightwear?"

"Certainly." Olivia rose to gather her extra pajamas and turned back to Teffeny. "I hope you're ready for this. I've a lot of baggage to unload, and since my friend Angie won't be here for another week, you're it."

"Bring it on," Teffeny said with a smile.

Olivia shared with Teffeny all that she had experienced the past year and a half. She told her new friend about the last extreme sports trip Ian had taken. He left with her disapproval, dividing their relationship. Something she hated and berated herself for repeatedly.

As Olivia shared, a liberating sensation flowed through her. She slumped against the sofa cushions, exhausted.

Teffeny stared at Olivia over the rim of her cup. "That's a heartbreaking story. I can see why meeting Luke was difficult for you. Even though more than a year has passed since your husband's death, emotionally speaking, meeting a new love interest couldn't have been easy for you."

Olivia stared at her, thankful that she understood the struggle.

"Thank you for that." She snatched a tissue and dabbed at her eyes. "I'm not sure I know any more now than when I first arrived in Trerose."

Teffeny placed her cup on the table. "Marrying Luke is a good decision. That I'm certain of. He's a good man and will treat you right." She tapped Olivia on the knee playfully. "Does this mean I'm maid of honor?" She flashed a wide, toothy grin.

Olivia smiled. "You're a good friend, and this evening has been a godsend. He definitely brought us together."

Teffeny clasped her hands and lifted them above her head, stretching from side to side. "Absolutely. But, hey, I know you'll want Angie to be your maid of honor. After all, she's been your closest friend for a long time."

Olivia started to speak, but Teffeny interrupted, "Do you think I'm too old to be a flower girl?" She teased.

Olivia sniggered. "Of course not! How about one last cup of decaf before bed?"

Teffeny rose. "Let's have it in the kitchen, so we won't nod off into our cups. This sofa is much too comfy."

They puttered in the kitchen, preparing the last cup of their gabbing session.

Teffeny sat at the table. "Have you considered buying the Sands and letting it to the historical society but keeping a section for your shop? You could still live above."

Olivia froze over the cups, the warmth of the steam heating her face. She swallowed and slowly turned toward her friend.

"That's something I would never have thought of. And marriage does center around compromise, does it not?"

That night, Teffeny's suggestion coupled with thoughts of a future with Luke sifted through her mind while sleep evaded her.

Could she tie herself so securely to the museum? Yes, she and Luke agreed they would not announce their engagement for several months, wanting to let the villagers get used to seeing them together for a time.

Olivia had to admit Teffeny's idea was wonderful. She would still own the Sands, allowing the museum to be in a portion of the structure. Initially, it could be a short-term lease to see how things transpired. She would live above the museum and her shop—with Luke still in his ancient cottage—and let time trot on until they made plans.

Yes, it could work.

She'd discuss it with him tomorrow. All tension about the Sands coming between them now faded into the recesses of her mind. She thanked God for His intervention via Teffeny.

An image of the antique journals tucked under Luke's arm flashed before her. They were about to pore over them, but she allowed her agitation to interfere in their relationship. That building had become the *extreme sports* of her relationship with Luke, and she had unknowingly welcomed it. And he had not called her.

Olivia had hurt him—all because of an old building. Shame coursed through her, and she wept herself to sleep as the sun slowly rose over Widow's Cottage.

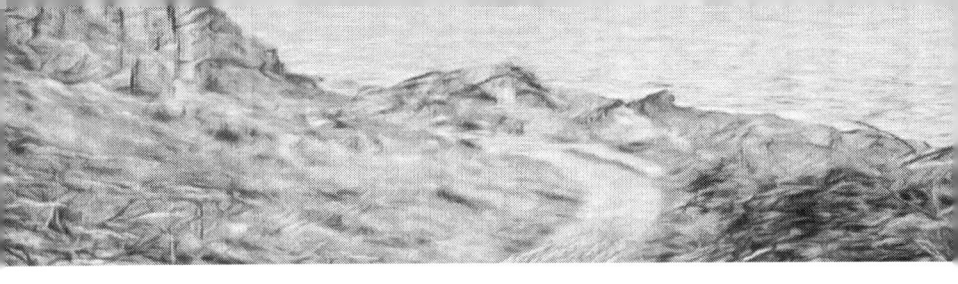

XII

Grace stood at the edge of the cliffs, head tilting toward the bright stars. The night was calm, cloudless, and cold. November was fast approaching, and her father would surely stir soon. Expecting Sebastian any moment, she would ask when they were to move into the cave. It seemed they were cutting the time far too close if they were to appear to be away before her father's rising.

The black velvet sky held numerous sparkling lights, and it took her breath away. How could a God who created this care what happened to an ignorant girl in a tiny part of Cornwall? She tugged her shawl closer. "God, if ye are there, please help us."

A shaky voice answered, "I do not believe He is there, Grace."

She whirled, fear gripping her. A few feet away stood Gerence Ellery appearing as a ghostly shadow in the starlit night. Speechless, she clung to her shawl like a rope dangling over the cliff.

He did not look her way, his hands clasped behind his back, as he watched the waves below, white caps faint in the night appearing and reappearing, as if they entranced him.

Grace's heart tightened. "In truth, do ye believe that?"

"Do not ye?" He then freed a coarse rattling cough from his chest.

Grace considered his question for a moment. "I believe in God, but I think He cares little about our small circumstances. Why should He?" She released her shawl and spread her arms wide. "He created all this. We are nothing."

Mr. Ellery coughed again yet longer.

"Are ye well, sir? Should I fetch someone for ye?"

Once composed, he laughed. "Nay, my child. 'Tis nothing. It does come and go. The winter approaching is the hardest time for me, but with the spring, all is better." His eyes swept over her face. "Glad I am that *ye* are well. I understand your father shall soon be about." Another cough sounded yet lasted briefly. "Pity."

Grace started at the remark. "Why say ye this?"

Mr. Ellery drew near. "Because he is a vile man and does not deserve your mother."

"Why would ye say such? I know he is not a man of character, but why do ye say anything about my mother . . ." Her breath caught, and her mind whirled—the name is Gerence—Gerry. She recalled what Mrs. Braddock told her of the Ellery brothers.

A slow awakening appeared on his face. "Aye, I can see that ye now know some of the truth. I have loved your mother since we were but children." He pulled his gaze back to the sea. "Yet she had eyes for none but my younger brother, William. When word reached us he died at Naseby, she married Radigan, though I begged her to wed me."

"Mr. Ellery, why *did* my mother wed him? 'Tis something I do not understand. She only tells me he was then a different man."

His sluggish answer came with a rasp. "Melior said she could not wed me because I looked much like my brother, and it would be too painful. She would see his face in me every day." He hesitated yet held her gaze. "Aye, Radigan was kind to her in the beginning before your brother was born." He raised his chin a notch in thought. "When Sebastian was near on three, he looked like . . ."

Grace waited for him to complete the sentence.

Mr. Ellery whispered, "Grace, I dare not reveal any confidence that ye have not heard from your own mother. 'Tis not my place." He half-turned to leave, paused, and said, "I miss him, ye know. It has become a habit to walk these cliffs each night, so that I may fall into exhausted sleep and not remember the terror of that day." His footsteps faded, his silhouette creeping along the edge of the sea.

His words about missing Nick caused slow, agonizing tears to trickle down her cheeks, knowing that her true love was gone forever. Before the tears turned to sobs, a familiar voice intruded upon her privacy.

"Are ye unwell?" Rig asked hoarsely. She moved away to hide her grief, yet he slipped an arm around her shoulders and drew her to him. "Who was that man?"

Grace did not pull away, yet she did not respond to his affection. Rig had awakened something within her. She drew in a shaky breath. "Mr. Ellery."

Rig stiffened and averted his gaze toward the sky.

"Please do not be jealous. He is a dear man, and his family has been friends with my mother's family long before I was born. My mother and he are of an age."

He remained silent, and Grace's concern mounted. Was he a jealous man? She turned and placed her hands flat on his chest. "Mr. Ellery is a kind man."

"Aye. I am certain he is." His voice, shaded with regret, held nay derision.

She cupped his cheek with one hand and placed the other on his shoulder. The stubble of a day's growth was not what she noticed most but the clench of his jaw. It was absurd for him to be jealous over a man of Mr. Ellery's age—the age of her father.

Slow anger bubbled, and she eased away. "I would not have taken ye to be a jealous man."

He dropped his gaze to hers. "Why are ye here alone?"

His question caught her by surprise. "Sebastian is to meet me here as he does each eve, dependent upon his shift at the mines." He stared at her, his eyes shaded by the dark.

"Again, I ask ye, why are ye here alone? Ye spoke to the sky." He swallowed hard "Then, Mr. Ellery came upon ye."

"Ye were *watching* me?"

His expression changed. "That sorry I am, Grace. I did not plan to spy on ye. I arrived before, but ye did not see me. Ye spoke with God. I wanted not to interrupt. Then Mr. Ellery appeared. The two of ye seemed rather intent on your conversation, though I could not hear the words."

Rig offered her a small bow. "Please accept my apologies."

Unsettled emotions tumbled inside her like the turbulent waves below.

"The psalmist wrote of God knowing how many stars there are, and He calls them by their names." Rig took another step from her. "The captain of my ship is a godly man and takes nay man aboard that will not hear the word of God. If God names the stars, think ye not that he knows yours?"

☙❧

The vicar ended the service with prayer, and the villagers filed out, the cold autumn air meeting them in gusts. They scurried a little faster to their warm homes as the sky darkened and a gentle rain fell.

Grace prayed it did not become ice. They would move to the cave tomorrow eve. A hand came upon her shoulder, and she turned to find Arabel.

"Arabel, I did not see ye in church. Where sat ye?"

"Sorry I am, but I did not attend. I came to find ye. Father began rising this morn and attempts to walk on the hour. I do fear he will rise fully by the morrow."

Grace took in this revelation. "Aye, but shall it not take a few days afore he has the strength to move down the stairs?"

"Most likely. But I do not want to count on that. He is most stubborn." She looped an arm through Grace's and whispered into her ear. "Adam did tell me it is time for us to *depart*."

Grace's eyes widened. They had only taken Arabel into

their confidence since the reconciliation. "When did ye speak with Adam?"

Arabel's gaze dropped, and embarrassment briefly flashed across her face. "We have spoken often since ye did tell me of Father's actions." She cleared her throat. "Adam is a most kindly man."

Grace gave her a sidelong look. "Aye. He is." A blast of icy wind buffeted them, and they huddled closer, tightening their cloaks. "I near forgot. Sebastian read your list of names from Father's business associates and has removed many yet three remain. He is trying to gain a sample of their writing, so we may compare." She lowered her voice more. "When in hand, he shall bring them to the cave."

Arriving at the tavern's rear door, Arabel placed a hand to halt Grace. "Adam did say their ship shall be ready to sail in less than a fortnight. He believes he and I should be the last to arrive at the cave, and much later, so as not to draw attention to our activity."

Grace could not decipher the feelings stirring within her. Did she feel fear, excitement, or both? Also, on the edge of her thoughts was what may be growing between her sister and Adam Gittens.

⚜

The day arrived for the five of them to begin life in the cavern, short though it may be. The men had done all possible to make them comfortable. A fire at night was questionable, afraid any small crevice may reveal a sliver of light. Cold would be their constant companion, but the men had provided well for their comfort by supplying blankets and cloaks.

Eulalia became her confidant with the approval of the others. The woman saddened for their absence, yet she was pleased they would end their lives of strife.

Grace noticed Wilmont was uncommonly nervous but did not question her. When Sebastian came into the kitchen near the end of the day, she noted a look passed between them. Something she had never seen before.

Did they have feelings for one another? Is that why her brother would not accompany his family?

She shook the thought away, believing it was her own unsettled emotions. Just as Arabel had told her what their father was about, near on every hour she could hear stumbling footsteps coming from his chamber. With each attempt, they sounded more sure and steady. Grace prayed he would not decide to maneuver the stairs on this day. A sudden image came upon her of him lying at the bottom of the stairs, taking his last breath.

Grace closed her eyes. "God, please forgive me for that thought. In truth, I do not wish him harm. Open his eyes to see what he has become."

A firm hand rested on her shoulder. "My dear, do not upset yourself. Your father's life is of his own making. But a prayer for him cannot hurt. God can change any heart. Remember the apostle Paul?"

Grace nodded. She wanted to believe her father could change but had difficulty convincing herself that he would ever desire it.

When she took a salver of food and drink to Sebastian, Adam, and Rig, they spoke few words, knowing what lay heavy upon each other's minds. The time was at hand.

The wind howled around the tavern, windows rattling. When a new customer arrived, the icy draught shot through Grace's shabby dress, making her shiver.

When the tavern was empty save for Adam, who waited patiently for Arabel, Grace cleared his table and spoke near his ear. "My sister said she would meet ye on the path at the appointed hour. We should all be settled by then." She made one last swipe with her cloth. "Adam, thank ye."

He presented her with his beautiful smile, sincerity shining in his coffee brown eyes.

As Grace made her way to the kitchen, the door of the tavern burst open and rebounded against the wall. A tall, burly man unknown to Grace shouted, "There be a murder at the cliffs. We need men, ropes, and torches."

When the man scanned the room and saw only Adam, he halted and stared at his meager choice of only one man.

Adam stood. "Aye, where are we off to? I have two strong hands." He sent Grace a look full of meaning. He would meet Arabel as agreed upon.

She nodded, and he grabbed his coat and left to aid the others. Her hands trembled as she carried the heavy salver to the kitchen. Eulalia was donning her cloak alongside Wilmont and Caye.

"Good eve." Grace met each woman's gaze and then rested on Eulalia's tearful one.

A slight hitch laced Eulalia's tone. "Good eve, child. Have a care."

The three women walked out together, Wilmont and Caye

chatting, their feet dragging from the day's weariness.

Grace arrived at the cottage, surprised to find the windows bright with candlelight and several men standing in front. What could be amiss at this late hour?

Mr. Cragoe, the constable, broke through the crowd and stood before her. He had always been kind—well, he had never been *unkind*—but he now wore a deep scowl. "Grace, where have ye been this eve?"

She peered over his shoulder at the men staring at her, some with sympathetic looks, some with questioning gazes. "At the tavern as always. I have been there since early morn, sir."

A glint of understanding passed fleetingly over his face before he pulled on his mask of authority. "Well, aye, but where be your brother and his new friend?"

"I am certain I have nay idea, sir. They were in the tavern earlier this eve."

He crossed his arms over his thick chest. "At what time did they depart?"

"Sir, I was but busy waiting on hungry and thirsty men and have nay chance to inspect the time." She tugged her cloak tighter against the frigid wind. "May I please know what 'tis about?" She lifted her chin toward the crowd.

"A body is being lifted from the rocks below the cliff now, and we shall soon know the man's identity."

Grace's mind immediately traveled to Mr. Ellery. Perhaps the poor man had slipped while walking the path in the night. She prayed it was not so.

A shout came from the dark, and all eyes turned toward the

man who had come to the Sands seeking help. He took long strides toward them.

"Aye, the man be dead." He caught his breath. "'Tis Radigan Atwood."

Chapter Fourteen

Olivia parted with Teffeny in the mid-morning light and hurried along the lane leading to the church. She'd thanked her for the insight regarding the possibility of leasing the Sands to the Trerose Historical Society. When she praised Teffeny on the clever idea, wishing she'd thought of it herself, the woman blushed with embarrassment.

Teffeny had replied, "Love is blind, my dear."

The comment had made Olivia laugh and complete it with something she'd heard long ago. "Love is blind, deaf, dumb, and has no sense of smell." Teffeny's laughter, most likely heard all the way through the village, lifted her spirits.

There was a lightness in her step as she skipped up the path when her mind twirled to the tea with Mrs. Atwood—Hortense—realizing she'd never gotten around to asking about her grandparents. They'd been too caught up in the old ledgers. She shrugged and made a mental note to have Luke remind her to ask.

Olivia stepped into the vacant church, sunlight slanting through the stained-glass windows sending swords of multi-colored light crisscrossing in mid-air. Her gaze slid to the floor in front of the altar. The effect was astonishing. It reminded her of an impressionist painting, the colors melting into one another. It was an awe-inspiring display, with the peaceful silence suspended around her.

"Looks like a tapestry, doesn't it?" She jumped at Luke's voice.

Her hand flew to her heart. "Luke! You scared the life out of me."

In two long strides, he stood in front of her. "I apologize, love. I thought you heard my footsteps."

He didn't touch her, but she felt as if he had. Their gazes stayed upon one another until voices drew nearer. The church door opened with a creak, and Beryl and Sheryl entered.

Luke took one pace away from her, breaking their contact.

The sisters strolled down the aisle, both giving them a 'good morning' greeting. Olivia held her breath, her gaze on Sheryl.

Beryl extended her arms. "We've come bearing gifts." She presented a prettily wrapped package, curling yellow ribbon bounced with the movement. "I've baked fruit scones."

Before Olivia could voice her thanks, Sheryl did likewise toward Luke. "Vicar," she cleared her throat. "I've baked your favorite—fruitcake. But I found a new recipe and want your opinion."

Luke smiled and took the cake from Sheryl. "That's very kind of you both. Thank you."

The quiet grew thicker. Sheryl's head dropped, and she tangled her fingers together. "I'd like to apologize." Her chin trembled. "Beryl explained what I cannot remember."

"Yes, we have banned the sherry from the cottage. Even for cooking. Just as an extra precaution." Beryl smiled at her sister. "Things will differ from now on."

Luke patted the top of the fruitcake box, then the scones Olivia held. "Why don't we take these treats to the kitchen and have a cup of tea?"

The twins' faces lit with pleasure. "That would be lovely, Vicar," Sheryl said with a nod.

He offered his arm, and she slanted a questioning look at her sister. Beryl nodded in agreement, taking Olivia by the arm, and led the way.

Just as they settled at the table with cups of smuggler's tea, the phone in the adjacent office trilled.

Luke rose to answer it, and Olivia leaned toward Sheryl. "Are you all right?"

Sheryl's face pinked. "I am. Thank you for being so forgiving. I honestly don't recall what I said to you and the vicar." She looked at her sister. "But Beryl told me all. I'm so ashamed. I wish the two of you the best." Her face blushed again. "Would it be proper for us—*me*—to come to the wedding?"

Olivia jerked her head around to peer at Beryl, then back at Sheryl. "What would give you the impression we're to marry?"

Beryl pulled a face. "Dear, we may be old, but we're not daft. It only takes a moment to see the way you look at one another."

Sheryl shrugged. "I hate to agree with my sister, but she's right. And we've known the vicar since he was in nappies. He's never, mind you—never, had a girlfriend before. Well, not for long. They've always been friends." She reached to tap Olivia's hand. "You're the one for him. That's enough about that."

Luke strode into the room and reclaimed his seat. "What's enough about that?"

Sheryl opened her mouth, and Beryl tapped her arm in disagreement. "Nothing. Just girl talk."

When her face heated, Olivia kept her gaze on her cup for a few moments.

Luke quirked a brow. "That was Hortense Atwood. She's on her way over. Said she had something to share with you." He looked at Olivia. "Something to do with your great grandparents."

"Really? I can't wait to hear."

Beryl and Sheryl sent her a curious stare.

Luke's brows rose. "I suppose we'll know soon. I'll get another cup and when she arrives, we'll tuck into those delicacies."

They chatted until they heard the church door open, accompanied by the sound of Hortense's wheelchair and a pair of footsteps. Luke jumped from his seat, and when he returned, he pushed Hortense into the room.

"I sent Laura to take care of the shopping while Hortense visits with us." He threw a glance at Olivia. "I told her we'd bring her home."

Olivia smiled at the woman. "That is certainly a good idea. I'm intrigued by what you have to share."

Luke situated the woman at the table and poured her tea.

Hortense peered into the cup and smiled at Luke with a deep sigh. "Oh, my boy. Smuggler's tea just as I prefer it. If I were fifty years younger, you wouldn't stand a chance. I was rather pretty at that age." She giggled and brought the cup to her lips, eyes closed with pleasure. "*Mmm* . . . lovely taste."

"Caffeine this late in the day!" Sheryl shot her a dangerous look. "Horty, that'll keep you up half the night."

Hortense blasted her with a killing look. "Sheryl, you really must rein in that tongue of yours. It's going to get you in a peck of trouble one day, my dear."

Olivia and Luke shared shocked expressions, waiting for the explosion to follow, turning their gazes to Sheryl. To their surprise, the woman released a hearty laugh.

"You've got me there, Horty. Already got the peck. I'm better now."

Hortense screwed up her mouth. "Ditched the sherry, did you?"

Beryl smiled and patted her sister on the back. "Yes, she has. Finally."

"Good." Hortense huffed. "Now on to bigger fish." She removed a thin navy folder from the pocket hanging on the side of her chair and placed it in front of Olivia. "Here are copies from my genealogy files. I used to be a real stickler for detail and organization." She tapped one temple. "I *was* quite organized."

Olivia refrained from voicing any comments, curious what the file contained. Her eyes caught Luke's. "Open it. Beryl and Sheryl may have some memories to share as well."

With trembling fingers, Olivia rifled through the papers. Seeing the Flowers and Knox surnames caused her heart to skitter in her chest. At a glance, she noted the article she'd seen about the RAF pilots. Hortense had done her homework. Olivia's eyes trailed across the pages each one more interesting than the last. When she finally brought her gaze to Hortense, moisture had gathered in her eyes. "Thank you for this." She waved a page in front of her. "I've just learned more about my grandparents in minutes than I have ever before. You are such a blessing."

The kindly woman squeezed Olivia's hand. "I'm so glad to help, my dear. These are copies, so please take them for your files."

Olivia thanked her, and during this interchange, Beryl and Sheryl perused some papers and shared a glance that Olivia caught. "Do you have something to share as well, ladies?"

Beryl's eyes widened. "Would your grandmother be Susan Flowers?"

Olivia's smile widened. "Yes, she is. We spoke a little of her the night you came to eat at the cottage—remember?"

"We know her!" Sheryl grabbed Beryl's hand. "Why didn't we recall our connection the night we discussed this?"

Beryl's eyes lifted as if deep in thought. "Seems like we were rather tired that evening." Her face squeezed into a grimace. "We don't do well in the evening."

"I'm sure they know why, Beryl. After all, we're no spring

chicks any longer."

"Nevertheless, Susan was but a small thing when her parents moved." Sheryl laughed. "We played together every day."

Olivia blinked as tears threatened. "How wonderful."

Beryl straightened. "We are a few years elder, but playing with our cousins was always a treat."

Olivia stared at her. "Cousins?"

Sheryl's eyes sparkled. "Yes dear. Although distant, we are relations."

Olivia grabbed Sheryl into a hug. "We are cousins!"

Luke's laugh echoed in the room. "This is amazing."

Beryl slapped her hands on the table. "Olivia, your great grandfather, Lawrence Steven Flowers, married our cousin Elizabeth."

Sheryl bent over the papers her sister perused. "After the war ended, your great-grandparents spirited Susan away to America."

Throughout the exchange, Hortense remained silent, her eyes misting. Olivia asked, "Are you okay?"

The elder woman shook her head, as if clearing her thoughts. "Yes, dear. I am in awe of how God brings circumstances together so seamlessly." She awkwardly stretched her hand toward the stack of information. Olivia helped by moving it closer to her side of the table. Hortense rifled through them until she hesitated over an ancestral chart, her crooked finger skimming until she stopped and tapped a name with a manicured nail.

"Sebastian Atwood was my husband's—" She turned her eyes heavenward, deep in thought. "—It's so hard to remember the numbers, but I think he was his eleventh great-grandfather or something like that. Hortense pushed the chart to Olivia.

Olivia scanned the names until she found Sebastian. Carefully noting the dates and family members, she released a small gasp and swallowed hard.

Luke rose and stood behind her chair, leaning over her shoulder. "Grace Atwood? His sister?"

A chill swept through Olivia. This had to be *her* Grace. The dates coincided with the dates in the diary. And she kept mentioning Sebastian.

Hortense's brows furrowed. "What diary are you speaking of?"

Excitement bubbled through Olivia. "My grandmother found a diary in my great-grandmother's things when she was a girl and thought it a ragged old book of no consequence. It stayed in the attic until a few weeks ago when I visited her and rummaged through her genealogy records."

Hortense's eyes widened with interest. "May I see it?"

"Certainly." She retrieved her bag and gently removed the prized book.

Hortense put on a pair of cotton gloves she retrieved from her wheelchair pocket and took the diary as if were a rare china cup. When she opened it, she gasped. "This is Grace Ellery's diary."

Olivia sat there stunned. "Ellery?"

"Look at the pedigree chart, my dear."

Olivia glanced at Grace's name again, noting it showed she was the sibling to Sebastian. She kept searching, then caught a footnote.

Grace Atwood married Nicholas Ellery . . . January . . .

The day and year were lost by wear and time. Olivia turned to another chart and found the Ellery name. She recalled the name from the diary and Nicholas noted in the same entry. Her breath caught. Grace had mentioned Nicholas's death some years before. But she ended up marrying Nicholas. How could that be?

Olivia voiced her confusion, and Luke agreed. "You're right. That's a mystery."

Hortense beamed. "I may be able to shed some light on that." She pressed her lips together, suppressing a laugh. "Could also shed some light on the fact that this chart says Grace's mother, Melior Atwood married Mr. Gerence Ellery, Nicholas's father." The woman tenderly flipped through the diary pages, occasionally releasing a note of approval or disapproval.

Luke watched her intensely. "Hortense, you can read that?" He pointed at the diary.

"My boy, I've been reading old handwriting since before your mother had any notion of you."

He kissed her wrinkled cheek. "Hortense, my love, you are an enigma."

"I know, dear." She kept flipping pages, her sharp eyes widening from time to time. "Mind you, they have passed stories down through the family, so I cannot prove all of it. But some are too juicy not to." She giggled like a girl.

Sheryl and Beryl busied themselves going over all the charts, occasionally commenting they didn't know *this* person was related to *that* one, or they weren't aware there were graves that old in the village cemetery.

Hortense sputtered, "I've a copy in there somewhere with the grave marker locations of each person."

Olivia started at the comment. "Truly?" The thought of actually seeing the last resting places of her ancestors that came from Trerose more than three hundred years ago sent a thrill through her.

XIII

Grace closed her eyes, fighting the dizziness attempting to overcome her. The cottage door creaked on its hinges, and her mother stood framed in the light. She stepped out, and Grace rushed into her arms.

Melior moved her daughter to arm's length, and their gazes held. "Grace, is what they say truth? Is your father dead?"

"Aye, Mother." Grace pointed to the man bearing the news. "He has just returned and confirmed 'tis truth."

Mrs. Braddock hobbled to stand beside them. "My dears, what goes on? Cragoe's men came to me cottage and said there be an accident. A stream of them keep appearing on me doorstep asking questions of what I know naught."

Melior led the old woman to the bench beside the cottage, shooed away the two men sitting there, and aided her to sit.

"Thank ye, dear Mellie. As I was saying, they asked me if I seen or heard anything. I telt them I have not, yet they keep coming. Wearing me to the bone, they is."

Grace gestured for her mother to sit, then knelt in front of them. "Mrs. Braddock, did they ask anything further?"

"Aye. Wanted to know if I seen Sebastian or that tall handsome friend of his come up the path today."

Grace and her mother shared a startled look.

"They said a man was murdered late last eve."

A fire lit in Melior's green eyes. "How could they possibly know at what time it occurred?"

Grace laid a comforting hand on her knee. "Mother, 'tis something we shall ask Doctor Keast. He would know of such things."

As if summoned, he appeared from the blackness and into the window's light. He nodded a greeting, then spoke with a calmness that defied his disheveled appearance.

"I would rather tell ye all a good eve but 'tis not to be. I was summoned to Penrose Manor to determine if the man found was to be revived, but he was dead before he hit the rocks below. Most likely soon after the sun did set."

Grace rose and stood at his side. "How do ye know?"

Doctor Keast sucked in a long breath and released it slowly. "When a man is stabbed so near the heart, it takes but minutes to perish."

Melior flattened her hands onto her chest. "Stabbed?"

"Aye. I fear so, though the knife was not found. Although, by daylight, it mayhap turn up."

"Humph!" Mrs. Braddock said. "Do not surprise me the man ended his days thus—someone helped him along his way." She tossed her thick ash-gray braid over her shoulder, eyes fierce.

Doctor Keast's posture stiffened. "Mrs. Braddock!"

"Do not snap at me, ye old goat! Ye are a beetle-head if ye believe there shall be any grieving going on 'round these shores for that hateful man."

The doctor opened his mouth, but Grace placed a hand on his arm. "'Tis nay need to pretend he was liked. A hard thing to say so, but 'tis truth."

His sympathetic gaze brought Grace some comfort. He gave them his condolences and left to return to his bed, advising they do the same.

Mrs. Braddock rose. "I am to my bed as well. Ye girls should be abed, though I doubt not sleep shall evade ye this eve." She hobbled away when Grace stopped her and asked one of the men who worked in the mines to escort the woman home.

One by one, the men slowly dispersed, leaving only the constable and Matthew. Melior strode to them and said something Grace could not hear, then came back to the cottage and made to enter. "Please stay here, Grace. I am to prepare tea for these men. Your father is at Penrose Manor. They took him there as it was the nearest place for the doctor to examine him." Her mother's breath caught. "He is being moved to the church . . . once prepared . . ." She went inside and thumped the door shut behind her.

Grace collapsed onto the bench, elbows on her knees, and buried her face in her palms. Tears would not come, but her entire body shivered. The cottage door opened, and her mother's voice sounded as if coming from faraway, calling the men in to have a hot drink.

Minutes later, a cup of tea was placed in her hand. Relief, fear, and gratitude all joined to create a storm inside her.

Mr. Cragoe's men asking about Sebastian and Rig troubled her. Were they under suspicion?

The image of Sebastian's angry face appeared to her when he discovered Grace had attempted to aid their mother against Radigan's drunken anger. Her mother had cowered before her father, blood on her hand.

Sebastian's words haunted her. *Lift not a hand to either of them again, or ye shall be sent over the cliffs.*

Fear, as she had never known, tore at her. Should Sebastian hang for his death, it would be unbearable. The murderer most likely sent the body over the edge with the hopes it would wash away—or vultures would . . . She gagged at the gruesome image.

A flash of insight came to her. Mayhap the murderer was interrupted by someone and had to do the most expedient thing. Her eyes widened, and she drew in a sharp breath.

Mr. Ellery. He said he had taken to walking the coastal path at night. Perhaps he met a man walking home from the mines, or a stranger, thinking nothing amiss as men traveled this way much.

Grace bolted to her feet, the cup of tea spiraling to the ground, and toward the manor, nay longer shivering, urgency rippling through her. Her skirts whipped at her legs as she turned inland across the moors. Spiked gorse snagged her dress, but she cared not. She prayed that Mr. Ellery had seen someone—anyone—that would take the blame from Sebastian and Rig.

The realization that her fear equally distributed between the two men alarmed her and pushed her faster toward the well-lit manor ahead, the lower windows ablaze with light. When she arrived, several men were astride horses stomping the ground as if eager to be away. Mr. Cragoe stood atop the broad steps of Penrose, directing the men to search for the murderer.

Horses shot across the moors in every direction, and Grace made her way up the steps to Mr. Cragoe. He crossed his arms over his chest. "Why are ye here, Grace?"

Her breath came in gasps. "I must speak with Mr. Ellery."

"Anything ye have to say about your father's death may be said to me, child."

Anger and frustration emboldened her. "Nay, sir. This is different. I must speak with him at once."

The man narrowed his eyes, nearly on her level. He was not large, but his awareness of the power he yielded in the county puffed him up like an angry brock. "Very well. Come along." He made for the door, expecting her to follow.

Grace was taken aback that he did not knock but simply entered. The butler, John Wyhon, walked across the entry, his gray hair ruffled, shoulders slumped.

"Where is Mr. Ellery? This young lady would like to have a word with him."

The servant smiled wearily. "This way, Mistress Grace. Mr. Ellery is in his study. It appears he shall have nay rest this night."

"Nor ye, Mr. Wyhon." She gave the man a smile. When she

drew closer to him, she whispered, "I am that sorry ye and the entire household will lose your night's rest."

"Thank ye." He stopped at the study door. "Please accept my condolences for the loss of your father."

She nodded and noted the glint in his eyes.

He knocked softly and waited until Mr. Ellery said, "Enter."

"Mistress Grace Atwood to see you, sir." He stepped back and made room for her to enter and closed the door behind him. His voice carried as he instructed the constable to wait in the parlor or step outside.

Mr. Ellery motioned for her to be seated in front of the massive oak desk. He shuffled papers in front of him until they were neatly stacked and rested his clasped hands on top.

"To what do I owe this pleasure at an unseemly hour?" His voice was not unkind but cool.

Grace eased onto the plush yet worn upholstered chair. The weariness of the day filled her as the comfort surrounded her. If only she could curl up and sleep for days.

"Sir, I am that sorry to disturb ye, but I must ask a question . . ."

The door burst open and in marched the constable. "Mr. Ellery, I must insist that I be privy to what this woman deems most important to seek ye about at such an hour. I am suspicious it involves this murder."

Mr. Ellery raised a hand, palm out, and stood. "Mr. Cragoe, how dare ye interrupt a private conversation that does not involve ye. Please leave."

At that moment, Wyhon entered. "Mr. Ellery, I must seek

your forgiveness. I stepped into the other room, and this man took advantage of my absence."

"There is nay need to apologize, Wyhon. Please escort the constable from our property."

Two servants, younger and stronger than the elderly butler, now stood at attention on either side of the doorway.

The constable straightened. "'Tis most unseemly—"

"Nay, Mr. Cragoe, ye have overstepped the boundaries of proper behavior. Until this moment I have given ye leave to near take over my home and grounds because a murder took place on my property, but I shall *not* have ye seizing anything any longer. Leave now. I shall contact the magistrate to speak of your conduct."

A flash of concern crossed the man's face, and he stormed out passing between the two guards, who promptly followed him.

Grace pushed herself from the chair. "I am most apologetic that I have caused such a spectacle. Please forgive me."

"Nay. Rest. Ye do appear weary, child." He regained his seat and rested his head against the back of the chair. "As would be expected, considering the circumstances, that man is over much full of himself. I care not for him."

One side of Grace's mouth lifted in amusement. The action astonished her. How could she find pleasure in any of this? Her heart thudded, and she sank onto her chair. She peered up to see Mr. Ellery's eyes on her.

"We shall not be interrupted again. Tell me what troubles ye."

Grace cleared her throat. "I am to understand that my

father was stabbed and then pushed over the edge of the cliff to conceal his body."

"Aye. 'Tis what I have been told." As he settled deeper into his chair, it released a creak.

"Ye told me walking the coast path each eve has become a custom of late." She considered how to form her next words.

"Aye?" His tone was impatient, fatigue etched on his face.

"The constable asked of Sebastian and Rig's whereabouts." She tarried over her thoughts. "Were ye on the path last eve?"

His brows rose.

"Nay. I meant to continue by inquiring if ye saw anyone else. Whether known or unknown."

Mr. Ellery levered himself from his chair and strolled around the desk to the wide window overlooking the front of the house toward the cliffs, his back to her.

"Why do ye ask me this?"

The question dismayed her. Was it not obvious?

"And who is Rig?"

Grace blinked rapidly. "He is a sailor that has befriended Sebastian." She tried to read his reflection in the glass.

"When ye said his name, there was fondness in it. Yet not with the same fondness ye speak of your brother."

Again, she grew confused at what this inquiry had to do with her reason for being here. "He is a kind-hearted man. I, too, have become . . ."

"Close?" He strode to stand by her chair. "Sorry I am. Other than our brief interaction at the cliffs, we have not spoken in years, and now we seem to be thrown together by providence."

Grace nodded as Mr. Ellery continued, "Ye are a lovely young woman and at one time I thought ye and Nicholas would grow . . ." He pivoted on his heel and recaptured his chair. "Nay need to revive old memories. God's will be done."

This time, his smile was tender and genuine—not forced. "Let me think on my most recent stroll." He leaned his head back in the chair and closed his eyes, remaining so as he spoke. "It was near on midnight when I left the manor, and I held to the same order as usual. First, straight from Penrose, toward the cliffs above the cave . . ."

Grace took in a shaky breath at the mention of the cave. Had he seen their comings and goings?

He kept his head reclined but opened his eyes. "Grace, are ye well? Ye appear wan of a sudden."

"Only fatigued. I am well." She fisted her hands in the folds of her skirt.

His brows drew closer, but he continued, "I paused there as I always do and thought of Nicholas." He hesitated. "I turned south and walked along the sea until I reached the stone fence at the border of my estate, then turned west to circle along the moors and pastures that lead to the manor."

She held her breath, waiting for him to reveal whether he had seen anyone.

"There were voices that night, but the darkness kept them hidden. Though they were on Penrose property, I see nay reason to hinder men and women from taking the path to and from their work. 'Tis understood among the villagers that I show them nay contempt in doing so."

"Did ye recognize any of the voices?"

"Nay."

Grace thanked him and stood, looking him directly in the eyes. "Thank ye for your time. I am that sorry ye have been so disturbed as well as your household. I was hopeful that ye may have seen some stranger that could have been the murderer and put all this to rest."

"I can see why ye would hope thus. Give my sympathies to your mother." Sadness shone from his glistening eyes. "I wished for nothing other than happiness for her. Life can be filled with such tragedy."

"Aye. Most assuredly." Grace strode to the door. "We have both had our share."

Grace departed Penrose Manor and returned home—her now peaceful home, which she had reflected upon much of the walk, yet she also remained troubled regarding Sebastian and Rig.

Chapter Fifteen

Olivia answered her insistent phone, one hand on Grace's journal. "Hello."

Angie's uninterested voice teased Olivia. "Can you pick me up at the train station tomorrow?"

"Angie! You're actually coming? Why didn't you let me know before you made your reservations?"

"Dear *friend,* I just this minute made them. I conned Jennifer into filling in for me." Angie slurped a drink, the sound loud in Olivia's ear. "With wedding season behind us, she can handle any photoshoots for a week without me."

"I'm glad you're coming, Angie. I have much to tell you."

"Rightly so, since you're always too busy to talk when I call." She cleared her throat melodramatically. "I also want to meet this man you found."

"I haven't *found* a man." Olivia closed the diary and

reached for her cup.

Luke came into the room with another local history book. "Love, I've—"

"Ah ha! I knew it!"

Olivia shot Luke a glare. "We're doing historical research. Don't get so suspicious."

"Me. Suspicious? Hardly," Angie said with faux hurt in her voice.

Olivia changed the subject while Luke watched her, wearing a wide grin. He loudly kissed her cheek.

"What was that noise?"

"Luke dropped a book."

"Hmm. Didn't sound like a book to me."

Olivia slapped at Luke's arm and placed a finger to her lips. "If you're through with the inquisition, give me your arrival time, and I'll see what I can do about picking you up." She coughed. "Unless I conveniently forget."

Olivia could envision Angie raising her hands in defeat.

"You win." Silence. "Until I arrive." She feigned an evil, dramatic laugh, and after giving the arrival information, she hung up.

"The infamous friend, Angie, I presume?" Luke sat beside Olivia and draped his arm over her shoulders.

"Afraid so." She leaned her head onto his shoulder. "I hope you won't be too irritated with her. Angie's very protective of me."

"A good friend to have." He kissed the top of her head. "Unless—"

Olivia lifted her gaze and sent him a wide-eyed stare. "Please finish that sentence."

"Unless she's overbearing."

She gave the statement some consideration. "No. I don't think so, although Angie will question you. It's all in how you respond."

Luke placed his right hand over his heart. "I'll do my best."

Olivia returned her attention to the journal. "Thank you."

"Hmm. Thank you . . ." He put his elbow on the desk and propped his chin in his hand. ". . . my dear, my love, the object of my desire, etc."

Olivia laughed. "You are incorrigible—my dear."

With an exaggerated sigh, he said, "That's more like it."

Their eyes held for a moment, and Luke focused on her lips. Olivia eased toward him. It was a while before they drew apart, Olivia's face heating.

"I love seeing your expression after we kiss. It's inspiring."

Olivia's hand lay against his chest. "How so?" She couldn't pull her gaze from his mesmerizing sea-blue eyes.

"Makes me want to do it again." He repeated the action.

She found the breath to speak again. "So, do I leave you with an *aftereffect*?"

A side of his mouth lifted in a heart-stopping grin. "You take my breath away."

ଓଃଡ଼

Olivia strode across the small car park at Looe Station and settled onto a bench at the end of the platform just as her phone chimed. It was Luke texting an apology for not accompanying her. A parishioner had called at the last moment requesting the vicar to call on him.

Luke said had it not been an elderly man who rarely called on him, he would have requested a visit later in the day.

She answered his text as Angie's train pulled into the station and rose to meet her friend, watching the passengers flow onto the pavement. When Angie's straight blonde bob first appeared, Olivia's grin widened until she saw a tall, well-built young man carrying Angie's brilliant yellow bag over his shoulder. She was lit up like a Christmas tree.

Olivia found her voice and called out to her friend. Angie turned in her direction, and she grabbed the man's arm and led him toward her. Teffeny suddenly appeared from the car park and headed toward them.

"Christian!" Teffeny flung herself into the man's arms. The kiss they shared told Olivia all she needed to know. Angie hung back, a sheepish smile on her round face.

Teffeny, her arm looped through the man's, bounded toward Olivia with Angie following.

"Olivia Griffin, this is Christian Salisbury. My friend from the States."

Angie came to stand by Olivia. "Can you believe we were seatmates? We got to talking and discovered he was coming to visit Teffeny, whom I've come to know via our phone conversations. Isn't it amazing—serendipity!"

Olivia stood in shock, her gaze vacillating from Teffeny to Angie, who introduced herself.

Still in bemused surprise, Olivia looked at Christian. "It's nice to meet you. It's astonishing how this all came about."

"Absolutely. Must be fate."

"God works in mysterious ways," Teffeny said, then turned to Olivia. "Why didn't you tell me Angie was arriving today? I would've come with you."

"Well, if my *friend* had given me some advance notice, I would have."

Angie grimaced. "Yeah. Sorry about that. Wanted to make sure I'd actually be able to come."

"All is well now," Christian said cheerfully. "And I'm starved. Got a good pub in Trerose?"

Olivia and Teffeny called out in unison, "To The Pilchard!"

CB80

Olivia steered her rental behind Teffeny, following her to Trerose. She briefly turned to look at Angie.

"Spill it. What's with you and Christian?"

Angie's expression shadowed with hurt. "Nothing. We met on the train and began talking about why we were in Cornwall. The next thing we found out was we're here to visit you and Teffeny."

Olivia chewed her bottom lip. "You just seemed awfully chummy."

"You've grown too suspicious. He's a nice guy. Too young for me, anyway."

Olivia started. "Teffeny is older than *you*."

"From what you've told me, it's not by much. What—three years?"

"Hmm. I guess you're right. But doesn't he look mid-twenties?"

Angie shook her head. "He looks young, but he speaks and acts a lot older."

Olivia shrugged. "Perhaps he's older than we think. Anyway, it's none of our business. Teffeny is a wonderful person. You'll like her."

Once settled at The Pilchard, Olivia's phone chimed, Luke asking where she was. She answered, and within five minutes, he came through the pub door. Her eyes lit when she spotted him weaving his way through the crowded tables.

Angie didn't miss it. "What's that longing look for? Did you spot a cheesecake?" She turned and saw Luke. "Oh, that must be *him*."

Olivia kicked Angie under the table, an 'ouch' escaping her friend before she stated her favorite witticism—*'Could eat him up with a spoon.'* Usually reserved for cute children, she occasionally directed it toward a handsome man. A sudden thought occurred—the quip could've come from Sheryl. She and Angie would probably get on well.

Luke pulled a chair from a nearby table and squeezed it between Olivia and Angie. He discreetly reached under the table and took Olivia's hand in his.

"Good evening to you all." He nodded at each person.

Teffeny gave Olivia a questioning gaze before introducing Angie, then Christian.

When Olivia recovered her voice, she thanked Teffeny for the introduction and peered at Luke. "It's a rather interesting story about Angie and Christian meeting on the train."

Luke pressed his lips together and nodded. "Ahh. Providence."

Angie perked. "Yes! I said serendipity."

An awkward silence hung over the table when a server approached. "What can I get you this evening?"

Luke looked at the middle-aged woman. "Hello, Mattie. Table service tonight?"

"Yeah, bit of a crush, so Bill thought it best." She notched her chin up. "What you having, Vicar?"

"Take the ladies' orders first while I have a look-see." He picked up Olivia's menu while the others ordered, her hand still clasped in his.

After Olivia ordered, she inspected Luke's profile until he lifted his menu to Mattie and gave his order. Her gaze traveled to Angie, and her friend narrowed her eyes, one side of her lips lifting, giving Olivia a smug *'Just as I thought'* glare. Shoving her chair back, Olivia released Luke's hand and rose. "I'll be right back."

Olivia zigzagged her way to the loo and locked herself into a stall. She rested her forehead on the back of the door. Tears were not what she needed now nor did she feel like crying. She pulled in a deep breath and released it. A lecture on forming such a serious relationship so soon after meeting was not something she wanted to hear from her best friend. How could she explain that this felt right? After praying about it, God had given her peace.

A timid voice called to her. "Olivia?"

She breathed a sigh of relief. "I'll be right out." She squared her shoulders and cleared her throat, stepping out to face

Teffeny.

"Are you okay? Luke said you looked pale and asked if I'd look in on you."

"He didn't ask Angie?"

Teffeny considered her for a moment. "I may be jumping to conclusions, but I sensed he thought she may be the source of your distress."

"He said that?" Olivia's insides warmed and twisted in equal measure. If he pegged her unease so precisely, he really did understand her—cared for her. Or was she too easy to read? "Is that what you think too? Am I that much of an open book?" A shattering thought struck her. "Do you think Angie read that as well?

"No. I considered nothing. I just thought you had to go to the loo." Teffeny's signature laugh echoed in the small space. "What is going on? Why would Angie make you anxious? She's your best friend."

Olivia washed her hands absentmindedly, her head bent, studying the sink.

Teffeny leaned against the wall. "Are you concerned Angie won't accept your decision?"

Olivia dried her hands, keeping her eyes averted. "Maybe."

Teffeny gently touched her on the shoulder. "Look at me."

Olivia obeyed, and she saw compassion in her friend's pale gray eyes.

"You and I have only known each other for a short while, yet we are the best of friends. Aren't we?"

Olivia nodded, her eyes stinging with unshed tears.

"Then why is it so hard to believe that you and Luke could have connected so quickly? Though at the very beginning it was a bit tumultuous, but there was definitely a reason behind that, and you've worked through it. He's an amazing man. You two are well-suited."

Olivia thawed at the kind words. She pulled Teffeny into a hug. "You are a good friend. Thank you for that—and your pep talk. It really doesn't matter what Angie thinks. I believe God brought us together. Not only Luke and me, but you and me as well."

"Yeah. God kinda knows what He's doing. Even when we don't. Take the gift He's offered you and live a brilliant life with the vicar."

"Hard act to follow. A vicar's wife. I never would've imagined I'd be in those shoes." Olivia's heart skipped a beat at the admission. A *vicar's* wife?

"Let's eat. My stomach sounds like my mum's cat right before she had kittens."

Olivia couldn't suppress a smile, and Teffeny returned it with a girlish laugh. "We'd better get out there before Luke comes in *here* looking for you. It would be the scandal of the village. Headlines read *'Vicar trips into ladies' loo'!*"

They arrived just as their food did.

Angie's eyes sparkled when Olivia looked at her old friend. Angie said, "Just like Livi. Right on time for the food."

A crowd across the pub sang happy birthday to a girl who beamed with joy. Luke joined in and soon the others at their table followed suit, reveling in the merry occasion. It was exactly what Olivia needed to lay her own problems aside.

Luke nudged her shoulder and whispered, "All well now?" His eyes held no ridicule, only concern.

Olivia answered, "All is well. Thanks for sending Teffeny."

His minty breath tickled her ear, making her insides tingle. "I'd like to kiss you right now."

"You scandalize me, Vicar. What would that do to your reputation?"

"Ruin me, most likely." He waggled his brows. "But it's worth the risk." His expression softened. "May I walk you home?"

Olivia felt the heat of him so near—wanted him close. A throat was cleared, and they looked up.

"We're ready for the vicar to say a blessing," Angie piped up. "I'm feeling outnumbered here. Surrounded by syrupy couples."

Olivia noticed Christian's arm over the back of Teffeny's chair, and with Luke whispering romantically in her ear, she understood what Angie meant. She mouthed an apology to Angie and inclined her head, nudging Luke.

He bowed his head. "Lord, we thank you for this precious fellowship among friends, new and old. Thank you for this food to nourish our bodies. Amen."

They tucked into their meal, but before Luke had taken his second bite, he quietly said, "You didn't answer my question."

She glanced into his welcoming gaze. "What question?"

"May I walk you home?"

Olivia groaned. "Sorry. My car is up the hill, and Angie is staying with me, you know?"

Luke's face fell. "I forgot." He took another bite, and while he chewed, his eyes lovingly studied her face. "You're beautiful."

Heat rushed to her cheeks. As wonderful as Ian was, he rarely told her that. She knew he found her attractive, telling her so occasionally. But seldom did he call her beautiful. She reached under the table, and his hand quickly found hers. Their gazes held for a time before resuming their meal. Between their praises of the food, they chatted amiably until Angie asked about Olivia's genealogy research, the reason she'd come to Cornwall.

Teffeny interrupted, "Did Olivia tell you she may buy the old Burning Sands building?"

Angie stiffened, her fork suspended half-way to her mouth, eyes somber. "No. She has not."

Olivia's stomach sank. "It's not final. Although Teffeny has some great ideas about what I'd be offering to customers." She sent a pleading look to Teffeny, asking for a lifeline, and she didn't disappoint.

"I'm sorry, Angie. I'm not trying to take Olivia away from home. We kinda got caught up in the excitement of reviving an antique that's in decline. If Olivia could open up a shop and sell items with her amazing artwork on them and exotic teas, she could revive the Sands. It's a shame such an icon should fall to ruin."

Teffeny took a long drink of water. "Olivia's considering leasing a portion of it to the local historical society for a museum."

Angie closely watched Teffeny's face during her speech.

When all was quiet, she turned to Olivia. "Livi, why didn't you tell me when we last spoke?"

Olivia nervously twisted her napkin but found no words.

Luke placed a hand on Olivia's arm. "I have to apologize. I've kept her too busy with research. I didn't give her much choice. But she can explain all the fine points when you two have a moment alone."

His explanation appeared to diffuse the tension when Angie released a miserable sigh. "I didn't mean to sound so accusing. I've just missed my best friend."

Olivia offered her a sympathetic smile. "Me too, Angie. We have a lot to catch up on."

Luke stood, then peered down at Olivia. He took her hand and pulled her to stand beside him. "Speaking of catching up. I may be in hot water over this, but I am proud to announce that I've asked Olivia to marry me, and she's accepted."

A wave of nausea coursed through Olivia, and her knees weakened as Angie's mouth dropped, anger flashing in her eyes.

Oh, Luke, what have you done?

XIV

When Grace reached the cottage, Melior was not alone. Her mother wore creases of pain around her eyes and mouth. Sebastian stood by the fireplace, an elbow propped on the mantle. Rig sat on the settle in deep conversation with her brother, but he stood when her mother bolted the door.

"Grace, where have ye been?" Sebastian asked, his voice tight, forehead furrowed. "Mother and I have been worried to despair with a murderer out among us."

Rig's regard never wavered, concern lining his handsome features. "Mistress Grace, shall ye please take a seat?" He motioned toward the settle.

She complied, her mother handing her a cup of tea, then she joined her. Rig sat across from them on the smaller settle and extended his booted feet toward the warmth of the fire. A spattering of rain pelted the window and gradually became louder and fiercer.

"'Tis good that ye came now. Afore long, it would have

soaked ye to the skin." Sebastian heaved an exasperated sigh. He crossed his arms over his chest. "Now tell us where ye have been all this while."

"I went to the manor to see Mr. Ellery." She straightened and cocked her head. "I needed an answer to a question that would not leave me."

She had their attention when a whimper flowed down the stairs, and all eyes traveled in that direction. Degory and Alsyn perched halfway down, eyes wide and curious. Her mother rose and went to them.

"My sweets, what brings ye down so late? Could ye not sleep?"

Alsyn rubbed her eyes. "We have been hearing voices for a time, Mother, and are scared. What has happened?"

"'Tis of nay concern at present. I shall take ye back to bed and tuck ye in tight, and ye shall have sweet dreams. We shall say a prayer, and when ye rise, all shall be well." They nodded, turned and edged their way to their beds, her mother following close behind.

Rig moved to sit by Grace, tossing Sebastian a look that confused her. She longed for them to depart, so she could ask her mother the question burning inside her. Rig took her hands and stroked warmth into them.

"What were ye thinking running off into the night through the moors without escort?" His green-gold eyes warmed her more than his hold of her hands. "'Tis not safe."

"Mr. Ellery walks along the coast each evening to forget." Rig's grip tightened on her hand. "Yet also to remember Nick. I recalled this outside while the constable's men were in here having a hot drink. Nay one was about, so I ran to the manor to inquire if Mr. Ellery had seen anyone while on the path this eve."

"Last eve," Sebastian corrected her. "Morn will soon be upon us."

She was so weary and yearned for her bed. "'Tis so." She inhaled deeply and released it. "I hoped he may have seen a stranger and could inform that *he* had been the murderer, releasing suspicion of . . ." A groan of regret escaped.

The men waited, but she did not go on.

Rig squeezed her hands. "Suspicion of what?"

The shivering returned—yet not of cold but dread.

Sebastian took one long stride toward her and dropped to his haunches. He took her hands from Rig. "Do they suspect someone?"

Timidly, Grace drew enough courage to speak. "One of the men asked Mrs. Braddock if either of ye came up the path today."

Something passed between the men, but Grace was too afraid to question further. "I am weary." She pulled free of Sebastian's hold. "I am to bed now."

She longed to have Rig's comforting arms around her, but it was not to be. As her mother returned and paused on the bottom step, Grace kissed her cheek, skirted behind, and dragged her weary body to bed. She could feel Rig's eyes on her, but she did not turn.

ଓଞ୍ଚ

Grace woke to the sun's light filtered through dark clouds. Her stomach rumbled at the smell of fresh bread, unable to recall the last time she had eaten. She rolled to her side and peered out the small window, desiring to lay long this morn. Something she had never done unless ill as the day after her father had found her beneath the gorse. He would harm them nay longer.

Rain pattered against the window. Once, their cottage had been part of the Penrose estate, though she knew not how it came to be in her father's possession. She sat upright with a start—one more thing to inquire of her mother. With all the excitement of the past two days, the question regarding Mr. Ellery returned.

Grace quickly dressed and tied her hair with a green ribbon. She took the narrow stairs faster than was safe, her mind spinning with questions. Her forthcoming words halted when she saw Sebastian sitting by the fire, Degory on his lap, both laughing. Alsyn sat at the table with their mother, preparing the morning meal. All eyes lifted to hers.

"Grace! I am that glad ye are now with us." Her mother slid a cup of tea and a plate of buttered bread to a vacant place at the table. "Come and eat. 'Tis a lovely morn."

Grace peered to the sky, the rain sending a sweet scent through the drafty cottage. *Lovely?* Grace looked at her mother, and the woman's expression clouded briefly. She went to the table and sat before the proffered meal.

"My dear Grace, I do not mean to be heartless, but I shall nay longer live by convention. What has been is nay more. We are free. I do mourn for the man Rad once was, but it was short-lived. He was like a dark cloud that hung over all he met—except those he used to his own good. Much like he did

Arabel for so long. It gives me much happiness to know the two of ye did reconcile before he died, and ye were able to make her see his true nature."

Of a sudden, sunlight beamed through the window, and the rain stopped. Her mother closed her eyes, the weary lines absent from her pretty face. Grace brightened at the thought of her mother's renewal.

Sebastian placed Degory on his feet. "Alsyn, will ye take your brother out to play?"

The girl tossed her glossy hair over one shoulder, walked to the settle, and took Sebastian's hand with a tug, a mischievous smile lifting the corners of her mouth. "Come, Brother."

Sebastian scooped her into his arms and raised her until their faces were level, Degory's laughter echoing. "Ye are a little monkey, my sweet sister." He kissed her cheek loudly and placed her next to her younger brother. "Now, off with ye two. And keep from trouble or ye shall hear of it."

For an instant, their eyes dimmed, but his teasing smile reassured them, and they each snatched a piece of bread and darted from the cottage.

Grace smiled at Sebastian. "Ye shall make a wonderful father one day." A glint of joy touched his eyes, then it was gone as quickly as it appeared.

"Aye. Someday." He grabbed his coat and approached the door. "Off to the mines. Have a good day, my lovelies." He presented an exaggerated bow and left them.

Grace and her mother shared a cheerful smile and returned to their repast. After a moment, Grace observed her over the rim of the worn cup. Placing it on the table, she mulled over how to ask the questions burning within her. She began by asking the milder of the two.

"Mother, how did this cottage come to be in Father's possession?" She took a small bite of bread and closed her eyes to savor the yeasty flavor.

Melior's brows rose. "Why do ye ask?" Her fingertips lightly tapped the tabletop.

"Today did it occur to me how Father could afford such a dwelling. Though 'tis not a fine one, it would cost a great deal, having been part of the manor estate."

Her mother began cautiously, hesitance in her voice. "Well . . . 'tis a long tale . . ."

They sat in silence for a while, many emotions playing across Melior's face. Grace read each one, wondering if she should have pressed the matter. "Ye see, when I was but a girl, not much younger than ye, I was in love with Gerence Ellery's elder brother, William." Her face softened, a distant look in her eyes, and Grace knew her mother was far away in another time.

Her mother's shoulders slumped. "We were to be married, but he left to fight against Cromwell's army and never came home." She tilted her head toward the sunlight beaming into the room.

Grace prompted. "And the cottage?"

"The cottage? Ah, yes. Did ye know it was once known as Grace Cottage?"

"In truth?" Grace smiled. "Is that why ye named me Grace?"

Pain flashed over her mother's face. "Nay. After Sebastian was born and grew to be a handful by the age of three, I then found I was with child again and needed grace from God to endure your father's wrath."

"When did he become so cruel? Ye once said he was not always as he . . ."

"After Sebastian was born. There was a gradual change. I saw it as he grew from the tiny baby into a lad."

It took a moment for Grace to realize she was speaking of her brother. Yet, what did he have to do with her father's vile temper? A slow creeping darkness expanded in the pit of her stomach. It was akin to the first time she went deeper into the cave that was to be their home, the blackness sending fear through her.

Her mother swallowed, and her eyes reddened. "Sebastian is not Radigan's son."

Grace gasped. "He is not my brother?"

"He is your half-brother, dear." Melior took her hand and squeezed. "That makes nay difference in your relationship. Ye love one another, and 'tis all that matters."

Grace stared at her mother. Shock and disbelief filled her.

Melior hung her head, her voice a whisper. "I am ashamed but have reconciled with God long ago. He forgave me, and I have suffered the consequences of my actions many times over."

The question burned to be released. "Why did ye not marry Mr. Ellery?"

Tears slipped from her mother's eyes, and she finally answered, "How could I? It seemed, somehow, disrespectful to both men. Gerry would have to raise his nephew as his own, and I would grieve the loss of Will every time I looked into Gerry's face."

"Yet Sebastian looks nothing like Mr. Ellery."

"Nay longer, but until he was a young man, they looked much alike. That is what your father could not abide. By the time Sebastian nay longer favored Will, the die had been cast. Your father could not forgive, though he knew of my condition when we married." Melior brought her hands to her face and sobbed, shoulders quaking. "He said it mattered not that I was *tainted*."

Grace embraced her mother, and they both wept.

An hour later, Grace viewed the sun glinting off the sea from her perch at the kitchen window. Her mother wore a smile as she stirred the pottage over the fire. She looked into her mother's gray-green eyes and saw they were bright, only a faint trace of the many tears she shed earlier.

Grace notched her head toward the window. "Appears we have a fine day ahead of us." She rose and washed their dishes, then retrieved her cloak.

"Where are ye going, dear?"

"To the Sands. We need the income more than ever now that . . ." She cleared her throat. ". . . things have changed."

Her mother stilled. "Is that wise? I mean only to say that 'tis a man's duty to run a tavern. Should we not sell it?"

Grace stopped, her hand on the door. "I had not thought of it. Arabel certainly is most capable of caring for the ledgers, and Eulalia, Caye, and Wilmont have had the running of the kitchen for a long while with my aid." She considered her words, standing rigid. "Aye. We can do this, Mother, and make a proper job of it in the bargain."

Her mother's smile lightened Grace's heart. Aye, *they* could do this. Mayhap Sebastian could quit the mine and be a part of it. Her spirit soared at the thought.

No more cowering at the cruel words of her father. Only freedom. Sweet freedom.

◦৪৯

The Burning Sands bustled with activity as Grace entered the kitchen. Laughter filled the room as the women hurried about their tasks. All heads turned upon her entrance, each with a broad grin.

"Grace!" Wilmont shouted. "Ye should see the crowd in there." Her chin lifted toward the dining room.

She strode to the door and peeped to see that every table was occupied, friendly laughter and conversations filling the air. Grace had never seen such a jovial lot. When she turned back, she noticed their demeanor was much changed as well. Sadness settled over her as she considered it took her father's death to bring so many people a release of worry.

A gentle arm wrapped around her shoulders. "Concern yourself not, child. He made his own bed. Ye shall mourn him in your own way, but ye are not responsible for another's soul and the choices they make."

Grace met Eulalia's moist eyes. "I know. Yet I cannot help but wonder if I could have done something to reach him."

"Nay, not even Vicar Olford could reach him. He did try."

Grace's eyes widened. "In truth?"

"Many times." Eulalia released her, returning to her duties.

Grace righted herself and headed to see Arabel and discuss her plan. Her sister was in agreement, and they made a list, agreeing that Sebastian must be consulted.

A knock startled them, and Grace realized the sun had shifted and the room began to darken.

Sebastian stuck his head around the door, straight brown hair falling over his forehead, his smile broad and teasing. "What are my sisters up to for such a long while? Eulalia did tell me ye have been here all the day."

Both women ran to their brother, throwing their arms around him. He squared his shoulders and pulled his head back. "What brings on this sentiment? I do not remember ever being greeted in such a manner."

They tugged him toward the vast desk and shoved him into the chair, both chatting excitedly.

Once he had absorbed all they shared, he reared back in the seat and looked up at them, eyes bright. "I must say, ye have done well."

Grace smiled. "May we get started? Are ye in agreement? Do ye have more ideas?"

Sebastian wrapped an arm around each of them. "One question at a time. I am as hungry as a bear. May we continue this at table?" He escorted them from the office, then he froze as the sound of breaking glass and men's shouts reverberated up the stairs.

He released them and rushed downstairs, Grace on his heels. She stopped at the door, gripping its frame, her blood chilling at the scene before her.

Chapter Sixteen

Frozen to her seat, Olivia swallowed hard, her face heating, as Luke's announcement echoed through her mind. Angie coughed and sputtered as if she had just taken a sip of her drink. Olivia couldn't look at her best friend.

What was Luke thinking?

Snapping from her stupor, she grabbed his hand and pulled him into the corner. She wheeled to face him. "Luke! What are you doing? I thought we agreed to wait to tell *everyone*."

Luke's gaze on her, he whispered huskily, "I'm sorry, but I thought it would be best. If we hadn't, Angie may make life challenging for you while she's here." He brought his mouth close to her ear. "You said she could be an interrogator. Your nerves are already strained as it is."

Olivia smiled. Her friend, the interrogator. Angie could definitely be that—and more. Yet she was like a sister. The truth was the news was out whether she wanted it to be or not, and now she would have to do damage control.

Olivia lifted on her toes to give Luke a kiss on the cheek. "Proceed." For courage, she gripped his hand tighter as they made their way back to the table.

Luke smoothed things over with a smile, though Olivia still couldn't meet Angie's gaze. "As I was saying, Olivia and I are to be married but have not set a date, wanting to have time for Olivia to settle into life in Trerose for a time."

Teffeny stood and lifted her water glass. "To Olivia and Luke! Cheers!"

Olivia forced herself to gaze at Angie. Christian followed Teffeny's lead and echoed the sentiments, and one by one, each person stood and lifted their glass except Angie, whose eyes held Olivia's with a pained expression.

Olivia's legs weakened. Her grip loosened from Luke's, and she collapsed onto her chair. When his gaze angled down to her, he wrinkled his brow and ran a hand over her shoulder.

"Are you ill? You look as if you'll faint." He handed over her water glass. She sipped, praying the lump in her throat would diminish.

"I'll be okay. Truly."

Luke turned to Angie as if he'd read her thoughts. Angie's face changed from censure to concern. The small reaction offered Olivia a modicum of courage. Turning back to Luke, she said, "I think you should accompany Angie and me home."

He nodded. "All right. I'll drive your car, so you don't have to walk the cliff path."

Luke escorted Olivia and a silent Angie to the carpark and drove them to the cottage. He carried Angie's luggage to her room while Olivia put a pot of tea on to steep.

Olivia leaned against the cottage door, the trailing vines trembling in the calm breeze. "Thank you for taking such good care of me. It's amazing how you know what will upset me when I've said nothing."

Luke placed his palm against the door just above Olivia's shoulders and leaned in. "I would do anything to protect you—emotionally and physically. No harm will come to you if I have any say in the matter."

She kissed him tenderly, and when they parted, her fingers brushed his cheek. "When we're alone, I'm afraid I'm going to wake from this wonderful dream."

"We never shall, love. There's nothing to fear when God has His hand in our lives." He studied her face. "You're still afraid of something, aren't you?"

The sound of the sea ushered back memories of that night on the cliff and the fear with it.

Luke rested his forearm above her head, his voice gentle. "Tell me."

In the quiet, he patiently waited, his fingers playing with a strand of her hair, his eyes sweeping her face. She swallowed.

"When Ian and I married it was like a marvelous dream, which would've continued had he not insisted on his extreme sports lifestyle. Before we married, I knew he loved it, but I never thought he would pursue it more passionately. I begged him to cut back on the activities, but he would not relent. Even when I tried to make him understand I feared for his life."

Luke remained silent, allowing her to vent the built-up frustrations, and she was grateful for it. "I'm afraid that will happen to us."

Luke's smile was sad. "I understand your misgivings. It's only natural. You think you really know someone, and then their true self appears. I've done enough marriage counseling to know that scenario. Couples date for months, years even, and within a short time after marriage, one of them invariably reveals bad habits or unwillingness to compromise and respect the other person's likes and dislikes—no matter how insignificant they may seem."

Olivia trailed a fingertip along his jawline and allowed her gaze to linger. Her voice trembled. "You give me hope, Luke Harper." She briefly pressed her lips to his. "I suppose I must go inside and face the music."

Luke ran a hand through his wavy hair. "I hate to leave you."

"I'll be fine. We'll talk tomorrow." Olivia turned but paused and said over her shoulder, "Pray for me."

"Always." He shoved his hands into his pockets and walked away.

Olivia slowly entered the kitchen to find Angie's blonde head bent over the genealogy notes, a mug of tea steaming in front of her. She brought her gaze up. "Must've been some goodnight kiss."

Olivia's face burned. "We were talking." She poured herself a cup of tea and placed a tin of almond biscuits on the table.

A fog of silence settled around them. Was their friendship at risk? Trying to draw courage, she molded her hands around the cup.

Angie continued browsing the materials, and when her voice broke the stillness, Olivia's hand twitched, splashing a few drops of scalding tea onto her thumbs. She bit her lip to silence the sigh.

Angie fixed Olivia with a glare. "Why didn't you tell me?" Her tone was taut—accusatory. "And why in the world did you accept the vicar's proposal? You *just* met the man, Olivia."

"What?" Olivia frowned. "Because I love him?" Even to her own ears, she could hear the ice in her tone.

Angie crossed her arms. "Sarcasm doesn't suit you, Olivia."

"And your tone wasn't harsh?" Olivia returned her cup to the table and stood. "It's late. I'm going to bed." She strode to the other room, hearing the scrape of a chair.

"Wait! I'm sorry. I didn't mean to sound that way."

Olivia twisted toward her. "Yet you called *me* sarcastic. Why shouldn't I find someone else? You're the one who keeps telling me Ian's been gone for over a year and to get on with my life!" She lifted her chin, the pulse in her neck quickening. "I didn't come here searching for a husband. God brought me here and led me to Luke."

She walked down the narrow hall, but Angie followed. When her friend pulled in a breath and started to speak, Olivia faced her. "Stop. I don't want to hear anything else about it. I know it's sudden, and I'm sorry I didn't tell you. But Luke and I are getting married with or without your support."

Angie wrenched her into a hug. "I'm sorry. Please don't

break off our friendship. It's going to take me more than an hour to digest that my best friend is getting married again, okay?"

Olivia's shoulder dampened, and Angie's body quaked. Her fury dissipating, she put her arms around her friend. "I know, and don't want anything to happen to our friendship either."

Angie eased back, swiping at her eyes. "Do you have tissues?"

With a box of facial tissues in tow, they returned to the kitchen and refilled their cups, quiet engulfing them once more. Olivia had no words. How should she handle the situation? It was uncharacteristic for her longtime friend to be so emotional.

Angie slumped in her seat and yawned.

Olivia repeated the yawn. "I think we should turn in. It's late, and you've had a long day of traveling."

They sluggishly headed to their beds, Olivia dreading the continuation of the upcoming conversation.

God, please tell me what to do. Guide my actions because I'm afraid I'll say something that will end our friendship—for good.

⋘⋙

Olivia's sleepless night had her up early preparing breakfast before Angie appeared, bleary-eyed and disheveled. She stood in the doorway, rubbing the sleep from her eyes.

Angie yawned. "What are you doing at this time of the morning? The sun's barely up."

"Couldn't sleep." Olivia waved a spatula in the direction of the hot pink teapot on the table. "Help yourself."

"Hmm. I suppose I may as well. I'll never get back to sleep now. What's on for the day? You're the resident tour guide now." She plopped into a chair and poured dark liquid into an enormous cup. "This looks like syrup."

"It's strong. The twins like their smugglers' tea."

"What's that?" She took a sip and scowled. "Bet a spoon would stand up in this stuff."

Olivia huffed. "That's the point. Guess smugglers needed something to sustain them through a night of sneaking."

Angie waggled her brows. "Like Ross Poldark?"

Olivia couldn't stifle the laugh. "Exactly."

"What's for breakfast? It smells good."

"Thought I'd make pancakes. It's been a while." She flipped a saucer-sized disc to brown on the opposite side.

The air stilled between them. Ian had loved pancakes.

Olivia and Angie shared a knowing look. Neither spoke. Olivia delivered the meal shortly and said grace over their food.

A few bites into the meal, Angie cleared her throat. "I don't want an instant replay of last night—"

"But?" Olivia added, fork hovering over her plate.

Angie pushed a bite of pancake around her plate, soaking up more syrup. "I . . . only want you to think about your engagement more deeply." Her emphasis on the word *engagement* was gentle.

Olivia noticed the inflection, but some emotion mutinied.

"Angie, I don't want to hurt our friendship. If you have something to say that is helpful, that's fine but keep it neutral please."

Angie swallowed. "I'll try. I only want what's best for you." She sipped her tea. "Please understand that you've not known the vicar long. He appears to be a wonderful guy, but you don't really *know* him." She held a palm out. "Hear me for just a few minutes."

Olivia sucked in an anguished breath and nodded.

"He's never been married—right?"

Olivia nodded again, dreading the forthcoming narrative.

"So, that means he's not experienced with women. His feelings—emotions—may be clouded."

"Clouded?" Olivia asked with a frown.

"You know—confused. He's attracted to your beauty, your sweetness, your vulnerability without realizing it."

Olivia summoned courage. "Angie, this sounds like some women's magazine self-test malarkey."

Angie screwed up her face. "Hardly!"

"Then get to the point—please."

"All right. *What if* he's subconsciously seeking you because he knows he wants the old tavern as a museum, and he knows the only way he can get it is to marry you and have you share it with the historical society? *What if* he's in need of a vicar-wife, and you're great material to fit that profile? *What if*—"

Olivia stood, clenching her hands at her sides. "I don't want to quarrel. I love him. Can't you understand that?"

Angie peered up at her friend. "But why can't you wait a

while? There's no rush."

Olivia's mood deflated, and she dropped to her seat. She glared at Angie long enough to soak up all she'd said. The revelation slowly seeped in, and her shoulders fell. "We haven't set a date. It *could* be a long engagement."

Angie's countenance relaxed. "That's a start." She reached across the table and clasped her friend's hand. "That's all I ask—time."

☙❧

Olivia entered The Pilchard with Angie, pausing inside the door to allow her eyes to adjust to the dimness. Angie pointed across the room. "There's Teffeny, Christian, and Luke . . . and someone else."

Olivia settled her gaze on Hugo. "That's Teffeny's cousin, Hugo. He's the estate agent I was telling you about."

"Hmm . . . not a bad-looking fellow," Angie commented with mild interest.

"I suppose not. Nice enough too."

When they reached the table, the men stood, and Olivia deliberately seated herself on Luke's left side, so it would force Angie to sit by Hugo. Maybe he would be her focus of attention and not the engagement. She lifted her eyes and sent God a silent thank you.

Luke shifted beside her and whispered, "What are you praying about?"

"Luke . . . you're making me nervous."

"What did I say?" His innocent expression didn't fool Olivia. "It's as if you can read my mind, and that's not a good thing."

He draped his arm over the back of her chair. "I'm not clairvoyant."

She smirked and reached for the lemon-laced water. "Did you order this for me?"

Luke lifted his brows but didn't answer.

Olivia nudged him with her shoulder. "*And* it's on this side of you."

She chuckled at his devious expression. "Okay. I'm being paranoid."

An exaggerated cough brought their intimate conversation to a halt, and they focused on the others.

Hugo stood and raised his glass. "I was not present at the impromptu celebration dinner last night, so I'll give my congrats now. To the future bride and groom!"

Olivia smiled and thanked him as did Luke, who leaned in. "Try to look a little happier, or you'll make me think you've had second thoughts."

She shifted a few inches. "I am happy. I have no second thoughts about *you*." She looked around the table at everyone chatting, Angie and Hugo's heads close in conversation.

Luke moved nearer. "What did Angie say to you last night? It's obvious you're not yourself."

Her face heated, and she dipped her head. "May we talk later? I'm sure I can get Teffeny and Christian . . ." Her gaze floated to Hugo and Angie. ". . . and Hugo to tour her around for a while this afternoon."

Luke's expression softened. "Certainly. I'll be at the

museum for the rest of the day. Bring your research."

"How romantic," Olivia added smugly.

Their lunch passed with Angie ensconced in conversation with Hugo. Teffeny sent Olivia questioning glances, notching her head in the seemingly new couple's direction.

Olivia answered her inquiry with a one-shouldered shrug.

Luke's brows rose. "Olivia, what's with you and Teffeny?"

She studied him for a moment. "Have your skills failed you?"

"Quite the comedian now, are you?"

"I'm amazed that you haven't noticed how Hugo and Angie have hit it off."

He smirked. "I've noticed."

"That's why Teffeny's been sending me signals."

"To what end?" He continued eating while his gaze swung to the other couples at the table.

Olivia longed to roll her eyes but refrained. "Teffeny, would you and Hugo be willing to give Christian and Angie a tour this afternoon?"

Teffeny swung her gaze to Angie, then back to Olivia. "If they'd like."

Hugo spoke up quickly. "I'd love to."

Olivia suggested Hugo show them the Sands.

"Good thought. I'll just pop over to my office and get my spare set of keys." He moved his gaze to Teffeny. "Do you want to take Christian and Angie and meet me there, or do you all want to go to the office?"

"I'd like to see where you work, Hugo." This was Angie, all

aglow with renewed energy.

Olivia narrowed her eyes at her friend with fresh curiosity. She'd never known Angie to be taken with a man so quickly. Hugo was nice, not an unattractive man, but . . .

Luke gently poked her in the ribs, his voice a whisper. "You're staring."

Olivia shook off the muddled thoughts running rampant in her mind. "Sorry. Just thinking."

They all stood, Hugo and Angie trailing behind Teffeny and Christian, and stepped out into the perfect afternoon, the wind creating tiny waves in the inner harbor. Luke and Olivia lagged behind.

She hugged Luke's arm closer to her side. "I've got to run up to the cottage and get my research."

Luke noted the time. "The museum opens in ten minutes. I'll meet you there."

Teffeny and Christian dropped back to walk beside Olivia, and Angie waggled her brows. "So . . . you and Luke are doing research?"

"So that's what you call it in Cornwall?" Christian smiled widely.

Teffeny slapped his arm. "He's the vicar, Christian."

"He's still human."

Olivia laid her hand on Luke's shoulder. "He's a perfect gentleman . . . always."

Luke shook his head, a mischievous glint in his eyes. "No, Christian's gone and done it now. He can come with us and chaperone if he thinks there's something untoward going on."

He crossed his arms over his chest and sent Christian a slanted look.

Everyone stilled for a long moment until Teffeny's laughter broke the ruse.

"I wish I'd had my phone in hand. Your faces would've made a priceless picture. This isn't the Victorian age, people. If our vicar wants to steal a kiss from his fiancée, we'll not take him to the gibbet."

Luke looked an apology at Olivia. "I'll see you in a few."

Olivia began the climb up the path. She dreaded telling him all Angie said about their relationship, but her friend had made some good points. But would Luke understand?

CAROLE LEHR JOHNSON

XV

A nightmare met Grace. One of the constable's men had a pistol focused on Rig's broad chest while Adam lay on the floor, blood oozing from a gash on his head.

Arabel screamed and dashed to kneel at Adam's side. She ripped off a strip of her petticoat and dabbed his wound. He moaned as she touched the gash.

Sebastian's voice, edged with fury, addressed the constable. "Cragoe, what is the meaning of this?" His voice rose with each word. "Since when do ye barge into a place and ransack and assault our customers?"

The constable stepped back, a flicker of fear etched on his ruddy face. It took but a few moments for his courage to return. "We be here to arrest the man what murdered Radigan Atwood."

All eyes shifted and remained on Mr. Cragoe.

Sebastian stepped toward the man. He placed his hands on his hips, fire blazing in his eyes. "And who might that be?"

"Rig Cooper." Then the man pointed to Adam. "We also be taking his dark friend in case he may be a partner."

Arabel blanched, tears falling down her ivory cheeks, Adam's head resting on her lap, as she pressed the cloth to his temple.

Grace moved to stand by her brother, eyes never wavering from Rig's. He sent her an imperceptible nod to stay put, but she could not hold her tongue. "What proof do ye have?"

Again, the constable's nerve appeared to flag. His head jerked to one side, and he motioned to a man who hung back in the shadows away from the lantern. Eudo stepped into the light, and Grace gripped Sebastian's arm.

Her brother threw the man a glare but said nothing.

Mr. Cragoe's voice cracked the silence. "Eudo, tell them what ye heard." His eyes grew steely as he sneered at Grace.

Eudo's face nay longer appeared handsome, the scorn he wore distorting his fine features into something sinister.

"When I was having a talk with Radigan, she . . ." he pointed to Grace. ". . . barged into the room and told him he belonged at the bottom of the cliffs, just as her brother said."

"And did she not call him by name?" The constable's face twisted into a sneer.

Eudo straightened, a dangerous glint in his eyes. "Aye, she did."

The room stilled, the only sound that of the fire crackling in the grate, while candlelight cast long shadows over the smoky room.

Grace froze, fear and shame gripping her. In her anger she had revealed something that could end her brother's life. It would be her fault. She hugged his arm close to her side and whispered, "Sebastian, sorry I am."

Eulalia's firm voice broke the quiet. "I do believe all ye men have gone mad. Is there not a single man in this room that has been at the wrong end of Radigan Atwood? Have ye not all said that one way or another he would get what was coming to him one day?" She sucked in a deep breath and blew it out. "If them words Eudo just spoke are what ye call evidence, then all that be present be guilty. Think on that!" The cook flounced from the room, Wilmont and Caye watching wide-eyed from the kitchen's threshold.

Mr. Cragoe shook his head. "Makes nay never mind what that old woman says. Eudo heard Grace rightly and that be just what Sebastian did. Whether he had it coming or not, 'tis a crime to murder."

He motioned for his men to bind Sebastian's hands behind him, then pointed to Adam, who still lay senseless, Arabel remaining by his side tending his wound. She stared at the men approaching and slung out her arm to stop them. They halted and shifted their eyes from Arabel to the constable.

"Have ye nay brains?" Arabel screamed and slapped them away. "He is unconscious!"

Grace went to her, but she shoved her sister away. "They shall take him, and he shall die in prison." She threw herself across Adam's chest, but he did not wake.

"Arabel," Grace whispered. "Please calm yourself." She stood and faced the men. "Let me fetch the doctor. Ye can leave a man here to guard him. He is not able to stand nor flee."

The constable faltered, considered her, and then agreed. "Aye, but he shall be guarded, and as soon as he can walk, he shall be taken to prison."

While the men were occupied with Rig and placing a guard on Adam, Grace strode to Sebastian and kept her voice low. "Slip out through the kitchen and go to the cave."

He measured her for a moment and shook his head.

"Sebastian, how can ye help Rig and Adam if ye are also in prison? Please do as I ask." Her eyes moistened. "Go to the cave and once things have calmed seek Mr. Ellery. He will help ye."

Her brother's brow furrowed. "Why should he aid me?"

Grace had nay time to explain, yet the truth must be told. "Because he is your uncle."

Her gaze swung to Rig, his eyes still on her. She mimicked moving bound wrists. He understood and struggled against the man binding him.

Sebastian's expression clouded, but Grace pushed him toward the kitchen while the others looked away, and through clenched teeth, she told him to go.

He hesitated but for a moment and slipped through the door, Wilmont and Caye parting to allow him past, then moved to fill the doorway again. Not a soul was the wiser. Grace faced the commotion and nodded at Rig to continue his struggle. He did so and added a few shouts into the mix.

Two men whom they trusted helped Arabel take Adam to a chamber to await the doctor, adding another element to the distraction. By the time the commotion calmed, her brother was well on his way to the hiding place.

The constable exploded, his face an unpleasant shade of purple, his breaths coming in gasps. The doctor arrived among his rantings and halted in front of him. "Cragoe, are ye determined to anger yourself into an early grave? The dropsy will get ye yet, man. Calm yourself."

"There be nay time fer ailin'." Mr. Cragoe surveyed the room. "Where be Sebastian?"

Everyone looked around. Rig punched one of his captors as they tried to subdue him, sending him crashing into a nearby table, adding to the chaos. Grace smiled, though her heart pounded with fear for Rig, Adam, and her brother.

The doctor pulled Grace toward the stairs. "Tell me what is amiss here."

Grace told all that had transpired as they made their way to the chamber where Adam was being guarded.

One man at the door whispered, "Mistress Grace, we are that sorry. 'Tis not of our doin'." His eyes darted down the hall and then returned to Grace. "We think Eudo may have passed the constable coin to be 'eard."

A cold sweat encompassed Grace. Eudo claimed to want to marry her but cared not that her beloved brother would hang. She thanked God for bringing this truth to light before she consented to wed him.

The realization that her father would have her wed such an evil man caused the old hate to resurface. She muttered, "Thank ye, Tom, for telling me. I knew I could trust ye and Matthew." She acknowledged the other man standing guard, and he sent her a sad smile.

"Aye, mistress. We be thankin' God we could help ye."

She nodded and turned to the door the doctor had entered moments before. Arabel sat on a stool by the bed while the doctor cleaned and stitched Adam's head. Thankfully, he remained unconscious.

Arabel's gaze found Grace. "He shall be well. Doctor Keast says he may be insensible for some time." She cut her eyes toward the patient and saw that Adam's eyes were wide . . . knowing.

The doctor brought a finger to his lips, silencing Arabel, and motioned for Grace to follow him. He stepped to the window and bowed his head, his voice barely audible.

"He is well, and we have hatched a plan to get him out of here, but we must keep up this façade until timely. I know we can trust Tom and Matthew, but 'tis best we do not include them so as not to cause them blame for his escape."

Grace looked from the doctor to her sister, taken aback by their scheming—and grateful for it. They could spirit Adam to the cave and, with Sebastian's help, find a way to help Rig.

She grasped his hand. "Thank ye. God bless ye."

He patted her hand. "'Tis my pleasure to help anyone in your family, Grace. Now that your father is gone it shall be much easier to do so." He hesitated. "While I wish nay one into Hell, your father has been given many times to turn from his wicked ways yet always took the wrong path. I prayed for him much. We were once the best of friends as we are of a near age." His head bobbed, and he exhaled a breath. "'Twas not to be as he made his own choice."

Arabel gasped, and the doctor walked back to his patient and leaned over him, whispering something she could not hear. Adam smiled, nodded, then winced at the movement. His eyes went to Arabel, and his countenance changed as quickly as the arrival of the pilchards, fondness in his eyes.

When Grace returned downstairs, quiet engulfed the large room. A few men sat, eating and drinking, while Caye and Wilmont served. All eyes turned at her entrance.

Several words of condolence and meaningful smiles of support warmed her. The day had been long and vexing. She set about aiding the women, and the men slowly filtered out into the dark, cloudless night.

Eulalia, Wilmont, and Caye sat at the kitchen table, a cup of tea in front of each. Eulalia pointed to a cup across from her. "Sit, child, this troublesome day be over."

The door from the main room swung open, and Arabel slogged in, shoulders drooping. Wilmont pulled out a stool. She sat and gathered a cup warming her hands around the chipped vessel. "Adam is sleeping." She lowered her voice and leaned over the table. "Doctor Keast says for him to rest 'til tomorrow eve. When 'tis darkest, he shall be strong enough to flee."

Wilmont's eyes widened. "How shall he sneak past the guards?" She wiggled her brows. "Mayhap Caye and me can distract them."

A cackle escaped Eulalia, and she slapped the girl's arm. "Go on now. There shall be nay goings on in this place."

Wilmont winked and shot her a one-sided smile. "I mean naught distasteful. Just a chat and a flirt to get their attention off the door."

Arabel grinned. "He shall not be leaving by way of the

door." They stared, mouths agape. The chamber was on the upper floor above the River Pol.

Once the tavern settled and the constable and his men departed except for the guards left behind, Grace skimmed over the details of the accounts and the fraud her father committed. What—or *who*—did it point to?

A recurring figure captured her interest in the numbers. The same amount appeared each month, a large number, yet not large enough to catch the eye of someone glancing over the accounts. Of whose acquaintance had such a sum to give her father and why? She tapped her finger atop the table, her gaze fixed upon the door leading to the tavern. When it opened, Arabel's wan face peeked around the edge, but her eyes sparked with something newly held.

"Grace, 'tis time ye were abed, but I dislike the idea of ye not having an escort home at this hour."

"I am staying with ye." Grace stacked the papers, placing the most recent upon the top.

Arabel sat and tilted her head in question. "Mother shall worry."

"Nay. I sent word to her by way of Caye's brother."

Her sister nodded and pulled the papers in front of her. "Have ye found aught?"

Grace drew her finger along a column. "Do ye see this recurring number? What is it for?"

Arabel pursed her lips, her eyes flickering back and forth. "I know not." She shuffled the papers and retrieved one.

"Here," she pointed, "'Tis when it began. I remember wondering and inquired but Father said not to worry. Said he sold something of a personal nature to an old friend."

"But they have entered this exact amount at the same time each month since . . ." Her mind flowed to the past. How long had Eudo been coming into the tavern each eve, paying her special attention?

Arabel looked at her. "What do ye see?"

"Do ye not find it odd that these monthly figures appear just as Eudo began to frequent the tavern *every* eve and pay special attention to me?" She slammed her hands on top of the stack. "He was selling me to that horrid man!"

She stood quickly, banging her knee into the leg of the table, sending a sharp pain through her.

Arabel cocked her head in thought for a long moment. "Mayhap. I remember when he arrived. Father is . . . *was* greedy." She fumbled with the quill. "Grace?"

Waiting for the question, Grace gripped the back of the chair, peering down at Arabel's black wavy hair. Involuntarily, as she did in childhood, her hand smoothed it.

Arabel tipped her head back and focused her ice-blue eyes upon her sister. "None of us have cried for Father."

The declaration pained Grace more than she would have guessed. He had been cruel for so long.

They stared at one another until Arabel broke the stillness. "'Tis nay matter. Father was what he was, and there be nay changing that now—he had many chances and passed them by."

Grace gathered the papers and shoved them into a canvas bag. "Let us take to our beds and begin anew tomorrow." She lowered her voice. "Tell Adam good eve, and we shall speak whilst we try to sleep as we did as girls."

Arabel edged closer to her sister and placed an arm around her shoulders. "And talk more of Adam's escape so he and Sebastian may plan Rig's rescue."

༄༅

The following day dawned with less mist in the air and an eerie light on the horizon. Adam was up, unknown to the two men outside his door. He was as quiet as a church mouse while Arabel chatted about what he could do when he was *able* to rise. The doctor spoke as if Adam would be abed for a few more days, his voice rising to convince the guards.

He smiled at Grace and Arabel, who aided Adam to walk around the room to regain his strength. They would soon be ready after night's darkness lay thick. The doctor made a show of telling them what to feed Adam, how to administer the medicine he left and for him not to stir. Grace followed him from the room.

She addressed the men sitting alongside the wall outside the prisoner's door. "Tom and Matthew, I shall send Wilmont with food and drink."

Both men straightened in their chairs, wearing apologetic smiles, and thanked her.

When she stepped into the kitchen, Eulalia wore a strained look and cut her eyes to one side. Grace followed the motion and found the constable hunched over a plate and cup at the table. He looked at Grace, a sly sideways grin on his bulbous face. "Aye, Mistress Grace, ye have a fine cook here . . . as I always been sayin'." He tipped his chin in Eulalia's direction.

The cook grunted and turned her back on him.

"What brings ye here, Mr. Cragoe?" Grace poured herself a cup of strong tea. "Mr. Gittens is barely moving and cannot leave today." She paused as she stirred milk into her cup. "Mayhap tomorrow." She looked at the man over the lip of her cup as she took a sip.

The constable spoke with his mouth full of eggs and cheese. "So ye say, Mistress, so ye say." He swiped his sleeved forearm across his mouth. "If he be not ready on the morrow, we shall drag him from here by the collar if need be."

He stood, stuffing the last bite of bread into his already full mouth, and stomped from the room, the door slamming violently behind him.

Eulalia spun around, a large wooden spoon in her hand held high. "That man makes me blood boil. Always was a bully when he was a lad. Now he just be a growed up bully!"

Grace bit her lip to squash a smile at the expression on her friend's face. Right, she was after all. Her mother had told her stories about the man's tendency to take out his frustrations on others.

The day dragged on, Grace's tension mounting. There were many people involved in what was about to occur. She feared something may get back to the constable. Was Sebastian able to go to Mr. Ellery when he had left the tavern? Somehow, she had to discover if he could help them without the constable discovering it. Dark would soon be upon them. Mayhap she could go at dusk and return before Adam made his escape.

Grace found Arabel sitting beside Adam's bed speaking in low tones, outlining their plan again. Did he think her sister a cod's head repeating the details?

She strode to the bed and whispered, "Arabel, the man is not deaf. Ye have told him this many times."

"Oh, Grace, 'tis not all we speak of." Her eyes took in the floor, and her face flushed pink.

Grace stood upright, embarrassment gripping her. "Sorry I am."

When she reached the door, she spun around and returned to her sister's side. "I must run an errand at dusk and shall be back as soon as possible. Do naught until my arrival."

Her sister nodded, and Adam clutched Arabel's hand tighter. In the kitchen, Grace retrieved her dark cloak and told Eulalia she was on an errand and would return soon. The woman shot her a concerned look but did not question her.

The song of the night birds carried on the soft wind ruffling her hair before she covered it with the cloak's hood, warding off the coolness and shielding her face should inquiring eyes peer from their windows. She took swift steps up the sloping hill, careful not to dislodge any pebbles. Upon reaching the rise that sloped toward the manor, she gathered her skirt to avoid rustling the tall drying grass and inched her way around to the servants' entrance. Wyhon, the elderly butler, answered her knock and smiled.

"Mistress Grace. A pleasure to see ye again." He waved his arm into the room and whispered as she passed him. "Mr. Ellery is in his study with your brother."

She started, opening her mouth to speak, but he did not give her the chance. "There is nothing to worry over. Nay servant in Mr. Ellery's employ would dishonor him by gossiping about what goes on under his roof. There are many

THE BURNING SANDS

secrets that have passed through these halls that nay one shall ever know of." He winked and led her to the study.

Sebastian sat companionably by the fire, one booted foot resting on the opposite knee, Mr. Ellery beside him, legs stretching toward the heat. They each held a steaming cup of coffee that filled the room with its sharp aroma. Their heads came up to stare at Grace.

Mr. Wyhon bowed out of the room and closed the door behind him, leaving Grace to stand alone.

Sebastian surged to his feet and strode to her, wrapping her into a brotherly embrace. "What are ye doing here? 'Tis not safe should the constable see ye."

Mr. Ellery stood, fondness flashing in his eyes. "Sebastian, I think she is most accomplished at avoiding Cragoe."

Grace sent him a sincere smile and looked at her brother. "He is right. 'Tis why I dressed in this." She lifted one side of the dark cloak.

A soft knock sounded, and the door opened. Mr. Wyhon entered carrying a salver, mist rising above the blue china teapot resting in the center beside a matching cup. "Mistress Grace." He gave a shallow bow and extended the salver toward her. "I do remember that ye are not partial to coffee."

She thanked him, took the cup, and followed Sebastian to a vacant seat before the fire. With Mr. Ellery's gaze upon her, she shyly took a sip.

"I am happy to see ye well. After Sebastian's revelation of what occurred at The Burning Sands, I grew concerned."

She settled her cup on the table and cleared her throat. "Ye are very kind, Mr. Ellery."

A noise from the entry made her jerk her head toward the door, but nay other sound came.

Mr. Ellery rose. "Pardon me for a moment."

Sebastian stood and moved to follow him, but he held his hand up. "Nay, Sebastian, stay here. Should it be the constable or some of his underlings, I shall need to address it alone. Dear old John has seen enough action in his time." He gave his head one dip, smiled, and left them.

Grace placed her cup on the low table. "Sebastian, how long have ye been here?" She gripped her hands together in her lap.

He sat and leaned forward with his forearms on his thighs, allowing his hands to dangle. His voice was low. "When ye told me to come here for help I fought the urge to seek him and made for the cave, staying in the woods until I could nay longer hide." He brought a hand through his unruly brown hair. The firelight made his blue eyes sparkle when he turned to his sister.

"I kept going over what ye told me. Memories returned, and they came like the stones gathered to build a wall—some of them stacked with skill, others not quite fitting, so I discarded them, and bit by bit I pieced together why Father hated me . . ." He dropped his head, eyes on the finely crafted Turkish rug under his feet.

Grace rose and knelt beside him, her hand on his shoulder. "Father did not hate ye. Ye were just two very different people."

"Nay, Grace." He shrugged off her hand and stood. Two steps took him to the fireplace, and he put his hand on the mantle and gripped it, his knuckles whitening. "He knew he was not my father, and it angered him."

Grace watched his pained features. "Mr. Ellery told ye all?"

"Aye. Well, most of it. Said Mother should tell me the rest."

Her heart ached for him. It *was* her mother's story to tell, and she would say nothing.

Mr. Ellery returned, but the line between his brows deepened. "Ye must go. The constable and his men are increasing their search for ye." He strode across the room and removed a pistol and short sword from above the mantle. "Take these. Do not use the pistol unless it is your last resort."

At his desk he lifted a black marble statue of a bird, tilted it, and removed a small key. On the side of the desk he inserted the key in what appeared to be a knot in the wood, and with a click a hidden drawer appeared. He retrieved two leather pouches and an envelope and extended everything to Sebastian.

"Take these. There is money enough for ye to survive for a few months and passage on a ship of your choosing. The papers in here," he lifted the envelope, "will supply ye with false identification should ye need it."

Sebastian's eyes widened, and he hesitated before accepting the gifts. "Thank ye, sir. I am in your debt, but . . ."

"But what, Sebastian? I am your uncle and want to do right by ye. Sometimes justice needs a nudge." His sad smile was tinged with pain.

"'Tis not that I am ungrateful, yet I shall not allow my friends to be blamed for something neither they—nor I—did." Sebastian brought his gaze to Grace, now standing nearby, her hands clasped at her waist.

Grace exhaled sharply. "Sir, Adam is to leave the Sands as soon as I return. He is to meet Sebastian in the cave. We have yet to plan how to get Rig from the prison." Moisture pooled in her eyes, and she turned her head away from them.

Sebastian placed an arm around her shoulder. "We shall think of something."

Mr. Ellery addressed Grace. "Is this the young man who met ye on the path after we spoke that eve?"

Uncertain how he could have known Rig was there that night, she stared at him, blinking in confusion.

"As I was leaving, I overhead him and waited to be certain the man meant ye no harm." He cleared his throat. "I soon found that he did not."

His sympathetic, endearing smile warmed her heart. She nodded in understanding.

Mr. Ellery smiled. "We must think of a way to get your young man from captivity."

He paced the room, hands clasped behind his back, head bent in concentration as Grace and Sebastian stood side-by-side watching him until he paused and faced them. They stood motionless in the quiet.

The wind whistled across the moors, the windowpanes rattling, bringing with it the scent of the sea.

Mr. Ellery stopped, meeting their eyes. "I may have a way. Come with me."

Chapter Seventeen

Olivia organized their research into chronological order, creating neat stacks on Luke's desk, beginning with the first entry date of Grace's diary. She could hear Luke's baritone voice as he guided a small group on a tour of the museum. The tourists had stumbled in on Grace's heels, and Luke had no choice but to assist them.

All the notes she'd taken from the diary lay before her. Most nights she stayed up late and went through them page by page and the next day gave them to Luke to go over. Whenever they studied together between kissing interludes, they would correct or add anything new. Olivia's cheeks heated with the memory. She placed a hand on the side of her face and smiled.

Luke dropped into his vintage desk chair, eliciting a squeak. "You look flushed, love." He cupped one cheek, and his face paled. "I think you have a fever."

Olivia bowed her head. "No."

He placed a finger under her chin and angled it to make her look at him. "What's wrong?"

She summoned a weak smile. "Where do I begin?"

Luke gripped the arms of his chair and pressed his back into it, his gaze intent on Olivia's. "I'm listening."

"First of all . . . my face is hot because I was remembering all of our, uh, *research* breaks."

His eyes gleamed, and he slid a foot to touch hers. Her stomach fluttered, and her pulse increased.

"Now I'm intrigued." He rolled his chair closer without changing position.

Olivia laughed but used her foot to roll his chair away from her. "No, Luke, stop flirting. I need to tell you something." She sighed. "Angie said—"

"Oh, no," He quipped, cutting her off with a frown. "I was afraid of this. Has she talked you out of marrying me?"

His pain became Olivia's. She took his hand between hers and brought it to her cheek. "Nothing will change the fact that I've fallen hopelessly in love with you. Please know that."

Luke gave her a tortured smile, making her heart squeeze. "But?"

"I'd just like to prolong our engagement, so we can get to know each other better."

His eyelids fluttered, and he stared at the floor, allowing

her to keep his hand against her cheek. They stayed this way for what seemed an age. "Are you going to say anything?"

He looked at her, his expression guarded. "I won't pressure you. It's our decision. I know we have not discussed dates, but I never assumed you'd want it to be a *long* engagement. Please define that."

"I don't know. Until Angie mentioned it, I hadn't given the time frame much thought."

He tilted his head back and stared at her through lowered lashes. "I see."

Olivia crossed her arms. "And what month were you considering?"

"To be truthful, I was thinking spring."

Olivia's chest tightened. "Spring? Really? That's months away."

Luke sniffed. "Does that disappoint you?"

"No," she said the word with more force than she intended. "I mean . . . that's great. Wouldn't you consider that a *long* engagement?"

Luke brightened a little. "I suppose so."

Olivia laid her forearms on her thighs and cupped his knees with her palms. "Are you okay with that?"

"Well . . ." He twisted his mouth to one side. "I'll be honest with you. I'm a little disappointed that you allowed Angie to sway your decision."

Tears burned behind Olivia's eyelids. "That hurt."

He placed a hand on her shoulder. "I didn't mean it to. It hurt me to know she could affect you so. I've trusted God through all of this."

Uncertainty overwhelmed her. "I know you have. I thought I had too."

Luke rose, pulling her with him, and took her into his arms. "Let's not quarrel." He tucked his head into her neck. "I love you and want to work this out. Agreed?"

His clean outdoor scent enveloped her, and she instantly calmed. "Agreed."

Another interruption split the moment. Once the museum bell died, Hortense Atwood's wheelchair squeaked out her presence. They rose and met the woman, greeting Laura, her driver. They agreed she could leave Hortense in their care for an hour or so.

Olivia knelt beside Hortense's chair and gently hugged her. "How have you been? I'm sorry we've not been to see you."

"Not to worry, dear. I heard about your friend visiting and am glad for you." She rotated her shining gray head to survey the room. "Where is the girl? I'd like to meet her."

Olivia wheeled Hortense to Luke's desk. He rolled his chair aside so Hortense's wheelchair fit between him and Olivia.

"Teffeny and Hugo have taken her on a tour of Trerose."

"And that adorable young man of Teffeny's as well?"

Luke chuckled. "My but you're well informed."

She patted Luke's hand and gave him a secretive smile. "I have my sources, Vicar. Word gets around when there's a handsome new man about the village. I may be old, but I'm not dead."

Olivia sputtered a laugh. "You are cheeky, aren't you,

Hortense?"

"Got a little life left in me, dearie."

Luke gave the old woman a kiss on the cheek. "You have a lot of life left in you. I hope I've got half that once I reach your age."

"Pfft!" Hortense briskly rubbed her hands together. "I came for research, my lovelies! Let's get cracking."

Luke's face puckered. "How did you know we'd be here researching?"

"Again, I have my sources." She lifted one brow.

Olivia patted her back. "Well, I'm glad you've come."

For a while, their heads bent over the desk, commenting, pointing out possible scenarios and making further notes. They were able to successfully merge some of Grace's diary entries with Hortense's family genealogy, verifying important facts to piece together life in seventeenth-century Trerose.

Hortense slapped her hand on the arm of her chair. "I forgot!" She tugged a ledger from her bag and slammed it on the desk, an envelope dropping to the floor. "Oh, my, that's for you, Olivia."

Olivia bent to retrieve the large brown envelope. "What's in it?"

Hortense waved a hand. "Some things about your grandparents you may find of interest. Open it when you get home, dear."

She tapped the ledger "Now! I stumbled upon another ledger last night, read a few pages, and discovered something of interest." She turned over a post-it note used as a tab to reveal a page with rows of numbers.

Olivia glanced at Luke with a slight, questioning shrug. They leaned closer, Luke now holding a magnifying glass.

Forgetting her prized cotton gloves, Hortense pointed with a gnarled finger. "This line near the top has small writing beside it, but I couldn't make out anything except the word *why*."

She slid her finger down the page. "Here the same writing says, 'Cubert?'" Her dark eyes sparked. "Is that a name or some sort of code?"

Luke frowned. "Seems the entries were written in the same hand except for these side notes. They appear to be different." He flipped the page and surveyed it for a minute.

"Although there are other entries . . . not many . . . but a few, and they are all corrections. Numbers crossed out, and lesser ones put in their place." He ran a hand across his face.

Hortense chortled. "Someone was cooking the books." A shadow passed over her eyes. "I've done a bit of bookkeeping in my day and this must've been the seventeenth-century version."

Luke took the paper in hand again and studied it. "You could be right. But what do these side notes mean?"

Olivia glanced at Hortense and saw fatigue settling in. "Could you take some time and decipher them, Hortense? That could give us some clues. She expressed a fake yawn. "I'm sorry. Could we reconvene tomorrow? Angie and I stayed up too late last night, and I'm tired."

Luke arched a brow. "You? Tired? That's—"

Olivia stood behind Hortense's chair and shook her head. His eyes narrowed, then widened with understanding. "That's a brilliant idea. Let's get you home."

Hortense drew the corners of her mouth downward. "I'm not tired."

"I need to check on Angie. I'd hate to totally abandon her on her first full day in Cornwall. I wouldn't be much of a hostess if I did."

The elder woman agreed. "Indeed."

It didn't take long for Laura to return, and they were soon away, Hortense telling Luke to keep the ledger and discover the meaning of the riddle.

Luke glanced at the black-ringed clock above the museum entrance. "Guess we can close now." He pulled a key from his pocket, strode to the door, and locked it. Nonchalantly leaning against the waist-high counter, arms crossed over his chest, Luke winked at her.

"Well done. I was so caught up in the research I quite missed her weariness. The yawn was a tad cheesy . . ." He joked. "But a nice touch."

"You really are smug, aren't you?"

He shoved away from the counter, arms still crossed, and came to stand in front of her. His head dipped and paused a breath away from her lips. "Now . . . where were we?"

Insistent pounding against the museum door made Olivia jump, banging her head into Luke's face. He groaned and grabbed his nose, blood dripping onto his fingers.

Olivia darted to the counter and snatched the box of tissues, plucking out a handful and rushing to him. He grabbed the tissues and applied them.

"Nod your head forward." She put her thumb on one side

of the bridge of his nose and her forefinger on the other. "Do this and pinch—" The pounding resumed, and Olivia shouted, "Hold on! We'll be right with you!"

Olivia continued her instructions. She observed for a moment, noting the flow had stopped. She jerked her phone from her bag and set the timer for five minutes.

"What are you doing?"

"After five minutes, the bleeding should've stopped. If not, you have to do it for another five."

He nodded with care and then handed her the key to the door.

"Go sit, and after I see who this is I'll get you a wet cloth."

Olivia opened the door, squinting at the sun. Teffeny, Christian, Angie, Hugo, Beryl, and Sheryl stared at her with varying expressions.

Teffeny gasped and pointed to the bloodstains on Olivia's pale blouse. "What's happened?"

The others stared, and Olivia ushered them all inside. "It's okay. I'm not bleeding. Luke just has a nosebleed, and I was tending to it when you banged the door down."

Teffeny had the good grace to wear an apologetic half-smile.

Luke sat with head tilted forward, nose pinched between two fingers, dried blood caked on his hands and shirt.

The timer on Olivia's phone sounded. "Ease the tissues away and let's see if it's stopped."

When he did, Sheryl gasped. "Oh, my. So much blood!"

Luke stood and faced the group. "It's fine, Sheryl. The

bleeding has stopped."

"How did it happen, mate?" Hugo asked in concern.

Luke frowned and took a step away from Olivia. "She hit me."

"You don't say?" Christian peered at Olivia with shock on his face.

"I did not!"

Teffeny laughed. "You two are a stitch."

Luke was not smiling, and his gaze hung on Angie. Her friend's reaction lacked amusement.

Olivia returned her attention to Luke, and he came to stand beside her. "I'll take that wet cloth now, love, if you please." The light in his eyes was unmistakable.

She felt like a deflated hot-air balloon. Why had she fallen for such a prank? First the trauma of seeing him bleeding so much, the urgent hammering on the door, now this? And Angie saw it all. She'd somehow twist this to Luke's disadvantage. On cue, Angie stepped forward, steely eyed.

"Luke, may I have a word, please?" Angie drew him to the furthest corner of the room out of earshot.

The laughter died, the newcomers quietly chatting among themselves. Olivia went to the lavatory, which was near the corner where the huddle took place. She allowed the water to warm for a moment. As she dried her hands Angie's voice rose enough for her to hear her declaration.

"Luke, you appear to be a good guy. But I don't believe Livi is ready for a serious relationship just yet. And that practical joke you just performed has told me a lot about you, vicar or no vicar."

Olivia heard Angie taking a deep breath to continue her set down. "I've encouraged Livi to get on with her life but marrying the next guy who came along is not what I meant."

Angie's voice lowered, and Olivia couldn't hear the rest of the conversation. Her heart ached at the betrayal. Nothing would ever be the same between them again.

After an early dinner, Olivia walked to the cottage with Angie in silence, the sun dipping toward the west. During the meal, Angie had chatted with Hugo and Olivia and Luke barely spoke two words to each other while Beryl and Cheryl had provided more than enough conversation to keep silence from descending over their table.

Luke hadn't offered to walk them home. Olivia wondered what all Angie had said to him at the museum for it had left quite the impact.

In the cottage, Olivia declined a cup of tea and told Angie she was tired and going to bed early.

"But the sun's still out, Livi. Why don't we watch a movie or something?"

Olivia avoided her friend's eyes, afraid either tears would surface, or she would lose her temper. Angie might mean well, but why did she feel compelled to interfere?

"No, thanks. You watch whatever you like. I'm done in."

With weighted limbs, Olivia made her way to bed, the sun still sending beams through the window like shards through her heart.

XVI

Grace and Sebastian followed Mr. Ellery as they strode across the room. He paused in front of the dark paneled wall and examined the portrait of a young Nicholas Ellery astride his new prized horse. Ever the adventurer, he had refused his father when he told him he would buy him a *pony*.

The memory was crystal clear in Grace's mind. Nick's face scrunched in confusion as he had stared at his father, and Sebastian, and her a few paces behind their childhood friend. They agreed the pony was magnificent. Yet Nick claimed he wanted a *man-sized* horse. After all, he was soon to be a man. She remembered the expression on Mr. Ellery's face that long ago day—a mixture of pride and fear. The man attempted to reason with him, concerned about him riding such a large beast. Nick had nay reservations at all, explaining that he would take proper lessons from their stablemaster.

Grace surveyed the handsome boy that she had loved as a child, his green eyes seeing her from the past.

Mr. Ellery stepped closer to the wall, reached out, and twisted one of the small, framed landscapes beneath Nick's larger painting. A narrow section of the panel popped inward like a door on its hinges. Grace's eyes widened, and her jaw dropped.

Sebastian sucked in a loud breath. Nay one spoke as Mr. Ellery grabbed a candle from the nearby table and stepped inside the pitch-black corridor. Without comment, they followed, and when they were all well within the space, he pushed the panel back into place.

"Follow me." His steps surefooted, he lowered his voice. "Keep quiet as I am uncertain if they can overhear us in the adjacent rooms." In the dim light, Grace turned now and then to search her brother's face in the candlelight, but he remained placid. It seemed they had walked quite some distance when Mr. Ellery stopped and held up a hand. "We must listen for any noise before we open the door."

They stayed this way for several minutes before he signaled for them to remain quiet and with gentle motions opened the door. A roughly hewn rock wall met them, appearing to block any further way out. Mr. Ellery made a sharp right turn and followed along the hard wall, his hand trailing along its surface.

Grace and Sebastian did likewise. After more than a dozen steps, Grace heard water trickling into a pool, the rhythmic dripping soothing her spirit. Without warning, the rock wall ended, and they were in a small cavern. On the far side, an opening no taller than Grace shone with hazy light.

Moonlight. The crash of waves against the cliffs met her ears. The beach.

Sebastian turned to their guide. "Sir, where are we?"

The man placed a finger to his lips. "We must keep our voices low. I trust nay one." He put the candle on a rock shelf near the hole and pointed through it. "If ye go through there, as soon as ye reach the sand, turn left and keep against the cliffs, stepping on the rock and not the sand. Eventually, ye shall find yourself by the cave where ye planned to hide. Stay there until I bring Rig to ye."

Mr. Ellery met Grace's gaze. "We shall discuss a plan to free Rig, then ye shall return with me and go to Adam and bring him to the manor. We shall bring him here to join your bro—my nephew." Mr. Ellery gripped Sebastian's shoulder. "My boy, have a care. I should like to get to know ye."

Moisture glinted in Mr. Ellery's eyes as the two men stared at one another. Sebastian nodded as he swallowed.

"Please do as he says, Sebastian. I do not want to lose a brother."

They shared a smile, and he slipped into the dark among the gentle ebb and flow of the tide against the sands.

Mr. Ellery blew out a breath. "Now. 'Tis done. Let us go create a plan of escape."

Grace dipped her chin and fell into step behind him, pondering what the future held for her—for all of them.

◊

Grace and Mr. Ellery sat in front of the glowing fire, a hot drink in their hands, a plan firmly in place. After discussing the options, he had accepted her proposal without question, telling her that it was brilliant. She basked in his approval.

Her thoughts strayed while listening to him. He would have made her mother a fine husband and she and her siblings a caring father. Fate was cruel. The vicar's scripture about all things working together for good to them that love God came to mind. Her mother loved God, so why did she have to suffer because of her husband's sins?

"Grace. Have I lost ye, my dear?"

She shrugged off her considerations. "Sorry I am. I suppose fatigue has overtaken me." Levering herself from the comfortable chair, she stood. "Thank ye for your compassion. I know this is nay small deed ye are undertaking. We are thankful." She curtsied and turned to leave.

With a hoarse voice, he told her, "I would do anything for your family. 'Tis the least I can do."

"Thank ye. Mother shall be most gratified, I am certain." The late hour spurred Grace to hasten her walk to the tavern and see Adam safely to meet Sebastian. When she arrived, the two guards were nodding off in their chairs but stiffened at the creak on the top of the landing. She wished them a good eve and went into Adam's room.

Arabel jerked up from her seat by the bed, her eyes cloudy from lack of sleep. Adam reclined on the bed, playing the weak, injured patient.

Grace stepped closer and whispered, "We have a plan." She dropped to her haunches and told them what they must do. "There is a small change to our scheme."

Returning to the door, she placed her ear against it, then came back to them. "Whilst Mr. Ellery and I contrived the idea for Rig, I remembered the potion Doctor Keast did give us to help Father sleep."

Arabel's eyes widened, and her lips formed a wide smile understanding the change. "I shall fetch our lovely guards a mug of ale. I hid the potion in the cupboard behind Eulalia's spices."

Grace nodded as she left and claimed her vacant chair, watching Adam as his gaze followed Arabel from the room. "I see how ye attend my sister. What are your intentions, sir?"

Adam's smile grew, his brown eyes glinting with affection. "If she shall have me, I shall ask her to wed me."

Grace straightened. Did he really love Arabel so soon? Did Arabel care for him? She hugged her middle and held his gaze. "Do ye have reason to believe she returns your affection? In truth, ye have known one another for such a short time."

"When God places love in front of ye, He shall make it most clear," he said without the slightest hesitation. "It was as if God put her into my heart, and I recognized it the moment I caught sight of her."

Grace pondered his declaration. How could she dismiss his claim? He was so very different from Arabel in appearance and in personality.

"Mistress Grace, do ye regard me as lesser because of the color of my skin?"

She considered the question. She had never judged others as inferior, or higher in status, whether they be poor, rich, a different color of skin, nor anything other than the way they treated others.

"Nay. 'Tis not what I believe at all."

Arabel's voice sounded in the hall, louder than usual. A

short while later the door opened, and she entered. Her brows lifted, and she flattened one palm to the other, placing them against her cheek and closing her eyes. Now they waited for the potion to render the men to slumber. Within half an hour, gentle snores came from the passage. Adam slung long legs over the side of the bed and reached for his boots.

Arabel brought him a long dark hooded cloak and draped it over his shoulders, looking up into his dark eyes. She held his gaze, and something passed between them that Grace found endearing.

Grace strode to the door and quietly pulled it open to see both men with their chins on their chests, breaths coming in a steady rhythm like the tide. They were kind by nature, and Grace knew they did not want to have this task, but when called to duty they did not shirk the responsibility. Had they their own way they would have let Adam go but could not afford to cross the constable. She glanced back at the couple and found them embracing. The small clock on the chest caught her attention. "Adam, ye must go now. Dawn will soon be upon us."

He nodded, kissed Arabel on the cheek, and came to the door. He peered over Grace's shoulder into the hall, then whispered, "Thank ye, Mistress Grace." He leaned and gave her a brotherly kiss on the forehead. "I shall see ye soon." His last glance was for Arabel before he departed.

When Grace spun toward her sister, she saw tears in her eyes and went to put her arms around her. "He shall be well. Sebastian is waiting for him, and they shall be safe."

"I pray that is so, Sister."

Grace stepped back and placed her hands on Arabel's

shoulders. "Now, we must take ale to the prison."

>><<

Although Grace and Mr. Ellery gave intense thought to their plan, she could not help but shiver at the task before her. Should something go wrong what would she and Arabel do? Mr. Ellery was to await them behind the prison in the shadows and take Rig to the cave. It was up to Grace and Arabel to take care of releasing Rig.

As the two women carried the bottle of ale down the cobbled, winding streets of Trerose, neither spoke. They glanced nervously at each other from time to time and with slight smiles encouraged one another. When they stood in front of the iron-studded oak door, they halted. Grace drew in a sharp breath and freed it. Arabel squeezed her arm and lifted the lion head knocker.

A metallic creak sounded as the small spyhole door opened, and a pair of black eyes peered at them. "What?" The voice snapped at them in irritation.

"Erth? Is that ye?"

His voice softened. "Who wants ta know?"

"'Tis Arabel Atwood. We have come to visit Rig Cooper." Her voice crooned, and she held up a bottle of ale.

His eyes widened, and he swallowed hard. "I b'law my innards could do with a sip of that there ale." The spyhole slammed shut, and the heavy door scraped open. He tipped his chin in Grace's direction and lowered his voice. "Best be givin' it me now so's Peter knows naught." Erth stretched his hand toward the bottle.

Grace held the other bottle in the air for him to see. "There is nay need."

The guard grinned with interest. "Shoulda knowed Rad's daughters would be as clever as he was." He chortled and took the bottle from Grace. "This way, ladies." He waved an arm with a flourish to point them deeper into the dank building.

Grace shivered as they walked down the damp, putrid-smelling corridor. She brought the edge of her cloak to her nose, shielding the scent.

"Peter, I broft some visitors for that Cooper fella so get your lazy hindend up, and let 'em in." He pointed to the man slumped in a chair by the meager desk centered in the room. Peter's head lifted from his chest sluggishly, and bleary eyes squinted at them.

Erth lifted the ale, so the man would be encouraged to comply. Peter was on his feet and alert in an instant, grabbing at the proffered bottle, licking his lips. "Come." The bottle tucked under his arm he led them deeper into the bowels of the prison.

As they passed a cramped cell the stench overtook Grace, and she gagged. Arabel took her hand. "All shall be well." She removed a handkerchief from her sleeve and shoved it at her sister. The aromatic scent of lavender welcomed Grace as she brought it to her nose.

"Thank ye. How are ye able to stand the smell?"

Arabel pressed a hand on Grace's shoulder. "I have always had a stronger constitution than ye, dear sister."

They shared a smile and trudged on behind the guard. At the end of the hall a sliver of light shone through the barred door from the torch illuminating the dismal cell. The iron key rasped an alarm to the prisoner who bolted from the straw-strewn floor.

"Visitors for ye, Cooper." The guard stood aside to allow the women to enter, but Arabel hung back. "Grace, I think I shall visit with Erth and Peter while ye speak with Rig." The guard's expression clouded briefly, then brightened as Arabel gave him a charming smile. "It has been a long while since I have seen either of ye."

He slammed the bars shut, locked the door, and looked at Grace. "Soun' out when ye be ready ta leave." He strutted away, taking a long swig from the bottle, as Arabel followed.

Rig stood in front of Grace, mouth agape, hands on hips. "What in blazes are ye doing here?"

Grace took two steps toward him. "We are here to free ye, but we must wait awhile." She glanced over her shoulder. "Let us sit and talk loud enough for them to overhear."

After a brief hesitation, Rig motioned for her to sit on the cot against the wall facing the door. "Adam is healing well, though he still cannot rise from his bed." She lowered her voice. "Once the guards have drunk all their ale it should take nay more than half an hour for them to sleep."

Rig looked a question at her.

Her voice rose once more. "Aye, Adam will survive his injury, but we must wait." She then dropped her voice again. "We have put a potion in their ale, and they shall sleep for time enough to release ye. Arabel will retrieve the key. Mr. Ellery awaits nearby to help get ye to the cave to meet Sebastian and Adam."

Bawdy singing could now be heard from the front of the

jail. The drink was taking effect on the two men.

"Adam?" Rig's eyes narrowed. "And Mr. *Ellery?*"

"Aye. We used the same potion on his guards, and he is now on his way to Sebastian. Mr. Ellery is helping us."

Grace saw a fleeting emotion cross Rig's face, but it was gone as quickly as it appeared.

They spoke for some time until they nay longer heard the guards talking and singing. They listened to the sound of jangling metal traveling down the corridor until they heard Arabel's voice. "Are ye ready?"

Rig took Grace's hand in his. "Aye."

Chapter Eighteen

Olivia awakened with a groan, a study in pain, her heart hurt as much as her body. The night had been torturous. Thoughts of Angie railing at Luke and he never uttering a word, taking the abuse like a lamb, played in her mind like a movie reel. She looked at the bedside clock, grabbed her pillow, and punched it a few times, finding it damp. Had she cried in her sleep?

Sliding from bed, her bare feet settled on the cold slate floor, and she scowled. What was she to do? Sit back and allow Angie to create unnecessary turmoil? She eased to the floor kneeling beside the bed. Her head wilted onto the mattress, arms extended, palms flat against the plush comforter.

"Lord, please help me. I'm a weary mess. Since Ian's death I've been at odds with every tiny decision. Am I doing *this* right, am I doing *that* wrong . . . on and on I struggle through each day. Once Luke and I figured out our feelings for one another, I felt at peace. Peace that you brought us together."

Olivia's sigh came from deep in her soul, strangling her emotions to the point of hysteria. Angie's face flashed before her, and a theory settled in her mind. Angie was *jealous*! Everything had been falling into place before her arrival in Cornwall.

She bolted upright, yanked on her robe, and sprinted into the kitchen. Angie wasn't there. She rushed to her room and banged on the door. No answer.

Jerking the door wide, her mouth opened ready to let Angie have it. The bed was made.

Olivia strode to the bathroom, feet slapping against the cold floor and found it empty, remembering Angie's morning jogs. She hurriedly brushed her teeth, ran a comb through her hair, and dressed. Rushing out the door, stopping on the front steps, she saw Angie powerwalking away from the cottage and raced to catch her.

"Angie!"

Angie braked to a stop and turned toward Olivia. The smile died on her face the moment Olivia drew closer.

"What's wrong? You look crestfallen."

Olivia placed fisted hands on her hips. "Yes, there is plenty wrong. And I mean to say something, and I don't want any interruptions or input."

Angie planted her feet and crossed her arms over her chest. Her eyes grew cold.

Olivia's body tensed, and her jaw clenched. She willed herself to calm and speak slowly. "Angie. You are my best friend—"

"But?" Angie ground out.

"But . . . you have overstepped your bounds. I overhead *some* of what you said to Luke at the museum yesterday."

Angie's face flamed red.

Before she could respond, Olivia continued, "You reprimand me about rushing into a new relationship when only a few weeks ago you told me it was time to move on because Ian is gone."

Her friend's mouth opened, but Olivia held up her hand.

"No. I will say my piece, and you *will* listen. I know I've always been the timid, quiet one in this friendship. Afraid of my own shadow. But that woman is gone. God spoke to me—and to Luke—about our relationship. It's not as if we're getting married tomorrow. It may be a year. The fact is we are together and will stay that way unless God reveals otherwise."

Olivia paused to catch her breath.

Angie asked, "May I speak now?" The red in her cheeks had not lightened. She dropped her hands to her side.

"No. I'm not finished. What about your own behavior with Hugo?"

"*My* behavior?" A vein in her neck pulsed.

"Yes, Miss High-and-Mighty! You were all over Hugo the minute we introduced you. I wasn't the only one to notice. So, what about that *quick* connection? At least Luke and I were not all over each other the moment we met."

Angie lifted her chin and narrowed her eyes. "How dare you!"

"Me!?" Olivia blew out an exasperated breath, whirled

from Angie, and jogged back to the cottage. By the time she'd reached her door, footsteps on gravel caught up with her. She glanced over her shoulder to see Teffeny coming up the path.

When Teffeny saw her face, she grimaced and pointed to Angie, who now sat on a rock about fifty yards away. "What's wrong? Did someone die?"

Olivia scowled. "Yes. A friendship." She met Teffeny's eyes. "Come in. I'm in need of caffeine. Would you like a cup?"

⚜

Olivia's trembling fingers snaked around the hot cup, her eyes closed. "I don't know what to do or say, Teffeny."

"Sounds like you've said and done enough for today."

"Too overkill on the speech?" The lump in Olivia's throat constricted. "I wasn't trying to be cruel."

"I don't believe you were. Especially after the way she's tried to crush your feelings for Luke and the relationship in general. That's not what a friend should do. She could've gently pointed out some pros and cons of a new relationship so soon. But her method was severe and just plain bossy."

Olivia smiled. That was Angie. A *boss-pot* was what her grandmother used to call her.

"Glad I could make you smile." She took a sip before going on. "What now? I don't necessarily think you should apologize for defending yourself or Luke, but maybe you could soften the impact by telling her you regret the *way* you presented your side."

Teffeny held out her palms and added, "I'm not trying to be bossy now."

A hard knock on the door cut Olivia's laughter short. When she answered, she expected to see Angie's angry face, but instead Luke rested against the post, a bemused expression in his eyes.

"Would you mind telling me what's going on with you and Angie?"

She widened the door for him to enter, but he didn't budge from his spot, holding her gaze.

Olivia looked heavenward. "Oh, just come in."

Luke shoved his shoulder against the post, pushing his tall form past Olivia. He pecked her cheek in passing.

The clink of glass came from the kitchen.

"Who's here?"

The answer came from the kitchen.

When they entered Teffeny immediately handed Luke a mug of tea. "You'll need this, Vicar."

Olivia shot Teffeny a pleading glance for rescue which prompted Teffeny into telling Luke the whole sordid story.

When she finished, he took one of Olivia's hands in his. "Angie came to see me, and I left as soon as she told her side of the story."

Olivia released his hold on her and straightened, shoulders back. "*Her* side of the story?"

"'Fraid so, love."

Teffeny leaned toward Luke. "Do tell."

His gaze flicked to Olivia. "Not a lot to tell. She believes she's right, and you should not have a serious relationship with me so early into our acquaintance. That you should go home and sort things out from a distance. Give it a few months and if you still feel the same way, return to Cornwall."

Olivia pinched her lips together. Her head throbbed, and the sudden urge to retreat to her bed and slam the door shut to the world grabbed her. Her stomach roiled.

"I cannot believe the gall of that woman! How dare she?"

Luke grimaced. "She said more."

Teffeny asked in a quiet voice, "Does Olivia really need to hear it?"

"Yes, she does. Angie said that's what *she* believes you should do, but as your friend, she will not say another word about it. It's your life to do with as you please—right or wrong."

"How generous of her," Olivia said sharply.

"You must know she sounded sincere. She said she wants you to be happy, and you were right about one thing."

Teffeny huffed but kept her thoughts to herself.

Over the rim of her cup, Olivia studied Luke's sympathetic eyes. "What *one* thing was I right about?"

"Her jealousy."

The revelation startled Olivia. In a more relaxed tone, she asked, "How so?"

Luke chuckled. "In her own words, 'You've met the *perfect* man for you.'"

Teffeny raised her brows and grinned. "She just earned a few gold points with me."

"What is that supposed to mean?" Luke asked as he tapped his lips with a finger.

Teffeny playfully shoved his hand away. "Simply that you two are perfect for one another. Even if neither of you realized it at first. You have more likes in common than dislikes." She hesitated. "Olivia, I'm sorry, but I must say this—the problem in your marriage with Ian was that there was one major dislike that created problems for you both. That was his love of dangerous sports that made you crazy with worry over his safety. I don't see that in this relationship. Unless Luke is keeping his diving in shark-infested waters a secret from us all." She laughed boisterously.

The expression on Luke's face never altered. "I suppose I must confess." He hung his head. "I've secretly been living two lives." He paused before going on. "I'm really a hitman with MI5."

Teffeny laughed again.

Olivia smiled. "*Ha ha.* You are so funny, Luke. That's on the same line as the bloody nose incident."

"If you say so, *dear.*"

CB&O

Olivia, Luke, and Teffeny strode to the village for lunch after their discussion. They searched for Angie, but no one had seen her. Luke walked Olivia home and lingered on the doorstep for several minutes, talking in hushed tones and kissing a long goodbye. After he left, Olivia peered at the dazzling blue sky, comparing the color to Luke's lovely eyes rimmed in gold.

A tiny brown bird perched on the vine growing around the porch entrance, just out of Olivia's reach. She stilled to watch the frail creature, and a Bible verse came to mind.

Are not five sparrows sold for two copper coins? And not

one of them is forgotten before God.

God would take care of the situation with Angie. She had but to trust Him. As she watched the creation of God, she prayed, "Lord, forgive my anger with Angie. What I said was true, but I should not have lashed out. Please give me the courage to apologize."

Olivia unlocked the door and walked into an eerily quiet cottage. "Angie. We need to talk—calmly. I'm sorry . . ."

No answer.

As she strode through the cottage each room was empty. Angie's door was open, but none of her belongings were present. An envelope lay on top of the bed, white against the cheerful yellow comforter.

With shaking fingers, Olivia lifted the paper with her name scrawled on the front. She perched on the edge of the bed and nervously slipped out a square notecard.

Livi,

I'm so sorry to have hurt you. I am still unsure why I attacked Luke so vehemently at the museum. It was as if I could not help myself. Something in me snapped when he played that ridiculous practical joke about the bloody nose.

I've caused enough trouble, so I've decided to leave. I'm taking the train to London and will return home tomorrow. Please tell everyone that it was a pleasure meeting them, but I had something unexpected come up. That's not a lie in the least.

You'll always be my best friend even if you choose to

sever our relationship. I believe I'll see Doctor Philips when I get back.

Ever your friend,
Angie

Olivia let the letter drop to her lap. She stared at the scribbled words and noticed they were not in her friend's usual perfect cursive. Was it because of the regret, or was something else going on with her—medically?

She grabbed her cell phone and quickly dialed Angie's mother, and the woman answered at once.

"Hello, Livi. How are you in lovely Cornwall?"

"Hi, Mrs. Timmons. How have you been?"

Olivia waited with patience to hear all of her local news. When she'd finished Mrs. Timmons asked, "Livi, what's wrong? Is Angie okay?"

"I'm not sure. I was hoping you could tell me."

Quiet stretched across the miles until Olivia could hear gentle sobbing on the other end.

The flat monotone voice mingled with sniffling told Olivia the full tale. "Angie is in denial. She snaps at everyone and suspects everything."

With trepidation, Olivia asked, "Do you have any thoughts about what it could be?"

"I do." Her sniffling calmed. "I pray it's only early menopause. Many of the women in my family have gone through it." Mrs. Timmons' voice strengthened. "I will not consider that it may be a brain tumor."

Olivia agreed. "No. Absolutely not. I will tell you Angie has sensed something wrong, and she told me she's going to see Dr. Phillips when she gets home."

Mrs. Timmons released a loud puff of breath. "Thank goodness. I am so grateful she came to you with it and is going to seek medical attention."

Olivia didn't enlighten the kind-hearted woman. "She's on her way home now. I suppose it got the better of her."

"I hate to hear that she wasn't able to stay for the delightful visit she'd planned with you."

"Me too, Mrs. Timmons. Yet I am relieved to know that she's getting help. Will you please keep me posted on the process?"

"I certainly will. Thank you for calling."

Olivia waited to hear the dial tone before she ended the call, relief washing over her. She quickly texted Angie.

Hi, got your note. Thank you. I'm praying for you and the visit to the doctor. Also, I apologize for telling you everything in anger. That was not my intention. Once you hear from the doctor please let me know. We'll reschedule your visit, and I'll give you a proper tour of Cornwall. With Teffeny's help, of course!

Love you,
Livi

XVII

Grace and Rig, their hands still clasped, slipped into the dark alley beside the prison. A heavily slurred voice came from the murky shadows. "So wha' do we have here?"

Eudo stepped into the dim light from a nearby window. "This be a cruel fine thing. The two of ye—'tis not fitty."

Grace dropped Rig's hand and took a step toward Eudo. "This does not concern ye. Please leave."

"Oh, but it do concern me. *Ye* concern me, Mistress Grace." He pulled a pistol from beneath his coat, cocked it, and pointed it at her. He swayed slightly but regained his stance. "Your father did sell ye to me, yet even after I sent him a message, he still did not fulfill our agreement. Said he could not force ye to wed me."

Eudo waved the gun erratically in the air between them. "I means to make it right. Too bad he shall not be at the wedding, Mistress Grace." He threw his head back and released a mirthless laugh. "We had a chivvy, and anger got the better of your father, so I telt him he would not see us wed. That was afore I kilt him and tossed him over the cliff."

Cold chills rolled over Grace's skin but changed into red-hot anger. "How could ye!"

Eudo laughed again. "Pretend not that ye mourn the man. He treated ye like a cask of French brandy. Sold to the highest bidder." His voice softened. "I woulda been kind to ye, Grace."

"Eudo Cubert, I would not marry ye if ye were the only man this side of Falmouth!" Against her better judgment, rage overtook her. She took two steps more, halted before the loathsome man, and slapped his face, the sound ringing in the enclosed alley. He shoved her backward, but Rig caught her before she tumbled to the rocky ground.

Eudo brought the gun higher and pointed it at Grace. "Ye are not worth the keeping."

As he pulled the trigger, Rig shoved Grace behind him. The shot split the air, and Grace screamed as Rig moaned, grabbing his shoulder and dropping to his knees, blood seeping through his sleeve. She fell and hugged him to her.

The click of Eudo preparing the gun made Grace flinch yet before he could complete the action, another shot rang out. Grace snapped her head up to see Eudo staggering not from drink. He fell against the stone wall of the prison. Red bloomed on his chest, and he stared at it with an expression of shock.

Out of the night, Arabel approached wearing a grim smile, a pistol in her hand. Behind her stood the constable and Mr. Ellery. Constable Cragoe skirted around them and went to Eudo. He stooped and examined his wound. "The scoundrel shall most likely live." He took the gun from him and tossed it a few feet away. He peered at Rig. "I suppose this makes ye a free man, Mr. Cooper. We . . ." He twitched his head toward Arabel and Mr. Ellery. ". . . heard his confession."

Rig nodded, his face growing paler by the minute. A crowd gathered at the entrance to the passage, voices murmuring questions.

Grace gazed at Arabel. "I shall take him to the tavern. Shall ye fetch the doctor please?"

Her sister nodded, lifted her skirt, and hurried away without a word.

Mr. Ellery came to Rig's side, removed his neckcloth, and handed it to Grace. "Allow me to assist ye."

"Thank ye, sir." Grace pressed the cloth to the wound. Rig moaned. He carefully placed Rig's uninjured arm over his shoulder and eased him upward.

"'Tis my pleasure. Once at the tavern I shall get Sebastian and Adam and bring them to ye."

She dipped her head and stood at Rig's side, holding pressure on the wound as they strode down the lane.

⋘⋙

An hour later, the doctor had dressed Rig's wound, and Grace, Rig, and Arabel sat at a table with coffee in front of them that Arabel had provided, the doctor having returned to his bed.

The door burst open with the dawn light behind Mr. Ellery, Adam, and Sebastian. Arabel jumped from her seat and hugged Sebastian first, then Adam. "I shall fetch more coffee."

Adam kept his arm around her. "I shall assist ye." Her

bright smile cheered Grace as her brother and Mr. Ellery joined them.

Sebastian gave Grace a hug and looked at Rig. "Well, old friend, I am glad to see ye among us." Grace silently thanked God for delivering them from danger.

Mr. Ellery's brows pinched, and his gaze met Sebastian's. "*Old friend*? I thought ye had just met."

Sebastian regarded Rig, who shook his head. "There are times when ye meet someone and feel as if ye have known them your entire life. This is the way with our friendship."

Arabel and Adam arrived with the coffee, and they sat in the heavy silence watching the early morning light spill into the room.

Mr. Ellery shattered the quiet when his chair scraped against the slate floor. He stood and raised his mug. "To a successful night for all." In unison, they lifted their drinks and repeated the sentiment. "I am to bed. It has been a long and arduous eve and am glad to have been a part of such a just endeavor."

Before Mr. Ellery reached the door, Sebastian stood, wearing an expression Grace had never seen on his face. Was it *pride*? "Uncle?"

Mr. Ellery turned abruptly toward him but said naught.

Her brother squared his shoulders. "Do ye mind if I reveal our relationship, sir?"

He grinned. "I think ye have just done so, nephew."

Rig's face froze, and his head reared back as if struck. "*Uncle*?"

Mr. Ellery returned to the table and stood over them. "Aye.

Sebastian is my brother's son. I fear Melior shall not be happy about the revelation, yet 'tis time. I nay longer have a son, and Sebastian shall be my heir." His eyes misted, but he pressed on. "I am certain ye are not aware, Mr. Cooper, but I had a son who was the best of friends with Grace and Sebastian. But fate would have it that I lost him when he was but a boy." The man hung his head, uncontrolled emotion gripping him.

All remained silent as the man grieved—yet again. As did she.

The kitchen door scraped open at Eulalia's arrival for the day. Grace jerked to her feet. She took a step away from the table, but a firm hand grasped her forearm, Rig's hand holding her in place.

He stood, his face unreadable. "Mr. Ellery?"

Before the man looked at Rig, he searched his pocket and retrieved a handkerchief wiping his eyes. "Aye, Mr. Cooper."

Rig released Grace's arm and took tentative, unsteady steps around the table. He halted a pace in front of the man, his injured arm tucked close to his side. His voice was nearly a whisper. "Father."

A gasp came from the doorway, Eulalia leaning against the doorframe, a hand over her mouth.

Mr. Ellery blinked rapidly, and Grace held her breath. *Rig . . . Nicholas?*

She swayed, head swimming, and her emotions shifted from curiosity to anger. How could this be? He had fooled her—and Sebastian—from the beginning. She sank onto the chair. Yet why?

The men's gazes held. Father and son. Reunited after years

of separation.

Mr. Ellery's tears became sobs, and he moved to grasp his long-lost son into his arms. Rig's face winced at the pressure upon his injury, yet he did not pull back. Instead, he placed his free arm around his father, and a tear slid down his sun-browned cheek.

༄

Still in shock, Grace gripped her skirts and stumbled up the hill toward home. She had been such a fool. Rig was Nicholas. Nicholas was alive!

Her heart gladdened that their childhood friend had somehow survived, yet why had he kept away for so long? He said he would explain all at the tavern for a midday meal. Betrayal and anger filled her as she tried to sort through her feelings toward Rig—nay, Nicholas.

Once Grace arrived home, she told her mother all that had occurred, relief and surprise shone in her eyes. When she was told that all now knew of her past indiscretion, fear blanketed her features yet softened when Grace relayed Mr. Ellery's declaration.

Grace slowly climbed the stairs to her bed and wondered if perhaps her mother may have feelings for Mr. Ellery after all. Halfway up she called to her mother, peeping through the stair's spindles into the kitchen.

"Aye, dear?" Melior stirred the porridge she prepared for the children's breakfast.

"Will ye join me at the tavern later? We are all to meet there and hear Rig—Nicholas's story."

Melior stopped stirring and stared into the pot. "I would

not care to leave the children."

"I am certain Eulalia would love to entertain them in the kitchen." She smiled to herself, remembering how they loved visiting the cook.

She waited, but her mother did not answer, so she began her ascent. When she reached her door, she caught the timid words that floated up the stairs.

"As ye wish, dear."

Grace warmed at the notion of the upcoming gathering. A homecoming of sorts. She longed to speak with Nicholas alone but knew it may be some time before that would happen.

The sweet slumber came quickly, and when she woke, she washed, dressed, and skipped downstairs.

Melior and the children sat at their small table, their voices low, faces freshly washed, and hair combed. Grace noticed that her mother had changed into her Sunday dress, and her hair was arranged prettily. She brought her gaze up to meet her daughter's.

"Grace, ye look well-rested, my dear." She rose from the table, and the children did likewise.

"May we go please? I do so want one of Eulalia's tarts. There are none better." Degory paled and stumbled over an apology. "Not that yours are not wonderful, Mother."

Melior ruffled his hair with affection. "There is nay need to apologize, my sweet. Even I know that Eulalia's are better than all others."

Degory took hold of Grace's hand, and Alsyn grasped her mother's.

The day was cold but fine, the wind fragrant with the sweetness of the broom plants lining the coastal path, the floral scent clinging on later than normal. It appeared a mild winter awaited them.

Once the inner harbor wall was in sight, Degory and Alsyn raced along the stone structure and rounded the corner toward the tavern, their laughter flowing behind them. They were such dear children despite the fear their father had instilled in them.

Melior took Grace's arm and hugged her. "Life has been most hard." She gently tugged her closer. "But I believe God brings something new and wonderful each day."

The River Pol bubbled beneath them as they crossed the bridge, its clear cold water soothing Grace. The children's voices could be heard as they entered the tavern, squealing with laughter as the cook greeted them with promises of tarts after their meal.

Eulalia greeted Melior with a hug. "'Tis so good to see ye looking so well. I see color in your face again, me friend." She brought her work-worn palm to caress her cheek.

Melior cupped her hand over Eulalia's. "Thank ye. 'Tis good to feel restored."

"That bunch in there are awaiting vittles, and if I can keep Wilmont from Sebastian, mayhap ye all shall be served soon enough." There was a glimmer of mischief in her bright eyes as she looked at Grace.

"Sebastian? What does he have to do with Wilmont?"

Melior and Eulalia chuckled and shook their heads. The kitchen door opened and in walked Mrs. Braddock, more spry than Grace had ever seen her. "Mrs. Braddock! How came ye to be here?" She strode toward the old woman and placed a hand under her arm. "Please come rest yourself."

"Pfft! I need not rest, Grace. That stroll down the cliff has invigorated me. I be here to listen to that boy's tale of the sea."

Grace pulled a stool from the table, but the woman refused it. "My, now, news does travel quickly in Trerose, Mrs. Braddock."

Degory and Alsyn burst into the kitchen, Caye following them. "We are ready for tarts, Mistress Eulalia!"

The cook chortled and pulled out two stools onto which they promptly settled. Caye poured milk while Eulalia placed bowls of fish stew and fresh bread before them followed by a platter of tarts. "Now see here that ye eat up the stew first."

Melior placed a hand on each of the children's shoulders. "Eulalia has provided us with a lovely midday meal, and I would have ye do as she bids. If ye clean your bowls, ye may have tarts."

Eulalia shooed Grace, Melior, and Mrs. Braddock into the tavern where Caye and Wilmont brought plates to them.

The men shoved two tables together, and they sat with Mr. Ellery at one end of the table and Nicholas at the other. Her mother timidly stood by, and Mr. Ellery jumped to his feet and pulled a chair out for her as did Nicholas for Grace. Her heart lurched in confusion over whether to be angry or elated. Indeed, she was happy to have Nicholas returned to them, yet he had not been honest in keeping his identity a secret.

When Grace sat, she turned to speak to her brother, but his eyes were only for Wilmont. Why had she never noticed his attention toward the young woman before? They had always been friendly, but now he appeared most attentive. She leaned toward Sebastian. "Would ye please tell me what is going on between ye and Wilmont?"

He kept his eyes on his tankard but answered her quietly. "Grace, I know ye are most intelligent and am astonished ye have not seen it before." He brought his eyes to meet his sister's. "Why else would I refuse to escape with my family?" He turned toward Wilmont and motioned her over. When she arrived, he took her hand and kissed it.

Astonishment filled Grace. How little did she yet know her own brother?

Wilmont's face fell. "Ye are not disagreeable for us to be together, are ye, Grace?"

"Indeed not." Grace took her friend's other hand and squeezed. "Yet why did ye keep this secret?"

Sebastian answered the question. "Because Father would have forbidden it. Ye know how he was about mixing classes."

Wilmont's eyes sparkled. "I was nay more than a lowly servant to him."

A loud cough intruded on their moment, and Grace brought her gaze around to see Nicholas standing. "Before we dine, I would like to suggest that someone say grace over our food. We have much to be thankful for this day." He reclaimed his seat, eyes on Sebastian.

Grace saw the panic in her brother's face, yet it passed quickly. He rose. "I must thank my *cousin* for placing me in such discomfort." He laughed. "But I shall attempt to thank our God for His bounty."

He bowed his head. "Father God, we come together today because of Your grace and mercy. Thank Ye for this food, fellowship, and the future Ye have for us. In Christ's name, we pray. Amen."

Several amens sounded around the table, and the clink of metal upon metal the only sound for a while.

Grace watched her mother's expression as Mr. Ellery stood. She believed she saw a flicker of admiration cross her face but was uncertain.

Mr. Ellery cleared his throat. "Well, my son, I believe your audience is ready for ye to share your sea adventures." He sent Nicholas a tender smile. "He, of course, shared some of it with me last eve. Neither of us could sleep, naturally. But I long to hear of it again."

Nicholas drank from his tankard, met Grace's eyes, and began his story. At once, she was swept away to that fateful day as a young girl playing in the sand.

CR&O

September 1656

Nicholas raced Sebastian toward the waves, tugging off their shirts, tossing them on the wet sand just out of the tide's reach. Grace sat huddled in the shade against the foot of the cliffs, her pewter cup piled high with sand. She filled and refilled the cup, packed it tight, turned it upside down, and tamped the molded form until it slid out. She repeated the action again and again, Sebastian watching her from time-to-time.

Occasionally, her eyes lifted to find them, and she waved a

tiny hand, her auburn hair blowing in the wind like the gulls overhead. Nicholas returned the wave, nay matter how many times she did so. He knew he was too protective of her, but she was like a younger sister, small and fragile.

Sebastian challenged Nicholas to swim farther out than they had ever gone—a goad he could not refuse. When Sebastian had reached their goal, he perched proudly on the cropping of rocks that rose from the sea, only twenty Cornish fathoms from shore, but the undercurrent was much stronger.

As Nicholas made to lift one arm in a stroke, he raised it high and waved at Sebastian. The hesitation in his rhythm faltered and a powerful tug of undercurrent pulled him downward. He struggled to maintain his momentum but failed, unable to release himself from the tow. It carried him further and further away from the shore, the rocks, and out to sea. Blackness overtook him.

When he woke, he could not move his limbs. Ropes entangled them, his head resting atop a wooden beam. He blinked salt-encrusted eyes toward the gray sky as it began to rain. The clean water revived him. He opened his mouth to take in the freshness of it.

Examining his trap, he figured it was the mast of a ship with pieces of the rigging and sails still attached. The vestiges of a shipwreck. Time was all he had now. He thought of the men who had perished, but their loss was his gain. For now. How long did he have to live?

When the rain became a deluge, he struggled more against his bindings, yet it made nay matter. He was trapped like the pilchards he and his friend used to catch in their nets. Though, he could not recall his name. When they had found the trap the next day, the animals were usually dead, but at times, they were not. It pained him now to think of their pitiful, struggling forms. Never again would he set a snare. His mind was foggy. Who was the boy that helped him? There was also a girl. A small girl with auburn hair. He squeezed his eyes tight, fighting to regain the memory.

Night came, and he grew faint with hunger. Barely able to turn his head from side to side, he stared up at the inky sky, jewels twinkling back at him. How peaceful it was. The lapping of the waves against something solid. A sound like water against wood greeted him, then the sudden whooshing of wind cooled his face.

Nicholas tried to scream, but his throat was dry with disuse. He cleared his throat, coughed, anything to make his voice of use. This time, he screamed above the waves. He screamed over and over again.

A boy's voice rose from far away. "I see it now!"

Rope fell into the water near him, but he could do nothing but continue to cry out. Soon, a dim light illuminated a boy swinging from it, a knife clenched between his teeth. The child dipped into the water beside him. The boy released one hand from the rope and took the knife in hand. "Hold on, mate." He deftly sliced through the rigging and the remaining net. "Take a hold of the beam whilst I tie ye to the rope."

Nicholas was so weak he could barely put his arms around the former ship's mast, but he hung on as he was told. The boy secured him to the rope in short order, and it pulled upward. Strong arms hefted him over the side of the ship, and a crowd of male cheers greeted him. The boy slapped him on the back. "Thought ye was done in for."

Nicholas wondered where they were from as the boy's accent was unrecognizable. Several men spoke, but their varied accents escaped him as well. Until an older man who was undoubtably the captain greeted him—he was most surely English.

The man dropped to his haunches in front of Nicholas. "I say, lad, glad we could be of service to ye. What is your name?"

He opened his mouth to answer, but nothing came. A deep breath escaped, and he shook his head. "I know not, sir." He fought back tears.

The captain placed a hand on his shoulder. "Worry not. Adam here will get ye dry clothes, food, and a warm bed. Just call me Captain."

Nicholas nodded, and Adam assisted him to his wobbly feet. He leaned on the boy until all the captain told was accomplished. The warm bed was the most welcoming after the hearty meal of fish stew that pleasantly filled his aching stomach. How long had he floated at sea? And, furthermore, who was he, and where was he bound?

☙❧

Grace watched Nicholas take a long drink and return his tankard to the dark table. "That is the tale of how I came to be lost from Trerose." He took another sip as if to fortify himself and let his eyes focus on something across the room before he returned to the story.

"It took some time before I remembered who I was. Something in me had shifted. I found I did not wish to return home." Sadness covered his handsome features. "All I could remember was my father's insistence on my being educated to inherit the manor and all its responsibilities." His apologetic regard met his father's. "I loved my life in Trerose, and I hated being in school and only coming home for short periods." His gaze moved to Sebastian and then to Grace. "I missed my friends."

Mr. Ellery cleared his throat. "Nicholas, sorry I am and regret forcing ye to go to school. I did it for your good as well. I needed someone capable to manage Penrose Manor." He hung his head.

"I know that now, Father. I, too, am sorry."

Mrs. Braddock sniffled and dabbed her face with a worn handkerchief. "In truth, I am glad God has brought this about to His good, but I want to know how ye came to be *Rig Cooper*, me boy."

Nicholas laughed. "My dear, Mrs. Braddock, I was just coming to that tale. Adam is the reason. As he is the one who cut me free of the rigging of the wrecked ship, he called me Rig. The captain said I needed a *surname*. Since I had become the apprentice to the cooper on board, the kindly man suggested that as the rest of my new name."

They all chuckled, but Mrs. Braddock was not satisfied. "How came ye to remember who ye were, lad?"

His countenance grew somber. "'Twas but a week or so, and we were bound for the West Indies, Adam's home, when I awoke in a cold sweat, remembering all. The anger at my father's decision to send me away to school took hold, and I decided I would never return." A faraway look shone in his eyes. "Years later, after traveling to many exotic ports, I confided in the captain. He is a godly man, and I valued his wisdom. After a sermon or two," Nicholas huffed, "he led me to accept Christ as my Savior, and my life has never been the same." He sent Grace an affectionate glance.

Adam lifted his mug. "Amen, Brother!"

Nicholas clapped him on the shoulder. "I also have Adam to thank for saving me from that horrid rigging!"

The evening ended soon thereafter, and each of them returned to their homes, full of joy and the many sea stories shared by Nicholas and Adam. In front of the tavern, Sebastian and Wilmont walked along the cobbled street, hand-in-hand. Grace and Nicholas watched them go and mimicked their behavior, laughing.

Once they reached the clifftop toward the cottage, Nicholas held her back. "Grace. *My* Grace."

She cocked her head. "I am *your* Grace now, am I?"

"Ye always have been, ye know?" He cupped her cheeks and brushed his thumb over her lips. "Since I *found* ye under the gorse. I didn't know it then. We were both too young to realize what God intended for us."

Grace leaned her head into his hand. "I was most angry with ye when ye revealed who ye were."

He brushed his lips against her forehead. "Were ye?"

"Aye. Why did ye not confide in me when first we met?"

"I was afraid and felt I should bide my time to see if the feelings I had gathered while on my journey home were real. It may have been a boyish dream—ye and me." He kissed her forehead again. "Yet I was wrong. It was truth. Most assuredly once I got to know ye again and saw what a beautiful woman ye have become. Inside and out. Upon my return, I tried to tell ye many times, yet God would not allow it." He smiled. "His timing is perfect."

"Aye, it is." She leaned into him.

"Grace?"

"Aye, *Rig*."

His smile told her everything her heart needed to hear. "Would ye be my wife and finish our journey here in Trerose? It shall be an adventure."

Grace smiled and brought her lips to his in a tender kiss, her answer one that needed no second thought.

"Ready I am, my love."

CAROLE LEHR JOHNSON

Chapter Nineteen

June 2022

Olivia perused Grace's diary while Luke found the local history book.

"There's an alphabetical listing here of names and any recorded happenings related to the name." He scanned the page and landed on one, bringing his head up with a snap. "Eudo Cubert."

Olivia jumped from her seat and came to look over Luke's shoulder. An entire paragraph outlined details of Eudo Cubert. Luke read silently while Olivia attempted to make out the faded print, finally nudging him in the back.

"Luke, will you please read it to us?"

He gazed over his shoulder. "Sorry, love. The author certainly did his homework by going through the old records.

This is fascinating."

Hortense twisted in her seat. "Luke, my boy, out with it."

"The researcher found records of the man's life from criminal records." He skimmed the paragraph—a rather long one—before continuing, "In 1671, he was brought before the magistrate for the murder of Radigan Atwood and for framing Sebastian Atwood, Rig Cooper, and Adam Gittens for the murder. During his initial time in the prison at—I can't make out the name—but it says they added the charge of smuggling to the murder charge."

Luke sighed. "The ink is smudged where the name of the prison is . . . and there's another mystery here." His finger tapped the page.

Olivia's curiosity got the better of her, and she knelt beside Luke and drew the book toward her. "There's another name written next to Rig Cooper's. It doesn't appear to be another person but a correction."

Luke turned in his chair and snatched a magnifying glass from an enormous cup. He flipped a switch on the handle and a tiny battery-operated bulb sparked on.

Hortense gaped at the tool. "Where did you acquire that?"

"Would you like one?" Luke asked with a cagey grin.

"Yes, I would." Hortense perked up, her eyes still admiring the glass.

Luke returned to the book. "It looks like a correction. See the faint image of a line drawn through the first name." He added the information to his notebook, then reread the entry. "The author has a comment."

It appears the name Rig Cooper was in fact crossed out

and the name taking its place is nearly illegible. From the original records, the Christian name appears to be Nicholas, yet the surname is not readable.

Olivia sank onto her heels, her mind whirling with questions. She remembered seeing the name Nicholas in the diary. She and Luke made eye contact.

"Nicholas Ellery!" they said in unison.

Olivia clasped a hand over her mouth, and for some mysterious reason, her eyes misted. Why should she feel such emotion about a man who had died over three hundred years ago?

Hortense leaned forward in her wheelchair and looked into Olivia's eyes. "My dear, why are you crying? Is this man one of your ancestors?"

Olivia took the tissue Luke handed her, dabbed at the tears, and shook her head. "No. Well, I don't think so." She turned back to Luke. "We still have a lot of research ahead of us."

His face brightened, and he turned to Hortense. "Would you remember anything about an ancestor of your husband's by the name of Radigan Atwood?"

The woman's faced scrunched in absorbed concentration. She slowly nodded. "Yes. I believe I do. He was the owner of the ledgers."

Luke opened one, searched for a date, and found it on the first page, which was dated 1669. The date of the murder charges was 1671. He then combed through the history book's index looking for the Atwood name and found several. Radigan was listed, and he found the page holding details of the man.

Radigan Atwood was the owner of The Burning Sands Tavern in Trerose, Cornwall. He met a bad end in 1671 when his illegal and immoral dealings with smugglers sent him over the cliffs near the village of Trerose, somewhere between Gwynne Cottage and Penrose Manor. Many rumors surrounded his death and were passed down as stories of entertainment. Whilst compiling this history, I was privy to many interviews with the local folks of said area. Since a mere one hundred years have passed, I do find that these accounts are, for the most part, wholly accurate. It was said the man to have been cruel in his dealings with his family and corrupt in business.

Olivia rested against the desk. "When was this history written?"

Luke flipped to the copyright page. "The year 1775." He continued reading silently while Hortense and Olivia discussed all they'd just learned.

Hortense drummed her fingers on the desk. "This means that—"

Luke jerked himself up, the book splayed open in hands. "You will not believe this! There's another reference to the Ellerys."

Upon further research, I have discovered the Ellery family was prominent in the region, having built Penrose Manor. William Ellery, the elder brother of Gerence Ellery, died in 1645 at the battle of Naseby during the civil war. Therefore, Gerence Ellery inherited the estate and passed it on to his son, Nicholas Ellery, in 1709.

Luke turned the page and read on.

Note: As of this reprinting in 1980 with added notes, the information the author states above was, sadly, water damaged beyond repair.

Hortense wilted at the revelation. "That's depressing. When we were so close."

"Not really," Olivia said. "We have the internet now. All those records are most likely online."

Luke shoved the book aside and logged onto his computer. "Let's hope what we're looking for is now digitized."

Olivia surveyed the woman's face. "Hortense, if you're tired, I can take you home." She glanced at the clock. "It's past time for lunch. And online research can take a long time."

Hortense stiffened her spine. "Not on your life. I'm staying."

Luke widened his eyes but said nothing as he typed.

"Olivia, why don't you be a love and fetch lunch so we may work through the afternoon." Hortense glanced around. "By the by, where is your pretty friend Angie?"

Olivia had shared the miserable news with Luke when they first met that morning, but she'd told no one else the details. Only that her friend had to hurry home. "Angie had something pop up and had to cut her trip short. She'll be back another time."

The woman seemed to take the news in stride. Olivia took their lunch orders and dashed away to the tearoom down the street. When she stepped inside, Sheryl and Beryl waved her over to their table.

"Good afternoon, ladies. Nice to see you." She joined them after placing her takeaway order. "So, how's the fundraiser going?"

Sheryl beamed. "Splendidly, I believe. Only two days to go." She forked a portion of pasty into her mouth and rolled her eyes dramatically. The woman was definitely a drama queen.

Beryl smirked at her errant sister. "We're looking forward to spending another day with Angie."

Olivia toyed with the handle of her bag. "I'm afraid it will have to wait. She had to rush home."

"We're so sorry," Beryl sympathized.

"She'll return as soon as she's able."

"Here you go, love. Tell the vicar to enjoy." The red-haired server gave Olivia a cheeky smile and turned.

"Not to worry, dear. It's a small village, and there are few secrets."

Sheryl blushed at her sister's words. Olivia thought of Sheryl's *problem* being revealed not so long ago, and her heart melted for her. She squeezed the woman's arm, told them goodbye, and took lunch back to her fellow researchers. When she arrived, Hortense sat at the desk alone reading the history book with the lighted magnifying glass. Olivia made a mental note to order one for her—a brightly colored one so it wouldn't easily be misplaced.

Luke's voice drifted from the recesses of the museum, his tone in tour-guide mode.

Olivia lowered her voice. "Does he have very many in the group?"

Hortense nodded. "Including one rather cheeky little boy who seems to know more than anyone else." She harrumphed.

Olivia placed the bag of food on one corner of the desk and sat next to the woman. "I say we eat. Luke could be awhile."

Hortense rubbed her hands together briskly. "Indeed. I'm famished."

It warmed Olivia's heart to see the elderly woman so involved in an activity, keeping her mind sharp. They blessed their food and ate while Olivia read notes Luke had taken to refresh her memory of where they were on the trail.

A half hour later Luke dropped into his chair and blew out an exasperated breath. "That was challenging."

"You're too nice, Vicar."

Luke said dryly, "That is a prerequisite for being a vicar, my dear Hortense." He bowed his head in silent prayer for a moment, then dug into his late lunch. "This pasty is wonderful," he said between bites. "Thank you for lunch, love."

Olivia kissed his cheek. "You're welcome. It's only fair that we feed our vicar."

Hortense patted Olivia's hand. "And our researcher." She took her last bite and dabbed at the corners of her mouth. "That was lovely. Thank you." She picked up the notebook Olivia had been perusing and read.

Hortense cleared her throat and looked at Luke. "Where did you find this information about the Olford name?"

"Hmm?" Luke chewed a bite of his pasty.

"You have *Olford* jotted here and a page number from the history book." She stroked the heavy volume.

Still chewing, Luke opened the book at the page in question and swallowed. "Yes, here it is.

In the parish records, I discovered Enidor Olford, Vicar of Trerose, 1631-1701.

Hortense gasped. "Is that the number of years he was the vicar or his birth and death dates?"

Olivia watched Hortense as she stared into the distance. "You are certainly quicker with math than I am."

Hortense shook off her musings. "What? Oh, yes dear. Thank you. Always had a good grasp on numbers."

She paused for a moment. "Enidor Olford was one of my ancestors. I'm trying to recall exactly what the connection is."

Luke's eyes widened. "That's amazing! We've discovered one of your ancestors. Can you consult your records to see if it may give us more clues?"

"I certainly can. Vicar, if you'll wheel me home, I'll look for my Olford peeps."

Luke and Olivia laughed to hear the woman use slang they would've never guessed she was aware of. Olivia stood with Luke, but Hortense stayed. "No, Olivia, time's wasting. You stay here and keep searching. Luke can get me home quicker. I'll also need to consult with Laura about our dinner plans. You two are coming tonight, and we'll compare notes. Also, may I borrow your looking glass?"

"Hortense," Luke said calmly as he handed her the glass. "Olivia may have plans tonight."

"Pfft! Too bad. Plans can be changed." She lifted her chin to stare up at the tall man and arched one brow. "Her *plans* are probably the two of you sitting on the sofa necking."

Olivia's mouth dropped, and Luke's face flamed. Hortense looked at them like the cat that caught the canary. "Good. I'll see you two at seven sharp. We have work to do."

◊◊◊

Olivia swung her and Luke's joined hands as they made their way to Hortense Atwood's house for dinner—and genealogy research.

Luke raised a tawny brow. "I've heard of dinner and a movie but dinner and genealogy?"

"Could be a coming trend," Olivia teased.

Luke halted. "It could be a new church activity. *Dinner and genealogy, discover your ancestor while you eat.*"

"I have the strongest urge to roll my eyes." Olivia tugged him on. "We'll be late if we have to stop for every one of your witticisms."

"I take that as a compliment." He sent her an arrogant look.

Laura answered the door, and when Olivia and Luke stepped over the threshold, she leaned toward them, her voice lowered. "She is on a tear. Already seated at the table telling me this is a working dinner. So please excuse the unorthodox table setting." She straightened and with a conspiratorial smile led them to the dining room.

Hortense twisted in her chair when they entered and frantically waved her arm, inviting them forward. "Come, come. I have found so many amazing things you will be . . ."

Luke gave her a mischievous smile. "*Amazed?*"

"Cheeky vicar."

Olivia saw the teasing light in her eyes as well as the admiration. She and Luke prepared to sit beside one another, but the elder woman instructed them where to sit, placing

Olivia on her right and Luke on her left.

"That's keeping you two from misbehaving. No holding hands under the table or snogging in my presence."

Luke sighed. "Hortense Atwood, we are not teens and need no instruction on how to behave."

For the first time, Olivia saw a hint of frustration in Luke's eyes, but it was gone as quickly as it appeared.

The woman softened her tone. "Luke, my dear man, let me play grandmother if for just a short while please."

Luke cupped her cheek. "If it makes you happy, dear."

"What will really make me happy, Vicar, is to get to work." She removed his hand and opened a folder in front of her. "I'll tell you what I've discovered. Some of it, mind you, is family history, but some of it is recorded."

As if on cue, and it most probably was, Laura served their meal of roasted beef, potatoes, carrots, and peas.

"Vicar Olford was my ninth great-grandfather." She took a bite of potatoes.

As they ate, Olivia detected a knowing look in Hortense's eyes. "I believe you're stringing us along. There's some very important news you have to share."

Her eyes twinkled. "You are correct." She took another bite.

When Hortense finished chewing, she said, "Oh! All right. Vicar Olford was a cousin to Melior Atwood and therefore a cousin to Grace."

Olivia looked at Luke and knew she must have worn the same questioning gaze. They glanced at Hortense.

She held a palm out. "I know, I know. Hurry it up." She hoisted herself up a few inches and reached to the center of the table, gripping a tiny black leatherbound book and held it in the air. "He kept a diary!"

Stunned silence filled the room as Hortense recovered Luke's magnifying glass and her cotton gloves. "This was a godsend." She waved the glass in front of her like a sword. "The writing in here is so tiny I would not have been able to read it otherwise." She opened the book but did not speak immediately. After a few minutes of scanning, while Luke and Olivia ate, she closed the cover with care.

"I'm going to nutshell this for you until you have time to read it for yourselves. At first, I thought it rather sinful for a vicar to keep a record of people and their personal issues, but in the end, he clarified why he'd done this. It seems he knew his time was at an end and wanted to clear up any misunderstandings."

She pulled in and released a breath. "He states that the only people he speaks of are relatives or anyone with a close connection to the family. Melior Atwood's first child actually belonged to William Ellery. They were to marry when he returned from the war, but as our research has uncovered, he died at Naseby. When he left, she did not know she was with child."

Olivia noticed Hortense's gaze light on hers, but she continued, "Vicar Olford says that Radigan Atwood married Melior because he'd always had his eye on her and was a handsome man. He was the owner of The Burning Sands Tavern. At the vicar's advice, she married him to save her reputation and provide her with a home. A few years later, he was sorry to have suggested it." Hortense took a deep breath and released it slowly. The narration was wearing the woman out after so many hours at the museum.

"Olivia, Luke, I want you to take this and make copies. It is an amazing account of life in seventeenth-century Trerose. You will find the connections branching from Melior and her husband to be astonishing. The Ellery family is another tale that should be a movie. Especially about Nicholas."

Olivia was on the edge of her seat. "Hortense, is it as hard to read as Grace's diary?"

With a tinge of pride in her voice, she said, "Not in the least. His writing is beautiful and very concise, not flowery at all. It has been well cared for through the ages so that certainly helps." She cradled the diary to her chest for a moment, then placed it before Olivia. She removed her gloves and lay them atop the book. "I entrust it to you until you may copy it."

Oliva put the gloves on and opened the diary to the end and read.

My life is soon at an end. I pray to my God that I have fulfilled His mission on the present Earth and look forward to eternity on the renewed Earth. I write these things for only my family coming in the future, so they will understand that we shall all suffer in the here and now, but should we put our faith in Jesus the Christ, we shall be redeemed. To my descendants, I pray you seek Him now and perish not.

Olivia's eyes stung. Her head bowed. "He was showing his future family how they had struggled but did not give up. They trusted God and are now with him." She held the diary in front of her. "This was his legacy."

THE BURNING SANDS

Luke reached across the table and wiped a tear from Olivia's cheek. A moment of silence passed, and as Hortense shifted in her chair, it squeaked and brought them around.

Luke's fingers still lay upon Olivia's cheek, and Hortense whacked him on the arm with the magnifying glass. "Enough of that touchy-touchy stuff, lad."

They all laughed, Hortense more so.

After finishing dessert—a decadent caramel-chocolate trifle—Olivia and Luke lethargically left the cottage. The night's breeze playing with Olivia's hair and the scent of the sea calmed her spirit. She thought of the precious diary wrapped in soft cloth in her bag.

Luke put an arm around her. "Quite the revealing."

"Yes. If you could guarantee one at each dinner-and-genealogy gathering, the church would soon outgrow its occupants."

He laughed. "Right you are. We'd have the whole parish talking."

They walked on in silence until reaching Olivia's door. He kissed her good night. "I suppose you'll be up half the night reading that diary."

She started to protest but knew it would be a lie. "Certainly. I'm so glad it's easier to read than Grace's."

"Say no more. If you can read half the night, I can stay up and decipher *your* Grace's. I have made a bit of headway but wanted to give it to you all at once. If that's satisfactory."

Olivia stood on tiptoes and planted a loud, smacking kiss on his lips. "You're a good man, Vicar."

Luke quirked a brow. "So, I've been told." He leered at her.

"But not quite as good as you."

Olivia narrowed her eyes. "How so?"

"By doing this . . ." Luke pulled her into an embrace and kissed her long and thorough, and Olivia didn't want him to let her go.

☙❧

The day after Vicar Olford's diary discovery, Olivia woke with a groan, stretching her stiff limbs. "Staying up late into the night is not a good thing to do once you pass thirty." She remembered her age and added, "Or forty." She gingerly got out of bed and took a long shower.

"Next up—smuggler's tea."

She wordlessly thanked the twins for introducing her to the strong brew. One cup and her day sped up. Cup two was her usual Earl Grey with lemon and scones with clotted cream. By the time she'd consumed all she was able, her mind cleared to recall what she'd read into the wee hours.

Olivia dressed, grabbed the diary and her bag, and jogged down to the village. She'd forgotten the museum was closed today and started toward the church to share her news.

The church was abuzz with activity. Another thing she'd forgotten—the fundraiser tomorrow. Guilt swept through her. If Luke stayed up, he would be exhausted and have a full day of festivities tomorrow.

Beryl spotted her and, for someone of her age, sprinted athletically toward Olivia.

"How nice you've come to help. I'll show you where your lovely painting will be displayed." She took Olivia's arm, not giving her a chance to voice a greeting. "We thought we'd put the fragile items inside the recreation hall in case of rain or wind."

Olivia nodded. "That's a good idea. Play it safe."

"Yes, dear. Indeed."

The recreation hall teamed with cloth-laden tables groaning with wares, foodstuffs, and gadgets—all to sell to aid the widows' fund.

"This is lovely, Beryl. You all have done a splendid job of it."

Beryl tittered, and Olivia gave her a questioning glance.

"Don't mind me. It's just that you're sounding like one of us now. And I'm glad." She hugged Olivia, quickly bounded off, and tossed over her shoulder, "I'll be back in a moment with something you may help with."

Olivia jumped when a voice close to her ear whispered, "Are you sleep-walking? I know I am."

She spun around and peered into tired but sparkling eyes.

"I want to hug and kiss you right now but that wouldn't be seemly since you are the vicar."

"What? No comment about the bags under my eyes. All done for love."

Olivia frowned. "Don't make me feel any more guilty than I already am. Only this morning did I remember this would be a busy day for you. I am sorry."

"No need. I'll make up the lost sleep the day after the event." He led her to a group of chairs against the wall and away from the activity. "Did you make any discoveries?"

Excitement welled within her. "I did. Rig Cooper *is*, well *was*, Nicholas Ellery! Nicholas and Sebastian Atwood were boyhood friends, almost the same age. They were swimming off Talland Sands beach while Grace, a few years younger, was playing in the sand. Nicholas was swept away, and Sebastian tried to save him but couldn't. The vicar's diary said Grace and Sebastian blamed themselves for not being able to help him."

Beryl bounded back with a large basket full of flowers and set it on the floor in front of Olivia.

"Here you go, dear." She pointed across the room. "The vases are there, already filled with water. We'd like a vase on the tables where the food will be." This time she pointed to the opposite side of the room. She said goodbye and slipped away with more spunk than possible.

"That woman is a marvel," Olivia said. "Now where was I?"

"Nicholas—"

"Oh, yes. Anyway, they assumed he drowned but never found his body. As it turned out, a ship down the coast rescued him, but he had no memory. The captain was a godly man and was a great inspiration to Nicholas. But, of course, he didn't know his name. Now get this!" She felt her face flush with the telling. "When they found him, he was floating on a piece of wrecked ship, tangled in the rigging! Get it? Rigging?"

Luke smiled indulgently.

Olivia huffed. "The captain called him *Rig*!"

Luke nodded. "I get that. But *Cooper*?"

"Oh, Luke. Aren't you excited? How many wonderful stories are lost in time and never discovered? This is a brilliant story."

He leaned close and glanced around the room. "You're making me want to kiss you more by the minute."

Olivia whispered, "Stop it. I want to tell you more."

He straightened and pulled his face into a stern, serious expression. "Yes, ma'am."

"That's better. There was a barrel maker on board who taught Nicholas. So, the captain called him Rig Cooper."

Luke studied her. "You're very proud of yourself, aren't you?"

"No. I'm just excited that we've found a piece of Trerose history. A very *personal* history."

He crossed his arms. "So, Rig aka Nick is also the lord-of-the-manor's heir, but he has an unknown cousin, Sebastian, who is Grace's brother—sorry, half-brother."

"Yes. But that isn't all. Grace and Nicholas marry in the winter of 1672 . . . *and* the pièce de résistance is the fact that Melior, Grace's mother, ends up marrying Gerence Ellery in late 1672. He was Nick's father and the uncle of Sebastian."

"Take a breath, love, or you'll get the vapors," he quipped.

"Aren't you the least bit excited about any of this?"

"Of course, I am. I'm just enjoying the performance of you telling it. You are even more beautiful when you're animated about something."

Pleasure filled her, and she clasped his hand.

He squeezed it. "Tell me more."

"Oh, yeah. The vicar believed The Burning Sands Tavern was named after incidents involving the shipwrecks of the 1650s. Although, he wasn't certain of the date the Sands was built. When there was a storm and a ship wrecked on Talland Sands beach, the villagers would salvage what they could and there was usually liquor involved in the cargo. They'd drink too much, build bonfires, and revel in their freedom to do so. Someone mentioned the sand seeming as if on fire. Hence the name *The Burning Sands*."

This time, Luke's eyes brightened. "Truly?"

"Ah. I finally have your full attention." She smirked. "And we haven't even kissed yet."

"You've had my full attention since the first time you snubbed me, love."

"*Ha ha.*"

"Seriously, that is brilliant." He nodded. "I mean it. Now you *must* buy the Sands."

The comment puzzled Olivia. "Why do you say that?"

"Only that you've been in love with the place since you first laid eyes on it." His voice held sincerity. "You deserve to have your dreams come true. God has and will continue to bless you."

"So does this mean you don't want it for the historical society?"

"Hmm. I didn't say that." He turned again to look around the room. "May we begin negotiations over dinner tonight?" He waggled his brows.

"Yes, Vicar, I believe so." She nudged his shoulder. "But prepare for tough negotiations."

⊗⊗

The negotiation dinner did not come to fruition as Olivia and

Luke planned. Angie texted Olivia and scheduled a phone call for the evening. It was a bittersweet reunion, Angie apologizing for her behavior. She gave Olivia the happy news that her *ailment,* as she called it, was only early menopause, and she was now on medication to ease the mood swings.

"I'm so glad, Angie. Please reschedule your visit. Teffeny said she wants to get to know you." Olivia laughed. "I think you'll have met your new best friend. Once you get to know her, you'll understand why she and I have hit it off."

The joy in Angie's voice lifted Olivia's spirits. "I can't wait."

Their conversation was short but deeply meaningful. Olivia told her about the village goings on including the church fundraiser the next day. She assured Angie she would continue to pray for her.

Olivia was true to her word. The next day as she walked from the cottage into the village she indeed prayed for her friend. When she reached the church for the fundraiser, she spotted Luke speaking with Hortense, who wore a bright smile and held something in her hand, looking at it as if she'd just been awarded a prize.

She slipped behind Luke and tapped him on the shoulder, eliciting a jolt of surprise. "Hello, Vicar."

He turned, and she saw the light in his eyes spark. "Hello, love."

"What's this?" Olivia noticed something on Hortense's lap.

The older woman waved the object. "My very own lighted magnifying glass! Isn't it glorious?"

Olivia laughed. "Yes, it is. I was going to order you one in hot pink, but I think the chartreuse suits you better."

"Indeed." She wiggled her eyebrows. "Who knows what I may uncover with this remarkable device?"

Beryl approached, all alight with the excitement of the day. "How are you lovelies today?"

Luke nodded, and Olivia said, "We're wonderful. Such a perfect day for an event." She glanced around the church courtyard. "Where's Sheryl?"

Beryl released an exasperated sigh. "She's as slippery as a lemon seed. We've only just arrived, and she's disappeared."

Luke nudged the silver-haired woman. "Has she found a new love interest?"

Beryl's expression was evasive. "Perhaps." She turned and strode away.

Luke asked Hortense to excuse them and pulled Olivia away from the festivities and whispered, "Have you considered my question from last night?"

Olivia smiled, took his hand, and nodded.

The day progressed happily, Luke and Olivia strolling through the village and church grounds, greeting people along the way. When they stopped at the tearoom, Olivia remembered something she'd forgotten to share with Luke. "I found a map at the back of Vicar Olford's diary." She sipped her tea and watched his face.

Luke gave her a sidelong glance. "Really?"

"Yes, it's quite good, actually." She pulled a sheet of folded paper from her bag, opened it, and placed it between them. "This is my rendition of what was in the diary."

The east Cornish coastline facing the English Channel with all the landmarks sketched along the path spread before them from north to south. First was Gwynne Cottage, south of that stood Atwood Cottage, then Penrose Manor—although it laid further inland. She traced the path from the cliffs down into Trerose Harbor and to The Burning Sands Tavern. In the corner of the map was the date—1689.

Luke stared at the page in wonder. "This is astonishing. Vicar Olford sketched this in the journal?"

"Yes, he did. And I'm so grateful."

He reached across the table and took her hand. "This is wonderful news, Olivia. You're going to have an amazing time opening the old Sands. You should enlarge this map and hang it in a place of honor."

"That's a great idea. Thank you."

He folded it and returned the map to her bag. "I guess we must get back to the church for the closing festivities."

They strode to the church, and Luke made his way to the podium and presented his brief thank you speech to all who took part. "Now I'd like to make an announcement with the permission of the person of whom I speak." He glanced at Olivia and motioned for her to join him. She timidly stepped up to stand beside him.

"I'd like to present Olivia Griffin, my fiancée. We are to be married next year, and I hope you will all be happy for us."

The round of applause escalated with loud enthusiasm.

Olivia watched Luke's proud expression and pondered all that happened to her since arriving in Cornwall. She thought of Grace and how in some ways their lives paralleled. God had worked in both their stories. He brought Nicholas home to Grace, and although God had not returned Ian to her, he'd brought her Luke.

A short while later, she found Luke carefully surveying her painting of the harbor which had garnered a hefty sum for the event.

Luke squinted at the canvas and pointed. "What's this?"

Olivia laughed. "You."

He looked at her, then back at the image of a small figure on the coastal path looking at the harbor.

Olivia looped her arm through his. "I thought we needed a reminder of how you pursued me until I agreed to marry you."

His cheeky smile warmed her heart as he leaned in to give her a gentle kiss.

Epilogue

Two years later . . .

Olivia crept into her husband's office, silently reaching his chair. She slipped her hands over his eyes but said nothing.

"My dear, how are you feeling today?"

"How did you know it was me?" she asked dryly. "After all, Sheryl is still available."

Luke spun his chair around and winked. "You are a cheeky monkey, aren't you, love?" He stood and helped her sit on the edge of his desk. "What was that noise?"

"I didn't hear anything."

He quirked his brow. "I believe the desk just groaned."

Olivia slapped his arm. "I haven't gained that much weight!" She patted her rounded stomach.

"Hmm. I'd say triplets." He tapped a forefinger against his

chin. "You know I'm only joking. You're barely showing."

Olivia frowned. "Luke, I'm about *ten* months along."

"Ten months is it now?"

She massaged her lower back. "Feels like it."

"Not to worry. The doctor says you're in great shape—for someone your age." He wiggled his brows.

"You insufferable man." Olivia's stomach dipped for a moment, the thought of her having a child at the age of almost forty-seven.

Olivia wrapped her arms around his waist.

"I must go. Angie's waiting at The Pilchard."

"How's she liking the twins' cottage?"

"Loving it. I'm so glad she could come and be here when Nicholas is born."

"Me too. Also, that her early menopause issue is in check."

"Luke! That sounded insensitive," Olivia whispered, not wanting the church secretary to overhear.

"Sorry. I didn't mean it that way. I'm thankful she's gotten medication. It wouldn't do for her to upset you in your condition."

Olivia sighed. "True. She seems her old self—and she and Hugo are still getting on famously."

He helped her to her feet and looped her arm through his, and they strolled to the door. "What does Angie think about the Sands and all your artistic products?"

"She loves them. Especially the map on the huge teacup."

"Have you told her about your and Hortense's latest historical find?"

Olivia gave him a sidelong glance. "Certainly. It particularly impressed Angie to find that mine and your ancestral lines crossed in the seventeenth century."

"What did she say?"

"She feels it's unlucky for cousins to marry."

Luke pinched his lips together and shook his head. "So, you're about my forty-ninth cousin?"

"Something like that." Olivia laughed. "She nearly spewed tea across the room when I told her we were naming the baby Nicholas after our shared ancestor."

Luke looked around. "Where's the car?"

Olivia hung her head. "I walked." She pulled her gaze back to his.

"*Olivia.* We've had this conversation. It's too dangerous for you to be strolling along that path over the cliffs—and it's too close to your time."

"Oh, Luke. This is not 1671. I've walked that path for over two years now."

A shadow crossed his face, and he pulled her into his arms, resting his cheek on the top of her head. "Oh, my love, you do make me fret over you."

"I'm sorry. The exercise is wonderful for me and Nicholas."

"That's fine but just humor me and don't walk on the path. Walk in the village where you'll be seen should something happen."

"All right. If it will make you feel better." She pulled away. "I'll need a ride."

He kissed her soundly. "The car's at the cottage, dear. I'll walk you to Angie."

They ambled along. "I wish you'd been there when Hortense and I discovered what happened to all the people in Grace's world. Her face almost glowed."

"I'm happy for her. And for those people. Arabel and Adam in the West Indies, Sebastian and Wilmont taking over the Sands, Nicholas and Grace living at the manor . . ."

"Don't forget Melior and Gerence Ellery."

"Right. I suppose we may never find out what happened to Grace and Arabel's younger siblings."

Olivia sighed contentedly. "Don't hold your breath. If Hortense Atwood has anything to say about it, that'll be next on her list."

They reached Gwynne Cottage and stopped to look out at the waves along the cliffs, sun shimmering on the water, a playful breeze causing the pink thrift to quiver.

"God has certainly worked in our lives, Luke, as well as those throughout history. We're blessed to discover His work in the lives of our ancestors as well."

She leaned contentedly against her husband's shoulder, her eyes on the vast sea stretching before her.

God had a plan far beyond what she or Grace could have imagined for their lives, the undercurrent of His love for them all moving to and fro as steady and recurring as the tide to the harbor, guiding ships safely back home.

That which is has already been,
and what is to be has already been,
and God requires an account of what is past.

–*Ecclesiastes 3:15 (NKJV)*

THE END

Author's Note

Thank you for reading *The Burning Sands*! I hope you've enjoyed this journey into the past of Cornwall, England. Several years ago, I visited Polperro, Cornwall for the first time. I had previously connected with the place via *The Rose Garden* by Susanna Kearsley. While not labeled Christian fiction, it is an outstanding historical time travel novel and a clean read. The setting was so interesting it drew me to travel to the old fishing village for vacation and research.

The map at the front of this novel is my rendition of fictional Trerose, which is based on Polperro. My visit there inspired me to write *The Burning Sands*. I've changed a few of the buildings, lanes, etc. to better suit my story. My friend Kellie Fox and I stayed in a lovely period cottage on The Warren located just off the harbor. I walked the coastal path many times, overlooking the surf surging against the jagged gray rocks, and up the thigh-crusher hill to the manor house mentioned in *The Rose Garden* (now privately owned).

My lifelong intrigue with history has become immensely helpful as a historical fiction author. I love the research almost as much as the writing. A few of my fellow authors cringe at the mention of research—but not me!

My list of resources is much too lengthy to note here, therefore I'll only mention a few. The online searchable version of the diary of Samuel Pepys (1633-1703) from the years of 1660-1669 was my number one source. Most of my characters' names came from history books or genealogy records.

The HMS Coronation built in 1685 shipwrecked off the coast of Cornwall on September 3, 1691. I changed the year to fit within my timeline, but the other historical notes are accurate. This was the means for Nicholas Ellery to be taken from his home and assumed dead.

The sermon by Victor Olford is in part from Thomas Watson's writings of that era. I changed it somewhat but kept the speech of that time to give it authenticity. He was a noted Puritan preacher and author.

Luke uses a local history book to help Olivia in her search. This is a fictional book I invented to move the story forward.

The historic village of Polperro has a long history of smuggling, mining, and fishing that I would have liked to include more of in the story, but there wasn't room to accommodate so much information. I strongly suggest if you ever find yourself in England to travel down to Cornwall and pay a visit to this lovely harbor town.

I'd like to thank my friend, publisher, editor, and brainstormer extraordinaire, Morgan Tarpley Smith. Since 2007, she has encouraged my writing journey, later becoming my writing/critique partner. Morgan, thank you!

I'd also like to thank Tammy Kirby, my writing partner and travel buddy. We've been on some interesting UK research trips and on occasion narrowly escaped trouble. Thank you for the fun travel excursions and your writing guidance.

A huge thank you to my beta readers for their time and input: Jennifer, Jo, Marguerite, Sherlyn, and Tammy. It is much appreciated.

Thank you also to my husband, Max, and my son, Daniel, for the support of my writing.

Finally, my deepest gratitude is to God for enabling me to write for His glory.

For more information on my other novels, research, travel, and to sign up for my newsletter, please visit my website, www.CaroleLehrJohnson.com

Enjoy *The Burning Sands*?

Here's a preview of another novel by Carole Lehr Johnson

A Place in Time

Chapter One

Stanton Wake, England
March 2021

Adela Jenks rummaged through a dusty crate, from time-to-time glancing across the room at her friends, Kellie Welles and Leanne Harcourt.

The pungent scent of incense nearly choked her, a thread of smoke drifting from the counter next to the cash register. Ever the optimist, she searched for what she hoped would be a memorable keepsake of this trip with her two closest friends.

The shopkeeper had told her the charity shop began as a

meat market five hundred years before, developing into many businesses through the centuries, and was reborn in the late twentieth century as Charity's Charity Shop. Not a clever name, to be sure, but one you wouldn't forget along with its history.

Everything was so much older, more historic in England—one reason Adela had longed to come.

She heard robust laughter and looked up to see Leanne plowing through a rack of vintage garments.

Leanne met her eyes. "Kellie, what's Adela doing in the corner? She sounds like a humongous pack rat."

Kellie held a long flowing silk robe up against her tall, curvaceous figure. "I have no idea . . . how does this look on me?" She twirled and tilted her head from side to side. "Hmm?"

"The two of you do *know* this is not a large shop," Adela said matter-of-factly. "I can hear everything you say about me. But—" She paused to sneeze.

"All you're doing is stirring up dust and aggravating your allergies," Leanne quipped.

"I'm determined to—" Adela sneezed again. "—find a keepsake that won't take up half of my carry-on."

Another sneeze. The potent incense had to be the cause. With a moment of reprieve, she looked at Kellie. "That silk thingy is beautiful. Don't you think so, Leanne?"

Leanne turned to Kellie. "Yes, the emerald complements your blonde hair, and the size of the print suits your height. You should get it."

"Really? I do like it, and it will please Adela since it doesn't take up much room in my bag." Kellie grinned and flung the garment over her shoulder.

Adela stood, dusting off her hands, and approached them. "I heard that." But she grinned and held up a small item in triumph. "I found the perfect keepsake."

Kellie and Leanne exchanged questioning looks, probably thinking of her penchant for *unusual* purchases.

"Don't give me *the* look," Adela admonished them. "It's something truly unique."

"What is it? A seventeenth-century fork for your cookbook project?" Leanne teased. "Whatcha gonna do? Pose with it for a picture?"

"Droll, very droll." Adela smirked at Leanne while Kellie chuckled.

Opening what appeared to be a small, thin antique book, Adela's lips curved into a smile as she took in the first page. "Oh, yes. This is exactly what I wanted."

A vintage passport.

CB£O

Seated in Lady Margaret's Tea House in the village of Stanton Wake, Adela chatted with Kellie and Leanne about their day over afternoon tea. Adela took out her new purchase and examined it. A ripple of brightly colored fabric slid over the page as Leanne flung her Celtic scarf around her neck. She glanced up. "What *are* you doing?"

Kellie answered, "Being ridiculous, as usual." She pulled the robe from her bag. "Not fair. I can't wear this around my neck."

Adela ignored their banter and jotted down a few notes in her journal of all they'd done since breakfast.

Leanne huffed. "I can't find my lip gloss." She plowed through her purse, piling things on the table.

Kellie pointed to the passport. "Why don't we have a look-see? Find out whose past you're delving into."

Adela tugged the leather tab from a tiny slit. The passport was close in size to a contemporary one, but when she opened the cover, the paper was blank, yellowed, and musty.

She noted Kellie and Leanne's disappointed expressions and smiled. They thought she'd purchased something of no value.

Adela gradually unfolded the paper to reveal one sizeable piece folded into ten sections. Two revealed faded black and white photos—one of a man and the other of a woman and a small child.

Leanne squealed with delight, and Kellie grinned.

Adela fixed them with a mock glare. "You both always seem so surprised when I find something of worth."

By the time their second pot of tea arrived, they'd learned the passport belonged to a man from Southampton and his wife and young son. They discussed the places the family had traveled to, then their conversation moved to the upcoming festival.

"I don't know what to expect." Kellie's expression clouded. "I hope it won't be a letdown."

"No worries, Kellie," Leanne said. "We'll have a great time. Just dressing up in those costumes Adela made will get us in seventeenth-century mode. Remember how hard we laughed when we tried them on the first time? All those layers. I thought I'd ache for days at how funny you looked when you got your arms stuck in that chemise, wriggling like trying to escape a cocoon."

"The least you could've done was stop laughing and helped me out of it. Adela had to rescue me while you lay on the floor laughing your fool head off."

Leanne's face lit up. "It *was* fun." She grew thoughtful. "With all those layers, we might need a two-hour start on dressing."

Kellie munched on her scone and nodded.

Adela studied the passport absentmindedly. Her thoughts went to the costume patterns ordered a year before their trip, and the time taken to sew the period garments. She'd been meticulous about the right fabric, colors, and patterns related to the era.

Taking a sip of tea, she glanced at her friends over the rim of her cup.

"Let's finish our shopping before dinner, go back to the cottage and crash," Leanne offered. She stifled a yawn. "Jet lag's still got me."

Adela signaled the waitress to pay and asked her to bag up the remaining scones. She tucked the paper bag in her tote, and they stepped out into the uncommonly warm March afternoon.

She closed her eyes and inhaled the sweet fragrance of wildflowers and foliage. The fresh country scents invigorated her as they strolled the lane toward their cottage.

Her gaze fixed on a pasture full of sheep, little ones running back to their mothers for safety.

Adela froze.

Beyond the field, the perfect example of a seventeenth century manor house stood at the end of a tree-lined gravel drive. Enough of the house was visible to glimpse its splendor. Something about the house called to her, inexplicably. She longed to rush up the drive. Foolish, she knew, but the urge was there nonetheless.

"Adela," Leanne called out. "You'll become a sheep if you stand there any longer."

Adela shook her head, awakening from a trance, but the connection, the pull of the house, stayed with her.

☙❧

The tiny tourist office stood at the center of Stanton Wake in a building dating back over three hundred years. Beryl, the short white-haired woman answering their questions, was most knowledgeable about the area. Having lived in Stanton Wake all her life, there wasn't a thing she didn't know about the village. Many of her ancestors had been born in the area.

Leanne whispered, "Let's find out about the Adela Jenks Manor House, so we can get some lunch."

Kellie elbowed her.

Adela ignored them. She had told them about the house and what she experienced, but she didn't expect them to understand.

She didn't even understand.

But maybe learning more about the place would somehow jog her memory about the connection to the house, perhaps one of her ancestors had lived there.

Beryl told them Maximus DeGrey built Dunbar Park about 1600. His father had bequeathed him one thousand acres. "He had no siblings—at least there is no evidence he did. His son, Henry, inherited. After his death in London, his son, Marcus, took charge of the house and brought his young daughter to live at Stanton Wake. The manor has never been out of the family's ownership."

"Do you think there's a possibility for a tour?" Adela's stomach clenched.

"Not likely. They only do tours during the festival and are probably booked. The family is protective of their privacy."

Leanne jumped in. "How can we find out? We *really* would like a tour." She placed a hand on Adela's shoulder. "Adela is a gourmet chef and history enthusiast and would love a tour of the house and its kitchen as research for her cookbook. Would you be so kind as to help us?" She turned on her winsome personality, which had amassed an enormous social media following and a career as an influencer along the way.

Beryl tapped her chin. "Let me see what I can do." She picked up the phone and dialed.

Leanne whispered to Adela, "That's a good sign."

Beryl stepped out of earshot and spoke quietly into the phone. Nodding, she walked back to the counter where they waited.

Adela held her breath.

The woman's mouth stretched into a wide grin. "You, dear American ladies, have an appointment to tour Dunbar Park tomorrow afternoon."

Adela gently took the woman's hand. "Wonderful! I don't know how to thank you."

"My pleasure, dear, my pleasure. It's nice for someone to take an interest in our local history. Everyone seems bent on tearing things down to put up something modern. Such a disgrace. I prefer visiting places that own morsels of history, not places where everything was built last week."

Adela laughed and bid her goodbye.

Walking along the cobblestone street, Adela marveled at their good fortune to tour the house, and she hoped it would reveal some of its secrets to her.

About the Author

Carole Lehr Johnson is a veteran travel consultant of more than 30 years and has served as head of genealogy at her local library.

Her love of tea and scones, castles and cottages, and all things British has led her to immerse her writing in the United Kingdom whether in the genre of historical or contemporary fiction.

Carole is the author of three inspirational novels set in England as well as a novella collection. Her second novel, *A Place in Time*, was a Notable Book Award finalist for the Southern Christian Writers Conference.

She is a member of the American Christian Fiction Writers (ACFW) as well as the president of her local chapter. She and her husband live in Louisiana with their goofy cats.

For more information, visit
www.carolelehrjohnson.com

Sign up for Carole's newsletter on her website for updates on her next release, U.K. travel features, recipes, book recommendations, and more.

Made in the USA
Monee, IL
13 September 2023